THE DEATH SQUAD

HOVANNES

Armed with a .38 revolver and twenty years of hate, he had a sure-fire plan to stop the New York Mobs.

OBREGO

He was loyal to Hovannes . . . even when it meant a murder a day.

SAVAGE

He had high ideals . . . and the squad gave him every opportunity to practice them.

POLITO

He joined for the most basic of reasons . . . he liked to watch the bodies fall.

"Compelling. A definite harbinger of things
to come in the very near future."
Robin Moore, author of *The French Connection*

CONTRACT ON CHERRY STREET

PHILIP ROSENBERG

AVON
PUBLISHERS OF BARD, CAMELOT, DISCUS, EQUINOX AND FLARE BOOKS

AVON BOOKS
A division of
The Hearst Corporation
959 Eighth Avenue
New York, New York 10019

Copyright © 1975 by Philip Rosenberg
Published by arrangement with Thomas Y. Crowell Company
Library of Congress Catalog Card Number: 74-23295

ISBN: 0-380-00591-3

First Avon Printing, May 1976

AVON TRADEMARK REG. U.S. PAT. OFF. AND
FOREIGN COUNTRIES, REGISTERED TRADEMARK—
MARCA REGISTRADA, HECHO EN CHICAGO, U.S.A.

Printed in the U.S.A.

for Charlotte

Acknowledgments

I WOULD LIKE to thank Ellen Fleysher of WCBS television and Frank Faso of the *Daily News* for technical advice and suggestions. I am also deeply grateful to my wife, Charlotte, my brother Stuart, and my sister-in-law Jacqueline for their helpful suggestions and comments.

PART ONE

Chapter 1

IN THE EARLY FIFTIES Jack Kittens had been a middleweight fighter who showed no particular promise. His real name was Castellano but back then Irish fighters were the big thing with New York promoters so he fought as Jake Costigan. Even so, he never did get on the card at the Garden, although he did have maybe a dozen fights at the old Saint Nicholas Arena. Mostly, though, he fought in small clubs in Queens, the Bronx, and out on the Island. While he was fighting, his contract was owned by Richie Saint, and when he finally had had enough of being beaten up by smooth-moving black kids fifteen years younger than he was, he continued to work for his old boss.

Richie Saint, or Richard Santucci, was a middle-level hood with lots of connections. Back when Jack Kittens was fighting for him, Saint had maybe three dozen fighters under contract, most of them better prospects than Jack Kittens ever was. In those days Richie Saint was a pretty big man in New York boxing circles, widely known and well liked by just about everyone who mattered in the New York mob. As his small-time boxing empire went downhill in the late fifties and through the sixties, he developed a number of new interests that kept him in touch with his friends in the mob, so that although he was a minor figure in the New York underworld, he knew a lot more than you might have expected judging from what he was into. And if Richie Saint knew a lot, then Jack Kittens knew almost as much.

When the observation tower at the Empire State Building opened at eight-thirty Monday morning, Jack Kittens was one of the first to get on the elevator. It was a gray, drizzly day and there would be almost no view from the top, so the elevator was empty except for Kittens and three touring Japanese businessmen who talked to each other slowly in very bad English the whole way up. They must have been told it was rude to talk Japanese in front of an American.

To get to the top you had to change elevators twice, and Kittens helped them out when they had trouble with the signs leading from one elevator to another. In the second elevator, one of them, a thick, solid man built a lot like Kittens, began to giggle nervously. He spoke rapidly in Japanese to his companions.

"Ears," another one explained for Kittens' benefit.

"Huh?"

"Ears," the man repeated, putting both hands to his ears. With his hands he pantomimed the ascent of the elevator and then drew little circles with his palms by the side of his head.

"Oh, yeah," Kittens said and the four men lapsed into silence for a few seconds. Then Kittens said, "Swal-low."

The stocky Japanese cocked his head quizzically.

"Swal-low hard," Kittens enunciated carefully, then closed his mouth and gulped a swallow. His three friends gave a smile of comprehension, tried it, and then nodded with satisfaction.

At the top the three Japanese hurried to the observation windows, where they peered intently into the thick overcast, looking down from time to time at the steel indicator embedded in the stonework that told them what they would have been seeing it they could have seen anything.

Jack Kittens walked slowly past the concession booth to the north windows, where he looked out for a few minutes without any particular interest. He could barely see up to Central Park and, anyway, he wasn't the tourist type. He checked his watch and saw it was only a quarter to nine, pulled a heavy, squat-bowled pipe with a short, straight stem from his topcoat pocket, pressed down the ashes on the top with his thumb, and lit it. With the pipe in his mouth he looked a little less like an ex-fighter—but only a little, because there was nothing else that would explain the thick layers of scar tissue over both eyes and the badly abused nose.

After a few minutes he walked back inside, past the concession stand with its little nickel-plated Empire State Buildings, past the elevator which was unloading eight or nine more people who looked like three generations of the same family, and to an unmarked doorway that opened onto a staircase. Two flights down he found himself in a narrow corridor and picked out a door that said EQUIPMENT ROOM NO ADMITTANCE. It was unlocked and he went in.

The room was dark but Kittens could see it was filled almost wall to wall with electrical gear. In addition to shelves stocked with various kinds of monitoring equipment, there were six-foot-high banks of something or other studded with intricate wiring. It looked a little like the switching machinery at a telephone exchange, but Kittens knew enough to know that it wasn't telephone equipment. This whole floor was occupied by the transmitting facilities of a large number of the city's radio stations, and whatever this stuff was, it had something to do with that.

He picked his way between two of the tall banks that stood half a foot above his head and came into a four-by-six alcove on the far side. There, seated at a cardboard folding table, was Frank Hovannes.

"You wanted to see me, Hovannes," Kittens said.

"Yeah, sit down."

Hovannes motioned him to a straight wooden folding chair leaning against the wall. He was sitting on a chair like it, smoking a cigarette and tapping the ashes into a styrofoam cup with a little black coffee at the bottom.

Kittens' pipe was in his hand by his side and he put it to his mouth but didn't draw on it. He glanced around for a few seconds, and although the pipe in his teeth hid any facial expression, his eyes showed that he didn't like being here. There was no denying that this was a good place to meet but it was, if anything, too isolated and Jack Kittens didn't like it.

There was a window in the wall behind Hovannes, and even on this gray day the little alcove seemed bright with a hazy, glary kind of light. Kittens took the chair Hovannes had indicated, flipped it open, and sat down heavily at the table facing the Inspector.

"Awright," he said, "whatdya want?"

"I'm interested in buying a typewriter," Hovannes said.

Kittens said, "Have you tried the yellow pages?"

Hovannes dropped his cigarette into the coffee cup, where it made a quick hissing sound as it died. He didn't say anything and neither did Kittens. After half a minute of this the ex-fighter put a thick, puffy hand into his pocket and came out with a pack of matches with which he relit the pipe. The tobacco had a heavy sweet smell that wasn't unpleasant in the stuffy room.

"Typewriters, Jack," Hovannes said. "I wanna talk to you about typewriters."

"What, you wanna write a book?"

"Yeah, I wanna write a book. You wanna be in it?"

"No thanks, Inspector."

"Then I think maybe you should tell me something about typewriters."

"If you wanted a couple cases of beer, maybe I could help you," Kittens said, his voice thick but mocking. "I'm in wholesale liquor you know, beer and wine."

Hovannes didn't respond, so Kittens went on. "But this, nah, it's not my line. I'm not in the typewriter business," he said.

Hovannes stood up, scraping the chair loudly on the concrete floor, and walked to the window. He stood with his back to the window and looked down at Kittens, a middleweight in his fighting days and probably not more than one-seventy now. Hovannes was much the bigger of the two, set heavy like Kittens but about six inches taller, a few years younger and in better shape, even though the ex-fighter worked out regularly. Like most boxers, Kittens carried himself well, and if the two of them had been standing together Hovannes wouldn't have made him feel small, despite the difference in size. But looking up at the Inspector from his chair Kittens did feel small and didn't like the feeling. He wanted to stand up, but if he did it would be too obvious why he did it so he kept his seat and looked away from Hovannes.

"Listen, Kittens," Hovannes said, speaking slowly, his voice tense and toneless and almost whispering, "you made it your business when you gave me certain information about certain people in the trucking business. So now you're into it whether you like it or not, and I want to know about typewriters. Like IBM shipped a truckful of them up from Kentucky to New York, only they got lost somewhere in Pennsylvania."

Kittens laid his pipe down on the table. "Don't push, Hovannes," he said, his voice halfway between firmness and complaining. "I didn't have to come here, you know. If I got nothing to tell you, I got nothing to tell you. I only told you that other thing cause my uncle said I should talk to you."

"Well *I'm* telling you to talk to me now."

Now Kittens did stand up. "You," he said, facing Hovannes, "you can't tell me shit."

"Jack," Frank said without raising his voice, "I am telling you."

"Come off it, Hovannes," Kittens answered, walking to within two feet of where Frank was standing by the window. "You know, you think I'm just a dumb pug but I ain't that dumb. When my uncle says to help you out I help you out, but I ain't on the fucking city payroll. I ain't gonna do your goddamned job for you. I laid it out for you four months ago, told you the man you wanted to see about them trucks was Big Sallie. And now you come crying with more questions. What the fuck do you want, Hovannes?"

His voice was a high, sneering, contemptuous whine as he kept talking. "I don't know if you know it, Hovannes, but the signals I'm getting tell me you blew it. You've had four fucking months since I told you what you wanted to know. And if you're coming back to me now it's because you couldn't do shit with it. I tell you where to look and you can't find anything and now Jackie Kittens is supposed to help the man out again? No way, Hovannes."

"You sure that's the way you want it, Jack?"

"It's not the way I want it, Inspector, it's the way it's gonna be," Kittens said and walked back to the card table to pick up his pipe.

Hovannes didn't move. "You like being in the wholesale liquor business, Jack?" he asked.

Jack Kittens turned slowly to face Hovannes. He didn't know what the question meant. "Yeah," he said cautiously.

"You like the policy business too, huh, Jack?"

So that was it, Kittens thought, and then he thought, So what? "I like what I'm doing, Inspector," he said. "Whatever I'm doing I like doing."

"Well, I like what I'm doing too, Jack. You're not gonna believe this but you can get a lotta kicks outta being a cop. Like when someone gives you trouble you can send a car out to thirty-eight sixty-two Queens Boulevard if you happen to know there's a numbers bank there."

"Ah, blow it out your ass, Hovannes," Kittens snarled

and put his pipe in his pocket. "You can't touch me and you know it. I'm registered."

Hovannes knew he was right. This pug was a registered federal informant. If the New York police took any action against him, a call from Kittens to his contact in the FBI would get the agent on the phone to the district attorney. The agent would explain that the FBI had an interest in this man and that he was to be left alone, and the district attorney would go along with it.

Hovannes still didn't move from the window. "Yeah, I know that, Jack," he said. "I know how it works. You get in trouble, your uncle helps you out. But like I said, I need my kicks too, and I would get a real kick out of being there at Valentine's when you try to explain how come we bust you and you're out on the street an hour and a half later. I'd like to hear you telling them about how good your uncle is to you."

Jack Kittens' eyes went dark. He had already started to walk toward the corridor out of the alcove, but what Hovannes said stopped him. Something in the Inspector's voice told Kittens he wasn't bluffing, and if he wasn't bluffing this could be serious.

No, Kittens said to himself, he's gotta be bluffing. A cop's not gonna put his ass on the line bucking the bureau. You could get in almost as much trouble fucking over their informants as you could fucking over their agents. On the other hand, you couldn't put anything past this Hovannes. Kittens had known him long enough to know he was capable of something like that. It'd be a shitty thing to do, but he could do it. Besides, it was probably true that he hadn't gotten a goddamned thing on Sallie Manzano in four months on the case. That was why he was here now, wasn't it? And if that was true, then he was probably getting a lot of heat on that score. So maybe his ass was on the line anyway, and in that case there was no telling what he might do.

Fuck it, Kittens thought, there's no sense finding out. He looked at Hovannes for half a minute without saying anything while he made up his mind, and then he said through his teeth, "Ya know, Hovannes, you are scum."

"That's right, Jack," Hovannes said, "I'm scum. But you, you're the May Queen. Sit down."

Chapter 2

"DID I TELL YOU, the word is Billy Mazes is back in town," Frank Hovannes said. He was stretched almost lying on the couch, his back caved toward the cushions and his long heavy legs reaching toward where his heels met the thin wool of the carpet almost a foot and a half past the coffee table. The slouch had something to do with the sluggishness he always felt after one of Dorothy Fleming's overrich meals, but also it was because this Billy Mazes business was the best thing he had heard in weeks and all through dinner he had looked forward to when the women would go into the baby's room and he could be alone with Ernie to tell him.

"Where'd you get that?" Fleming asked. "You want another cup of coffee?"

"Jack Kittens. Yeah, I'll get it myself."

"Kittens? You must've had to lean on him pretty good," Ernie observed, laughing slightly as he climbed out of the upholstered chair facing Frank and shuffled slowly into the dining room. He filled Frank's half-empty cup at the table and one for himself and carried both carefully back into the living room. "Is he still juicing?" he asked as he handed the cup to his partner.

"Kittens says no. Steady as a rock. Dresses nice, too."

Ernie shrugged skeptically. "Maybe it means something," he conceded, "but I wouldn't put money on it. Manzano'd never have him driving for him again."

"That's not what I get from Kittens," Frank said with a trace of smugness. Ernie shrugged again as he sat down, a gesture so slight that if Hovannes hadn't known him for over twenty years he probably wouldn't have been able to see it. But he did see it and it bothered him, so he took a couple of seconds to think before trying to answer Ernie.

Billy Mazes was a small-time hoodlum who used to be Big Sallie Manzano's private driver. He had a bad drinking problem, though, and hadn't driven for Sallie for maybe four or five years. At first Sallie just demoted him to the role of occasional messenger and courier, but as the drinking got worse Sallie had less and less use for him. Then Frank busted him and he got zip to seven at Greenhaven on a gun charge and when he got out three years later Sallie wasn't having anything to do with him. That was maybe two years ago and he hadn't been heard from since.

"I know you're gonna tell me I've got my head up my ass, Ernie," Hovannes said at last, speaking slowly as he stared past the cup and saucer he was holding cradled on his stomach. "But I got this feeling says Billy's our man. The way I read what Kittens tells me, Billy's back in the club. Has lunch in Valentine's every afternoon and you know what that means. That's Frankie Diamond's place and Frankie and Big Sallie are pretty tight, so what would Mazes be doing there if he's not on Sallie's payroll again?"

"Frank, maybe he likes the food," Fleming said with a sarcastic emphasis on the last word. "Big Sallie's not gonna touch a wheelman who likes to get stewed five days outta the week plus weekends. Be serious."

"Well, yeah," Hovannes answered, realizing the sense of Ernie's argument, "but maybe Sallie's got a heart. Or maybe Mazes has got himself straightened out. Christ, if he's sober, there isn't anyone you'd rather have driving for you than Billy. And trucks—hell, he could drive a garbage truck so the flies couldn't follow it."

"You think he's doing those jobs?"

"Hell no," Hovannes said. "He's too chickenshit for that and anyway it's not his style. But the stuff is coming into the city and he'd be a natural for driving it at this end. I can see him doing that. Whatdya think?"

"Could be," Ernie said. "You told the Chief about this yet?"

Frank was thinking about the time six years ago when Billy Mazes, driving a rented eight-ton truck, shook a tail in the middle of Manhattan. It might have cost two of Frank's detectives their gold shields if he hadn't known what kind of a driver Billy was.

"No," he answered, "why should I? If I have to tell him, I'll tell him."

"It might take some of the heat off."

Frank looked across at his partner, who was sitting in that oddly prim way he had, his feet flat on the floor and together, the coffee cup balanced on his knees and his back away from the upholstery even though it was a soft chair. He looked like he knew something Frank didn't, and it made Frank uncomfortable, so he said, "Jesus, how long's it take to change a baby? They've been in there a half hour."

"Aw, they'll be a while yet," Ernie answered and smiled, stretching his legs out in front of him. As he did so his whole body seemed to change, thickened and softened and sank into the chair. "You know, Frank," he went on, his voice friendly and confiding, "when you have your first kid at my age—Dorothy's age too, I mean—you'd be surprised how much you just wanna watch him and play with him and things like that. It makes you realize you missed out on a lot before. I'll tell you something else, too, you wouldn't think of unless it happened to you. It makes you realize you're not getting any younger. Some ways that's not true—I mean, sometimes I see Dorothy holding him and I feel like, I don't know, like we're twenty-one years old again. But sometimes I say to myself he's gonna be growing up soon and Jesus Christ I gotta get moving."

He said all this from deep in the upholstered chair, and Frank wasn't sure he understood why Ernie was saying it, especially when he added, "If you tell Halloran, it might take some of the heat off for a while, cause I hear he's pretty pissed about the way this thing is going. But I don't know that it'll do you much good for long. Even if Billy is doing the driving, what's it gonna get you? If we're lucky, we can send Billy away again, but I got a feeling we'll never be able to tie this thing to Big Sallie Manzano's tail. I got a feeling Billy Mazes turning up doesn't change all that much. We've been on this since May and we've still got nothing."

"Yeah," Hovannes said slowly, "yeah, I know it. I think I'll look up Billy anyway."

Monday, October 7

"That Rickie is a cute little kid," Emily Hovannes said brightly, leaning her head back and looking across the seat at her husband. It was a warm night and the wind through the open window on her side of the car blew her hair across her face. She reached up to brush it back.

"I don't think Ernie likes you calling him Rickie," Frank answered.

Emily didn't say anything. It seemed like all you had to do was just mention the subject of children and there was no talking to Frank. Why was it, she wondered, that something so simple and so important you couldn't talk about? And ever since Dorothy and Ernie had their baby, the subject came up every time they went over there. It couldn't be helped—but then why did they go there all the time if it made Frank so uncomfortable? God knows, it wasn't Emily's idea. She didn't really trust Ernie, who somehow didn't seem to be the same kind of cop she thought she knew her husband was. Yet Frank's friendship with him dated back to his Academy days, and she could remember that even before she married Frank there had been a special closeness between him and Ernie. During Frank's first few years of patrol the two of them were stationed in different precincts and didn't see much of each other, but they both made detective at about the same time and had been partners off and on ever since.

Emily knew enough about what police work was like to recognize that the bonds formed between men who share the same fight for a long time are especially intense. Years ago she had been jealous of Ernie, but she got over that. Recently, though—over the past two or three years, but especially since Frank got promoted to Inspector—she had begun to get feelings about Ernie she didn't quite like.

Rolling her head away from Frank to look out her window, her eyes squinting against the wind so she could barely see the tall gray apartments on Riverside Drive, Emily pointedly remembered that at dinner tonight Frank and Ernie hadn't once mentioned the job or the case they were working on. There always had been things about the job they wouldn't discuss in front of the women, and Emily understood that. But this was unnatural. It had gotten so there was nothing they could say to each other except when they were alone. Maybe they didn't even talk about it then, she thought, and the idea made her uncomfortable because she didn't understand it. She knew that the case concerned some trucks stolen somewhere out of state, but she didn't know anything else about it and she used to always know a lot, or at least a lot more than this.

Even Dorothy seemed to have noticed it, because she tried to bring up the subject once. There had been an item in the *News* this morning about a mobster in the Bronx named Vincente Robustelli or something like that, and during dinner Dorothy asked Ernie, in a way that sounded almost nervous to Emily, if this guy had anything to do with Ernie's investigation. Emily was looking at Frank when Dorothy said this, and she got the feeling he looked away from her. Maybe not, but it seemed that way. Then she heard Ernie say, "No," very softly, and Frank looked up from his plate and asked whether Ernie had decided anything about the car he was thinking of buying.

The whole relationship made her uncomfortable, and added to it was the fact that she found herself more and more set against Dorothy Fleming, who always seemed to remind her of things she didn't want to think about herself. Dorothy was altogether too mousy and accepting, too willing to put up with all the neglect and disorientation you had to put up with if you were a cop's wife. Even the way she asked that question tonight was a part of it, like she knew Ernie wouldn't answer her and was willing to accept that. The trouble with Dorothy was that she played the part to the hilt, as though there were some special privilege involved in waiting dutifully at home for when your husband had time for you in the middle of whatever secret things he was doing. It was the secrecy more than anything else that bothered her, and she honestly believed that it didn't bother Dorothy nearly so much. Maybe it was because she was Catholic, Emily thought, with a certain snideness. Being a cop's wife was the next best thing to being a nun, all sacrifice and self-effacement.

The snideness made Emily feel ashamed of herself, because she knew she never used to be that kind of a woman. She closed her eyes firmly and inched closer to the window, letting the wind take her hair and trying to put the whole thing out of her mind.

That was the trouble though, because everything about Dorothy made her feel ashamed. After twenty-two years with Frank she ought to have adjusted better than she had, and when she was forced to think about it she had to admit that it wasn't Frank's fault she wasn't more like Dorothy Fleming. And of course the baby didn't help any.

It wasn't fair for a man to be the only thing in your life when you weren't the only thing in his. Weren't even the most important part—because when you came right down to it the job of course came first. Some day, she thought bitterly, feeling tears behind her tightly closed eyelids, it will kill him. That was a fact she had known for a long time, just as she knew that her tears were for herself as much as for Frank. The little booklets the Department sent out every once in a while about what was expected of a police officer's wife said you weren't supposed to think about that, but if you knew your husband was running up against gangsters every day of his life you had to face the fact that sooner or later it would catch up with him and you would be left with a widow's pension and a little duplex in Riverdale. It would be stupid not to think about it.

So one day Frank would die for the Department, Emily thought, and she couldn't imagine him dying for her. That was a strange and sickening way to put it, but it just about told the story, didn't it?

She opened her eyes and turned toward Frank, who was staring at the road in front of him as he drove. They were just passing under the George Washington Bridge and would be home in a few minutes, she thought, again closing her eyes, which were dry now.

Chapter 3

VALENTINE'S WAS a small tavern and restaurant on Cherry Street just a few blocks from the Lower East Side waterfront. It was said to be Frankie Diamond's place, although Frankie didn't actually own the papers on it because, with a record like his, it would be impossible to get a liquor license. For this reason it was owned by one of Frankie's nephews, who had never seen the inside of the place and probably didn't even know where it was.

When Frank Hovannes came in, around one o'clock Tuesday afternoon, the lunch shift at Valentine's was going full swing. Hovannes hadn't been there for six or eight months, and as he walked in he again noticed, as he had the last few times he had been in, that the customers had changed a lot in recent years, ever since they put up those housing projects on Madison Street. It used to be that in the afternoon the place looked like they were holding a class reunion from Greenhaven, Attica, and Sing Sing. If you wanted to know what was moving on the waterfront, Valentine's was the place to find out. Now almost all the men at the bar were Puerto Ricans from the project, so that if he hadn't looked farther, past the bar and the booths opposite it, to the small cluster of round tables at the back, it would have been easy for Hovannes to have assumed he had come to the wrong place.

Years of undercover work give a man a knack for sizing up a room quickly, and by the time he got to the end of the bar Hovannes could have picked out any one of the dozen men there from a lineup if he had to. This was just habit, though, because it wasn't any of these sullen Puerto Ricans drinking beer from tall straight glasses that he was interested in.

Frankie Diamond wasn't there, Hovannes noticed, but that was okay because Frankie's office hours usually didn't start till around supper time. Billy Mazes wasn't there either. But Phil Runelli was. He was seated with three other men at a large round table in the far corner of the restaurant, directly under the clock. Two of the men had their backs to Hovannes and he didn't think he recognized them. The third was Johnny Lombardi.

Like Frankie Diamond, Phil Runelli was one of Big Sallie Manzano's top lieutenants, but unlike Frankie he never seemed to have anything better to do than sit in Valentine's with whoever happened to be there, usually not even his own men. Hovannes had known Runelli for a long time but had a curious feeling of indifference when he saw him. Probably no one had more money out on the street on the east side of Manhattan than Runelli, and in addition to his loan-sharking operations Runelli had a reputation for being the most vicious labor racketeer on this waterfront since the fifties. But there was something about the man that made you not want to bother with him, and Hovannes didn't seem to be the only guy in the Department who felt that way.

If you thought about it, it was funny the way cops tend to pick out favorite targets and shy away from others. This was true not just in the Organized Crime Control unit to which Frank was attached but in general among detectives throughout the Department. It didn't seem to have much to do with how much shit a man was into or how well he ran his operation, although of course that counted for something. Johnny Lombardi, for example, was a sloppy operator, and whenever somebody needed a collar it was always easy to shake a couple of Lombardi's people out of the trees. But that wasn't the main thing, because if you wanted to it wouldn't have taken that much more trouble to go after Runelli, or at least bust one or two of his enforcers.

For some reason or other, though, Phil Runelli had never been high on anybody's priority list. Maybe it had something to do with the way he looked, with his small soft body invariably draped in an inexpensive gray suit, his face soft around the jowls, and his thinning gray hair. He came across as a genuinely friendly guy—not that he went around like he was everybody's pal, the way a lot of successful mobsters did. He had a quieter, less self-assertive way about him, like a not particularly bright man who happens to enjoy people. Phil Runelli, Inspector Hovannes thought, is probably the only guy in the Mafia whose shoes need a shine.

Sitting next to Runelli, helping himself to thick brown spoonfuls of *calamari* from a large serving dish in the center of the table, was Johnny Lombardi. About a dozen years younger than Runelli, Lombardi was a man in his middle forties who was only just now starting to move up in the mob. Although he was close to Sallie Manzano, mostly as a result of his friendship with Big Sallie's brother Eddie, he wasn't an important part of Sallie's operation. Hovannes knew a couple of narcs who were trying to tie him up, but no one had anything big on him.

As Frank slid onto a stool at the end of the bar, he saw Lombardi nudge Runelli and nod in his direction. He pivoted away from the foursome at the table and caught the bartender's eye, ordering a beer. As he did, Runelli's voice came slicing through the white noise of the tavern, cutting off all conversation with a suddenness that was startling. "Inspector," he called, "what can we do for you?"

To his left, looking down the length of the bar, Frank could see a dozen suspicious eyes turned toward him. He wheeled slowly toward Runelli's table and noticed that the two men with Runelli who had their backs to him hadn't turned. "I just came in for a beer," he said, making a mental note to find out who those two were. Punks, probably—the kind of wise-asses who thought it was cool to ignore a cop when he walked in.

"By all means," Runelli called back. "If you're in a sociable mood, Inspector, get your beer and come over and say hello."

Hovannes nodded and turned back to the bartender, who hadn't moved since Runelli had first spoken. When he saw Hovannes looking at him he pulled at the tap, letting the beer slide slowly down the side of a heavy glass mug until it was filled to the top with no head at all. Hovannes put a dollar on the bar, picked up the stein, and walked over to Runelli's table.

"Sit down, Inspector," Runelli said, motioning toward an empty chair between Johnny Lombardi and the older looking of the two punks, who sat with his eyes glued to an ashtray into which he was tapping a cigaret.

Hovannes didn't move for the chair.

"I don't suppose I can offer you some *calamari*, Inspector?" Runelli went on, knowing that Inspector Hovannes would neither sit at their table nor eat their food. The offer was made just to be polite and it didn't require an answer.

"I don't think we've all been introduced," Hovannes said, looking down to his right. The older of the two punks had short sandy hair and a sharp nose. When Frank spoke he looked up slowly, turning his neck to stare into Frank's face for a few seconds, then turning back to whatever interested him in that ashtray.

Tommie Minelli, Frank thought, making the connection. He had heard that Frankie Diamond had this wise guy named Tommie Minelli working for him who thought he was bad news, and this punk seemed to fit the bill. Then the other one must be his kid brother.

"Sure, Inspector," Phil Runelli said. "This here's . . ."

". . . just a friend of Mr. Runelli's," Tommie Minelli cut in without looking up again.

"If that's how you want it, Tommie," Hovannes said, and then added, to the brother, "You must be Mickey. Nice to meet you."

Tommie Minelli ground out his cigarette and reached for another. Hovannes noticed that both Runelli and Johnny Lombardi smiled quickly and then hid their smiles in the tense silence that followed. If they got a kick out of seeing a cop put down Tommie Minelli, that told him something about where Minelli stood with them and he filed it away for future use.

Tommie Minelli must have seen it too, because he stood up and said, "Come on, Mickey, let's get outta here. I kinda lost my appetite." Then the two Minelli brothers stalked out of Valentine's.

"I don't wanna tell you how to run your business," Hovannes said when they were gone, "but whatdya want with a coupla wise-asses like that?"

"To be perfectly frank with you, Inspector, I don't want nothing with them. You know better than to think guys like that work for me. You ever see guys like that working for me?"

"They work for Frankie Diamond, huh?" Hovannes asked, knowing he was crossing a line with that question and Runelli couldn't answer it.

"You wanna know that, Inspector, you ask them or you ask Frankie Diamond," Runelli said. "If you got some business with Tommie Minelli," he went on, inviting Hovannes to leave, "it's no skin off my ass. But then maybe you oughta go see where he went, huh? There's nothing I can do for you."

Hovannes swung the empty chair next to Johnny Lombardi around so that its back was toward the table and sat straddling it. "I got no business with Minelli," he said. "At least nothing I know about. Course, you probably know something I don't. You must be wondering so I'll tell you—this is just a social call. I heard Billy Mazes is back in town."

Johnny Lombardi glanced quickly over to Runelli and then back to Hovannes. It told Frank what he wanted to know. Runelli, though, didn't flinch at all.

"That's right, Inspector," he said, after a long pause during which he took stock of the situation. "He comes around in the afternoon a lot. Stick around if you wanna see him."

"I think I'll do that," Hovannes said and reached across the table for an ashtray. He lit a cigarette and the three of them sat for about ten minutes while Hovannes smoked slowly and sipped on his beer. No one said anything. Johnny Lombardi was getting more fidgety by the second and Frank enjoyed watching him twisting his coffee cup around in its saucer, although his impassive face showed no sign of enjoyment. It was a temporary stand-off.

Runelli meanwhile was as poker-faced as Hovannes, but he was doing a slow burn. He always thought it was good policy to be friendly to cops, but on the other hand they were supposed to know their place. Hovannes clearly didn't, but then he never had. For Runelli cops were a fact of life and you had to learn to live with them. Tough ones like Hovannes were a fact of life, too. You had to face the fact that whenever they wanted to they could more or less call the shots, but even they had ways of doing things you could learn to adjust to. Everything in Runelli's book said that if Inspector Hovannes wanted to talk to Billy Mazes he could just find him and talk to him. But he had no business sitting at this table all afternoon, no business at all. Yet here he was and there was nothing Runelli could do about it, because he wasn't ready to order Hovannes out and, unlike Tommie Minelli, he wasn't about to go anywhere himself and leave his table to this son of a bitch.

At about one-thirty Billy Mazes walked in, said hi to the bartender, and loped to the back of the restaurant with his long rolling strides. He stopped dead about ten feet short of the table when he saw Hovannes.

"Come on over, Billy," Runelli said, all his geniality intact again. "Got an old friend here wants to say hello."

Billy had put on some weight since the last time Hovannes had seen him. At the time he had been doing a lot of drinking and always seemed pallid and shaky. But now the premature lines were gone from his face and he looked ten years younger.

"Hello, Cap'n," he said cordially but noncommittally.

"Inspector, Billy," Runelli corrected. "You been gone a long time. The Captain's an inspector now."

"Yeah," Mazes said, loosening up a little and turning to Hovannes, "that's nice. Congratulations."

"You're looking good too, Billy," Hovannes said. "Life treating you okay?"

"Can't complain." Then, after a pause, "What can I do for you, Cap'n?"

"Nothing at all, Billy. Just heard you were in town and wanted to say hi. No hard feelings, I hope?"

"None at all, Cap'n," Mazes said and meant it. "Best thing ever happened to me was the last time you sent me up. Haven't had a drink since and I feel like a new man."

"It shows, Billy, you look it. Glad to hear it. What've you been up to?"

"A little of this, a little of that."

"That's what got you in trouble before, Billy," Hovannes said, knowing he was crossing that line again. In a way, cops and hoods were like rivals in the same business. Their dealings made it necessary for them to talk with each other all the time, and each side was more or less used to the way the other operated. Talk like this was never friendly but it was civil, except that there was this thin but clear line and if you crossed it you weren't rivals anymore but enemies.

No one said anything and Hovannes felt that slight thrill he always felt somewhere down the middle of his chest every time that fragile membrane of civility ruptured and he looked at the enemy face to face, each side knowing who the other is.

"Well, I gotta be going," he said, standing up. "Just wanted to say hello and it's good to see you again, Billy."

He turned and walked three steps from the table, then walked back. "I'll keep in touch," he said and walked out of Valentine's.

The three men at the table didn't say anything till after he had gone.

Tuesday, October 8

"Hi, Roberto, get me the yellow sheet on Tommie Minelli, will ya?" Frank Hovannes said as he picked his way through the clutter of desks in the wardroom outside his office. "You know if Lieutenant Fleming's around?"

"Yeah, Inspector," Roberto Obregon said. "He was in about a half hour ago looking for you. Said he'd be up at the pistol range if you wanted him. Did you say Tommie Minelli?"

"Yeah, Tommie Minelli," Hovannes repeated, stepping into his office.

Obregon followed him. "I can tell you what's on his sheet if you really wanna know, Inspector," he said.

"Yeah I really wanna know," Hovannes answered, moving around to the back of his desk and pushing some papers around looking for something. "That's why I asked for his sheet."

He looked up at Obregon, who stood where he was in the doorway without moving. "Awright, you wanna tell me, tell me," he said and smiled.

Obregon had been working for him for almost a year now and he was a good man. For a young guy he knew a helluva lot. Usually detectives his age try to tough it out. They take each case one at a time and bust their balls on it, but it doesn't dawn on them till they've been in the job a long time that the trick is to keep all your chips stacked in little piles and to know how many you've got. Maybe that wasn't true in Homicide or Burglary, but it was for shitsure true in OCC, because if you didn't have the big picture you didn't have anything at all. From the start, though, Obregon had taken Frank as his model and Frank knew it. That was why Roberto worked so hard at keeping track of all the mobsters in Manhattan, and it was also why Frank liked watching him work. He couldn't remember the last time he had seen a young guy operate the way he liked to see his men operate. Obregon got a kick out of being able to tell the Inspector, off the top of his head, things the Inspector asked him to look up, and Frank was usually willing to indulge him.

"What we got on Tommie Minelli is mostly diddleshit," Obregon said. "His juvenile sheet goes back to when he was about twelve years old but he didn't start to get interesting till about a year, year and a half ago. Up to then it was all nickel and dime stuff. Started out running numbers, boosting cars, a coupla pennyante break ins. Then maybe a year and a half ago all of a sudden he's working for Vin Robustelli, which is pretty fast company for a kid whose idea of the big time is boosting a rack of fur coats. Anyway, he's up in the Bronx working for Robustelli for maybe six or eight months. Mostly as decoration, I think, cause from what I hear he comes across tough as hell. But Robustelli didn't see much of a future for him and cut him off. The kid's a little on the psycho side. Walks around with two forty-fives and thinks he's Jimmy Cagney. So Robustelli must've figured he didn't need the kind of trouble you can get from having a psycho asshole like that around. So he's back on the street a coupla months and the next thing you know he's hitched onto Frankie Diamond. Which is where he is now. It's gotta be a comedown for him, working with Frankie Diamond after he was right next to Vin Robustelli, but that's show biz."

Obregon stopped talking for a minute to see if there was anything else, then added, "Oh yeah, and there's his brother. The brother's not connected at all. Just hangs around with Tommie all the time." He paused again. "How's that?"

"That's good, Roberto," Hovannes said. "Someday they'll replace you with a computer."

"You still want the sheet?"

"Yeah, I still want the sheet."

"Whatdya want Tommie Minelli for?"

"Nothing really," Hovannes said. "I just ran into the little turd this afternoon and wanted to know what's what."

"Oh sure, Inspector," Obregon said and then added, trying to be helpful, "There's not much to him, but if you ever wanna put him away, you can always nail him for those forty-fives."

"A waste of time, Roberto. A guy like that the thing to do is to wait till he uses them and then put him away for that. Kills two birds with one stone."

Obregon wasn't sure whether or not Hovannes was kidding, but he smiled anyway. "Oh, Inspector, I almost forgot," he said. "The Chief called, wants you to call him back."

"Halloran?"

"Yeah, Halloran. Chief Sitting Bull."

Hovannes laughed. "That what they call him? Not bad. Remind me later, I'll give him a call."

Obregon said, "He said it was important."

Hovannes bristled momentarily, then relaxed into a smile. "You ever wanna make Inspector, Roberto?" he asked. "Then let me give you a little advice. Three things. First, you gotta figure out what's important yourself. Halloran's got two stars and he could have twelve stars, but you know as well as I do what his idea of important is. When you're working for me, I'll tell you what's important, not Halloran. And when you're working for someone else you can figure it out for yourself. Second, don't ever call a guy like that on the phone if you don't have to. There's something about a telephone, Roberto, I don't know what it is, but those stars come right over the wires. You've been here a year now and have you ever once seen me pick up that phone and call Halloran? I go down there, right? Get a guy like that one-on-one and he's a pussycat. Memorize those two rules, Roberto, and you'll be an Inspector by April. Probably have my job."

"What's the third one?" Obregon asked.

"Third one? Oh yeah, watch your mouth. You make a crack like that Sitting Bull line once too often or to the wrong guy and they'll have you back busting fags."

"You got the wrong boy, Inspector," Obregon said. "Picking fruit is one detail they never had me on."

Hovannes sometimes puzzled Obregon, made him feel not quite sure how he was supposed to react. Sometimes the Inspector would say things that sounded flippant but when you answered him that way you found out he wasn't kidding at all. He'd look at you like he was trying to melt the shield in your pocket. Other times you could tell he was kidding, and this had looked like one of them.

"Yeah, sure, Roberto," Hovannes said. "Me neither. Ask around—no one's ever been on that detail. Must've been some other police force."

There was an almost startling bitterness in Hovannes's voice all of a sudden and Obregon realized he had guessed wrong. Had the Inspector ever worked vice, he wondered. There were some guys who could work vice their whole lives and actually got to like it. It was a soft detail, you could say that for it. But any cop Obregon knew who got anywhere in the Department either never worked vice or hated it when he did. Really hated it. Obregon thought he knew what the Inspector's background was and he didn't remember, from when he looked up his scorecard a year ago, that Hovannes had ever been in the Vice Squad. But maybe he was, and that would explain the icy sarcasm in the way he spoke. Whatever it was, Obregon figured he'd better drop the subject. "That all, Inspector?" he asked.

"No, it's not all," Hovannes said. "There's something I want you to do. You know who Billy Mazes is?"

Obregon shook his head.

"No, of course not. He was before your time. Billy Mazes is a wheelman for Sallie Manzano. He's sitting in Valentine's right now. We got someone around who's not doing anything?"

"I don't know about not doing anything, but Fred Gallagher's down at the corner."

"Yeah, Gallagher's fine. Okay, you drag Gallagher away from the trough and go over Valentine's and wait for Billy Mazes to come out. Gallagher probably knows who he is but get his picture out of the file anyway. Then tail him. Nothing heavy. I don't care if you lose him so much but I don't want him to know he's got company. That's the important thing. Don't waste too much time on it. Put in a couple of hours, and if he goes home, forget about it."

"Where's home?"

"How should I know? You're the ones tailing him."

"You want that right away?"

"Yeah, Gallagher's fat enough already."

"Okay. I'll get you the sheet on Minelli and then I'll go get Gallagher."

"Forget Minelli," Hovannes said.

Tuesday, October 8

Bob Halloran was Assistant Chief Inspector for Organized Crime Control and Frank Hovannes's immediate superior. When OCC was formed during the Department shakeups in nineteen seventy, Halloran hadn't been the Deputy Commissioner's first choice as ACI. At first the job went to an Inspector from Narcotics, but he lasted only about eight months and then was forced to retire in order to head off some sort of a scandal. The Department managed to hush it up so successfully that Hovannes and a lot of men even higher up in the Department never did find out what the story was. If the guy was a narc it had to be money, but you couldn't be sure.

Anyway, when the first ACI was canned, Frank had figured that maybe he would get the job, especially since he had seniority over the other inspectors in Organized Crime Control. Instead, they picked Halloran, who was already an ACI in Intelligence. Even Frank had to admit that if you looked at it from the Commissioner's office the choice made a certain amount of sense. Frank had a reputation as a loner and he knew it. When the brass wants to pick someone safe for a job they want someone they know pretty well. They had already been burned once with the division's first ACI and the best way to keep from being burned again was to take someone who had been around Headquarters for a long time. The rule was if you had to choose between someone who was brass all the way and someone who was a cop all the way, take the brass every time. So Halloran got the job even though it was no secret he had already put in for his pension while he was still in Intelligence. They must've sold him a bill of goods about how his city needed him and could he just put in another year till they had the Organized Crime unit on its feet.

Everybody expected Halloran would be retiring soon but Frank wasn't particularly looking forward to it. When you wear out your third swivel chair they put you on pension automatically, he heard one of the men say, but as far as he was concerned he'd rather have Halloran in there than someone else. Frank knew he wouldn't get the job next time either, and he was better off with someone who would let him run things his own way without bothering him too much.

So far Halloran had been little more than a pain in the ass. If he had been a patrolman he would've been the kind who always went for the easy collars, and so he expected his men to run up a good score each month. He never could understand why Hovannes was willing to tie up eight or ten men for months at a time on a single case, and if he could have had his own way he wouldn't have permitted it. For Frank this meant that he had to spend a fair amount of his time making sure that Halloran didn't have his own way.

The ACI's office was on the first floor of Headquarters, directly under Frank's. There was a small stairway leading downstairs in the corner of the wardroom past the lockup where prisoners were supposed to be kept while the arresting officer did the paperwork prior to booking. It led directly into Halloran's outer office and Frank always went that way whenever he had to see the Chief.

Halloran's secretary, a policewoman with sergeant's stripes, told him the Chief would be free in a minute and Hovannes stood by her desk while he waited. As soon as her intercom buzzed he walked in.

"You wanted to see me, Bob? What's up?" he said.

In the Department you generally called an Assistant Chief Inspector Chief unless you outranked him. Hovannes usually went along with this kind of protocol, but for Halloran he made an exception. And Halloran, who only had four months to go to finish out the year he had promised the Commissioner, was beyond caring.

"Good news and bad news," Halloran said. "Sit down, Frank."

"That's all right, I only got a minute. Give me the bad news first," Hovannes said, standing behind the empty chair that faced Halloran's desk.

"I'll give you the good news first. We just got the FBI reports on that job in Pennsylvania. The IBM stuff. Two guys did it and the driver gave them pretty good descriptions."

"Yeah," Hovannes said flatly.

"Figured it might help, Frank. The sergeant has all the information for you. Pick it up on your way out," Halloran went on.

"I'll work on it," Hovannes said, "but you didn't call me down here for that. It would've come up on the tube anyway."

"No, I didn't. That's the good news," Halloran answered. He was speaking more slowly now, picking his words carefully. "How long does it take them to get rid of a load like that?" he asked and saw at once that he had made a mistake.

"I don't know, Chief," Hovannes said. "They don't send me their delivery schedules."

"You know what I mean, Frank," the ACI bristled. "They can't hold onto this stuff forever. Now what's reasonable? And think before you give me an answer, Frank, because whatever you say, that's what you've got."

"You gotta be kidding," Hovannes said.

"Do I sound like I'm kidding?"

Frank turned and walked away from the Chief's desk toward the bookcase on the far wall. He fished a cigarette from his pocket and lit it and then turned back. There were maybe twenty-five feet of space, maybe more, between him and Halloran, and for the first time Frank was impressed with the size of the ACI's office. His own probably wasn't ten by twelve and you could hardly have put Halloran's huge oak desk in it without having to climb over it to get in and out the way he and Emily had practically had to climb over the bed in their first apartment. He wondered if the men got smaller as the offices got larger or if it only looked that way. Sitting behind his desk, almost ten yards away, Halloran looked ridiculously small and old.

Give him the benefit of the doubt, Frank thought to himself with more contempt than pity. Maybe ten years ago—no, make that fifteen—Halloran could've said something like that and made it stick. Then again, maybe not.

Frank took a drag from his cigarette and started to move toward Halloran's desk as he spoke.

"Look, Bob," he said, "I explained to you once before how it works. It all depends on what kind of facilities they got. If they're just boosting the trucks and unloading them, then three, four days at the outside and they're rid of the stuff. If they got decent warehousing they could hold it for a long time. Now what do you want me to tell you—that I'll round 'em up in two weeks? This isn't television, you know."

"I know it's not television," Halloran said, surprising Frank, who hadn't expected him to say anything. "On television you always get your man; here we don't. How long you been on this thing? Three months? Four? And what've you got? Nothing, Frank. You're already running into the eleven o'clock news and you got nothing to show for it. They're pitching a shutout at you, Frank. Why don't you admit it?"

"Aw, shutout—shit!" Hovannes said and flicked his cigaret into the ashtray on the Chief's desk. "They're doing a million bucks worth of business a year, you know that. And I'm supposed to give it another month and then call it off? Then what do I do? Drive out to Sallie Manzano's house in Tenafly and tell him he's home free, the statute of limitations has run out of him?"

"There are other people working on it, Frank," Halloran said, trying to get the discussion back to a more reasonable level.

"Yeah, the Pennsylvania Highway Patrol and the FBI. If you want to tell anyone to call it off, tell them. This is where the stuff is coming, Bob, and this is where we're going to have to nail them. If we pack it in they could fucking well draw up papers and sell stock in Sallie Manzano Enterprises."

"All right, Frank," Halloran said. It was almost three o'clock and there was no point spending the whole afternoon on this. "You wanna chase your tail around some more, chase your tail around some more. But I'm not giving you forever."

Hovannes turned to leave. Some of this, he knew, was just a lot of ritual horseshit, the Chief coming down on his men, letting them know he wanted results. He was supposed to thank Halloran for showing a little confidence, for giving him more time. But how could you thank a man for making you waste a half hour trying to get you to feel grateful for permission to do your job? As far as Frank was concerned the only good thing about it was that he hadn't been forced to tell Halloran about Billy Mazes. If things had really gotten hairy he would've told Halloran that he had a new lead he wanted to develop and then he would've had to tell him what it was. But the way it worked out was fine, Frank figured. He still had that card in the hole and could play it later. Anyway, the less Halloran knew the better.

"I don't need forever," he said at the door. "But it's gotta take time, Chief. Everything else is on their side. Time's the only thing we got going for us."

Chapter 4

THERE WAS a firing range in the basement of Police Head-quarters, but Ernie Fleming didn't like to use it. Too many cops who can't shoot work out of Headquarters, he used to explain, but Frank Hovannes knew that the real reason was that Ernie liked to be alone when he was shooting and the Headquarters range was always crowded. So when-ever he could, Ernie went up to the station house in the Central Park precinct, where apparently cops didn't believe in pistol practice. Late in the afternoon you usually could have the pistol range pretty much to yourself, and Ernie was the kind of guy who could spend half a day squeezing off shots.

Like many cops who weren't especially good with their guns, Frank knew that if his life ever depended on getting off one perfect shot he'd be in a lot of trouble. Ernie, though, was something else. A long time ago, when he and Ernie were working together in an Upper West Side bur-glary squad, Ernie had given his sergeant a rifle and then matched him bullet for bullet with his service revolver at seventy-five yards in the basement firing range at the two-four. For some reason that scene passed through Frank's mind as he hurried downstairs after leaving Halloran's office. As far as being a cop was concerned, he had realized a long time ago that being that good a shot didn't matter very much. It was nice for winning bets but you didn't really need it.

But these things were important to Ernie. Although he didn't look the part, short and overweight, his hair thin-ning, in a way he was like a cop out of the movies, deadly with any kind of a gun and not afraid of anything. He was also surprisingly strong, especially in the shoulders and arms. When they had both been in the two-four, years ago, there wasn't a man there who could arm wrestle Ernie, and most of them were a lot bigger.

Back then Frank had been jealous of the way Ernie

could handle himself, but now he could honestly say that those things didn't matter so much. He would have liked it if he could shoot better than he could, but it never seemed worth the hours of practice it took. He had only had to use his gun twice in all his years on the force and on both occasions it turned out he was good enough. That was all you needed.

Hovannes left Headquarters by the basement exit on Centre Market Street, a narrow alleylike street one block long between Broome and Grand. Police vehicles were parked on both sides their curbside wheels well up on the sidewalks so traffic could pass. Frank climbed into his car and started uptown. At Houston he cut over to First Avenue and then sped north, moving easily until the traffic thickened when he passed Thirty-fourth Street. When he had to slow down for the traffic, he got on the radio and told Communications to page Obregon's car and have Obregon call him on the telephone at the Central Park station house. There were a number of leaks in the police communications system, and if you wanted to by-pass them New York Tel was a better bet.

After he clicked the microphone back onto its hook, Frank realized it would be at least another half hour till he could get to Central Park. The First Avenue lights were staggered, but even so he was only making a block or two each time the light changed. He thought about using his siren and decided against it. In the first place, you weren't supposed to if you didn't have a reason, and in the second place, he wasn't in any hurry to meet Ernie.

If Frank had been in a better mood, he might have been able to see the meeting he had just come from as a kind of victory, but the way he felt now it was impossible to get any satisfaction from having stalled off Halloran till the next time. So far the Chief was right. Sallie Manzano was pitching a shutout against him, and yelling at Halloran didn't change that. The only way to change it would be to break the case, and Frank realized the odds weren't too good. Even if Billy Mazes was doing the driving for Manzano's hijacking operation, the case could still drag out for months, and maybe even then nothing would come of it. So far Frank hadn't even been able to find out what kind of facilities Manzano had for moving truckloads of hot merchandise. Things like typewriters, television sets, electronics equipment he'd probably want to hold for a while to let them cool off. That means he has to have warehousing for it, which is where Billy Mazes comes in. Having someone like Billy to tail meant maybe you had someone who might lead you to the shop. But then what?

Realistically speaking, it was as good as certain that whatever warehouses Manzano had weren't in his name. He'd never touch any of the merchandise or go anywhere near it. The only chance to make any kind of a case against him was Billy again. Faced with a third conviction, maybe he'd be willing to make a deal—his ass for Big Sallie's. The trouble with that was that he'd be as good as dead if he did, so the choice for him would be Greenhaven or the Harlem River, and Hovannes didn't have anything to offer him to make the river seem more attractive.

And even if he did, Billy would not exactly make the kind of witness who could put Sallie Manzano away. Frank remembered a time about six years ago when he and Ernie spent what seemed like a lifetime on a case involving Carmine Leone, the Brooklyn boss. They were both working in Intelligence at the time, and the case was big enough for the DA's office to be in on it with them the whole way. Mostly just dragging their feet of course, but Frank and Ernie kept pushing them and finally they had a case they thought they could go to court with. When it came down to the end, though, the two assistant DAs went over the whole thing and told Frank to forget it. They had turned a guy around who knew the whole Leone operation inside out, but the DA's people didn't think he'd make a believable witness. "Those chicken-shits won't go into court until they have a written confession from Leone signed by two witnesses and a priest," Frank complained bitterly to Ernie the night the case was dropped.

And Ernie had said, "The only fucking way we're gonna get rid of Leone is just the two of us go out and waste him."

If this was going to be the same thing as the Leone case all over again, Frank didn't want to think about it. But why should it be? There were a lot of differences. Like now Frank was an inspector and had ten men in his detail, where then it had just been him and Ernie. But more important, he wanted Big Sallie more than he had ever wanted anyone. When he got right down to it, it was that simple: he had the men to do it, he was in charge, and neither Halloran with his little old man's ideas about the safe, easy collars, nor Ernie for that matter, with his cocksure skepticism, were going to stop him. After twenty-three years Frank knew he had made it as far as he was ever going to make it in the Department. He was never going to get command of OCC, but at least he would get Sallie Manzano. It could have been anyone—Big Sallie, or Vin Robustelli in the Bronx, or Leone, who still ran Brooklyn, or Tony LaGarda, the East Side boss who was Sallie's main rival in Manhattan. But Hovannes had picked Big Sallie and he was nowhere near ready to turn back yet.

Frank turned left on Eighty-fifth Street and headed for the park. The transverse was sunk below the ground level of the park, surrounded on both sides by a brick wall like a roofless tunnel with thick-leaved elms and plane trees poking over where the roof should have been. About a third of a mile into the park Frank pulled into the station house parking lot. There were about a dozen unmarked cars there and almost as many patrol cars and vans, but Frank recognized Ernie's tan Chrysler at the far end near the equipment sheds. He parked next to it and walked to the side door that led directly into the basement. The clerk in charge of the pistol range was stationed behind a counter just inside the door.

"Is Lieutenant Fleming here?" Frank asked.

The sound of a pistol popping dully behind the wood and glass doors down the corridor answered the question.

"Yes, he is, sir," the clerk said. He was a uniformed patrolman who looked barely eighteen years old, like a kid playing a cop in a high school play. Had this kid ever been out on patrol, Frank wondered. Maybe they were keeping him down here till he got older.

"What do I get? Fifty bullets?" he asked.

"Yes, sir. Just sign for them," the patrolman said, sliding a register toward Frank. He turned and took a small cardboard box of bullets from a low shelf behind him and put them in front of Frank. "Excuse me, sir," he said. "Are you Inspector Ho-vanes?"

"Hovannes," Frank corrected.

"Sorry, Inspector," the kid apologized. "There's a message here for you. A Detective Sergeant Obregon called and left a number for you to call him at. Said if he wasn't there he'd call you every fifteen minutes or so till he got you."

"Thanks, Officer," Frank said, and stood facing the young patrolman, waiting. The patrolman was waiting too.

"Excuse me, sir," he said tentatively after half a minute, "but you have to sign out for those bullets."

Hovannes smiled. "The telephone number," he said.

"Huh?"

"The telephone number. You said I was supposed to call Sergeant Obregon. You didn't give me the number."

"Oh. Yes sir." Flustered, the young patrolman groped around the countertop, then slid a piece of paper to Hovannes.

"Do you have a telephone?"

"Yessir," the patrolman snapped with military crispness.

"Well? Where is it?"

The young officer pulled a telephone from under the counter and placed it facing Frank, then stood behind the counter at parade rest. Frank waited for him to get the idea that he was supposed to leave but the patrolman wasn't moving.

"This is confidential police business, Officer," Frank said, trying to make it clearer.

"Yes sir." The patrolman's face brightened with curiosity.

Frank picked up the receiver and started to dial. "Officer, would you go tell Lieutenant Fleming that I'm here and I'll be with him in a few minutes, please," he said.

Disappointment crossed the young man's face like someone had turned off a switch. "Yes, sir," he said, and moved down the counter, into the corridor and off toward the range.

Hovannes finished dialing and the phone rang only once. A heavily accented Spanish voice said hello.

"Obregon?"

"Si."

"Awright, where are you? You gotta talk Spanish or something?"

"Naw, just kidding, Inspector," Obregon said, his accent gone. "Just keeping in practice. I used to be an undercover. I went around disguised as a Puerto Rican."

Hovannes laughed. "Where are you?" he said.

"Corner of Greene and Spring."

Greene Street was in the middle of an old neighborhood consisting mostly of run-down warehouses and factories in the southern part of Manhattan.

"Did you see our friend?"

"That's what I'm doing here, boss."

"What gives?"

"We got to Valentine's just in time to pick him up. He was on his way here and we tailed him. You know the neighborhood?"

"Sure."

"Well, he went into this warehouse or something at one-oh-two Greene Street about a half hour ago. Hasn't come out since. No other cars around so he's probably alone in there. He had keys to the place and let himself in. We're around the corner on Spring Street. Gallagher's keeping an eye on the place and I've been waiting for you to call back since."

"He didn't see you?"

"You said he wasn't supposed to know he was being tailed."

"I know what I said."

"Well, then he didn't see us."

"That's beautiful, Roberto. Look, here's what I want you to do. Keep an eye on him and follow him if he goes someplace else. This is important now, I don't want you to lose him. Don't let him know he's being tailed but don't lose him."

Obregon laughed. "Yeah, I know," he said. "Don't give him anything to hit but don't walk him either. Thanks, coach."

"You got it, Roberto," Hovannes said. "Who do we have free?"

"I don't know about free, but I think there's Stu Rhodes and there's that guy Lieutenant Fleming had you borrow from Marco."

"Savage?"

"Yeah, Savage."

"Awright. Look, you stay with our friend and have Rhodes and Savage put a surveillance on that place. It's all empty warehouses around there so they should be able to get a place across the street where they can see what's going on."

"Sure, Inspector. What's up?"

"I just told you what's up," Hovannes said. "You and

Gallagher take Billy, and Rhodes and what's-his-name get the warehouse. Oh, yeah, and look, tell Rhodes and that other guy to stay there till they're relieved. We'll arrange something for them for later tonight. I want everything in and out logged. And tell them to get right on the horn if they see anything. Have someone do a check on that address. Put Saladino on it. I want to know who owns it and how he's tied in with Sallie Manzano. Tell him if he comes up with any interesting names to check out anything else they might own."

"That's it?"

"Yeah, that's it. Keep in touch."

Hovannes hung up just as the patrolman was coming back down the corridor. He picked up the box of bullets from the counter, signed the receipt, and walked slowly toward the doors to the pistol range.

"I told him you were here, Inspector," the patrolman said as they passed in the corridor. Hovannes nodded.

Inside, Ernie was reloading. The pistol range was a long, dimly lit room about the size of a small gymnasium except that it had low ceilings covered with acoustical tile. It was divided up into shooting lanes that made it look something like an old-fashioned bowling alley. The paper targets at the far end were hooked to a pulley system so the officers could reel them in when they were finished shooting. The Central Park range hadn't been modernized since about the Second World War; it had none of the fancy partitions between the lanes that in the newer ranges put each shooter into his own isolated alcove. About the only concession to modern police science was the fact that they had taken out about three quarters of the lights after a Department study revealed that most of the times when a cop would have to use his gun it would be dark.

Ernie Fleming didn't look up from reloading his revolver. "Frank," he said.

"Yeah, hi."

"What's up?"

"Obregon and Gallagher tailed Mazes to a warehouse down on Greene Street. How's that sound?"

"Sounds okay," Fleming said. "What'd Halloran say?"

"The usual shit," Frank answered, waving the Assistant Chief Inspector out of his mind with an impatient gesture of his hand. "I think he wants us to close down the investigation if we don't get them on this IBM job. I put Rhodes and that new guy from Narco to watch the place at Greene Street."

"Savage?"

"Yeah, Savage."

"How's he working out?"

Hovannes shrugged. "He's awright, what can I tell you," he said. "Seems pretty gung-ho. I guess he didn't like it in Narco."

"Well," Ernie said judiciously, "I think they had him doing undercover. You'd have to be crazy to like that. I saw another guy you might wanna check out. I saw him a coupla weeks ago and I've kinda kept my eye on him ever since. His name's Polito, he's in Tactical now."

After Frank's promotion to Inspector, Ernie had come up with the idea that Frank ought to have his own squad. When he took over the unit there were twelve men in it, including himself and Ernie, and maybe three or four of them were ringers. Ernie's argument was that if you could get rid of deadwood like Gallagher and bring in new men like this guy Savage, you would have a squad of handpicked men you could use however you wanted. OCC was a prestige outfit and they'd be grateful to whoever brought them over, which would make it very different from working with men who were already there when you took command.

Frank could see the sense to this, but it didn't have the importance to him it had to Ernie. "Don't need him," he aid. "We already got enough men."

"Yeah, I know, Frank," Ernie answered, his voice sharp with impatience. "But Christ, if I ever got my hands on a command like you got you can damn well make book that inside of six months every goddamn one of the men in it would be my own man. Your trouble is, Frank, you still think of yourself as a detective, but you're a fucking commanding officer."

That part was right enough, Hovannes had to admit. Some guys knew how to do their own jobs and some guys knew how to use men. Ernie probably would have been a better choice for the Inspector's stripes, and in a way they both knew it. So through Frank the lieutenant was trying to run the squad the way he would have done it if he had been given the command, and as long as what he said made sense Frank was willing to go along with it.

"Okay, give me his name and his shield number and I'll get him from Tactical," Frank said.

Ernie didn't answer. Without warning, he turned quickly, raised his gun, and got off three shots toward the target. In the dim light and at that distance Frank couldn't see where they hit, but just after the blast of the third shot, while the room was still echoing, he could hear the dull thud of the bullet against the wood backing of the target cutout that told him the bullet had gone home. Ernie lowered the gun and peered across at the target, then raised it slowly, taking careful aim this time. Now he held the gun with two hands, the way you were supposed to, and steadied it on the dim paper outline across the room. Frank braced himself for the explosion but it didn't come. Instead, Ernie said, "Take a couple of shots, Frank. It'll do you good."

Hovannes pulled his service revolver from the clip at the small of his back and flipped it open. He spun the chambers, checked them, clicked it closed, and then raised the gun toward the target, Ernie holding his position beside him without moving all the while.

"Okay," Frank said, and the two of them blasted away, three shots each. Frank hit his target low with two of the shots and couldn't tell where the third went. But it did feel good, getting them off like that. He could almost see why Ernie got such a kick out of it and wondered if it helped to think of the target as someone. Did Ernie do that, he wondered, and if he did, who was he shooting at?

A momentary shiver passed down his back and he quickly said to himself, What the fuck does it matter who Ernie thinks he's shooting at? He raised the gun again, and this time he tried to see Big Sallie Manzano's heavy moon-like face at the top of the target. Keeping this idea in his mind, he emptied the pistol with a sudden remembrance that twenty-three years ago in Korea he had always tried to put faces on the men at the other end of his rifle. A lot of the soldiers with him said you couldn't do that, that you had to shoot at a uniform because if you saw a face you'd never be able to get your shot off right. But the enemy had to be more real to Frank that that, and so he would put faces on them. Once when one of his buddies was shot by a North Korean not thirty yards away, Frank put about a dozen rounds into the Korean a few seconds too late. For the next three days that slender, bony face with almost transparent skin was who he shot at every time he raised his rifle.

The gun felt like it was still jerking in Frank's hand as he lowered it and turned to Ernie, feeling something that he wasn't quite sure of but it was almost like embarrassment. His face felt hot and flushed but he was sure it didn't show in the dim room. So he said, "What're you doing tonight, Ernie?"

"Nothing really," Fleming answered. He was reloading his gun and his voice sounded soft and distant. "I told Dorothy I'd be home," he said evasively.

"Oh sure," Hovannes said, still feeling strangely awkward and embarrassed, unable to completely put out of his mind how real he had been able to make the shooting feel. "I just figured maybe ten, eleven o'clock we could go relieve Rhodes and that other guy."

"Sure," Fleming said, "sure," his voice suddenly quick and eager, almost incongruously so for what promised to be a routine stakeout. "I'll come down around ten o'clock, we can go over from Headquarters together."

Hovannes turned to leave but his gun was still in his hand and for a moment he wasn't quite sure what he was supposed to do with it. He flipped it open, ejected the spent casings, and reloaded it from the box of cartridges. Then he slid it into the clip under his jacket.

"I signed out fifty bullets," he said. "You want 'em, take 'em. I don't need them."

Chapter 5

EVEN STAKEOUT DUTY with this detail was something to be thankful for, as far as Lou Savage was concerned. A month ago he was thinking he had just about had it with Narcotics, when all of a sudden this new assignment came through, transferring him for two weeks to Organized Crime Control. Then, when the two weeks were up, the transfer was extended indefinitely on an as-needed basis.

Even though Lou had spent most of his time in OCC on surveillance duty, he didn't find the assignment dull. In the first place, you didn't often get to build a case slowly like this in Narco, and there was something about the pace of it that appealed to him. In Narco you were always hopping up and down like the Keystone Cops—bust a guy, turn him around, use him to set up a buy, and then bust the next one. Twenty-five collars a month sometimes. Of course you weren't expected to make that many, but the fact that you could do it showed how ridiculous the whole thing was.

Then, in the second place—but for Lou this was really what mattered most—this month in OCC was that much time away from the junkies. After a while it got hard to think of them as the victims of the dealers anymore. Thrown in with them day after day, you got the stink of them on your clothes and on your skin and you learned to think like a junkie so you could stay one step ahead and keep your ass alive. But you got to hate yourself for it, so you ended up hating them, and whenever that happened it made it hard to get exercised about the dealers.

Lou pulled over to the curb on Wooster Street and cut the engine and the lights and looked around. In his rearview mirror he could see traffic passing on Houston, but Wooster Street was absolutely deserted. The block was part of the Charlie sector of the sixth and Lou thought patrol here must be a piece of cake. A few blocks to the east the neighborhood had started changing, slowly evolving into something like Greenwich Village used to be before the hippies hit it. Empty lofts were being rented out to artists at a good clip, so in the daytime the streets were fairly busy with trucking traffic from the warehouses and factories and at night there was a small but more or less steady stream of rather strange-looking pedestrians. But these changes hadn't reached this far west yet and there probably weren't more than a dozen occupied lofts in the whole three-block stretch of Wooster he could see, and maybe that many on Greene Street too, one block to his left. There was no telling how many of the buildings were vacant. During the day the truck traffic was light here and at night absolutely nothing moved.

Lou reached down around the steering wheel and slid his gun up out of his ankle holster and along his calf. It was a heavy Browning automatic but he preferred it to the service revolver. On stakeout duty like this the extra weight was no problem. Reflexively, he snapped the clip out to check it but didn't really look at it, and then snapped it back until it seated. With his gun back in the holster, Lou stepped from the car and locked it.

The street was dark, and it was hard to tell one dingy building from another, but after three weeks in the same place Lou knew where he was going and found the doorway to number one-eighteen. The padlocked latch was open and he pulled a key from his pocket for the Segal lock, opened it, and went inside, closing the door behind him and turning the deadbolt. Every time he stepped through that door the sharp musty smell hit him like an unpleasant surprise. He breathed out heavily through his nose but couldn't manage to get the prickly sensation out of his nostrils. Through an open door he could see cutting tables stretched with cloth, which was where the smell came from. Even the air here had a fibrous, filamentary texture that you could taste on your mouth and feel against your eyes and inside your nose.

He found the staircase and started up, sorry for about the twentieth time that he hadn't brought his flashlight from the car. Four flights up an iron door led to the roof and the padlock there was unlatched too. Outside on the roof it was lighter and Lou moved quickly across the gravel and tar paper toward the shed on the roof of one-oh-five Greene. There was a musty smell here too, but it was different because the building was empty and had been empty for a long time. The smell here was just dust, which was less annoying.

On the second floor he found the doorless room where he would spend the night and walked in. Fred Gallagher was seated by the window and he turned slowly when he heard Lou's footsteps. "Jesus, what is this?" Gallagher said with good-humored surprise. "I got eleven-thirty. You crazy or something?"

There was another man standing next to where Gallagher was seated, but Lou didn't know him. With Gallagher's thick jowly face at about his chest level, the new guy looked very tall and skinny and the effect the two of them made was almost comical. The tall man had his jacket off and Lou noted his shoulder holster and figured he must be new because almost none of the detectives wore shoulder holsters anymore.

"Just trying to show a little enthusiasm, Fred," Savage said, and then, to the other man, "My name's Lou Savage. We on together tonight or am I your relief?"

"Oh, you two don't know each other, huh?" Gallagher said. "This here's Ron Polito. You're working with the boss tonight."

Gallagher put his hands on the arms of the old wooden swivel chair he had found a few weeks ago downstairs and pushed himself into a standing position. "Unless you wanna go for a walk or something, I'm gonna cut out," he said. "There's nothing going on down there."

"Sure, go ahead," Savage said. "Anyone down there?"

"Not now," Gallagher answered, moving for the doorway already. "It's all on the log there." Then he added, "If you wanna use my chair, go ahead."

Gallagher walked to the doorway and Lou and the new man heard his heavy footsteps as he started down. They looked at each other and smiled. "That sonofabitch," Lou said, "so that's why he was in such a hurry to get outta here."

Inspector Hovannes didn't want anyone coming or going by the front entrance on Greene Street in case there was anyone at one-oh-two, but Gallagher must have figured if he could get out before the Inspector showed up he could save himself the climb to the roof and back down on the next block.

"I don't think it matters very much," Ron Polito said. "There's no one down there."

Lou walked to the window and looked down to see Gallagher shuffling up toward Houston Street. There was a yellow legal pad on the sill that was kept there for logging purposes and Lou picked it up. As he did, Polito said, "That guy who comes here all the time, Billy something, showed up around six o'clock with another guy. Gallagher knew the other guy's name. It's down there. They just stayed maybe half an hour and there's been nothing going on ever since."

In general it was hard for Polito to talk to these detectives. Most of the time they just told him what to do or where to go and that was that. It annoyed him the way Savage just picked up the pad to see what was logged there when he could have asked, and Lou sensed his annoyance. "Thanks," he said and put the pad down without looking at it.

Something struck Polito as almost friendly about the way Lou said it, and he thought to himself that for the first time since they put him on this goddamned detail maybe here was someone he could talk to.

"It's funny, isn't it," he said. "This kinda work drives me up the wall, just sitting here like this. I was telling Gallagher that before and he was saying he didn't mind it. Then you show up early and he splits like they just let him outta jail or something and I'm still here."

"You wanna go, go ahead," Savage said. "The Inspector'll be here in a couple minutes, I'll be all right."

Polito's face flushed white as he realized that Savage thought he was asking for permission to leave. That wasn't what he meant at all, and he wanted to say something else to make himself understood, but all he could think to say was, "Nah, I'll stay. I don't mind."

Savage shrugged and for about five minutes neither spoke. Then Polito said, "Hey, Lou, are you a detective?"

"Yeah, sure," Savage answered stiffly, put on guard by the question because it sounded like Polito was trying to make some point or other and Lou couldn't figure out what it would be. Like when people say, "Hey, were you ever in the army?" or "How long you been in the job?" they usually don't want to know so much as they want to use your answer to make some kind of a point.

But Polito really wanted to know, because he said, "I was just wondering. I'm not."

"Then what're you doing here?"

"Fucked if I know," Polito said, a slight whine in his voice indicating his perplexity and irritation. "I just got assigned over here a coupla weeks ago."

"Yeah, me too," Lou volunteered. "I guess they're kinda short of men or something."

"Yeah, I guess so," Polito said, not really satisfied with the explanation. "Where'd they get you from?"

"Narco."

"No shit. Then this must be as much of a drag for you as it is for me. You can go fucking crazy sitting here looking out a window all the time. I was in Tactical. That probably doesn't seem like much to you, I mean it's not like being in Narco or something, but at least there's something's going on all the time. I'd like to get into something like Narco."

"Go ahead," Lou said.

He wasn't trying to be surly, but he didn't want to get into the kind of conversation Polito was trying to get him into. This was the way they all talked when they were rookies, usually sitting in the squad room before roll call. There was something about the job that made you talk about it all the time, and Lou had done it himself too, even though it annoyed him. At first he thought it was because there was so much dead time, but then he realized that that wasn't it. Hell, car salesmen sit around the showroom all the time with nothing to do, but it didn't seem likely to Lou that they talked about selling cars. Then he thought maybe it was because there was so much to learn, not just about your job but about the Department itself. Almost everyone in patrol figured he'd get out of a patrol in a few years, so the rookies were always trying to find out what else there was and what the other guys were thinking. By the end of your rookie year, though, you either made up your mind where you wanted to go or decided to just wait and see. You didn't hear three- or four-year men sitting around talking about wanting to go into Narco or undercover or Special Services.

"I mean it's funny," Polito went on, either not noticing Savage's disinterest or not caring, "but I always figured I just wanted to make detective, it didn't matter where. Tactical's okay, don't get me wrong. It beats patrol—at least where I was. But I wanted that gold shield, I guess everybody does. Now I'm not so sure. I mean, the way I see it, it matters a lot where you are. Like Narco's probably okay, but this—shit, you could go crazy. If they told me I could have a gold shield tomorrow if I stayed here, I think I'd tell them I wanted to go back to Tactical."

"Depends what you like, I guess," Savage said, walking away from the window and lighting a cigarette. There was no one down there, so it probably wouldn't hurt to smoke at the window but Lou was glad for the excuse to get a few steps away from Polito, who hadn't moved from where he was standing next to Gallagher's chair. Besides, he didn't want the Inspector coming in and finding him at the window in the dark with a lighted cigaret.

Lou didn't even hear any footsteps until the Inspector was practically in the room. Hovannes stepped through the doorless doorway holding his flashlight, which was turned off. He saw Savage first, who was in the middle of the room, then Polito by the window. He looked around quickly.

"What the fuck is this?" he said sharply.

"What? Hi, Inspector," Savage answered. Polito turned to face Hovannes.

"Where's Gallagher?"

"Oh. Well, I got here a little early so he left," Savage explained, knowing it wouldn't wash. He and Polito were both new men, so if anyone was going to leave early Gallagher should have let Polito go and he should have stayed so there'd be one experienced man from the unit there.

"Yeah, all right," Frank said. "It's not your fault, Lou, but next time you gotta relieve Gallagher don't go showing up early." To Polito he said, "Anything moving?"

Polito glanced down at the log to get the names. "Yeah," he said, "Billy Mazes showed around six o'clock with this other guy. Angie Morello. The two of them stayed about a half hour and then left. Since then there's been nothing."

Hovannes thought it over for a minute. "Well, I can't figure it," he said finally. "We must have the right place, huh? Unless Mazes is playing games with us. You think he knows we're here?"

"I don't see how he could," Savage answered quickly, trying to sound confident. As soon as he said it he realized his mistake and hoped the Inspector wouldn't pick him up on it.

"You don't see how he could, huh? Your fat friend, Polito, he left by the front, didn't he?"

Polito didn't say anything.

"Yeah," Hovannes said, making his point. He moved to the window and looked down at the street, first across to one-oh-two, which was dark, and then up toward Houston. Polito stood next to him. Without turning from the window Hovannes said, "You can go now, Ron. See you tomorrow."

Maybe there's more to this than I figured, Polito thought to himself as he looked at the heavy silhouette of the Inspector, almost as tall as he was even leaning forward, his foot on the sill and his elbow resting on his knee. Framed in the soft yellow-white light that came up from the street lamp, it seemed to Polito that maybe the Inspector knew something he didn't, that maybe even the fact that they had seen nothing out that window at all since six-thirty meant something.

"Yeah, thanks, Inspector," he said, moving for the doorway. His jacket was on a wooden crate toward the middle of the room, and when he stopped to put it on he said, "Nice meeting you, Lou. See you tomorrow, Inspector."

When he left, Savage walked to the window and stood by Hovannes, taking the same position with his foot on the sill. The two of them stared out without talking.

Chapter 6

THE HOSPITAL in Trenton was a grim granite building eight stories high. It was just after midnight when Ernie Fleming drove around the front of it to find the emergency entrance. Most of the lights were off, giving the hospital the cold and hostile look of a prison. The emergency entrance was on the south side of a one-way street, which struck Ernie as a dumb arrangement, so he turned left onto it the wrong way and pulled into the parking lot, parking the car where it would leave the ambulance clearance to get out.

Inside, two ambulance attendants were drinking coffee from styrofoam cups. In an open alcove off the main corridor a team of young doctors and a middle-aged black nurse were working over a man on a wheeled table which was already bloodied where his head lay. Ernie couldn't tell whether the man was conscious.

Three Trenton cops were leaning against the built-in cabinets beyond the victim and one of them looked up slowly from the table, peeled himself away from the others and walked quietly, almost tiptoeing, over to Ernie as soon as he saw him.

"Lieutenant Fleming, NYPD," Ernie said. "Where is he?"

"You're looking at him," the Trenton cop said matter-of-factly. He was a man in his middle thirties, about Ernie's size. His blue uniform looked stiff and new but his face had the sullen look it takes at least ten years in the job to acquire.

"You gotta be kidding," Ernie said, looking across to the table where the man's cheeks and temples were covered with blood. Something about the way his head was lying looked terribly wrong and Ernie guessed that the back of it must have been mostly caved in. "I got here all the way from New York."

"Well," the cop answered laconically, "it happened

way the hell out toward Allentown. Christ knows why they brought him here."

"How's it look?"

"You see what I see, Lieutenant. Not good, I guess."

"Can I talk to him?"

"Couldn't say. No way he's gonna talk to you though, from the looks of it."

Ernie walked over to the table and said to anyone who would answer, "How's he doing?"

One of the doctors was swabbing at the man's head with some sponges. He looked up at Ernie and a flicker of distaste passed across his mouth, then he looked down to his work again without answering. The other doctor said, "Hurry it up, let's get him upstairs. Hamilton here yet?"

"Yeah, I think so," the doctor with the sponges answered, and then he said, in what Ernie assumed was a response to his question, "Maybe, maybe not. If you can stick around till they finish with him upstairs they'll be able to tell you. You a cop?"

"Yeah."

"Well, get over there with the other ones. You can't stand here."

Ernie turned from the table and walked over to the cabinets. "What do you know about it?" he asked.

"The guy's a trucker," the cop who had spoken to Ernie before said. He pulled a notebook from the slit pocket in his pants and flipped it open. "Name Leon Gregory. Someone found him lying next to the cab of his truck on the Turnpike, trailer was gone. That's all I can tell you."

"Know what he was hauling?"

"No, but someone called the company he worked for. I think I heard they couldn't get in touch with anybody, but you can check that yourself. Know where the station house is?"

Ernie shook his head.

"I'll be checking back in soon as we leave here," the officer volunteered, "You can follow me."

"Yeah, okay. Any blood in the truck?"

"They tell me no. I wasn't out there."

Ernie said, "So they shot him outside. He must've tried to put up a fight."

One of the other cops, who hadn't spoken yet, said, "He wasn't shot. They bashed his head in with something."

"I heard he was shot."

"Yeah, I know, that's what they said at first. But he wasn't."

"Were you there?"

"No, me and Mike here are in the same car," the officer said, indicating the patrolman who had been answering all the questions so far. He was younger than his partner, a lot younger, maybe in his early twenties, and would have been good looking except that he had very bad skin and the same sullen look in his eyes and around his mouth that his partner had. Shit, Ernie thought looking at him, this town must be worse than New York.

There was nothing to be learned from any of them, so Ernie said, "Awright, let's get over to the station house."

As the four policemen stepped into the corridor they were passed by an orderly rushing into the alcove and then by the two doctors going the other way, down the corridor toward the elevators. Ernie heard a squeak of rubber wheels and turned to look. The orderly was turning the table around so it would come out head first and the nurse scrambled to stay beside it. The three Trenton cops walked together toward the exit but Ernie stayed a few seconds behind until the table was wheeled past him.

The truck driver's head passed right below Ernie, who could see that his eyes were open now. They looked surprisingly clear but something in them told Ernie that the man was going to die and knew it. There were clean towels under his head now and no more blood seemed to be flowing. Down the corridor Ernie could see the two young doctors holding the double doors of the elevator open, and as the table swung to the left the corner of it bumped Ernie in the thigh. He turned to catch up to the Trenton cops and heard the orderly say a soft, low, "Sorry," over the squeak of the table, which was moving rapidly now toward the elevator.

Tuesday, October 29

"Everybody's here, Inspector," Roberto Obregon poked his head through the door to announce.

"Yeah, fine," Hovannes said from behind his desk, "I'll be there in a minute."

As soon as Obregon closed the door Ernie Fleming said, "You'll think about it, Frank? That's all I want to know."

"Let's see what happens," Hovannes answered for the second time in the last few minutes, knowing what Ernie would say.

Ernie stood up and moved toward the door. "Sure," he said, "but you know as well as I do what's gonna happen. We can write off that load of typewriters already, right? You gotta figure in four weeks they've gotten rid of them. And I can't see we've got any more going for us on this new job that we didn't have on any of the others. So what's gonna happen is nothing."

"Maybe," was all Hovannes would say. He moved quickly around the desk and joined his partner at the door.

Ernie's suggestion hadn't surprised him. In a way, he had known it was coming for a long time. What did surprise him, though, was how easy it had been for him to listen to Ernie. He had just said, "Frank, I've been thinking, if this case folds, we oughta get Sallie anyway. We're too fucking old to play games, and if that truck driver dies, I can't see letting him get away with murder."

Hovannes had thought the same thing himself many times. What cop hadn't? But there was a line you crossed when you moved from thinking about it to talking about it, just like there would be another line to be crossed when you actually went and did it. Right now, though, the important thing in Frank's mind was that it wasn't unthinkable, even though he didn't want to talk about it yet. But just having it out in the open gave him a feeling that was almost like relief, and he realized it gave him an option that he hadn't had before.

Obregon and Gallagher were at their desks when Frank opened the door, and Lou Savage was bent over Obregon's desk leaning on his knuckles and listening intently to one of the Puerto Rican sergeant's stories. Stu Rhodes, who was seated on Gallagher's desk, stood up when the Inspector's door opened. Ron Polito was standing by himself, a few feet to Frank's right, leaning against the thin glass and panel wall that separated the Inspector's office from the cluttered squadroom. When Hovannes looked at him he turned quickly and walked toward the small conference table at the far left corner of the room. Mike Ferran,

Bill Menaker, and Tony Saladino were already seated around it.

Lieutenant Fleming followed Hovannes out of the office, and the ten men gathered around the table, which was too small to seat all of them. Rhodes and Savage stood.

"Okay," Hovannes said when everybody was settled, "I don't want this to take long. Last night our friends hit a truck on the Jersey Turnpike. Looks like they might be branching out into the homicide business. They worked the driver over pretty good and right now it doesn't look like he's going to make it. The truck was filled with television sets and so far as we know they got three places it can come to if it's coming into the city. I don't think they've got any more. Now you guys all know we've been watching all three of these places for the last couple of weeks, but this is the first time we've had them all covered right after a job, so there's a pretty good chance if we sit tight the pieces'll start coming together."

The Greene Street warehouse had been staked out since a few days after the IBM job, but Jack Kittens had warned Hovannes that the typewriters might not have been ticketed for New York. Since then Frank had also learned of the existence of a trucking depot on Eleventh Avenue that was owned by Star Realty and Investment, a corporation that OCC knew to be under Sallie Manzano's control. A surveillance had been put on the depot as soon as Hovannes found out about it, but if the typewriters came to New York they might have already passed through there before Frank had a chance to put some men on it. The third place was another warehouse on Front Street, in lower Manhattan near the East River waterfront. The check on the Greene Street address had disclosed that it was owned by Alvin Schulman, whose brother Gerald was one of Sallie Manzano's lawyers. Ferran and Saladino spent almost a week, full time, going over property records and turned up the fact that the same Alvin Schulman also owned the Front Street establishment, so a watch was put on it. Obviously, the typewriters could have gone through there before Hovannes's men uncovered it.

"This could be what we've been waiting for," Hovannes went on, "so I don't want any mistakes now. As soon as we finish here, this is what I want. Tony, you and Polito take the place on Front Street. About ten o'clock, Obregon and Menaker, you relieve them. Ferran, you and Lieutenant Fleming got Greene Street. I'll relieve you tonight, same time. Gallagher, you're going with me over to Eleventh Avenue now. Savage, Rhodes, you'll take over there when we leave. That all straight?"

The men muttered and nodded their comprehension.

"Any questions so far?"

"Yeah," Obregon said, "whatdya want us to do if something comes in?"

"I was just getting to that. What you do if you see anything is get on the horn right away and the Lieutenant and I'll come over. Don't make a move. We don't want to have to go in for them if we don't have to. All we'll get ourselves is a bunch of truck drivers if we do that. I don't have to tell you guys, this isn't the fucking lost and found department. If we move too soon we get the stuff back, but we don't get Manzano. So if you see anything, send up some signals and take as many pictures as you can get. We'll figure out where to go with it from there. Any other questions?"

Gallagher said, "Do you really think something might come in tonight, Inspector?"

"I don't know, Fred. I think we've got all the bases covered. We don't really know how they work it yet, but we've had that place on Eleventh covered since three days after the Pennsylvania job and Front Street since maybe six, seven days after that. Which means that if the stuff came in it came in quicker than that—they're not holding it. If they follow the same pattern, then the next couple of days are critical. But who knows. Maybe they're still holding the typewriters somewhere else, maybe they went to Chicago, which I heard is possible. We've gotta go with what we've got and what we've got is they just boosted a truck in south Jersey and three places to wait for it. Anything else?"

No one spoke.

"Okay. You guys who got assignments now, get to them. Those of you that relieve them, get some rest. But look, I want all of you somewhere you can be reached."

Hovannes stood up and the others did also. As they started to disperse, Hovannes said, "Oh yeah, look. Don't worry—if this thing lasts more than a couple of days

I'll get some more men on it. The next few days some of you may have to do some double shifts, but it won't be for long."

The men broke into pairs as they were assigned. Savage arranged with Rhodes to pick him up that night and the two of them left, along with Obregon and Menaker, who agreed to meet back at Headquarters around nine-thirty. "Hey, Ron," Tony Saladino called from the doorway, "get your ass in gear." He put on his jacket. His shield case was in his shirt pocket, the gold shield hanging outside, and he took it out, flipped the case closed, and stuffed it into a jacket pocket.

Ron Polito was still standing by the conference table, looking toward where the Inspector, Fleming, Mike Ferran, and Fred Gallagher were gathered by the door to the Inspector's office. He took a short, hesitant step like he wanted to go up to them, but then changed his mind and hurried to join Saladino. As they got to the door Obregon was coming back in, and from the corridor they could hear him shouting across the squadroom. "Hey, Inspector, do you want me to set it up with Communications?"

"Yeah, thanks, Roberto," Hovannes called back.

"Anything else?"

Hovannes smiled weakly, then looked over at Ernie and back to Obregon again. "Nah," he said, "just tell me something's really gonna move tonight, will ya."

"Something's really gonna move tonight," Obregon said with a mock solemnity that made Hovannes laugh. Obregon laughed too, but Ernie Fleming just said, "Cmon, Frank, we gotta get going."

Tuesday, October 29

Fred Gallagher sat at a second floor window of the Shield Box and Paper Company, his feet on the sill and a paper cup of hot coffee cradled in his lap. Between his shoes he could see a narrow corridor of the block of Eleventh Avenue that ran between Twenty-eighth and Twenty-ninth. At the Twenty-ninth Street end, a block away, there was a low garage big enough for one truck. To the south of it, stretching toward him, lay a set of eight back-to-back loading bays in a narrow covered pier.

The bays facing Eleventh were far enough back from the avenue to allow a truck to back in and have its cab clear the sidewalk. The back bays opened onto a large gravel lot off Twenty-eighth Street. There were six or seven empty trailers parked in the lot.

Normally a loquacious man, by about five o'clock Gallagher had grown tired of dropping conversation down a bottomless well, and so he contented himself watching the sky quickly darkening and almost forgot about Inspector Hovannes standing behind him. Barely forty years old, Gallagher looked perhaps a decade older and felt even older than that. He was thinking about that kid Polito, who had been with him on that Greene Street stakeout two weeks earlier, complaining through the whole tour about the tedium of it, while Gallagher, for whom a stakeout was almost like a paid holiday, listened uncritically.

There were two good things about a stakeout. One of them was that they were no trouble and the other was the conversation. Mostly Gallagher did the talking, but that made no difference to him and he could be just as happy letting someone else carry the ball, even someone like Polito, who seemed to look forward to insane shootouts with gangsters like on television and who reminisced —the fucking kid couldn't be twenty-five years old and he was reminiscing—about covering the Columbia riots during his rookie year in the Tactical Squad. It seemed to Fred Gallagher, as he took a long hissing sip from his coffee, that kids hadn't been crazy gung-ho like that when he was a rookie. At least he knew he hadn't, that was for shitsure.

Now this Hovannes, he thought, is a completely different bird. You certainly couldn't describe him as the gung-ho type, but on the other hand he was a pain in the ass to have as a commanding officer. The worst kind of guy to have over you was the kind who took the whole thing personally, and that seemed to be Hovannes's problem. How anyone could look at it that way after over twenty years in the job was a mystery to Gallagher, but not one he particularly wanted to understand.

He did a little quick figuring and computed that over the next three days the squad would need three shifts a day at three stakeout locations, two men each. That would be fifty-four shifts. There were ten men in the squad, which meant thirty shifts in the three days, leaving twenty-four to make up. Hovannes and the lieutenant would probably take double shifts every day, so that took care of six of them. The little Spic would do anything the Inspector asked him to and that nut Polito would probably want to do double shifts even though he hated stakeouts. That still left twelve extra shifts to be divided among the eight of them. This, of course, was figuring that Hovannes meant it when he said he'd get some extra men in a couple of days.

Gallagher's computations were interrupted by a gray Plymouth that pulled into the back lot of the depot. "Inspector," Gallagher whispered, nodding toward the window. He took his feet off the sill and sat forward to look.

Hovannes moved up behind him, stooping to look over his shoulder. No one got out of the car and from where the two detectives sat on the second floor they couldn't see in.

"Know the car?" Gallagher asked.

Hovannes grunted a negative.

After about ten minutes of waiting, during which nothing happened, Frank said, "Wait here," and walked out of the room. Gallagher could hear his footsteps on the stairs and then he didn't hear anything else for about a minute or two. Then he heard the Inspector coming back upstairs.

"Yeah?" he asked.

"We need this, huh?" Hovannes said. "It's two kids, a guy and a girl. They're having a fight. A whole city to have a fight in and they have to pick this parking lot."

Gallagher said, "Hey, let's radio for a patrol car to chase them out." But Hovannes decided to give them another ten minutes. Before the ten minutes were up the Plymouth drove off, leaving rubber on Twenty-eighth Street as it raced for Tenth Avenue and turned north with a sharp screech of the tires.

"Good for us, not good for them," Gallagher said lightly, but Hovannes didn't respond.

Chapter 7

THE MORNING HAD TURNED to drizzle when Frank Hovannes got home shortly after dawn. He pulled up to the garage door but felt too tired to bother with it so he left the car parked just clear of the sidewalk, slid out across the passenger's side, and climbed the eight steps to the front door.

Inside it was dark. Emily had pulled the blinds in the living room, as she always did when she had to stay alone at night, and the gray morning sent only a damp, weak light into the house. Without taking off his topcoat, Frank walked into the kitchen and opened the refrigerator door, not knowing what he was looking for. Last night's dinner was still there, uncooked, two thick chops on a plate covered with waxed paper. A small pool of blood had collected on the plate and Frank took the chops out, uncovered them, and poured the blood down the sink, rinsing the drain with cold water. When he put the chops back in the refrigerator he found a small cardboard basket of freshly shelled peas and scooped out a handful. They tasted sweet, dry and mealy like the kind of apples he liked, so he took another handful and closed the refrigerator door.

Upstairs, the drapes in the den were opened, which meant that Emily must have gotten up already. Opening them was always the first thing she did in the morning because the front end of the house faced east and she was like a plant about sunlight. Even if she was going back to bed she would open the drapes, because she liked the light to be there for her when she got up for good.

Frank took off his jacket and his topcoat together and laid them across the back of the recliner. Then he snapped the holster off his belt and carried it into the bedroom. With the holster and gun in his hand he walked to the bed and looked down at Emily, sleeping on her stomach, her face deep in the pillow and her hair scattered across

56

her cheek. With his free hand he reached down to brush it back and Emily said, her voice blurred with sleep, "I'm awake, Frank, I was just going to get up in a minute."

As Frank sat down next to her, she slid her body over toward him until she could feel the pressure of his hips against hers through the blankets. He reached to put the gun on the end table and then bent over to untie his shoes.

"What time is it?" Emily asked.

"About seven-thirty."

"Are you hungry?" she asked. "Do you want something before you go to sleep?"

"No," Frank said, "don't get up yet."

He stood to undress, leaving his clothes in a pile on the floor. The pants would have to go to the cleaners anyway. Then he climbed in beside her and lay on his back. Thank God Emily wasn't one of those women who started to wear nightgowns to bed when they approached forty. Her body had a steamy, sweaty smell under the covers, a pleasant smell that made Frank want to go limp with relaxation, but he stretched himself taut, stiffening his back and pointing his toes to get the last sensation of his tiredness before letting the limpness take over. As he did Emily turned on her side and moved toward him. She put her head lightly on his shoulder and his arm went around her back, his hand reaching down to find a resting place just below her waist, where he could feel the curve of her hip beginning. She lay her right leg across him, her thighs crossing his so he could feel her warmth in his genitals. With his left hand he pressed her thigh against him, and the heavy softness started a stirring in him that they both enjoyed.

"I'm glad I got home before you got up," he said softly.

"Me too," Emily answered.

Frank closed his eyes and was already starting to fall asleep when the feeling of her breast against his chest suddenly brought an image to his mind that he couldn't get rid of. It was from years and years ago, a young woman with heavy breasts like Emily's. He was still in uniform at the time, on patrol in the two-four, teamed with a sergeant named Harrold—yeah, that was it, Bert Harrold. One night the two of them found this hooker crumpled up in a phone booth on Eighty-eighth Street just off Broadway. She was slashed all over, her face, shoulders, neck and breasts, and her dress was open to below her ribs—not ripped open but cut. Frank and the sergeant had seen her on the street fairly regularly for a few weeks and had spoken to her two or three times, and Frank had joked once that her heavy rounded body reminded him of his wife and made him want to get home in a hurry.

Before the ambulance got there she died. Her pimp was in a bar on Amsterdam Avenue and Frank and Sergeant Harrold walked over there to get him. Harrold was an old guy with a thick gray and red mustache, which was practically unheard of in the Department in those days, and just before the two of them went into the bar to get the pimp he said, "You sure you wanna do this, Hovannes?"

"Sure, whaddya mean?" Frank asked.

Harrold said, "I was just thinking instead of busting him maybe we could find him later and give him some of what he gave her."

Frank didn't say anything, so the sergeant said, "Forget it, it was just an idea. That little prick isn't worth it."

They took him out of the bar and neither one of them ever mentioned the incident again. For a long time Frank couldn't forget the way that girl had looked in the phone booth, with smooth brown breasts dripping blood onto what was left of her bra. But he hadn't thought about it for years, and now what he was remembering was what Harrold had said, and for the first time he wondered if the old sergeant, who was probably dead by now, had meant it.

Wednesday, October 30

When the relief team arrived at the Greene Street stakeout, Ernie Fleming declined Frank's offer of a ride home. Instead, he walked back to Headquarters, going south two blocks on Wooster to Broome and then six blocks east on Broome to Centre. After being cooped up in that warehouse since early yesterday afternoon, Ernie felt like he needed some time alone on the deserted sidewalks in the cool early morning drizzle.

When he got to Headquarters he went inside to see if Chief Halloran had arrived yet, but the ACI wasn't expected for hours so Ernie left by the back door. He was hoping he would find someone in a patrol car on Centre Market Street, but when that didn't work out he proceeded to the coffee shop at the corner of Broome and Mulberry. At that hour all the stools at the counter were filled with cops just coming on duty, their tunics unbuttoned and hanging loosely like bathrobes. He said hello to the three or four men he knew and found himself a seat at one of the small booths by the Mulberry Street windows.

In a way, he was annoyed with Frank for not having mentioned his suggestion again. He had known since the other night, when he saw that truck driver with the back of his head smashed in and the Trenton cops who were pissed off at him because he had not been brought to Allentown, that they would have to do something like this. It wasn't the murder so much that got to Ernie—that is, assuming the guy died. This trucker wasn't anything like the first the Manzano operation had killed. Twenty would be more like it. It was just the first connected with these hijackings. No, murder had nothing to do with it. It was the principle of the thing, and the principle right now was that Big Sallie Manzano was into heroin and coke and prostitution and numbers and shakedowns and hijacking trucks and beating truck drivers senseless, and there wasn't a thing that OCC or any of the thirty thousand men in the Department were able to do about it. Ernie could see that clearly and he was sure Frank could too. If you didn't want to put up with it, that gave you only one choice, and that was the choice he was offering Frank now. Of course there was one other choice and that was just to make the best case you could, and if you nailed them you nailed them and if you didn't that was just too bad. But that choice amounted to saying forget about it, and in that case you might as well forget about being a cop too.

"Good morning, Lieutenant," the waitress said. She was a tall, flat-chested young woman in her late twenties with a very pretty face. She knew most of the Headquarters cops by name and always addressed the officers by rank. "Just coffee, or do you want some breakfast, Lieutenant?"

"Good morning, Judy," Ernie said pleasantly, putting Sallie Manzano out of his mind and smiling up at her as she poured steaming coffee from a glass pot into the cup in front of him. "Yeah," he said, "lemme have some breakfast. A coupla scrambled eggs and some toast."

"You want bacon with that?"

Ernie considered it a few seconds. "Nah," he decided, "be a little greasy. I think I better not."

"Been up all night?" Judy asked, more as an expression of sympathy than as a question.

"Yeah," Ernie laughed. "My stomach can't take this any more. Guess I'm not getting any younger, huh, Judy?"

"Who is?" she said, turning and walking back toward the counter.

Ernie sipped at his coffee and then looked around the restaurant. The place had emptied very quickly in a matter of minutes without his noticing it, and now there were less than a dozen men at the counter. By the register a patrolman in street clothes stood holding his uniform in front of him, folded into a square pile like the way the army issues clothing. His gun and holster were on top of the pile and a counterman was trying to balance a paper container of coffee on top of the whole thing, leaning it against the patrolman's chest. About eight or nine other officers stood grouped around the register waiting for coffees to go.

Ernie glanced restlessly around and spotted a copy of the *News* at the next table amid a clutter of uncleared dishes. He got up and brought it back to his table, leafing through it from the back to get to the sports. It was a terrible time of the year; the World Series was over about a month ago, football was only played once a week, and even the bookies couldn't take basketball seriously this early in the season. He tossed the paper impatiently aside and started to think about Frank and his plan again, but all that came to his mind were the same things he had told himself before. So he forgot about it and just stared absently into his coffee cup until Judy arrived with his breakfast.

He ate quickly, left a dollar bill and two quarters on the table, and headed back for Centre Market Street. Half a dozen patrolmen were standing around their cars, killing time until they started their tours. Ernie found a pair from the one-oh and talked them into giving him a ride home.

He lived on Twentieth Street, in the Chelsea district two blocks from the river, and he had the patrolmen drop him off at the Getty station on the corner of Twentieth and Tenth Avenue. It was about twenty past eight and Ernie saw a few men he recognized as neighbors hurrying toward their cars in the parking lot west of Tenth. He was no exception to the generalization that cops usually don't have friends who aren't on the force, and he didn't know any of these men by name. But he nodded to them anyway and they nodded back.

A few doors before he got home he noticed a green Chevy parked in front of his door. There was no parking on the south side of the street that morning because of the alternate side of the street parking regulations, and the Chevy was the only car there. Ernie could see a man behind the wheel. It wasn't the sort of thing that would make the average person look twice; maybe the guy's wife wasn't ready to leave on time and he went down to sit in the car at eight o'clock so he wouldn't get a ticket. But on the other hand, you couldn't take anything for granted, especially a man waiting in a car in front of your house.

Ernie unbuttoned his topcoat and his jacket so he could get at his gun, and he felt the cold drizzle wetting his shirt and sticking it to his chest and stomach. The car was parked facing Ninth Avenue, away from Ernie, but as he got closer he could see that the man in the car was looking in the outside rear-view mirror. From the back the guy looked a little familiar, but Ernie couldn't place him.

When he was just by the car, the door opened and the man stepped out. It was Ron Polito.

"Lieutenant Fleming," he said in that sheepish, mushy voice he had, "I've been waiting for you. I wanted to talk to you."

"Yeah, sure," Ernie said, pulling his coat closed, "come on inside."

"It's, uh, private," Polito said hesitantly.

The lieutenant raised an eyebrow and gave his small invisible shrug. Dorothy would be up already, Rick never let her sleep. "Awright, how about here?" he said and walked around to the passenger side of the car.

Inside he said, "Hey, put on some heat, Polito, I'm fucking numb."

Polito turned on the engine and adjusted some switches on the dashboard. "I'm sorry to bother you, Lieutenant," he said, "I know you were on all night, but this is kind of important."

Ernie pushed in the cigaret lighter and fished in his jacket pocket for a smoke. He didn't say anything. Polito watched him until the lighter popped out and Fleming lit his cigaret. Then he turned to stare out the windshield. He raised his arms to grip the steering wheel with both hands, and as he did he could feel large drops of sweat rolling down his sides.

In a low voice, unsure of himself only for the first few words, he said, "I heard what you and the Inspector were talking about, Lieutenant. I want in."

Ernie hesitated a moment, trying to think whether he and Hovannes could use someone like Polito. Then he said, "We were only talking, Ron."

"Yeah, I know," Polito said. "But I want in."

Chapter 8

ERNIE FLEMING SAT in Gallagher's chair, hunched forward with his elbows on his knees. The window in front of him was open about ten inches and the cold November wind blew into his face. From time to time he squinted against it as he stared at the lighted window across the street on the first floor of one-oh-two Greene.

"Hey, Frank," he said, without turning from the window, "what about it? It's been almost a month now, whatdya say?"

Hovannes walked around behind his partner and leaned against the wall to the right of the window. Ernie turned to look up at him and their eyes locked on each other for a few seconds. Then Ernie, who had decided not to tell Frank about his conversation with Polito until he had Frank's answer, turned back to the window. He spoke in a low voice, carefully and tentatively. "If you don't want in, Frank," he said, "maybe I'll go ahead without you."

He didn't say it like an ultimatum and Frank didn't take it as one.

"You couldn't do it yourself, Ernie," Hovannes said flatly, thinking that Sallie Manzano had two bodyguards. Getting at him would be hard enough for two guys to pull off, impossible for one man by himself.

"Why not?" Fleming asked. "You wouldn't stop me, would you?"

"No, I wouldn't stop you. It can't be done, that's all."

Ernie shrugged and Frank knew he was still waiting for an answer. Instead of thinking about what he would tell Ernie, though, Frank found himself remembering the run-in he had had with Halloran that morning. It was just short of official now that Halloran would be retiring at the end of the year, just six weeks away, and Frank had been counting on the fact that in his last few months as ACI he would lay off about the Manzano case. What could it matter to him now?

When he came in this morning, he found a note from Obregon on his desk telling him to report to Halloran's office. As soon as he got downstairs the sergeant outside the Chief's door sent him in. Even before he had closed the door behind him, Halloran said, "They knocked off another truck in Jersey, Hovannes," and then ordered Frank to sit down.

Frank walked slowly across the large, high-ceilinged room and sat in the straight-backed chair by the side of the Chief's desk. Halloran placed his elbows carefully on the black blotter in front of him, joined his hands together, and looked sideways at Frank. But all he said was, "See the sergeant on the way out. She'll give you all the information."

Frank nodded and waited for what seemed a long time.

"I want this clear, Hovannes, I want you to know where you stand," the Chief said at last. "This is it, bottom of the ninth. Get them on this or you don't get them at all, and I'm not kidding this time."

"What? Tonight?" Hovannes said, his voice expressing not so much incredulousness as anger.

"I ought to say tonight, tomorrow night, a week at the outside," the Chief answered levelly. "You've got every place you know about staked out. So either the stuff shows up where you got your men or it's going somewhere you don't even know about. If it's going someplace you don't know about, you've had six months and you've come up with shit. Enough is enough, Hovannes."

Frank said, "What are you telling me?"

"I'm telling you you've got till the end of the month. After that you pick two men and assign them to the case and you get yourself and the rest of your squad onto something that makes sense."

"You know this isn't just hijackings," Frank protested, even though he knew what the Chief's answer would be. "They killed that truck driver. This is homicide."

"It's a Jersey homicide," Halloran answered predictably, "it's not your homicide. Two weeks. That clear?"

Frank didn't say anything.

"I want to hear you say Yessir," Halloran said, and the change in his tone was so sudden it took Frank by surprise. There was a kind of malicious vindictiveness in the way he said it, and Frank sensed that for some reason or other the Chief wanted to make this into a personal thing.

"Tell you what," Frank said, trying to ignore it, "if we don't get any leads in the next two weeks I'll call it off. That's fair enough. But if we're making any progress, I'm not calling it off, there's no two ways about it."

"What kind of progress?" Halloran asked skeptically.

Frank decided to push his advantage and tell him about Billy Mazes.

"Well," he said, "we just found this guy who's probably driving some of the rigs. We've put a tail on him and so far everything fits in. He goes to all the right places. We've got the warehouses covered and we can use this guy to tie the whole thing to Manzano."

Halloran leaned forward at his desk so far that he was almost out of his chair. "What kind of shit are you handing me, Hovannes? That's Billy Mazes, huh? You've had him for a fucking month and a half and I know it! Don't play games with me."

"Who told you that?"

"Not you, that's for goddamned sure!"

Hovannes didn't say anything and Halloran settled back in his chair. He picked up a ballpoint pen on the desk and looked at it absently for a few seconds, then looked up at Hovannes. When he spoke his voice was soft and level again and Frank knew he had lost.

"Hovannes, I don't like the games you're playing," he said. "But that's not why I'm telling you it's got to stop. I could bring you on charges for what you did—holding back information, trying to con me—but I've got no interest in that. I'm stepping down at the end of the year, maybe you know that already and maybe you don't. Maybe that's why you figured you could get away with trying to play games with me about what's happening on this case. I can understand that, I'll give you the benefit of the doubt."

Halloran paused, tapping the ballpoint on the blotter for emphasis. "But the thing is this," he went on. "I'm not leaving this office so whoever sits in this chair next can come in and wonder what the hell we've been doing here. I've always given you a pretty free hand to run things the way you like and you know it. But I'm not having someone step in here and think I was running some kind of asshole operation. Before I leave, you're gonna be doing something that if someone asks you can tell them. I don't want to hear later that Bob Halloran let his prima donnas chase their tails around for a year and a half without putting a stop to it. So that's it, Hovannes. Before I'm gone you either nail this thing down or you pull your men off and put them to work. If that's clear, get out of here."

Frank knew that if he told Ernie any of this it would corroborate everything Ernie had been saying, and before he even got back to his office he decided not to let his partner know that the investigation would be cut off in two weeks.

He called the squad together, briefed them on the latest hijacking, and assigned stakeout teams, putting himself with Gallagher again at the Eleventh Avenue depot and Ernie with Mike Ferran at Greene Street. He didn't want to be alone with Ernie for a whole tour.

Then, about nine-thirty, Al Jenner's voice came over the radio from base communications. "Frank, this is base, you reading me, Frank?" the voice said.

"Yeah, I'm reading you. Go ahead."

"Post two called in, said Subject arrived."

"Subject one?"

"No," Jenner's voice came back, "two."

Post two was the Greene Street stakeout, where Ernie and Ferran were stationed. Subject one was Billy Mazes and two was Angie Morello, the guy Polito and Gallagher had seen coming in with Mazes a few weeks before.

"Awright," Hovannes radioed back, "tell them I'm coming right over. And let me know if anything else pops."

Frank signed out and put the microphone back in its cradle. This had to be it, he said to himself. Morello was waiting for Mazes to show up with the truck. It had to be, especially after all that shit Halloran had given him. Frank figured he had this much of a break coming.

He raced to the Greene Street post and sent Ferran to join Gallagher, who was alone watching the depot on Eleventh. "Morello still there?" he asked Ernie, looking down to where a light was burning in a first floor window at the Wright Storage Company building at one-oh-two.

"Yeah."

"Anything else?"

"Naw, that's it."

Frank radioed base and ordered Jenner to brief Obregon and Savage, who were on the Front Street stakeout just ten minutes away. He wanted them ready in case they were needed.

That was about ten o'clock and now it was past one and nothing had happened. Morello was still inside and the light was still on and the two detectives had barely spoken until Ernie told Frank he wanted an answer.

Hovannes leaned forward, his head above Ernie's, and looked across the rutted street and broken sidewalks toward the light at one-oh-two. He knew what that light meant to him but wondered what it meant to his partner.

Just then a door down the street opened and a man in a gray suit stepped onto the sidewalk. He wore no topcoat and his tie hung unknotted around his neck. He pulled his jacket closed against the cold and started to walk rapidly north toward Houston Street, passing under the window where the two detectives were stationed.

"Cleaned out, huh?" Frank suggested.

"I guess so," Ernie said flatly.

Every Thursday night, they had noticed for the last six weeks, one of the lofts, which was vacant the rest of the time, apparently was used for a poker game, and Frank and Ernie generally got a kick out of watching the early losers leaving. When the game broke up, usually around two or three o'clock, the players all left together, with the one or two men who had brought cars driving the others home. But someone always would be wiped out early and wouldn't want to hang around an hour or two watching the others play. So you could always count on someone stepping out onto the sidewalk some time after midnight, looking like he had just come from being mugged, and heading up the abandoned street toward Houston, where he could catch a subway—or a cab if they had left him enough money.

"What do you think those guys do?" Frank asked when the poker player had rounded the corner onto Houston. He was just trying to make conversation.

"How would I know?" Fleming answered.

"I mean, that guy looks kinda like a businessman or something. Probably works downtown. How do you figure he comes to be in a place like this?"

"I don't know, Frank, and really I don't give a shit," Fleming said.

Hovannes shrugged and walked away from the window. There was a sink at the far end of the loft and he filled a cup with water from the tap and then rested his immersion heater in it. When the water was boiling he unplugged the heater and shook a huge helping of instant coffee into the cup, gave it a stir with the heater, and came back to the window. Except for Gallagher's chair, the only domestic amenities any of the ten men who were using this loft had brought into the place were Frank's cup and immersion heater and the jar of coffee.

"You know, you really ought to bring in a cup, Ernie," Frank said. "I don't know how you can make it like this without any coffee."

"If I wanted coffee I'd get a cup," Ernie said without turning around.

Frank sat down on the sill, his knees almost touching Ernie's. The two watched in silence, Frank looking over his shoulder out the window and Ernie still hunched forward with the wind blowing in his face. After a half hour Frank's back started to ache from the cold draft and he got up to rinse out his coffee cup. "Christ," he said as he walked back toward the sink, "how long does it take them to get up here from south Jersey! I hope they show up pretty soon."

"You really think someone's gonna show up?" Ernie asked, his voice dull and cold and mocking.

Frank thought a minute before answering, because ever since Halloran told him about the hijacking this morning he had been counting on the fact that things were finally going to start turning his way. And when the call had come in from base telling him that Morello had shown up at Greene Street, he was certain of it.

"Yeah, Ernie," he answered carefully, "I really do. I've had this funny feeling all day that they're going to come driving right up here. They're going to park their truck right down there so fucking close you could piss on it from here. I mean, look at it," he went on when Ernie didn't respond, "there's Angie Morello sitting down there waiting for Billy and we're up here waiting for both of them. Beautiful."

Ernie couldn't help smiling in spite of himself. He and Frank had been through a lot together, and he couldn't hear his parter talking like that, excited and eager and hopeful, and not have some of it rub off on him. Sometimes Frank was like a rookie who didn't know the score yet. Maybe it was these illusions that made him such a good cop, because when you were up against the mob day after day you had to believe that busting some of these guys made some kind of a dent in their operation. Ernie didn't have any of Frank's illusions left, but something in what his partner just said reminded him of what it had been like when the two of them first started in the job. So he just said, "Be nice, wouldn't it?" and laughed quietly.

"You better believe it," Frank answered gratefully.

Five minutes passed while Frank paced briskly around the back of the loft. He was starting to feel good and thought about getting on the radio and checking with base to see if either of the two other teams had anything. But if anything happened there, they would get in touch with him, so he decided not to bother. Besides, it wasn't going to happen at either of the other places. It was going to happen here.

Then, abruptly, like he had just changed his mind, Ernie swiveled around in Gallagher's chair and stopped facing Frank, his back to the window. It was almost a signal that he had decided he didn't care what happened out there. Frank knew what he was going to say.

"Frank, what about it?" he said, his voice almost pleading. "I want your answer, I gotta know."

"Let's see what happens," Hovannes replied. "Maybe we'll get something tonight. Let's see."

"See what?" Ernie shot back. "Billy Mazes driving up here with a truck full of hot stuff? So what does that get you? It gets you Billy Mazes. Oh, yeah, and you get Angie Morello too, who is about as big a shit in the mob as I am in the police department. If you think there's any way you're gonna nail Big Sallie Manzano, the hell there is. Because that guy is into so much shit that if it would have been possible to nail him he would have been nailed a long time ago. So what you're gonna get is Billy."

"Yeah, I know," Hovannes said, his voice dull and numb.

"So what you're gonna get is Billy," Fleming repeated. "Look, Frank, you did that already. You've been in the job what?—twenty-three years? I figured it out the other night and between the two of us we must have collared about twelve hundred guys. And eleven hundred of them are in town right now and it didn't do them any harm. You walk into Valentine's or Vickie's or Cannonero's or the Dugout any afternoon or night and you're gonna see them all there. They're still in business at the same stand,

So you want to bust Billy again, and by Christmas he'll be in the van on his way back up to Greenhaven. But I'm gonna tell you something. Five years from now you're gonna walk into Valentine's some afternoon and there'll be Billy again. And Frankie Diamond'll be there and Phil Runelli. And Billy'll still be driving for Sallie Manzano."

Frank didn't move from where he was standing through Ernie's speech, about thirty feet away at the far end of the loft. "I'll tell you what," he said, realizing he was replaying the scene he had had with Halloran just that morning, "if this case folds, I'm with you. But we've got to give it a chance."

"How long?" Ernie asked.

Frank figured that if Halloran was willing to give him until the end of the month, Ernie owed him at least that much. "Two weeks," he answered.

"Make it this job," Ernie said, pushing his advantage. "If we don't get anything on this shipment, you and me go after Sallie. Whatdya say?"

There was nothing Frank could say, so he nodded his assent. As he did, the sound of footsteps came in through the open window. Ernie wheeled to face the sound and Frank raced across the room to the window. But it was nothing, just six men on the sidewalk in front of the building with the poker game. One of them was locking the door with a padlock while the others stood joking amiably in a group clustered around a tomato-red Pontiac with its wheels well up on the sidewalk to allow traffic to pass on the narrow street. The driver climbed in and unlocked the other doors, and in a few seconds the tail lights had disappeared onto Houston Street, following the course taken by the loser an hour before.

Ernie could feel Frank bending over his shoulder. His voice was tense and husky in the darkness as he said, "It's the only way, Frank. You know that, don't you? It's either that or we just give up and start collecting our pensions. Cause I've had enough of this shit."

"Yeah, I know," Hovannes answered, putting it in words this time, "me too."

His voice was soft and he was starting to become afraid. In a way, what frightened him was not so much his promise to Ernie. The idea of gunning Sallie Manzano didn't seem wrong or evil to him at all, not compared to letting Sallie have things his own way. Anyway, that was still in the future, and maybe things would work out so they wouldn't have to do it. What was frightening was what he had just confessed about the past. In telling Ernie to count him in, he was admitting that up to now he hadn't been really fighting Sallie Manzano. He was on the take, the same as a lot of other cops were, because all he was for Manzano was just an overhead expense. Like if he nailed this shipment of goods and busted someone like Angie Morello or Billy Mazes, what was it to the mob except an overhead, part of the price they paid for operating, like the money they passed out in white envelopes to cops who at least weren't fooling themselves about what they were doing?

Suddenly the radio started crackling from the middle of the room. Frank moved quickly away from the window toward the receiver and picked up the microphone. As he did, he heard Ernie call to him, "Hey, Frank, the light just went out."

"Frank, this is base," the radio was saying. "You read me, Frank?"

"Yeah, I'm reading you," Hovannes said. From where he stood, about ten feet behind Ernie at a cardboard folding table that held the radio, he couldn't see across the street. "What's doing, Ernie?" he yelled, his microphone still open.

Jenner's voice came back. "You got something there, Frank? What gives?"

"Nothing. I don't know. Why? What've you got?"

"That's what I called to tell you, Frank. We struck out."

Ernie at the window heard the words and wheeled around toward Frank like he wanted to say something. But there was nothing to say. He stared hard at Frank and Frank thought he understood. Ernie was telling him that it was time now, that he had crossed that first line two minutes ago when he said he would do it and it was already time to cross the second because there was nothing on the side he was standing on. Then Ernie turned slowly back to the window again and Frank could see him reaching into his pocket for something. What did Jenner just say? Frank wondered. Or hadn't he said anything after "We struck out"? Frank thought he heard something else but couldn't be sure.

"What did you say, Al?" Hovannes asked. He held

the microphone right to his mouth and his hands were wet and sweating.

"I said we struck out. They picked up that truck in Jersey a little while ago. State troopers found it, abandoned with the stuff still in it. Someone must've got cold feet or something. Anyway, it sure as hell isn't showing up there tonight."

Frank didn't say anything. Ernie had slid the window open another foot and a half and was leaning forward now with his elbows on the sill. He had his gun in both hands and Frank could see the barrel of it, with a long silencer attached. The silencer sent a shiver down Frank's back. He didn't even know Ernie had one. Christ, Frank thought, he's really gonna do it. How long has he had that thing?

"Hey, Frank, you there?" Jenner's voice came through again.

"Yeah, I'm here."

At the window Ernie wasn't moving and Frank's eyes were riveted to that silencer, aimed downward and across the street, toward where Angie Morello would come out of the warehouse at one-oh-two. It looked incredibly sinister and fascinating at the end of Ernie's gun. Ernie, he realized, had already crossed the last line. The moment he bought that thing he crossed it, and now he was taking Frank with him while Frank stood and stared at those four inches of dark metal.

"Whatdya wanna do, pack it in?" Jenner's voice asked.

"Yeah," Frank said into the microphone. "Send the others home. There's nothing on tonight."

"You coming back here, Frank, or you wanna call it a night?"

It didn't look like Ernie had moved, but Frank wasn't sure, because all he could see clearly was that short tube of gray metal. Then there was a flash from it, like flame, which surprised Frank because it looked just the way a gun barrel looks when it's fired at night and he had expected it would look different. But the only sound was a dull ping, like the sound of a hard punch to the stomach, only a little higher, a little faster.

"We'll be in later," Frank said into the microphone. "We just gotta straighten up around here and we'll be in. Send the others home."

Chapter 9

THE DOORBELL RANG late Saturday morning and Emily Hovannes answered it. A pleasant-looking young man, sturdy and muscular, stood facing her. He was wearing a blue nylon windbreaker unzipped over a cotton shirt in a darker blue. The morning air was brisk and comfortable, a gorgeous day, all autumn, with not a trace of winter in it.

"Mrs. Hovannes," the young man said, "my name is Lou Savage. I'm in your husband's outfit."

Emily blanched momentarily and her eyes closed involuntarily. But the young man went on, "Is the Inspector home? I wanted to talk to him, it won't take a minute."

Emily's eyes opened—they had been closed only a second—and her first thought was, How stupid of me. Of course they would have sent Ernie. She said, "No, he's not. But he should be home soon. Please come in."

Emily moved back from the door and Lou stepped inside, walking behind her to the living room. "Sit down and make yourself comfortable," she said, not indicating any place in particular. "Can I get you some coffee?"

"No, thank you, Mrs. Hovannes," Savage answered, taking a seat in the middle of the long Naugahyde-covered couch. Behind him were floor-to-ceiling sliding glass doors opening onto a shallow patio about eight feet deep, at the back of which stood a low stone wall. Above the wall the land rose steeply and Emily had planted a rock garden there. "I hope I'm not bothering you," Lou added. "I can wait to see him Monday if that would be better."

Emily said, "No, that's all right. He should be home any minute. Excuse me, what did you say your name was?"

"Lou Savage."

"And you're in my husband's squad?"

"Yes, I am."

The name wasn't familiar to Emily and she was sorry she hadn't asked to see some identification, but she was embarrassed to ask for it now. Lou guessed what she was thinking and said, "I'm not really attached to your husband's squad. I'm actually in Narcotics, but I've been working for the Inspector on temporary assignment the last two months."

Emily nodded, accepting the explanation. Not that it mattered. Frank told her so little about the job these days that it didn't surprise her that she didn't even know the names of the men he worked with.

No one spoke for about half a minute, and then Lou broke the silence, saying, "My girl and I were going up to the Cloisters for the afternoon and I knew the Inspector lived up here in Riverdale somewhere. We've been pretty busy, I guess you know that, and sometimes it's hard to get to see him. So I figured maybe I could catch him at home now."

Emily was wearing blue jeans and a loose brown T-shirt and she was trying to decide whether to excuse herself and go change her clothes. She never liked to let anyone see her dressed like that and always changed to something she considered more suitable, even if it was only to run up the block to the market or to the dry cleaner. She was comfortable dressed in this way, with no shoes and no bra, but she was afraid of looking like one of those women who try to wear young people's clothing when they're well past the age for it. Then she realized what Savage had said, and she said, "Did you say your girlfriend was with you?"

"Yes, she's in the car," Lou answered, surprising Emily with the offhanded way he said it.

"Oh, please ask her to come in," Emily said earnestly. "I'll make some coffee."

"That's all right, Mrs. Hovannes," Lou explained, "there's a supermarket right down the street and she said she might go over there and buy some stuff for a picnic. It's such a beautiful day and we thought when we left the Cloisters maybe we'd drive upstate."

"Yes," Emily agreed, "it is a beautiful day. Nice day for a picnic." Then after a pause she added, "Why don't you go see. If she's not at the market she can come in, or she can come in when she gets back. You can't leave her sitting out in the car."

Lou hesitated a moment and then said, "To be perfectly frank with you, Mrs. Hovannes, I don't think she wants to come in."

Emily looked at him quizzically. She hadn't sat down yet, but had remained standing in the middle of the living room in front of Lou, still not sure whether she should change her clothes. But now she decided that it didn't matter and sat in the brown upholstered chair about six feet from the couch, facing it at an angle. She pushed the hassock away, planted her bare feet on the carpet, and waited for an explanation. She liked this young man, who reminded her of Frank about twenty years ago. Her husband, too, was the kind of man who could say "To be perfectly frank with you" to someone he had just met.

Lou said, "She doesn't like what I'm doing. She thinks I shouldn't have transferred out of Narcotics."

"But you didn't transfer," Emily protested, surprising herself with how easily she came to this young man's defense. "You said you were assigned to my husband's unit."

"Yeah, I know," Lou said, "but I could get back if I wanted to. All I'd have to do is ask my CO in Narco and he could say he wants me back. It's only a loan thing. The thing is, I don't want to go back. In fact, I'm thinking of putting in for a transfer and she doesn't like it."

"Why not?" Emily asked, and then added, "Do you mind if I get some coffee? I'd like some. Are you sure you won't have any?"

Emily walked around to the look-in kitchen behind the chair where she had been sitting. The counter where the percolator stood faced into the living room, and she could watch Lou as he talked to her.

"Well," he was saying, "she had some friends who really got themselves messed up with drugs. Two guys she knew since she was a kid oh-dee'd and a couple of her friends are strung out. So when I was in Narco it really meant a lot to her."

"Yes," Emily assented, "but they're the same people, aren't they? I mean, the men my husband—you and my husband—are investigating, they're the same people who are behind the narcotics traffic."

"That's what I try and tell her," Lou said. "But it's not really the same, I can see her point."

Emily pushed the plug into the percolator and came back

to the living room, sitting down again in the same place. "What's her name?" she asked.

"Celia."

"She sounds very nice," Emily said, sensing that Lou might want to hear that from her.

"Yes, she is," he agreed eargerly.

They both heard a key move in the front door lock and turned to look. They heard Frank call Emily's name and she called back, "I'm in here, Frank."

In the living room Frank's first words were, "What's up, Lou?"

Savage, who was standing, explained that he had some information, that he was passing by on his way to the Cloisters, and that he thought he'd stop by instead of trying to find the Inspector on Monday. Frank sat down on the arm of Emily's chair and motioned for Savage to sit down. "Em," he said very softly, with a short sideways nod of his head.

"I don't think it's that kind of a thing, Inspector," Lou said tentatively as Emily started to get up. Frank nodded and said "Okay," still very soft for Emily, who let herself sink back into the chair. She looked across at Lou and smiled gratefully, conscious of feeling a little jealous of Celia and sorry she had not met her.

"This may not be much," Savage began, "but last night this informant I used to use in Narco got in touch with me. This guy's pretty well connected. I mean he's not on the inside, but he's not a street dealer either and he's always been reliable. I used to work in the ninth, and you know that's Tony LaGarda's territory. This guy Gagliano is running the heroin business for LaGarda. You know him?"

"Yeah, Paulie Gagliano. Sure," Hovannes said.

"Well, my man tells me—I can't tell whether he's getting it straight from Gagliano or not—that maybe there's going to be a panic on soon. LaGarda's been edgy for years about having Sallie Manzano and his brother for neighbors. He thinks either LaGarda's planning a move against Manzano or he's already started it or something. He wasn't very clear. But what he wanted me to know was that there might be some shakeups in the way the traffic was being handled."

Frank didn't particularly like Emily hearing all this, but since she was listening he wanted her to understand. "Sallie Manzano," he explained, getting up from the arm of the chair and moving across the living room so he could face his wife as he spoke to her, "is the guy we're investigating now. Not in connection with his narcotics business, though. He's a real old-style hood, came up the hard way in the forties. He's not a top boss, but he's got a lot going for him in Manhattan, mostly on the West Side. And this Tony LaGarda that Lou just mentioned, he's an ambitious type, not as big as Sallie but he wants to be. They're different as night and day. Sallie's hotheaded and kind of crazy and LaGarda is the coolest guy you could imagine, very careful about everything. They call him Tony the Lawyer. Anyway, like Lou said, LaGarda's a big man on the Lower East Side—that's where the ninth precinct is. Okay?"

Emily smiled and nodded.

"All right," Frank said to Lou, mostly to test the young detective and let him show off a little, "what's this got to do with us?"

"Well," Lou answered carefully, "I'm not sure. But if my man thinks that whatever's brewing between LaGarda and Manzano might be enough to mess up LaGarda's drug business, then there's a good chance Manzano's got to feel it too and it could change the way he's handling that hijacking operation. You know, those two warehouses we've got staked out are really in LaGarda's part of the world. Manzano might want to stay out of them if he's getting trouble from LaGarda, and then we'd be wasting our time watching them."

"Good," Frank said, pleased with the way Savage thought matters through. He walked to the glass doors behind the couch and looked out over the patio. The sun sparkled brilliantly on the shiny myrtle leaves in Emily's rock garden and Frank thought to himself that it wouldn't be a bad idea to see about having Savage transferred permanently to OCC. With his back to the room, he said, "What's this you said about it might have started already?"

"Well, that part wasn't very clear," Savage answered, "but my man said some people are saying that some guy who worked for Manzano was hit and maybe LaGarda had something to do with it. He didn't know any more about it than that. He didn't know who or where or what, or at least he wasn't telling me. I didn't put too much stock in it. It was all very iffy, but I thought you should know."

"You don't believe it?"

"Well, I don't know," Lou said. "If LaGarda wanted to move against Manzano, he wouldn't want to put him on guard by going after some smallfry, would he?"

Frank knew that what Lou was referring to was the hit on Angie Morello, and he knew that he and Ernie had done it, not Tony LaGarda. But he said, "Maybe, maybe not. One of the ways these things sometimes work is you use a small hit like that to send a message. That'd be one way LaGarda could tell Sallie he's not wanted on the Lower East Side, and maybe if he's not prepared to fight it out he'll get the message and pull out."

That seemed reasonable to Lou. A lot of this stuff was new to him and he liked having it explained. "Could be," he said.

"Yeah," Frank echoed. "Could be."

Chapter 10

THANKSGIVING MORNING FRANK SLEPT until after eleven, which he almost never did. He and Emily had arranged to spend the day at his mother's, and Emily had made him promise that he wouldn't cancel their plans. She had wanted to go to her mother's. It had been three years since they had had Thanksgiving there and not once since her father died, but she thought that somehow it would be harder for Frank to back out of it if it was his mother and she wanted the day with him away from the job.

When he came downstairs he found Emily in the kitchen making cranberry jelly and an apple dessert she was planning to take. The kitchen smelled of cranberries and cinnamon, and the tense irritability Frank had felt upstairs as he dressed began to evaporate. At the stove he tasted the apple mixture and dipped a wooden spoon into the hot cranberry syrup, sampling it carefully with his tongue. Then he poured himself a cup of coffee and sat at the kitchen table to watch. They talked cheerfully for a few minutes, until Frank said tentatively, "I think I'll just call in and see if everything's okay."

"Oh, Frank, don't spoil the day," Emily pleaded. "Everything's okay."

"Yeah, I know. I just want to check in, make sure nothing's happening."

"What could be happening, Frank? Even gangsters take Thanksgiving off," Emily said, trying to make a joke.

"Yeah," Frank answered sullenly, "you know that, huh?"

"They do if they have families," Emily said brittlely.

Frank picked up his coffee cup and walked out of the kitchen. "I'm going to see if the football game's on yet," he said, moving to the living room and clicking on the television set. It was still too early for the Thanksgiving Day game and Frank stared absently at some parade while he thought about what was probably going on at Eleventh

Avenue. In the week since the shooting of Angie Morello he had been concentrating his men on the Imperial Trucking Company, on the assumption that this was now the most likely place to catch a contraband shipment. Manzano probably would be staying away from the Greene and Front Street warehouses to avoid any confrontation with Tony LaGarda, whom he must have figured was responsible for icing Morello.

Through the week Frank had been trying desperately to make some progress with the case. His deadline from Halloran was running out and somehow he sensed Ernie knew it. He doubted that Ernie was in contact with the Chief, but his partner hadn't even once mentioned the plan to get Manzano or the Morello incident. It was almost as though he was waiting for something and knew it wouldn't be long. But a break in the case would settle everything, with Halloran and with Ernie.

Frank had left Fred Gallagher and Stu Rhodes at Shield Box, the factory whose upstairs windows provided a view of Imperial's loading bays, but what if they let something get by them? Today was the first time in a long time he would be away from the place for a whole day and he was nervous about it. It wouldn't hurt to call in, he said to himself, but decided against it. There was no point in compromising with Emily on this. What he wanted to do, if he could, was go down there, but since he couldn't do that he didn't want to call in and let Emily think she had let him have his way.

At twelve o'clock the football game came on and Frank watched it dully through the first quarter. Then Emily said that she would be ready to go as soon as she changed her clothes and Frank answered that he was ready already. "Do me a favor, then, Frank," she said. "Could you find that carving board we used to use? Your mother asked me to bring it. It's in the back closet, I think."

Frank was in the closet when the phone rang. He wanted to get to it before Emily did, but it stopped ringing after two rings and he knew she had picked it up upstairs. He waited in the kitchen for a minute to see if Emily would call him, and when she didn't he headed back for the closet. Then he heard her yell from upstairs. "Frank, it's for you."

"Hovannes here," he said into the phone in the living room.

"Frank, hi. You haven't left yet?"

"No, going in just a minute. What's up, Ernie?"

"Look, I didn't want to bother you today, but I just figured Dorothy wasn't going to be ready for another hour—we're going to her sister's—so I thought I'd take a run over here and see if everything's okay. I got here about ten minutes ago and Stu and Fred were just about going crazy. This truck came in and they're unloading television sets. Admiral television sets. Maybe it's that Jersey Turnpike load from last month, the one where they killed the trucker. It's all Admiral television sets. I can read the fucking boxes from here."

"Who's there?"

"The only one I know is Billy Mazes. There are two other guys but we draw a blank on 'em."

"I'll be right over," Frank said and hung up quickly. He raced upstairs and found Emily trying to zip up her dress. "Turn around," he said and zipped it for her. "That was Ernie," he said.

"I know."

"Something's on. I think it could be what we were looking for. I'm going over there."

Emily didn't say anything.

"Look, Em," Frank said, sensing he had to explain, "you know what the score is. We've been watching this place for a long time, and now Ernie says there's a shipment coming in and he thinks maybe it's this truckful of television sets we've been waiting for. I gotta be there."

"Can't they handle it?"

"No, they can't. And besides, I wouldn't let them."

He paused and pulled a cigarette from his shirt pocket but didn't light it. "Look, Emily," he said, trying not to sound like he was losing his patience, "I went along with you when you said not to go down today. I didn't call in this morning, like you said. He called, I didn't. You can't blame me for that. But I can't help it if these guys pick today to move their stuff. We've worked this case for almost seven months, and I'm not going to let someone else blow it. That's all there is to it."

"No it isn't, Frank," Emily said, but she knew it was.

"Yes it is, Emmy," Frank answered sharply. In the back of his mind he was aware that he didn't have to say anything else, that she had given in already. But he went on anyway. "I don't have time to explain," he said. "We're going to need all the guys we can get and it's Thanksgiving for every goddamned one of them. If they take this stuff back out, we've got to decide whether to arrest them there or follow it and I don't want someone else making the wrong decision. They could lead us to forty-seven tons of stuff, and if someone makes a wrong move, they're just going to waltz right out of there and that'll be the last fucking thing we see of them."

He stopped himself, because he didn't usually swear in front of Emily, and then he turned to go. For the first time since he had put it on that morning, Frank was conscious of his gun under his shirt. Emily, though, had known he had it since he came downstairs, because he never wore his shirt outside his pants except when he had his gun.

"Frank," she said, "I'm going over to your mother's and I'm going to have Thanksgiving dinner with her. If you're not there when we finish dinner, I'm going over to my mother's. She's all by herself. I just want to have my Thanksgiving dinner and I want to visit my mother for a while. Is that okay?" She was trying not to cry.

"Emmy, I'm sorry. Don't be upset. We'll talk about it when I get home. I gotta go," he pleaded.

Emily said, "All right, Frank. Good luck." She wasn't crying but she turned away from him anyway, facing toward the window.

Frank turned, too, and ran down the stairs. At the back door he stopped and went back to the closet and in a few seconds he found the carving board and freed it from the boxes on top of it. He set it on the kitchen table and left.

Frank raced south on the West Side Highway, pulling off at the Twenty-third Street exit ramp less than a half hour after he had hung up the phone at home. He took a right at Twenty-fourth and cut over to Eleventh Avenue, where he took a left against the light and drove to Twenty-seventh. He turned the wrong way onto Twenty-seventh, passed the Otis Elevator building, and pulled the car, tires squealing, into the Otis parking lot. Except for an old Oldsmobile which probably belonged to the Otis watchman, the lot was empty. Frank scrambled from the car as the watchman, a gaunt black man in his sixties wearing a police uniform that hung loosely from him, walked slowly toward him.

Frank reached for his shield in his back pocket and flashed it toward the watchman, who was still fifteen yards away. "Police," he said. "I'm gonna leave my car here awhile. Watch it, will you?"

"Sure thing," the watchman said.

Frank started for the street and then stopped. "Do me a favor," he said. "Will you turn it around for me? I may need it in a hurry."

"Sure thing," the watchman said again, walking slowly toward the car. Frank tossed him the keys.

Stu Rhodes was standing at the door to the Shield Box and Paper Company on the north side of Twenty-seventh Street. Frank hurried across the street and into the dingy factory, with Rhodes swinging in around him and closing the door behind them. Shield Box and Paper ran the whole block from Twenty-seventh to Twenty-eighth and the elevator was at the north end. They crossed through the factory and into the elevator, which was waiting. Frank shoved the door closed and pulled the chain and the ancient hydraulic elevator rose slowly. Inside, Rhodes briefed him quickly. There seemed to be only three men unloading the truck, but there might be more inside. Ernie Fleming had come about forty-five minutes ago and had sent for some more men. They were probably there already, Rhodes thought, but couldn't be sure since he had been downstairs waiting for Frank for the last ten minutes.

The elevator jolted to a stop and Frank and Rhodes walked quickly to the window, where they saw Ernie Fleming with a pair of binoculars and Fred Gallagher next to him. Gallagher had a walkie-talkie.

"What's up?" Frank asked, taking a position at the window between Gallagher and Fleming. It was a bright day and the factory they were in was unlit. The sun stood behind them and in the dark they wouldn't be visible from the loading platform, which they could see beneath them. The truck they were looking at was in the front lot, backed up from Eleventh Avenue to the first loading bay from where they stood, almost directly below their window. At first Frank saw no one, but within a few seconds a man he recognized as Billy Mazes walked out from the covered pier onto the platform and into the trailer.

"Billy Mazes," Frank said. "Who else?"

"Don't know 'em," Gallagher said. "Probably just hired help."

"How many?"

"Two, far as we can tell. But there might be more. Mazes and the two guys doing the unloading came in the truck, but there might be someone else in the office." There was an office in the back part of the garage at the Twenty-ninth Street end.

Frank scanned the yard beneath him. He counted six trailers in the back lot, and a car. "How long has that car been there?" he asked.

"That's what we don't know, Frank," Fleming said. "It wasn't there when we left last night, was it?"

"Shit no."

"Yeah, that's what I said. No one saw it come in. That's why we figure there might be someone else in the office."

Frank looked from Rhodes to Gallagher, but both of them were staring out the window and didn't say anything.

"Did you make the plates on it?"

"Can't see me from up here, and we figured we'd wait till you got here to do anything downstairs," Rhodes explained.

"Yeah, good," Frank said. "Who else's here?"

"We got Ferran and Polito over across Eleventh in that Erie building," Fleming said, motioning with the binoculars toward an ancient brick building with broken windows on the corner of Eleventh and Twenty-eighth, directly opposite the cab of the truck. "And Obregon and Menaker are up on Twenty-ninth in the bottom of that warehouse across from the Shell station. You can't see them from here."

"Anyone in cars?"

"No, Frank. I figured we couldn't risk it. You see any cars out there?"

Ernie was right. Except for very light traffic up and down Eleventh Avenue, there were no cars on any of the streets he could see. This was a district made up mostly of factories and trucking companies, and on the holiday the streets were virtually abandoned. A parked car would have stood out like a sore thumb, and anyone watching from the garage could have counted the vehicles going by, there were so few, and easily might have noticed if one passed more than once.

A minute or two passed in silence, and then Fleming said, "Whatdya think, Frank?"

Instead of answering, Hovannes asked, "You figure they almost got that thing unloaded?"

"Yeah, pretty soon. Shitload of television sets," Rhodes said. "They've been at it almost an hour. If they had a fork truck they'd of been gone a long time ago."

The men were unloading the truck with a hand dolly, two or three sets at a time, and only the two men Hovannes didn't know were working. Billy Mazes just walked in and out of the trailer from time to time.

"All right," Frank said after a few seconds more thought, "we got two choices. You're sure these are the sets from the Jersey Turnpike job?"

"If they're not, Admiral makes one helluva lot of television sets," Fleming said.

"Yeah, okay. Then we hit them now or we see what they do with them. Anybody got any warrants?"

"No," Fleming said, "but if you think we oughta hit 'em, I don't think that's a problem. If that isn't one big truckload of probable cause I've never seen one."

"I don't know," Frank said. "I'd sure hate to lose them on that. The other possibility is we don't hit them now. Whatdya think they're unloading this stuff for?"

"Well," Fleming said, "they're either gonna reload it or they're gonna break it up."

"Whatdya mean?" Rhodes asked as Frank nodded agreement.

"If this is the end of the line," Fleming explained, "then they'll break up the shipment and a bunch of small trucks'll come pick up three, four, six sets, whatever they contracted for. Or they could load the whole fucking truck back onto another truck to ship it someplace else. If they're breaking it up, we oughta get 'em now cause we'll never have the whole load together again. But if they're reshipping it, maybe it'd be nice to know where it's going, huh?"

"Right," Frank said. "So we wouldn't want to move in till we see what they're doing. That still leaves us two choices. If a panel truck comes up, or something like that, then they're breaking up the shipment and we have to move on them. But if they start putting it in another trailer we gotta figure whether we want them now or want to risk losing them to see if we can find out where it's going. Christ, I wish I knew how many guys are in there."

"I'd like to follow them, Frank," Ernie Fleming said.

"Yeah, me too," Hovannes agreed. "You know, we've probably got another hour at least till they can load up another truck. Maybe we could send Obregon and Menaker to see if they can get warrants."

"Today? You gotta be kidding."

"They're not doing anything down there. They can't even see the fucking place from where they're sitting. If Billy Mazes and his friends'll give us a couple of hours, maybe they can get them. And if something moves before they get back, there's still six of us here, which oughta be enough. Gallagher, get on that thing and send those two for warrants. And don't take any shit from them. Just tell them I said they'd better find themselves a judge."

Gallagher muttered into the walkie-talkie and a minute later Frank could see two men who must have been Obregon and Menaker walking across Eleventh Avenue and then up to Thirty-first Street, where they got in a car and drove off. Frank looked back down to the loading platform right underneath him.

"Hey," he said, "where's Mazes?"

No one knew.

"I haven't seen him in maybe five minutes," Rhodes said.

"More like ten, I think," Gallagher said.

"Where'd you see him last, in the truck or in the loading bay?" Frank asked. Fleming thought it was the loading bay and the other two agreed.

"That's what I thought," Frank said. "What's he doing in there so long?"

"Watching television, maybe," Rhodes said. Frank looked at him. "Well, he's got enough of them there," Rhodes added lamely.

"Can they see in there from that Erie place?" Frank asked.

"Not too good," Gallagher said. "The truck blocks 'em out."

"Well, ask them if they can see Mazes."

Gallagher radioed the question and then reported, "They haven't seen him in maybe ten minutes. He might be right in back of the truck, they can't see there, but Polito thinks he went up to the other end a little while ago."

"Polito *thinks* he went up to the other end? What are those guys doing, playing with themselves?"

"He went up to the other end about ten minutes ago," Gallagher corrected, making it definite.

"So either there's someone in the office or he's gone to take a crap, right?" Frank said.

"Let's figure there's someone there," Fleming advised.

"Let's figure we go find out," Hovannes answered.

No one said anything. Frank felt it was important to know how many other men might be in the Imperial Trucking Company, in case they had to move in on them. When he explained this to Gallagher and Rhodes, whose carelessness about the car parked in the back lot was responsible for the fact that the team was now operating in the dark, Gallagher volunteered to go over and wander around the lot to see if he could learn anything, but Frank vetoed the idea. He and Ernie would go.

The four men left their observation post at the window and rode down in the elevator. Frank stationed Gallagher at the first floor window on the Twenty-eighth Street side of the factory, where he could look directly across the street at the loading platform. Rhodes stood about six feet away behind a heavy fire door, ready to come out onto the street in case there was any trouble. They radioed across to Polito and Ferran to come down to the first floor level at the Erie building so that they too would be only a few seconds away, across Eleventh Avenue, in case they were needed.

When they were all in position, Frank and Ernie crossed the box factory to the Twenty-seventh Street side, then walked briskly east to Tenth Avenue, around the block up to Twenty-eighth, and then back west, on the north side of the street, toward Billy Mazes and his truckful of television sets. When they were about a hundred feet from the end of the back lot, they slowed to a very leisurely stroll.

The loading bays closed with vertical gates, and now Frank and Ernie had the right angle to see for the first time that the gate to the back bay opposite where the truck was unloading was open. Frank glanced quickly at his partner and he could see that the same thought was passing through both their minds. If they could get up

close they might be able to see down the length of the long
pier toward the office. Billy Mazes wasn't anywhere in
sight.

Frank stopped to light a cigaret while the two truckers
headed toward them out of the truck onto the platform
and into the bay. One of them was pushing a dolly with
two large console-size television sets on it, and the other
walked beside him. Frank got a good look at them and
was sure he didn't recognize them. The larger of the two
pushed the dolly into position beside what looked like half
an acre of similar cartons, and his partner leaned the
boxes slightly so he could free the dolly. Then the two
walked back into the truck, their backs turned away from
Hovannes and Fleming.

"Come on," Frank said, softly but firmly.

He and Ernie cut quickly into the lot and stopped beside an empty trailer that paralleled the long pier of loading bays. With the trailer between them and the loading
bays, they couldn't be seen by anyone in there. The car
they had been wondering about was just a few feet beyond
them and Frank memorized the license plate. They could
hear the truckers talking, but couldn't make out what
they were saying.

"You wanna get closer?" Ernie asked in a whisper.

"Yeah, I think so," Frank said.

Both men reached to their sides to feel their guns
under their coats and then moved around to the back of
the trailer and then toward the loading pier. They were
about ten yards from the sidewalk now, so the truckers
still couldn't see them through the open back gate. Quickly
they passed three trailers this way, and when they got to
the last one separating them from the pier they ducked in
beside it so that only the one empty trailer and fifteen
feet of space stood between them and the workmen.

The truckers' voices were clear now, indicating they
were inside the covered pier. Frank could hear one of
them say, "How many we got left?" and the other answer,
"Four." He looked at Ernie. That meant they'd be finished
in three or four minutes.

Shit, Frank thought, what are we doing here? If they
leave when they're finished, that means there must be
someone else in the place because they wouldn't leave all
this merchandise with no one to watch it. And if they stay
after they have the truck unloaded, that probably means

there's no one else there except them and Mazes. For the first time Frank realized he had been too impatient. He could have learned this without risking going into the yard, simply by waiting to see what happened when the loading was finished. He looked at Ernie to see if Ernie had realized the same thing, but he couldn't tell anything from his partner's expression.

"Let's get outta here," Frank whispered.

He started to move toward the north end of the lot in order to go around the empty trailers and leave the same way they had come in, as far from the loading pier as possible. Ernie was right behind him. Suddenly Ernie's left hand grabbed Frank's shoulder and in a second the two of them were standing alongside the trailer, Ernie right in back of Frank, their guns drawn. They could hear footsteps on the gravel heading toward them.

They were less than ten feet from the back of the trailer when Billy Mazes stepped in front of them. He was heading toward the car parked beyond the empty trailers, and when he stepped into the opening in front of Frank he was looking straight ahead. But he must have seen something out of the corner of his eye because he wheeled toward Frank, whose gun was leveled straight at his chest. Instinctively his right hand started to move for the gun under his jacket but stopped almost at once. "Don't try it," Frank said anyway, and a second later he heard someone shout, "Watch out, Billy. Cops!"

Then there were shots, two shorts at first, one right after the other, followed by maybe eight or ten all at once, and somewhere in the middle of the shooting Hovannes heard Ernie say, "Jesus, Frank." And then it was all over and Frank, who hadn't taken his eyes off Mazes, heard Fred Gallagher come up behind him saying, "We've got him covered, Frank. Ernie's hit bad."

So little had happened, it seemed to Frank, and it had happened so quickly, that at first he couldn't understand. Later he put it all together. Ernie had realized the moment Mazes stepped around the back of the truck in front of Frank that it was all over and they would have to arrest whoever was in the shed. He couldn't tell from where he stood between two trailers whether Gallagher and Rhodes could see them, so as soon as he saw that Frank had Mazes covered he headed for the sidewalk to signal them to move in. In fact, Gallagher had seen the whole thing from his vantage point on the ground floor of the box factory. He had seen Billy Mazes come out of a small door on the north end of the loading pier near the garage, and as Mazes walked down the stairs to the parking lot level, Gallagher realized he must be going to the car and would walk right into the two detectives crouched on the far side of the first trailer. "Let's go," he said to Rhodes, and the two of them pushed through the fire door and onto Twenty-eighth Street with their guns drawn just as Mazes stepped in front of Frank. The truckers hadn't seen what was going on in the parking lot, but they saw Rhodes and Gallagher come charging out of the box factory. The bigger one pulled a gun and yelled his warning to Mazes while the other one ran into the shed and out on the Eleventh Avenue side. It was just then that Ernie stepped from behind the truck. The trucker on the platform spotted him, hardly twenty feet away, and opened fire. Two shots from the loading bay ripped into Ernie's side, smashing into his ribs just four inches below his armpit. Ernie was dead, and Rhodes and Gallagher both opened fire on the trucker and didn't stop until he was dead, too.

PART TWO

◆◆

Chapter 11

FRANK HOVANNES STOOD in the phone booth at the corner of Third and Forty-seventh, talking to no one. His right hand, in the pocket of his windbreaker, held his thirty-eight and his left hand held the receiver to his ear as he listened to the dial tone. Ten minutes was all he would wait. In ten minutes maybe the doorman at the Russell would notice him or maybe one of Manzano's boys was in the lobby and would see him.

He glanced over quickly to where the panel truck was parked across the street about twenty-five feet down Third Avenue, directly opposite the hotel entrance. He could see Roberto Obregon behind the wheel and knew that Lou Savage was in the back. Then he looked east down Forty-seventh again to where Manzano would come from. He would be walking with two of his boys, one on either side of him. Probably Louie Silvera and Al Palmini. Silvera and Palmini would be armed, Manzano wouldn't. The time to hit him would be right when he turned down Third, his back to the telephone booth.

It would be a lot easier, Hovannes thought, if they could do the job from the truck. But there might not be a good shot from the truck. If it was going to be done right, they couldn't take a chance like that. The idea was that as soon as Hovannes shot Manzano, Savage would open fire from the back of the truck. If Hovannes hit his quarry fast and started moving, Savage could keep the bodyguards pinned there so that Hovannes could get away. Either up Third or straight across the avenue to the truck, depending on how it looked.

Frank's mouth was sticky and dry and he ran his tongue across his teeth trying to rub away the sour taste. This was the third time he was here, but somehow it felt like this one would be it. The first time, just a week ago, he waited the scheduled ten minutes and when Manzano didn't show he left. Savage told him later that Big Sallie

—Savage had taken to referring to Manzano as Big Sallie
—had shown up less than three minutes after Frank left.
"I could of hit him myself," Savage said. "It would of been
easy. But Obregon said no, we had to do it the way you
said. Shit, it would of been easy."

Yes, it would have, Frank thought, and that night he
had been sick thinking about it. Being out on the street like
that, in the open, scared him but he wanted to be sure and
this was the only way. So three days later he was back in
the phone booth, the panel truck back across the avenue.
This time Manzano showed up on time and rounded the
corner less than fifteen feet from Frank. But just as he
was ready to shoot—he was going to shoot through the
pocket of his windbreaker—these four girls came out of
nowhere and crossed into the hotel right in front of him.
Out of nowhere. It would have been impossible to hit
Manzano without a pretty good chance of hitting them,
and if he didn't get them Savage sure as hell would from
the truck. It was as important not to hit anyone else as it
was to hit Manzano, so he turned on his heels and walked
quickly down Forty-seventh, feeling sick again.

Now this was the third try, and Frank didn't hide from
himself the almost fearful panic he had felt the first two
times and was feeling again now. He had hardly slept the
night before—in fact, the whole last week had been bad,
ever since the first time he had taken his position here
waiting to gun Manzano—and his nerves were showing
the strain. What he felt now was the panic you feel before
going into combat, the gut-souring acid panic that is in
part fear for your own life and in part an instinctive re-
vulsion at the whole situation, at the killing. He hadn't
felt anything like it since Korea, even though on two occasions he had had to kill a man since coming back to
the States.

If it didn't come off again this time, he told himself,
they wouldn't try again. They'd have to figure out somewhere else to hit him. He couldn't keep coming back to
the same phone booth all the time, like he was booking
bets in there. Anyway, Manzano, who looked where he
was going all the time, would probably recognize him if
this went on too long. So this had to be it.

All these things were going through Frank's mind when
he saw Manzano, Silvera, and Palmini coming toward him
about halfway down the block. Silvera must have

weighed about two hundred eighty pounds and you could see him a mile off in his white suit. Who the fuck does he think he is, Sidney Greenstreet or something, Frank thought. Silvera was walking about the middle of the sidewalk, Manzano to his right, and Dumb Al Palmini to his right, so that whenever they came to one of those little plots with a scrawny tree and some dirt and dog shit around it, Dumb Al had to step behind Manzano and then do a little skip to catch up to him. The three of them looked pretty silly, Frank thought, and that made it easier for him.

When they were about thirty feet away Frank started talking into the telephone. He didn't know what he was saying but he wanted his mouth to be moving. The three of them seemed to be approaching very slowly, like when you see a subway up the tracks and the headlight just seems to hang there, not getting any closer. Then all of a sudden they were almost on top of him and it seemed for a second like they were going to walk right through the phone booth. They couldn't have been ten feet in front of him, and Frank could see their eyes. Manzano was looking straight past him, Silvera was talking, his eyes shooting quickly up the avenue and then back to his boss. Dumb Al Palmini wasn't looking at anything, his head kind of hanging down in his stupid round-shouldered way.

It didn't seem like they had come this close the last time, and for a moment the thought flashed through Hovannes's mind that they weren't going to the hotel, that they would cross Third Avenue and just keep walking. If they did that they would cross right in front of the truck and there wouldn't be a thing Hovannes could do about it. Savage was in the back, and he wouldn't even get a shot at them. Besides, like the first time, Savage wouldn't do anything unless it was going just like they planned. Frank could feel a burning acrid taste at the back of his throat as he waited to see what would happen. All this didn't take three seconds but it seemed a lot longer.

Then they turned, and as they did Dumb Al practically walked into the phone booth, just missing it by hopping in back of Manzano and then skipping around to his side again. They were about fifteen feet ahead of Frank now and he stepped from the booth, his hand deep in the windbreaker pocket holding the thirty-eight for all he was worth. Quickly he pulled it from his pocket—fuck, I wasn't going to do that, he thought—and opened fire. The first shot hit Manzano and he went down. The next three followed him to the sidewalk. Silvera and Palmini wheeled toward Frank, reaching for their guns, and as they did he hit Silvera once in the side. The fat man just stared at him, his hand groping toward the gun under his jacket while a red stain started to spread under his armpit. Frank wanted to hit him again but the thing to do was to make sure of Manzano.

By this time Palmini had his gun out. Just then Savage opened fire from across the street. Palmini stood there a second, his gun aimed straight at Frank, a look of animal bewilderment crossing his stupid face, and then he made up his mind and whirled away from Frank toward where Savage was shooting from. It was that close.

Frank turned and ran up Third Avenue, leaving the two hoods crouched down over their boss, returning Savage's fire. He could hear the bullets screaming against the truck, making a sharp tearing sound. Frank ran into the avenue and was racing uptown, his gun still in his hand. Once he was off the sidewalk he was out of their line of fire, which was nice to know even though they were too busy with Savage to try shooting at him. When he was halfway to Forty-eighth, Obregon put the truck in gear and sliced across the avenue to pick him up. The truck rolled up beside him, moving slowly, and Lou Savage swung open the rear door. Frank jumped for it, Lou pulling his arm and yelling up front to Obregon, "Let's get the fuck outta here!"

At Fifty-ninth Street they turned right and headed for the bridge and into Queens. On the other side of the bridge they parked the truck a block from the BMT station and took the train back into Manhattan. No one had said a word.

"Did you see him?" Savage asked on the train, meaning did you kill him?

"Yeah," Frank said. "I think so. Fatso too, I think."

Then they split up.

Chapter 12

"I JUST DON'T FIGURE IT," Eddie Manzano was saying. "I mean LaGarda's gonna get his. There's no way he's not gonna get his. But I just don't figure it."

"Maybe it wasn't him," Phil Runelli suggested.

"Whatdya mean it wasn't him? Of course it was him. Ever since that sonofabitch had Morello hit I knew he was gonna be real trouble some day. But this? I never figured this."

Runelli tried again. "I mean I was just talking to Paulie Gagliano, you know him, just the other day, and he's in pretty tight with LaGarda. I mean if something was on he'd of known it. And he didn't say nothing. I mean I know Paulie maybe twenty years and we was always pretty tight. He'd of said something."

"It was him," Eddie Manzano said, mumbling the words, not so much answering Runelli as saying that he didn't want to hear any more about it.

They were in the big study upstairs in Salvatore Manzano's house in Tenafly. As soon as he heard, Eddie had come right over to tell Ruth. Runelli and Frankie Diamond showed up together a little later, while Eddie was still downstairs in the front room with Ruth, who was crying. Runelli and Frankie Diamond went right upstairs to the big study to wait for Eddie. There was nothing to say till Eddie came up and told them what was going to happen, so they poured themselves drinks from the decanter and sat down to smoke and wait without talking to each other.

They sat there most of the evening. Occasionally they could hear Eddie's voice from downstairs, and sometimes they could hear Ruth crying. She just didn't stop crying. Around eight o'clock they heard a car pull up in the gravel driveway and Frankie Diamond went to the window to look. "It's Helen," he said.

Helen was Big Sallie's daughter. She jumped from the

MG almost before it had crunched to a halt and raced across the gravel toward the front door. Frankie Diamond saw a kid, maybe twenty at most, scramble from the driver's side and catch up to her before she reached the door. He was a good-looking kid, tall with long wavy black hair, and he spoke to her earnestly for a few seconds, facing her and holding both her hands in his. Helen stood tensely, shaking her head no, then turned and bolted into the house. The kid stood until the front door had closed behind her, then turned and walked slowly back to his MG.

"It's gonna be rough on her," Frankie Diamond heard Runelli say.

He turned from the window but didn't answer.

"I mean she and Sallie was real close," Runelli went on. "This is just gonna break her up. I mean, my Terry and me, we ain't like that. But she was real close with the old man."

"Shut up, Phil," Frankie Diamond said.

"Poor kid."

"I said shut up."

They both fell silent. Then Frankie Diamond asked, "Do you think she knows already?"

"It's on the radio," Runelli answered. Then they waited some more. Around ten o'clock Eddie came upstairs and poured himself a drink. They waited to hear what he would say.

"LaGarda," he said at last. "It's gotta be." That was when he said he couldn't figure it and Runelli said that maybe it wasn't LaGarda, but Eddie would have none of that. So they sat like that a few minutes, Eddie smoking a cigar while Frankie Diamond and Runelli drew nervously on cigarets.

"How's Ruth taking it?" Runelli asked.

"She'll be all right."

"And Helen?"

"Helen's a good kid," Eddie said.

"I got some boys'll hit LaGarda tonight, maybe tomorrow, if you just say so Eddie," Frankie Diamond volunteered, his voice soft and consoling. He meant, I know how you feel, losing your brother like that. Don't worry about anything. We'll take care of the arrangements.

"Maybe we should take this up to the top," Runelli

suggested. "You know Robustelli ain't gonna stand for this kind of trouble. He'll take care of it."

Eddie leveled him with a stare, took a deep drag from his cigar, and blew the smoke toward Runelli.

"Phil," he said, "sometimes you give me the creeps. That cocksucker wastes my brother and you sit here telling me we should let Robustelli handle it! Helen's an orphan. You realize that? Just went out to the pictures with her boyfriend and comes home and her father's dead. And Ruth's crying her eyes out right over there in his bedroom," he said, motioning toward the door, "and maybe we're gonna have to get the doctor for her, and you're sitting here telling me Eddie Manzano can't handle it when some cocksucker kills his brother! Jesus, you give me the creeps."

Then he turned to Frankie Diamond and the anger seemed to drain out of him. "Thanks, Frankie. But not tonight. He'll be expecting it. We'll figure out a way and then we'll hit him for sure. Then I'll tell you when. And when I do, Frankie, I'd like you should tell your boys to cut the little fucker into pieces. But not tonight."

Another car pulled up and this time it was Runelli who went to the window. "It's Johnny," he announced.

They could hear the butler telling Johnny Lombardi they were upstairs and then Johnny's footsteps running up. He came into the room and closed the door behind him.

"You been to the hospital?" Eddie Manzano asked.

"Yeah, sure. That's where I'm coming from."

"How's Louie?"

"He's in pretty tough shape. They took three slugs out of him. He'll be okay, the doc says. But he's in pretty tough shape."

"Did you talk to him?"

"Yeah, I talked to him."

"So?"

"So, he says he got no idea who hit him. Never seen the guy before. There was one guy out on the street, big guy, and Louie says he got a pretty good look at him but he never seen him before. No idea who he is. And there was some guys over in a truck across the street shooting a machine gun."

"Christ, I know that from the radio. Everyone knows that. It was on the fucking radio. What else he tell you?"

"Nothing. He just says he don't know who the guy is. That's all."

"Maybe it's some guns from outta town," Runelli suggested.

"Must be," Eddie Manzano said. "It sure don't figure. How could LaGarda get guns from outta town without us knowing it? I never would of figured the son of a bitch for anything like this. What about Dumb Al? Where's he?"

"He ain't talking to no one. They scared the shit outta him. He's got himself a room at the Blackstone and he ain't talking to no one. I tried to go see him but he has the door locked and he won't let me in. Me, for chrissakes. I don't think he knows who they was either. Fat Louie says as soon as that truck drives away Dumb Al says, 'You okay, Louie?' and Louie says, 'I'll live,' so Dumb Al says, 'Then I'm getting the fuck outta here, Louie,' and he takes off. I don't think he was hit, but if he was maybe it wasn't much. I ask him, 'Look, Al, do you need anything?' and he says, 'Get lost, Johnny.' So I say, 'Do you need a doctor? I'll get you a doctor,' and he says, 'No, Johnny, just get lost.' So I tell him he knows where to find me if he wants anything. Wouldn't even let me in. They really scared the shit outta him. But I don't think he saw anything. If Fat Louie don't know who them guys is, it's for sure Al don't."

There wasn't much else to say but Eddie said, "I hope all you guys tell your boys to be careful. LaGarda wouldn't gun Sallie unless he means to make something big out of it, so all of you gotta be very careful."

"Sure, Eddie, we know that," Runelli said.

"Yeah, well, you just make sure you tell your boys."

Johnny asked, "Have the cops been here yet?"

"No," Eddie Manzano said. "Jersey cops. They won't be here till tomorrow."

"Yeah, well I just thought I'd tell you. They was already looking for Frankie here. I called your place, Frankie, and Tommie Minelli tells me they got cops there asking questions."

"What kinda questions? They don't think Frankie'd shoot one of his own, do they?" Manzano asked.

"Naw, nothing like that. Just asking questions. Minelli couldn't talk—they was there when I called—but they're just asking questions. They got nothing better to do, I guess."

"Yeah," Eddie said, "I guess so. Jersey cops'll be here tomorrow. What the fuck they want from me I don't know. But they'll be here. They probably know less about this thing than we do."

"Maybe, maybe not," Frankie Diamond said. "They might know if there was some guns from outta town hanging around. Maybe I'll get one of my boys to see if they know anything. Funny we wouldn't know if there was some outta town guns hanging around. But maybe the cops know something we don't."

"Yeah, check that, Frankie," Eddie Manzano said. "I'll see you boys tomorrow."

Phil Runelli, Frankie Diamond, and Johnny Lombardi all stood up together and walked out of the room without saying anything. Runelli, who was last, pulled the door closed behind him. Eddie Manzano reached up over his shoulder and turned off the floor lamp beside his chair and the big study was dark except for the red point of his cigar.

Monday, April 14

Tony LaGarda was stuffing shirts into an attaché case in his office at the back of the Caffe Fidelio, the restaurant he operated on Elizabeth Street. Paulie Gagliano was watching without saying anything when Jimmie Monks came in.

LaGarda, who was now behind his desk bent over in the swivel chair searching for something in the bottom drawer, looked up quickly. "What?" he asked.

"Nothing," Monks answered. "Nobody knows nothing. Just that Big Sallie got hit, that's all."

LaGarda pushed the drawer closed violently and sat up, looking angrily at Monks. Then he didn't say anything but waited a moment to collect himself. He was called Tony the Lawyer because he had built a reputation for staying cool under any circumstances, for always figuring out the smoothest way to handle any situation. He liked to think that when it came to being hard, when it was a matter of muscle, he could hold his own with any of the bosses, but he knew that he had gotten where he was by using his head when guys like Eddie and Salvatore Manzano would turn their guns loose. Besides, he didn't anger easily and this gave him an advantage if he knew how to use it.

"Jimmie," he said, "this doesn't make sense. Somebody hit him so somebody's got to know who did it. And we got to find out fast."

"Eddie Manzano thinks you done it," Paulie Gagliano suggested timidly, afraid of what Tony's reaction would be.

But Tony the Lawyer just leaned back slowly in his chair, looking toward the ceiling. "That's what I'm talking about," he said. "I've tried to figure it every way I could, and there's no one I can come up with. Robustelli's got nothing to gain by knocking off Big Sallie like that, nothing at all. Same for Leone. We had this thing all worked out, and I don't think they'd cross me up like that."

"Whatdya mean, worked out?" Gagliano asked.

"I don't mean nothing," LaGarda shot back. "When you gotta know something, I'll tell you."

No one said anything for a few seconds and then Gagliano tried again. "What are you gonna do?" he asked.

"What am I gonna do? What do you think I'm gonna do? If you think I'm getting into a war with Eddie Manzano and God knows who else, you gotta be crazy!"

Again nobody said anything for a while, and then Jimmie Monks sat down in the chair beside LaGarda's desk. "Tony," he said, picking his words carefully, "maybe you got no choice. Maybe you just gotta have it out with Eddie. No, listen to me," he said to stop LaGarda from interrupting, "I think Eddie's gonna be looking for you. I think unless Eddie finds out for sure it was someone else did this thing to Sallie, he's got to go for you, and unless we're ready there's gonna be hell to pay. See what I mean?"

Monks was as old as Tony and had known him since they started as soldiers in the mob together more than thirty years ago, so Tony listened to him, thought about it for a minute without answering, and then said, "Maybe you're right, Jimmie. We're sure as hell gonna have some trouble from Eddie and I guess we gotta give him trouble if we're gonna keep our asses alive. But I think we gotta see what happens first. There are some things we gotta find out, like who hit Sallie and what he's gonna do next. That's the thing that got me, cause I got a funny feeling going for Eddie is just what he wants us to do. See what *I* mean?"

"Yeah, I guess so," Jimmie Monks said. Gagliano nodded.

"Okay. Then here's what we're gonna do. I'm going down to Vineland. There'll be no heat there, none of them knows about the place, and I can figure out what to do. The thing for you boys is to find out whatever you can. Maybe this thing will be straightened out. But find out whatever you can and get all the boys ready. And be very careful. Stay away from any of Eddie's boys. I mean that, Paulie. You know who I mean. I don't trust that Phil Runelli and I never have. And if you trust him you're gonna get us all killed. So stay away from him. You get Richie Saint and you get Rusty from the Bronx and maybe Artie and you get them all ready. Eddie's gonna be looking for me, but I'm not gonna be here. Now when I get back from Vineland we'll see how Eddie's handling this and we'll be ready to move. If you find out anything you know how to call me."

He picked up his attaché case and started for the back door. "Paulie," he said, "I'm taking the bus. I'll pick it up in Jersey. I don't want to go in no car. You drive me to Jersey and take the car back. Then call Vineland and have them pick me up."

Tony the Lawyer and Paulie Gagliano left by the back door and climbed into Tony's Imperial, Paulie driving. Jimmie Monks moved to the chair behind LaGarda's desk, put his feet up, and waited.

Chapter 13

WHEN THE POLICE DEPARTMENT MOVED to its new head-quarters near Foley Square, a few units, including the Organized Crime Control Squad, stayed behind in the cavernous old mausoleum on Centre Street. Except for a small grassy park at the north end, the four-story turn-of-the-century structure runs the whole of the long block between Broome and Grand streets. A makeshift scaffolding, of the sort that contractors put up around a building to keep debris from falling on the sidewalk, follows the old headquarters for virtually its entire perimeter, even though no work is being done. Put up in the sixties to make it difficult to toss molotov cocktails into the second story offices, the scaffolding has become permanent, cutting the lions that guard the Centre Street entrance in half, so that only their lower extremities are visible from the street.

The Centre Street entrance itself, at the top of a short flight of stairs, is a surprisingly narrow doorway with a round guard booth immediately inside it, so close to the entranceway that only one person at a time can walk by into the main lobby. The guard stationed in the booth demands identification and a pass from all visitors. In the morning as the skeleton staff still stationed in the old building arrives, they file around the booth in a steady stream, then gather in clumps for a few moments of sociability in the huge lobby before proceeding up the double set of massive stone stairs that head upward to the north and south at the back of the lobby.

As Assistant Chief Inspector Lawrence P. Flynn mounted the stairs at eight-thirty on Tuesday morning, he had in his right hand a sheaf of reports on Monday afternoon's shooting. The people with first floor offices had all moved upstairs, leaving the ground floor vacant, so the new ACI's office was now at the far south end of the second floor. Halfway down the corridor Flynn could see a small group of reporters waiting for him in front of the heavy oak doors to his office.

"Good morning," Flynn said amiably. Half a dozen perfunctory good mornings came back.

"What can you tell us about Manzano?" someone asked.

"Not very much right now, gentlemen," Flynn said. "I'm just getting here myself."

"You can do better than that."

"Well, in fact," Flynn said, "I had some preliminary reports sent over to my house this morning and I've looked at them on the way over. But there's still not very much I can say because at this point we don't know very much."

Three or four reporters asked questions simultaneously and Flynn chose to pretend he didn't understand. Instead he just launched into a simple narrative of the events, telling little more than had been available to the press from the precinct the evening before. One or more unidentified persons had opened fire on Salvatore Manzano and two of his associates. Manzano was dead when the police ambulance arrived and one of the associates, Louis Silvera, known as Fat Louie, had been taken to the hospital with gunshot wounds. The other associate fled and has not been identified. It was not known whether or not he had been wounded. The assailant fled in a blue panel truck which apparently had been parked across the street. It seemed that shots also had been fired from the truck. No eyewitnesses could be found to identify the gunmen, the truck had not been identified except as to color, and it had not been found. "Other than that, gentlemen, there's nothing I can tell you," he concluded.

"It's nice to see you watch the eleven o'clock news too, Inspector," one of the reporters said archly. Flynn smiled.

"Inspector," another asked, "would you call this a gangland killing?"

Flynn smiled sardonically again and looked pointedly at the lettering just above eye level on his door where it said ORGANIZED CRIME CONTROL LAWRENCE P. FLYNN ASSISTANT CHIEF INSPECTOR. "What would make you think that?" he asked.

"Inspector, do you think this is going to be the start of a new round of mob wars?"

"I'm afraid you're going to have to ask your contacts in the mob if you want an answer on that one," Flynn said.

Then he added in a more conciliatory tone, "Look, you know how these things work as well as I do. But right now we don't have a goddamned thing. And until we do I'm not saying anything. If you'll excuse me, I have a lot of work to do."

He pushed past the reporters into his office, swinging the door behind him. It was still a few minutes before nine and his secretary wasn't at her desk in the outer office yet. The door to the inner office was open and just before he stepped in he smelled cigarette smoke.

Frank Hovannes was stretched on the couch to his left. He slowly raised himself to a sitting position as the Chief made his way to the desk in front of the window. "Good morning, Frank," Flynn said. "I guess you know what I wanted to see you about."

"Yeah. The Manzano thing."

"Right. What we're afraid of is that it means something's starting, and I guess you know the kinda heat we get about things like that. You remember what those Gallo wars were like, and now another one. If we don't get on top of it pretty soon the Commissioner's gonna want all our asses."

Hovannes didn't say anything.

"He gets a lot of heat too, you know, Frank," Flynn went on awkwardly. Frank Hovannes always made him feel uneasy, but he wasn't alone in that. Frank made a lot of people in the Department uncomfortable. Talking to him about the political pressures in a case was like talking to a priest. You couldn't expect him to understand and he made you feel guilty for wanting him to. But Flynn wanted Frank to know that if people were going to lean on him, then he was going to lean on Frank. So he said what he said even though he knew that Hovannes despised him for it. In Frank's book, a cop who gave a shit about that sort of thing was in the wrong business. "I just want you to know where things stand, Frank," Flynn added apologetically after he had said his piece.

"I know where things stand, Larry," Hovannes answered, not giving an inch.

"Okay, just so it's clear."

Flynn shuffled some papers on his desk to keep from saying anything else and to keep Hovannes from saying anything. "So far all I've got is the precinct reports," he said, "and they turned up absolutely nothing. Nothing.

They don't even know who the third guy was. Can you beat that? Hoods like Manzano, Palmini, and Silvera show up every fucking Monday and Thursday in their precinct for two years and they give me this." Flynn pulled a sheet of paper from the sheaf he held in his hands and then read, " 'A third member of Manzano's party, possibly also wounded, fled the scene. Identity unknown. Refer to OCC.' "

He tossed the reports back onto his desk and looked up at Hovannes. He felt their positions were clearer now. He was the chief and Hovannes was his senior field officer. If he kept it that simple, if he didn't let himself get loused up worrying what Hovannes was thinking, then he could just give Hovannes orders and that would be that. He wasn't going to let Hovannes intimidate him like he had done with Bob Halloran.

"So that's it," Flynn said. "All we got now is what you see in the papers. It's our baby now and I'm giving it to you."

Hovannes stood up and turned to leave. "I'll get some men and get on it," he said, moving for the door. "When we get something I'll let you know."

Chapter 14

TOMMIE MINELLI and his brother Mickey were sitting in Tommie's car on Elizabeth Street across the street from the Caffe Fidelio. Tommie was one of Frankie Diamond's soldiers, and his brother, who was only nineteen, was his informal apprentice, following him around constantly and accompanying him practically everywhere. It was Tuesday night and Tony the Lawyer LaGarda was already safe in south Jersey, but the Minelli brothers had no way of knowing this at the time.

They weren't really looking for LaGarda, though. Without specific orders they wouldn't have got themselves involved in anything as serious as a hit on Tony the Lawyer. But the word had gone out in a general way to be on the lookout for any of LaGarda's people, and Tommie knew there was no better place to look out for them than at the Fidelio. So the two of them sat there, Mickey behind the steering wheel, Tommie smoking continuously and snapping the butts against the window of the bakery in front of which they were parked. For two hours they sat without speaking, except once when Mickey said, "Who do you think's in there, Tommie?"

Tommie just looked at his kid brother, took a long drag from his cigaret, and snapped it at the bakery, barely missing a young couple walking past the car. "Hey!" the boy exclaimed and turned toward the open window of the Buick, stooping to look in. Tommie looked straight at him, sizing him up, and then turned contemptuously away to look out the windshield. Mickey didn't say anything and the girl, who sensed something menacing about the brothers, pulled on her escort's sleeve and urgently whispered at him to forget it. Slowly he straightened up and walked away. When he had gone a few steps, her hand still clutching his sleeve, he turned to look in through the windshield and saw Tommie staring straight

108

at him. Mickey was laughing. Then the couple rounded the corner onto Hester Street and were gone.

This happened at about ten-thirty. A little after eleven Mickey said, "Hey, Tommie, I don't think anyone's coming out. They probably seen us here. Maybe we should just drive down the block and wait. They see us drive off, they'll think we're gone."

Tommie didn't say anything.

"Huh?" Mickey asked.

"Sit tight."

"But Tommie, nobody's coming out. I think they seen us."

"So? I want em to see us. I want em to know we're here."

Just at that moment, almost in refutation of his logic, the door of the Fidelio opened and two men walked up the three shallow steps and onto the sidewalk. One of them Tommie recognized as Richie Saint, or Richard Santucci, the ex-fight manager and a friend of LaGarda's. A thin, almost emaciated man in his middle fifties, his invariable costume was a rumpled dark suit and a broad dark tie that completely obscured his shirt.

Richie Saint had had a run-in with Tommie Minelli about a year and a half ago. Minelli spotted Saint one night at the fights in Madison Square Garden. Tommie had just picked up with Vin Robustelli, the Bronx boss. He was sharply dressed and full of his own importance. Richie Saint, who still had some of his boxing connections, had a fighter on the card in one of the preliminaries. Tommie approached him ostentatiously and asked him for a tip, and Richie Saint turned to the man he was standing with at the back of the Garden, someone Tommie didn't recognize, and asked, "Who's the kid?"

"Tommie Minelli," Tommie said before the stranger could answer.

"He's with Vin Robustelli," Richie Saint's friend explained.

"That right?" Richie Saint asked.

"Yeah, I'm with Robustelli," Tommie boasted.

"Well, for a friend of Vin Robustelli maybe I can suggest that Red Folkers is a promising young fighter," Richie Saint said and turned back to his partner, leaving Tommie standing there.

Tommie put fifty dollars on Folkers—he would have

made it more, but even fifty dollars was a lot for a six-round preliminary—and Folkers was knocked out in the second. After the fight Tommie found Richie Saint and his friend again at the back of the Garden. He started to make a scene.

"Tell Vin Robustelli's friend," Richie Saint said, turning away from him and talking to two toughs lounging against the wall whom Tommie hadn't noticed before, "that sometimes if you gamble you lose. Explain to him that that's what makes it fun." Then he walked away. It probably wasn't the kind of scene Richie Saint would remember, just a harmless prank on a swell-headed punk. But it wasn't anything Tommie Minelli would forget.

"The skinny one's Richie Saint," Tommie hissed to his brother. "I don't make the other one."

The man Tommie Minelli didn't recognize was Leo Goffman, a small-time burglar and bad-check artist from the Bronx with no mob connections except for his friendship with Richie Saint. For some reason, Richie Saint had dispensed with his regular wheelman and had been traveling with Goffman for the past week or two. They stood at the top of the steps to the Fidelio for a minute, scanning Elizabeth Street in both directions. When Richie Saint spotted the Minelli brothers across the street in their yellow Buick he nudged his friend in the ribs with his elbow and nodded toward the car.

"The cocksucker!" Tommie hissed at the gesture.

Then the two men on the sidewalk exchanged a few words and, turning to their left, walked briskly the few paces up to Hester Street, crossed Hester, and then quickly turned right and crossed Elizabeth, heading east down Hester.

"Fuck 'em," Mickey Minelli sighed, secretly relieved that they were gone. Hester was a westbound one-way street, so it would be difficult to follow them in the car.

"Get going!" Tommie almost screamed at his brother.

"What?" Mickey asked, incredulous.

"Get going. Come on!"

Mickey started the engine and threw the Buick into drive, flashed across Hester Street and up to Grand. He turned right and right again at Bowery, then slowed down so they could have a look. At first they saw nothing, but then a block and a half ahead there was the unmistakable pencil-thin shape of Richie Saint. He was standing on the sidewalk by a black Imperial while the man with him was unlocking the driver-side door.

Mickey Minelli pulled the yellow Buick to the curb and he and his brother watched Richie Saint and his friend climb into the parked car. On the nearly deserted street they could hear its engine start and saw its headlights flash on. The Imperial pulled away from the curb and Mickey was about to pull out and follow when the Imperial suddenly made a U-turn and headed straight back up the Bowery toward them.

"Sit tight," Tommie growled.

The Imperial passed them and they could see Richie Saint's friend driving, the red ash of a large cigar glowing faintly in the darkened car. When the Imperial was about a block north of them, Tommie said, "Okay," and his brother made a crisp U-turn and started following. The two cars, about a block between them, drove easily up the Bowery until Astor Place, where Bowery becomes Fourth Avenue, then up Fourth to Fourteenth Street. Richie Saint either didn't know he was being tailed or didn't care, because his friend, who was doing the driving, was cruising along main streets and taking no evasive actions. He turned left on Fourteenth and headed crosstown all the way to Tenth Avenue, then up Tenth to Twenty-third, then west again to the on-ramp up to the West Side Highway.

Mickey Minelli followed easily and was right behind his quarry as the Imperial waited for an opening in the midnight traffic headed north up the West Side Highway and out of the city. Then the two of them pulled out evenly and Mickey let about a hundred feet of space open between the two cars. They drove like that along the whole length of Manhattan, up the ramp to the George Washington Bridge, and across the upper deck into New Jersey. The Imperial swung off at the first exit on the Jersey side, cruised through the well-lighted plaza where the toll booths used to be, and picked up speed as it headed north on the Palisades Parkway, which soon became an unlit divided highway following the Hudson River. Out the passenger window Tommie Minelli could see the river down below the Palisades and, beyond that, apartment lights glittering across from the Bronx. Ahead of him he could see the taillights of Richie Saint's Imperial, which his brother skillfully kept a steady hundred yards ahead.

This went on for about ten miles, and soon they were the only cars on the highway. Except for an occasional set of oncoming headlights on the other side of the meridian, which in some places was as much as fifty yards across, the Minelli brothers were surprisingly alone with Richie Saint and his friend.

"Think he knows he's being tailed?" Mickey wondered out loud.

"Why don't we make sure he does," Tommie answered.

Mickey eased his foot down on the accelerator and soon had closed the gap between the cars to a few feet. Tommie chuckled audibly when he saw Richie Saint twist in his seat to look back at them, then speak animatedly to his friend, who took a quick look behind him and then slammed his foot to the floor. The Imperial lurched forward and started to open space, but soon Mickey Minelli closed it up again.

Apparently Richie Saint had been dimly aware that the Minelli brothers were following him, for he had seen them outside the Fidelio and must have noticed when they U-turned behind him on the deserted Bowery. And apparently, too, he hadn't given it any importance. Small-time soldiers in rival families did this sort of thing when they had nothing better to do, and it never constituted more than a petty harassment. Although it was less than thirty-six hours after the murder of Big Sallie Manzano and he might have been more cautious, Richie Saint had an extremely good connection right into the inner circle of the Manzano family who had informed him just that evening that even though LaGarda's people were Eddie Manzano's prime suspects, for the time being Eddie had given no orders. Indeed, that was the message he had gone to the Fidelio to deliver. He didn't know whether or not he would be warned when Manzano decided it was time to hit back at Tony the Lawyer, assuming it ever came to that, but he trusted completely the assurances he had received that Manzano's soldiers were not authorized to do anything yet. Besides, he knew the Minellis to be cheap punks and felt he had nothing to fear from their tailing him around Manhattan.

But when he saw the headlights of their yellow Buick right behind him twelve miles into Jersey he had second thoughts. Usually when chickenshit mobsters like these guys went joyriding after him they would give up when he pulled up the ramp to the George Washington Bridge. A long ride back from Jersey and a dollar toll had no attractions for restless punks out to kill some time before picking up some broads or finding themselves a crap game. But since the Minellis were this far out, maybe they meant some trouble.

He said some of this, just a little, to Leo Goffman, who quickly began to panic. The Imperial was doing eighty-five by this time, and the space between it and the set of headlights behind wasn't getting any wider. Every minute or so the nervous driver turned back to confirm that the tail was still there, and this frightened Richie Saint almost as much as the Minellis did. "Keep your fucking eyes on the road," he said. "I'll tell you when they're gone."

"Richie, next exit we come to I'm getting off."

"You crazy? Whatdya wanna do that for?"

"Christ, Richie, there's houses there. We pull off, we'll be somewhere. They wouldn't do nothing in the middle of some fucking town."

"Just keep going. As long as you keep driving we're all right."

Leo Goffman was silent for half a minute.

"They still there?" he asked.

"Of course they're still there. Where the fuck would they be?"

"I'm getting off, Richie. Next exit."

"Just keep driving, Leo," Richie Saint said. "This as fast as this shitheap'll go?"

"Christ, I'm doing ninety-five, Richie. I don't like this."

Meanwhile in the Buick Tommie and Mickey Minelli weren't saying anything. Tommie had taken his forty-five automatic out from where he kept it clipped under the front seat.

They sped by a sign that warned of an exit in half a mile. "I'm getting off here," Leo Goffman said in a shrill, frightened voice.

"Keep going, Leo," Richie Saint barked.

Leo tried to put the exit out of his mind, decided that his friend had more experience in these things and knew what he was doing. But when he was just about beside the exit ramp his panic got the better of him and he cut the wheel sharply to the right, hitting the brakes. The big

Imperial moved into the exit lane but then Leo lost control of it as the rear end fishtailed around. For a horrifying second they were going sideways, and then the front wheels slid off the pavement and onto the grass and the rear end came all the way around. When they came to a stop they were looking straight into the front of the Minelli brothers' Buick.

Chapter 15

LOU SAVAGE FOUND a message in his locker when he reported for duty at the Police Headquarters Annex on Broome Street Wednesday morning. It read "A.B. wants to talk to Mr. Burrows at the Liberty P.M." A.B. was the code designation of Fran Marks, an informant Savage had been using since his days in the Narcotics Bureau. The name Mr. Burrows referred to himself and the Liberty was the Liberty Tavern, a seedy bar on Front Street near the East River waterfront. Marks was a small-time drug connection who had demonstrated over the years his knack for developing reliable information on gangland narcotics traffic.

Savage doubted that Marks could have anything to report that would help him with his current project, Operation Counterthrust, but when an informant as good as Marks called it was best to make the contact so as to avoid the risk of alienating him. Lou was certain that when he finished with this assignment for Inspector Hovannes he would be transferring back to Narcotics—it didn't seem to him he could stay in OCC after a thing like this—and so he didn't want to lose a valuable contact like Marks. Besides, these informants didn't help the police out of any sense of civic responsibility. They did it because they needed the money a particular piece of information would bring them, or because they would be wanting favors some day. Often the guys who worked for money would sit on something for a week or two if they weren't short of cash, saving it for when it would come in handy. But then when they wanted to sell something they wanted to sell it right away. Savage knew that if he didn't keep the appointment Marks would probably peddle whatever he had to someone else. Anyone with gangland intelligence was always in a sellers' market, and Lou didn't want Marks developing new channels of communication if he could help it.

At the age of twenty-eight Lou Savage had eight years on the force behind him and still managed to look maybe five years younger than he was. With his short, muscular body and his thick mat of curly black hair, he had only to peel off his shirt and put on his nylon windbreaker over his T-shirt and he would fit in perfectly with the crowd of longshoremen and miscellaneous toughs who populated the Liberty Tavern.

The letters "P.M." in the message from Marks meant only that Marks would be at the Liberty sometime in the afternoon, but, as was his custom, no time was specified. So Savage, who had the morning to kill, busied himself reading some reports. Ron Polito came in around ten and Roberto Obregon shortly thereafter, and the three of them spent about half an hour in general exchanges of speculations. Each had his own theory about what sort of action Eddie Manzano could be expected to take and what their own next move would be. Then, around eleven o'clock, Frank Hovannes walked in and the conversation stopped.

"You guys got anything better to do than sit here bull-shitting?" Hovannes asked.

"Sure, boss," Obregon said. The others were silent.

"Listen," Hovannes went on, "you've got investigations of your own going and I want you to work on them. I don't want anyone around here wondering what you're doing. And I don't ever want to catch you guys rapping like this again. If I heard you, someone else could hear. This isn't a fucking high school prom you're planning. You sound like a bunch of girls planning how to decorate the goddamn gymnasium."

No one said anything. Obregon slid a clipboard on the table around in front of him and started to read.

"And another thing. I want you guys here at three o'clock. I got some plans I want to go over with you," Hovannes said, and then added, "if you're not too curious to wait till then."

"Frank, I gotta go meet a contact this afternoon downtown," Savage said.

"What about?"

"I don't know. He just left word he wants to meet me. Should I go?"

"He got anything we need?"

"I doubt it."

"Fuck him."

"I don't know, Frank," Savage said. "He's a good man and I wouldn't want to lose him. Like you said, we wouldn't want him wondering what I'm doing so important I don't have time for an old friend."

"Maybe you're right," Hovannes said after giving the matter a moment's thought. "Sure, go ahead. Then come back up and Roberto'll brief you."

Hovannes turned and left the room. As soon as he was gone Polito tried to engage Obregon in a discussion about what they could expect from the three o'clock meeting, but Obregon turned him off, saying, "Look, the Inspector don't want us talking about it. Let's wait and see." Polito then turned to Lou, who quickly lowered his head and plunged into some paperwork. Obregon busied himself with his clipboard and a tense silence prevailed.

Without Polito's saying anything, Savage knew what he was thinking. He was thinking that if another hit was planned, goddamn it, he wanted to be in on it. With the operation only a few days old, Savage knew that already Polito was building up a charge of sullen resentment, directed especially against Obregon, and he thought to himself maybe he should say something to Polito, something friendly and encouraging, something with a team spirit, like, "I guess we're really getting down to business, huh, Ron?"

It was strange that someone so hard and unapproachable, so wiry and tough and cold as Ron Polito should need such coddling, but Savage sensed he did. He remembered the first time he met Polito, last winter at the Greene Street stakeout, and how quick he had been to be offended when Lou checked the log instead of asking him what was going on. And he remembered how quickly Polito had become bitter when the first plans were presented to them and he had been excluded from the actual hit. Polito's job had been to get the truck from the pound, get a set of plates for it, and then to pick it up in Queens after the raiding party had used it in the attack on Manzano and return it to the pound.

"Christ, Lou," Polito had said at the time, "if I'd of known all they wanted was a goddamned truck driver I never would have signed on for this thing."

"Somebody had to do it."

"Yeah, I know. But why me? Why not Obregon?"

"Or me?" Savage asked.

"That's different."

"How's it different?" Savage asked, bristling.

"Look, Lou, don't go looking for things I didn't say. It's not that at all. I mean, I just wanna be in on the action, that's all. I joined this thing figuring it'd be more action. That's all."

"Before this is over there'll be enough action to suit anybody," Savage said, trying to get off the subject.

"Not me," Polito threw out.

Lou Savage hadn't answered anything at the time, but he made a mental note to leave Polito alone and to have as little to do with him as possible, given the long-term nature of the assignment and the close teamwork that would be required. Now it seemed to him he should say something, but his resolve to stay clear of Polito came back to him and he decided to keep quiet. Whether it was because Polito resented having Obregon, a Puerto Rican, assigned to the hit in preference to himself, or whether he was just so eager to be in the gunplay, it all came to the same thing as far as Lou was concerned. Guys who were gung-ho like that scared him, and he often wondered what it was they thought they were doing. Sometimes it seemed like they weren't even in the same line of work he was. And then he remembered what Operation Counterthrust was all about and he had to admit to himself that maybe he didn't know just what line of work he was in. Maybe guys like Polito were what an operation like this needed.

For about fifteen minutes after Hovannes left, Polito just sat at the long table fiddling with a pencil. Then he said, "Awright, I'll see you guys at three," and walked out of the room. Both Savage and Obregon turned to watch him leave, and as they turned back to the reports before them, their eyes met. Obregon shrugged and shook his head mildly, and Savage smiled, and they both could feel the tension evaporate. Obregon wanted to say, "Hey, Lou, I think we've got a problem. I think we should tell the Inspector," but somehow he felt it wasn't his place and he hoped Savage would say something. In his experience, whenever two officers had a problem and one of them was Puerto Rican, he was the problem. He didn't think Savage felt that way, but still he didn't want to say anything until he had some clear sign from Lou.

Around noon Savage said, "Hey, Roberto, I'm going for lunch. Wanna come?"

"Thanks," Obregon said, "but I never eat lunch. Go ahead, I'll see you later."

Savage got up to leave. "Okay," he said, "I'll be back after I meet my man."

Lou left the Annex and then, when he was out in the air on Broome Street, he decided against lunch. Lighting a cigaret, he paused for a moment before setting off with his brisk bullish strides down to Canal Street, where he took the BMT south to Fulton. Lighting another cigaret as soon as he emerged from the station, he quickly crossed the six blocks of progressively seedier neighborhoods that brought him to Front Street and the Liberty Tavern. It was a quarter to one.

Lou walked the length of the bar, checking the occupants with the quick, almost imperceptible glances that come naturally after years of undercover work. There were six longshoremen, all short, wiry, and Irish, in their forties or fifties, on the first six stools. Each had a shot glass and a glass of beer in front of him. The last four stools were empty and so were the two around the elbow of the bar. Two middle-aged blacks in workmen's clothes sat at one of the tables drinking beer from heavy mugs. Marks hadn't shown yet.

Lou slid onto one of the empty stools at the waitress station around the elbow of the bar. Unless the place filled up no one would sit next to him there and from this vantage point he could see the front door.

The bartender, who looked like he had tended bars like this in all the old movies, turned toward Savage without moving from where he was standing in front of the longshoremen. Lou pointed vaguely toward the drinks on the bar; without acknowledging his sign, the bartender drew a glass of beer, poured out a shot of whiskey, and carried them ponderously along the length of the bar. He didn't hide the fact he was pissed off at having to walk.

If this fucker doesn't show up pretty soon I'm gonna have to spend the whole afternoon here drinking, Lou thought, and immediately was sorry he had skipped lunch. Where he was sitting he could smell the sour uriny stink from the men's room just a few feet to his left at the end of the bar, and he gulped down the whiskey to erase the smell. Then he lit a cigarette and settled in to wait.

Around two o'clock the front door opened for the first time since Lou had come in and Fran Marks stepped through it, holding the door open with bright sunlight pouring in from the street around him while he studied the place. Then, spotting Lou at the other end of the gloom, he gestured toward him ostentatiously and loped into the tavern. "Hey, Billie," he bellowed genially, "knew you'd be here. How ya been?"

If he thinks he's an actor, Lou thought, he's got another guess coming. Marks must have been six feet tall, maybe six-one, and couldn't have weighed more than one-sixty-five. He had more hair on his head than the nine other inhabitants of the Liberty put together and an oily, acne-scarred face. He was wearing tattered blue jeans and a red checked woolen shirt even though it was probably eighty degrees out.

Jesus, Savage thought, he couldn't look more like a pigeon if he had feathers. But Lou went along with the act and greeted him profusely, and before Marks was seated the longshoremen were back in their conversation. The two black guys at the table were staring at Marks, but they tired of this too after a minute. "Say, gimme the same thing up here, will ya?" Marks called to the bartender, who pretended not to have heard for a couple of minutes. Lou and his pigeon swapped information about their imaginary families—"How's Edie?" "Oh fine, fine." "And the kid?" "Aw, the kid's terrific."—until the bartender arrived with Marks's drinks and another round for Lou. Then he steamed on back to the longshoremen and the two of them got down to business.

"Ya know, Billie, we had a death in the family. Didn't know if ya heard," Marks began.

"Yeah, I heard."

"Kinda sad, Aunt Sallie going like that."

"Sure is. You know, I didn't even know she was sick. What she die of?"

"I don't know," Marks said into his beer glass. "None of the doctors seem to know either."

So what the fuck did you drag me down here for? Savage wondered to himself. There must be a line out on it, and Lou wanted to know what it was. Marks must know but he wasn't telling until he had some sense of what Savage knew already. Lou decided to send up a trial balloon.

"Poor old Sallie, she had a tough life," he ventured. "We heard she was really getting shafted by her lawyer."

"Shit no, the Lawyer wasn't giving Sallie no trouble," Marks shot back.

Savage was shocked by this answer. Everyone was supposed to think Tony the Lawyer made the hit. So how come it wasn't working that way? Damn it, Hovannes is not going to be happy to hear this, he thought, but figured he'd better not pursue it any further right away. Marks still thought Savage was in Narcotics and Lou didn't want him to know how interested he was in the Manzano incident.

"Naw," Marks went on, "not the Lawyer. Who told you the Lawyer?"

"Just something I heard."

"You heard wrong," Marks said with uncharacteristic finality. The two of them sipped at their beers silently.

"Say, Billie, ya know who was in town for the funeral?" Marks started in again.

"No, who?"

"Cousin Al. You remember good old Al, dumb Al."

"Sure do. I didn't know he was in town. Where's he staying?"

"Uptown. On Broadway. The Blackstone."

"Aw, gee, that's terrific. I'll have to look him up."

Then they were silent again. Two minutes passed without Marks offering anything new. "So far this isn't worth the price of the drinks," Lou whispered into his beer glass.

"There's more," Marks answered softly. "But not here."

"No problem," Savage said. "I'll put some music on the machine." He nodded toward the jukebox.

"It don't work."

"All right, then let's get outta here."

Savage left a five dollar bill on the bar and the two of them walked out into the sunlight on Front Street, then down to the waterfront.

"Ya know, Francis," Savage began, "you're gonna have to do better than that. I don't give enough of a shit about Dumb Al Palmini to drag my ass across the street to see him."

"I got better, but it's give and take, ya know, Lou."

Savage pulled a slender roll of bills from his pocket and peeled off two tens. He stuffed them into Marks's shirt pocket but Marks pulled them out and examined them dubiously. "Shit, Lou, I come all the way down here, I need bus fare home," he said.

Bus fare was thirty-five cents. Lou reached into his pocket again and pulled out another ten and a five. Then, thinking better of it, he stuffed the ten back into his pocket and handed the five to Marks, who took it, shaking his head and snorting some sarcasm.

"Make it good," Savage warned.

"Richie Saint was in town last night."

"So? Richie Saint's in town every night."

"Yeah, but last night he didn't make it home."

"What are you telling me?"

"He's parked somewhere up on the Palisades Parkway." Marks could see the surprise on Savage's face. "No hurry," he added. "He'll stay parked till you find him. Him and a friend."

"Who?"

"Don't know. Just a friend. He's not connected. Anyway, that's what he gets for hanging around with Richie Saint. Never could stand that prick."

"Who hit him?"

"No telling. Maybe Tommie Minelli. Maybe one of Johnny Lombardi's boys. Maybe none of the above."

Savage digested this information and figured Tony the Lawyer was worth another try. "Richie Saint was tight with Tony," he said. "If somebody wasted Richie, then it must of been because Tony hit Big Sallie."

"Nope."

"Then how do you figure it?"

"Look, Lou, I don't wanna do your work for you. For that I get extra. Just take my word for it. The Lawyer's not in this."

"Then you tell me how to figure Richie Saint."

"Easy. Richie was hit because Eddie *thinks* it's the Lawyer did his brother. But Eddie Manzano didn't get famous for being smart. Eddie's wrong. That's all."

"Maybe."

"Maybe nothing. Look, you know Tony's outta town. Now does that make sense? There's nothing in hitting Big Sallie if you don't take care of his brother too, so there's no way Tony's gonna gun Big Sallie and then go on vacation."

"Makes sense."

"You better believe it."

Savage's instincts told him he had gotten his twenty-five dollars' worth of information and the two of them split up. Lou walked quickly back toward the Fulton Street subway station. I'm gonna be ten years into my pension, he thought, before I figure out how these shit-assed quarter-pound connections always know so much.

Then he realized that if he got back uptown fast enough he could still catch that meeting. If nobody was buying the line about Tony the Lawyer, they had better know about it before they planned anything else. He flagged down a cab and settled into the back seat. Jesus, he thought, spacing the words in his mind for emphasis, Hovannes is gonna be royally pissed!

Chapter 16

THE BLACKSTONE IS a residential hotel on Broadway in the low Nineties. Rooms are rented mostly on a weekly or monthly basis and the clientele consists to a fairly large extent of the elderly lower middle-class people on pensions who, during the daylight hours, populate the benches along the mall that runs down the center of Broadway. A fifteen-story brick structure, it is in a lot better condition than most of the other hotels in the neighborhood, and when Hovannes learned from Savage that Al Palmini was in hiding there he was surprised, because during his five years of duty on the Upper West Side he had always figured that the place was clean. But maybe that had changed, since it didn't seem likely that Dumb Al Palmini would go somewhere that hadn't come recommended to him.

A check with the twenty-fourth precinct, however, indicated that the hotel still was considered relatively clean, although along with the elderly crowd there was also now a younger element, some of whom were known prostitutes and drug dealers. Palmini, it seemed likely, knew about the place on his own hook.

At ten o'clock on Wednesday night Ron Polito and Roberto Obregon walked into the well-lighted lobby, with its banks of potted plants in chest-high troughs, turned left, and headed for the room clerk's cage directly opposite the elevators. The lobby was done entirely in a grainless plastic paneling that is supposed to look like wood. The desk clerk's station, which used to be a counter but was completely closed off by floor-to-ceiling paneling a number of years ago in order to prevent stickups, is at the far left of the lobby. An eye-level porthole-type window in the cage faces the front door and another, with a removable grate below it, faces the elevators.

Polito walked around to the grating and Obregon moved in behind him. The night clerk hadn't heard them

come in and was sitting at ... ... the cage
Thursday morning's *News*. Polito rapped on the window
and the clerk, startled, hurried forward.

"Police officers," Polito said, pulling his shield in its
leather case from his jacket pocket and flipping it open
in front of the window. "We're looking for someone we
have reason to believe is staying here."

"Yes, sir?" the night clerk said nervously.

"White guy, about five-ten. Short black hair. Very thin,
weighs maybe one-fifty. Long neck. Very long neck."

"Sorry," the clerk said, "but that doesn't ring a bell.
I only work nights. Maybe if you checked with the day
man."

"He checked in Monday," Polito went on. "Mind if
we look at your records?"

"I don't know," the clerk stammered. He was getting
more nervous by the minute, a beefy man with soft features, a bad shave, and the top button of his shirt missing
below where his tie was knotted. "I think you'll have to
check with the day manager."

"Where's the night manager?"

"There's no . . . ," the clerk started to say, but then
corrected himself. "I'm the night manager."

"You'll do. Let's have a look at your register."

Polito took a step to his right toward the door to the
cage. The clerk hesitated a moment, then opened the door.

"What's this guy's name?" the clerk asked as Polito and
Obregon walked in and seemed to take over the office.

"His name's Palmini but he might not be registered
under that. Maybe Palmer or maybe Porter. Let's just see
who registered Monday."

"I'm sorry, I don't know if I can do that. I wouldn't
want to do anything wrong. Don't you need a warrant or
something?"

"We don't . . ."

"Hey, don't do that," the clerk called sharply to Obregon, who had moved over to the counter behind the
grating where the register sat open and had begun leafing
through it.

"We don't need a warrant unless we want to search the
premises," Polito began to explain. The clerk glanced nervously from Obregon to Polito and back to Obregon
again. "If you insist, we could get one for the whole

...t I don't........ guests'd like it if we did a ...om-to-room search."

The clerk wasn't listening. He was trying to figure out what to say to stop Obregon.

"How long have you worked here?" Polito asked.

"Huh? Five years."

Polito reached into his jacket pocket and the clerk stiffened, his eyes riveted to Polito's hand. He was visibly relieved when Polito pulled out a small wad of folded money and peeled two tens from it. He set them down on the desk and pulled the clerk's copy of the *News* over them.

"Either way, it comes to the same thing," Polito said, and a sharpness came into his voice that hadn't been there before. "You make us go back downtown and it's just a lot of trouble for everyone. Or you help us and everything's simpler."

"I don't know," the clerk still hesitated, but for twenty dollars he didn't intend to do anything now to stop Obregon from checking the register.

"Twelve-oh-six," Obregon said just then.

The two officers moved for the door, and before the clerk fully understood what had happened they were in the automatic elevator and the door was closing behind them. He went to the desk and reached under the newspaper for the bills, which he put quickly in his pocket and then hurried across the cubicle to close the door, which they had left open.

Walking quietly down the uncarpeted but well-lit corridor on the twelfth floor, Obregon and Polito quickly found room 1206. Polito took a position directly in front of the door and placed his hand carefully on the knob. Obregon stood against the wall to his left. Polito kicked hard at the door twice and jumped back to the wall on the other side so that he and Obregon were facing each other with only the door between them. "Open up, Palmini. Police," he said.

For a minute there was no response, but they could hear faint sounds of movement from within the room. It was an old hotel and the walls were thick, but the rooms had cheap wooden doors that Polito and Obregon could hear through easily. Breaking one of these down would be no problem.

"Don't try anything, Palmini. It won't work," Polito said when the room had become quiet again.

"Whatdya want?" a tense voice from inside said. He was standing near the door and there was no defiance in his tone.

"Open up."

"What for?"

"We gotta ask you some questions."

"I ain't done nothing."

"Open up."

No answer.

"If we have to come in and get you it's not going to be good for you, Palmini."

"You guys got a warrant?"

"We ain't arresting you. We don't need no warrant. You're a material witness. We just gotta take you down for questioning."

"You can't come in without a warrant. I know my rights."

"Palmini, your rights won't be worth shit if we have to come through that door."

No answer.

"You got five seconds, Palmini. I'm telling you, we're not arresting you, we don't need a warrant."

"That right?" a hesitant voice asked from behind the door.

"That's right."

The door opened and Dumb Al Palmini stepped quickly away from it and raised his hands above his head automatically as the two officers pushed into the room with drawn guns. Polito grabbed him by the arm just above the elbow and spun him around, pulling his arm down as he did.

"On the bed," Palmini said.

Obregon stepped past him to the bed and picked up the thirty-eight Police Special Palmini had left lying there, checked the safety, and stuffed it into his belt. Polito, his gun in Palmini's back, was patting him down.

"I wanna talk to my lawyer," Palmini said. Polito shoved him with the heel of his hand and he came to rest next to the door to the bathroom, then turned to face the two officers.

"Save it," Polito said.

Obregon said nothing. Instead, he searched the room

quickly while Palmini watched his movements sullenly. It didn't take him two minutes because, as they had expected, there was absolutely nothing there. Palmini was wearing the pants from a gray suit, now badly rumpled from three days' continuous wear, his shoes and socks, and a sleeveless undershirt. His suit jacket hung on a wooden hanger in the closet and his shirt hung next to it on a wire hanger. Except for these two articles of apparel in the closet, a necktie on the bureau top, and the gun Obregon had taken from the bed, there was nothing in the room.

Obregon pulled the bureau drawers open rapidly, slamming them shut when he had ascertained they were empty. He stood on tiptoe to check the closet shelf, patted down the jacket and pulled a wallet from it, checked its contents, and replaced it. The bathroom turned out to be equally void of signs of habitation, except for an unwrapped bar of soap in the soapdish by the sink and the wrapper in the wastebasket. No shaving equipment, no suitcases, no changes of clothing. Palmini hadn't come out of his room since he checked in on Monday.

"We're not arresting you, Palmini, so we're not gonna put the cuffs on you," Polito said when Obregon came out of the bathroom. "Get your stuff and let's get going. And don't give us any trouble."

Palmini had regained some of his composure while Obregon was conducting his search. "I want a lawyer," he said, firmly and with conviction.

"We asked you anything yet?" Polito responded.

Dumb Al didn't answer.

"Let's go," Polito said as soon as Palmini had put on his shirt and suit jacket and stuffed his necktie in his pocket. Polito waved him toward the door with his gun.

As they moved into the corridor Polito holstered his gun and the three of them walked to the elevator and waited after Obregon pushed the button.

"How'd you find me here?" Palmini wanted to know.

"You're here, ain't you?" was all Polito would answer.

Downstairs they walked past the room clerk's cage. The clerk, who was watching the elevator from his desk over the top of his newspaper, pulled the paper up and pretended not to see them. When the trio stepped onto Ninety-first Street Polito and Obregon quickly scanned the street in both directions and immediately spotted

Frank Hovannes and Lou Savage across the street and to their left, parked at a fireplug in front of the Chemical Bank. Hovannes, on the driver's side, nodded crisply but the two officers with Palmini didn't make any sign of recognition.

"This way," Polito said, poking Palmini in the back and motioning him toward an unmarked Plymouth parked a few doors east of the hotel entrance.

Palmini, who apparently knew the routine, walked around the car with Polito while Obregon slid in behind the wheel. Then Palmini climbed into the back seat and Polito followed. Obregon took the microphone from the portable two-way radio and muttered something into it Palmini couldn't understand. A transmission he also couldn't understand came back and Obregon replaced the mike and pulled away from the curb, driving west on Ninety-first Street all the way to Riverside Drive.

"Hey, where we going?" Palmini asked when he noticed they weren't heading for the twenty-fourth precinct station house, which he knew was on One Hundredth Street.

"I told you," Polito said. "We're taking you in for questioning."

"Where?"

"Downtown."

"Oh."

Dumb Al lapsed into silence again. So they were probably taking him to Headquarters. But why? Where they going to book him? On what? At least if they would book him he could get a lawyer, which would be better than this, he thought.

Wednesday, April 16

Lou Savage waited in the car with Hovannes for a half hour after Obregon had driven off with Polito and Palmini in the back seat. As they waited, mostly in silence, Lou tried to get himself to talk to Hovannes, to raise some of the questions that were bothering him. He trusted the Inspector completely, not only for his tactical judgment, which he respected, but also for his probity. Yet doubts were beginning to claw at the back of Lou's mind, and he knew that Inspector Hovannes could answer them if anyone could. He thought back to how Frank had recruited him for this project, and how open and candid he had been.

Lou had known about Frank Hovannes for a long time because of the reputation Frank had made for himself in the Narcotics Bureau before Lou got there. There were widespread rumors in the Bureau about detectives on the take; some men were known to be receiving payoffs, others were suspected, and others were suspected to be clean. But with Hovannes it wasn't suspected he was clean—it was known. He had had an arrest record with Narco that hadn't been matched since he left, and the Department is big on tradition and has a long memory. So even though Lou didn't come to Narco until sixty-eight—years after Hovannes had transferred out to Intelligence—the detectives Lou worked with, at least those of them he respected and admired, had a way of talking about Hovannes that made Lou eager to meet him, and to work for him if that would be possible.

Then, last fall, when Lou got his orders temporarily assigning him to Organized Crime Control, where he would work under Hovannes, he was delighted—and not simply because he was finally getting out of Narco. His CO told him that Hovannes had specifically asked for him from Narco for the job and Lou felt honored by the request. He was puzzled that Hovannes even knew who he was and had no way of knowing it was actually Ernie Fleming, with whom he had worked for a few weeks the summer before, who arranged the transfer.

While Lou was in OCC, Hovannes ran him ragged, working days and nights in an effort to link Sallie Manzano with a series of truck hijackings. Although the FBI was technically heading up the investigation into the hijackings, with the NYPD responsible only for related activities in the city, it was pretty clear from what Lou could see that the only people really working on the case were Hovannes and his men. After each of the incidents, which occurred in half a dozen different states up and down the eastern seaboard from Virginia to Jersey, a report, rarely more than a page, would come in from the Bureau and then they wouldn't be heard from again until the next truck was ripped off. Hovannes had had some choice things to say about the federal agents and their lack of diligence in following things up at their end.

One night, while the two of them were watching the Manzano warehouse on Greene Street, Frank explained to him that to the FBI this was just another case, and not a big one at that, so that if it was going to be cracked it would have to be cracked right here in New York. "Lou," he said, "I wish someone would say to me, 'Hovannes, the FBI is yours. Those fuckoffs are going to take their orders from you until this thing is all cleared up.' If I could have three weeks to run the show in Jersey and Pennsylvania and Virginia, Big Sallie Manzano would never know what the fuck hit him! That's the only way to make a case like this. You've got to follow the stuff from where it's coming from, not sit here and wait for it to come in. They probably know we're here, for chrissakes, so they're rerouting everything. The way it is now, our only chance is to pick up on something here and follow it around for a while and maybe we can find out how the whole operation works. And believe me it's a shitty little chance."

Shitty little chance or not, Lou had thought, this guy doesn't let up.

Then, on Thanksgiving, a shipment finally did come in and Frank's partner got killed. All they got for it was that one hot truck and a couple of truck drivers, but even though the arrests were made at a trucking company they could tie Sallie Manzano to, there was nothing they could use to convict the Manzano brothers themselves.

After that the investigation didn't last long. Fred Gallagher told Lou once, just before Christmas, that some of the men were saying that Hovannes was on a personal crusade, that he was wasting his time and that of his men because Ernie Fleming had been killed on this case and Hovannes couldn't bring himself to admit that the case was a dud. There were even hints that it was Frank's carelessness that had gotten Fleming killed, and that was why he was making such a big thing of it.

Lou became incensed whenever he heard talk like this, and although he didn't say anything he found himself more and more intensely rooting for the Inspector, hoping for the break that would lead them to some hijacked shipments and show that Hovannes had been right. Crusade or not, the Inspector's passion for the case was beginning to rub off on him.

And then it was over. Without receiving any explanation from anyone, Lou was assigned back to Narcotics. For a while he was bitter about it. He told Celia that the investigation had been killed by one of those shortsighted decisions the Department was always making because it didn't have guts enough to trust the few investigators on the force who really deserved its confidence. The Department, he felt, had stabbed Frank Hovannes in the back.

"If that's the way you feel," she had said, even though she had wanted him to go back to Narco all along, "why don't you go up and talk to him about it? He liked you, Lou."

But Lou didn't think there was anything to talk about and let the matter drop. Then, about a month later, toward the end of January, he was surprised to receive a call at home from Frank Hovannes, with whom he hadn't spoken since the trucking case was closed. Hovannes wanted to talk with him, and they agreed to meet later that evening at a steakhouse on lower Fifth Avenue near Lou's apartment on University Place. Three hours later, sitting over gristly steaks and steins of beer in a corner booth, Frank told him what he wanted to do and invited him to join.

At first Lou was too shocked to know what to say, and he just ground away mechanically at his tasteless steak without saying anything. Before even commencing the conversation, Frank had explained that he needed Lou's strictest promise of confidentiality, that he was about to propose something to Lou, and that regardless of whether Lou declined or accepted he must never reveal a word of this conversation to anyone. For a fleeting second Lou wanted to say, "I can't do that, Inspector. Whatever it is, if it's got those kinds of strings on it, I don't want to know about it." Instead, he gave Hovannes the promise he wanted.

As he thought back on it, what was surprising about the Inspector's explanation of Operation Counterthrust was its candor. From the first, Hovannes made no effort to conceal or gloss over the hard parts. For ten minutes he spoke, laying out the scheme in great detail, and then he said, "Lou, I don't want to kid you about what you'd be getting into. You know I think this is a right thing to do or I wouldn't be doing it. But you've got to know right off that if any of this ever comes out, we've got absolutely no legal cover. None at all. I want you to think about that, Lou. Everything I just described to you is one hundred percent illegal. You can't forget that for a minute. And another thing. If you go into this thing, it's got to be completely voluntary. You go into it with your eyes open, and there'll be none of this you-was-just-following-orders shit."

Hovannes stopped talking abruptly and Lou didn't know what to say. The whole idea was shocking and crazy, and yet there wasn't anything crazy about Frank Hovannes.

"Let me think about it, Frank," Lou said, using the Inspector's name for the first time. "I don't think I can give you an answer tonight. Is that all right?"

"Sure," Frank said. "Yeah, that's fine. I want you to think about it. Take a couple of days, as much time as you want."

Lou fumbled with his dinner. There were questions he wanted to ask but he wasn't sure what they were. It seemed strange sitting over a meal and discussing this plan like the Inspector had just asked him to go partners with him in a business when what Frank really was asking him to do was to sign on as a hit man. That was what it came down to, wasn't it?

After almost five minutes of silence, during which the waiter cleared the table and brought coffee, Lou had a better idea of what he wanted to say. "You mind if I ask you a couple of questions?" he asked.

"No, fine. Go ahead. You oughta have some questions."

"Well, I don't know how to say this, Frank. I'm sure you've thought about this whole thing. But do you really know what this is you're asking me to get into? I mean, we're gonna be a bunch of hit men, isn't it? Are you sure that's all right?"

Frank pulled his spoon from his coffee cup and gestured with it as he spoke.

"Yeah, I've thought about it," he said. "But you've got to think about it yourself, because what I think doesn't count for shit."

Then the spoon went back into the cup and Frank watched his own hand stirring vaguely as he spoke. "Lou," he said, "I'm serious about this. The only way you can sign on is if *you* think it's right. I think it is. Right and necessary. Take that for what it's worth."

"Okay, Frank, thanks," Savage said, grateful that Hovannes hadn't tried to make it too easy for him. "There's one other thing. Say it is right. I'm not saying it is, but just say for a minute that that's out of the way. Then what I gotta know is do you really think we can do it. Do you really think we can start hitting guys and covering it up and getting away with it?"

Hovannes didn't answer for a long time. Then he said, "Lou, I can't tell you anything about that except this. We've already started. Take my word for it, we can do it."

Lou could feel the force of what Frank had just told him like something hard in his stomach, and more than anything else that answered his questions for him. There was something about the way Hovannes said it, something grim and fierce and determined, and Lou liked it and wanted to be a part of it.

He didn't give the Inspector his answer that night, and the next three days were a period of intense confusion for him during which he worked his way around all the things he had ever heard about right and wrong, about taking the law into your own hands, about whether anyone could ever be above the law, and about whether any ends could justify a handful of men in killing at their own discretion. And he decided that, yes, people could be above the law, that in fact one had a duty to oneself to put one's own sense of right and wrong above the law. This was, in a sense, sort of a policeman's conscientious objection, a recognition that there was a sort of higher law to which one could appeal, and that this higher law said that it was possible that a man who was willing to bear the responsibility could in good conscience take steps he knew to be illegal if those steps would accomplish an end which he knew to be good.

He even dug up from his memory the idea he had learned in college that the way to test a principle is to ask yourself, What would happen if everyone adopted this principle? His first answer was that this would be chaos, the end of all law and the breakdown of society. And then he realized that this wasn't so at all, for the principle at issue wasn't whether or not any person is legally entitled to do whatever he thinks is right. No, Frank had spelled that out very clearly when he insisted that from the start Lou had to acknowledge that the operation was illegal. So the issue here was whether one could go ahead with it in good conscience, even in the face of its illegality.

Strangely, Lou found that it helped a lot not to have to argue about whether believing in the operation strongly enough—that is, believing that it was justifiable, "right and necessary," as Frank had said—could make it legal. That was an argument he suspected he couldn't have brought himself to make, couldn't have believed in. Because if your conviction made it legal, then you had a right to do it, and that would be chaos. But you weren't putting yourself above the law if you recognized that your own beliefs had nothing at all to do with its legality. If you kept the two things separate, the law on the one side and your own sense of what it was right to do on the other, then the law remained intact. That was what conscientious objection was, wasn't it, and although Lou had never thought before that he agreed with the conscientious objectors, he could see the validity of their point.

After thinking about Frank's proposal for three days, Lou finally brought the problem to Celia, telling her nothing about Frank Hovannes or the specifics of the plan, but talking about it in an abstract, high-toned way that didn't come naturally to him at all. And although Celia was puzzled by his sudden plunge into philosophy, he could tell that she liked hearing him talk this way, perhaps because it was the type of discussion he knew she used to enjoy with her friends when he first met her. It was this sort of thing, he sometimes guiltily suspected, that she must have missed ever since she moved in with him and lost contact with most of her old college friends.

As much as she could without knowing specifically what it was he was talking about, Celia had agreed with him, and he took her concurrence with him and reported to Frank Hovannes that he was to be counted in. He asked Frank a number of questions, detailed questions about planning and strategy so that Frank would be sure to notice that he had given it careful thought, and Frank answered them all.

Lou remembered all this as he and Frank waited for Polito and Obregon to be gone a half hour with their prisoner, and there was some question in the back of his mind he wanted to ask. He wasn't even sure what it was, but if he could just talk about it maybe he would find it and then Frank could answer it for him.

It hadn't bothered him at all when he stood in the back of the truck three days ago, sighting down a machine gun to where three men would be on Third Avenue, and when the time came he had opened fire on them with scarcely more than the slightest moment of hesitation. He had decided beforehand that the first hit would be the hardest, and that once he was initiated the rest would follow easily. But somehow it wasn't getting easier. The thought that Dumb Al Palmini, whom he had seen at the end of his machine gun barrel just three days before, was at this very moment among the burned-out piers underneath the elevated section of the West Side Highway below Seventy-second Street, the thought that Ron Polito was with him right now and would kill him, maybe had killed him already, sent a shiver of nausea running the whole length of his body.

It was strange that killing wasn't the hard part to stomach, but the thought of Ron Polito killing was something Lou couldn't adjust to. Maybe if he could just say to Frank, "Hey, Frank, do you think Polito's okay?" Frank would know what he meant and would answer him. But he couldn't say it, and while he was still thinking about all this the half hour passed and Frank said, "Let's get going."

Lou hurried around the back of the car and he and Hovannes crossed Ninety-first Street together and walked into the lobby of the Blackstone. As they crossed toward the clerk's cage, the clerk scurried from his desk and asked in a high-pitched, nervous voice whether he could help them.

"Police officers," Hovannes said, flashing his badge. "We'd like to ask you some questions."

"What is this?" the clerk asked, annoyed and incredulous.

"Were two guys here asking questions about someone staying in the hotel?" Hovannes deadpanned.

"Yeah. Don't you guys get together? About a half hour ago."

"You'd better let us in," Frank said solemnly, stepping sideways toward the door, which the clerk opened. The two officers walked into the cubicle. Inside, Frank asked, "Where'd they go?"

"Upstairs."

"Where?"

"Twelfth floor. Twelve-oh-six." Frank and Lou both turned quickly and started to move toward the elevator. "Hey, what is this?" the clerk shouted after them.

"You wait here. We'll want to talk to you when we come down," Frank answered.

"Sure. But you won't find them up there."

Frank stopped in his tracks while Lou, who was already in the elevator, held the door open. "Whatdya mean?" Frank asked.

"They left."

"Left? When?"

Lou almost felt like laughing, but instead he stepped out of the elevator and followed Frank back into the tiny office.

"Like I said. About a half hour ago."

"Which way'd they go?"

"How the fuck do I know? Don't you guys talk to each other?"

"What kinda shit are you giving me, mister?" Frank glowered at him. "Those guys weren't cops."

The clerk, who had been working himself up to anger, deflated as though he had been hit. "Sure they was cops," he stammered, confusion spreading across his soft, dingy face.

"They leave alone?" Frank asked.

"Naw, they left with the guy they was looking for."

"And you don't know which way they went?"

"Naw," the clerk drawled, almost pleading. "I can't see the street from here. Look for yourself."

"You'd better get a call out on this," Frank said, turning to Lou, and Lou hurried out to the street, raced across to the car, and then lit a cigaret while he waited for Frank to finish covering Polito's and Obregon's tracks.

Frank took the clerk's name.

"You sent these guys upstairs?" he asked.

"Sure. Look, officer, they said they was cops. They showed me their badges."

"Did you get a good look at them?"

"Yeah, sure."

"A good look?"

"Well, yeah. I mean, they looked like real badges."

"Mister, you could be in a lot of trouble," Frank said after a slight pause.

"What for?" the clerk protested. He was scared and Frank didn't say anything. "They said they was cops," the clerk repeated again.

Frank just shrugged. Then, like it was an afterthought, he asked, "Did they give you any money?"

The clerk didn't answer.

"Cops, huh," Hovannes said derisively. Then he added, in a mollifying tone, "All right, if we catch up to these guys tonight it'll be okay. But if they're gone, somebody's going to catch some shit for it and I'll tell you right now, mister, it's not going to be me."

Frank turned and walked across the lobby. When he was almost to the door the clerk stepped from his cage and called after him. "Hey, officer," he said, trying to get it all straight in his mind, "which ones of them you looking for? Them two guys said they was cops or the guy upstairs?"

"All of them," Frank said.

Chapter 17

THE BLACK IMPERIAL RACED down the New Jersey Turnpike carrying two grim and silent men. Once they had left the heavy traffic at the New York end behind, they were able to cruise easily at eighty-five or ninety miles an hour, and they passed the Camden exit while the April sun was still high in the sky.

"What time you got?" Paulie Gagliano asked.

Jimmie Monks glanced at his watch and at the dashboard clock. "Quarter past three," he said.

"We'll be there by four, huh?" Gagliano asked.

"Yeah."

"That what you told him?"

"I told him around four, yeah," Monks said absently. He reached forward and fiddled with the air conditioner vent, but although the cold air was blowing right into his face, the sun shining through the windshield was hot and he could feel drops of sweat under his arms and down his sides and his shirt was sticking to his chest.

"What he say?" Gagliano asked.

"He didn't say nothing," Monks said and pulled a cigar from his suit jacket pocket. He bit the end and lowered the electric window a few inches to spit out the tip.

Gagliano pulled the Imperial into the right-hand lane as a sign warned that the exit they wanted was approaching. Soon they were speeding down Route 47, past Glassboro and south through the southern Jersey farmland. When they started to see the large sheds full of chickens they knew they were almost there, because Vineland is unmistakably in the heart of chicken country. Gagliano reached down with his left hand and pressed the button to open his window. "Smell them chickens," he laughed, taking a deep breath.

"That's chicken shit, not chickens," Monks protested. "Close that fucking window."

They turned east off Route 47 and drove through the

town of Vineland without stopping. About four miles east of town they turned left onto a two-lane county road. Gagliano was driving slowly, looking for Tony LaGarda's farmhouse. It was just a few minutes past four when they got there.

Tony the Lawyer was waiting for them in front of the house, dressed, like they were, in a dark suit. With farm-land all around them, green and shimmering in the sun and chicken sheds on the horizon, the three of them looked incongruous standing by the black Imperial in their dark suits. Jimmie Monks never failed to sense this every time he came there, but after a few minutes the feeling always went away.

"Come in the house and cool off a minute," Tony said. They followed him to the side door and found themselves in the large cool kitchen. "Want some lemonade?" Tony asked, taking three glasses from the cupboard and pouring out the drinks. Then they sat down at the table.

"I guess we know where we stand now, huh, Tony?" Jimmie Monks began.

"Yeah," Tony sighed, breathing the word slowly. "Whatdya know about this?"

"Well," Monks said, biting off the tip of another cigar and walking to the sink to spit it out, "the other night Richie Saint comes down to the place with that guy he's hanging around with, Leo Whatsisname. Me and Paulie have a couple glasses a wine with them and then Richie says he got something to tell us. So we have the boys make this Leo a nice dinner and we leave him sit-ting there and Richie and Paulie and me go back to your office."

Tony LaGarda had learned a long time ago that Jimmie Monks told a story his own way, like it was one of those long involved jokes where you had to get all the crappy little details right, so he sipped on his lemonade and lis-tened patiently.

"Then Richie says he hears Eddie Manzano thinks it was you had Big Sallie whacked out," Monks continued, "but he says that's not the way they're figuring it uptown and that's not what Robustelli thinks."

"He really said that?" LaGarda interrupted.

"Yeah, sure, Tony. He says that what he hears from uptown is that Leone's going crazy trying to figure it be-cause he's not buying the idea you did this thing. And Robustelli don't know what to make of it either, but he's listening to Leone."

"Well, that's good," Tony the Lawyer said. He finished his lemonade and carried the glass to the sink. "What else?"

"Well, then Richie says that Eddie Manzano has you pegged for it, but Eddie told his boys not to do anything so there's no heat on yet. He says he heard it straight out of Big Sallie's living room that Eddie Manzano told his people not to make a move."

"He say who told him?"

"Naw, he wouldn't say, but I figure it's probably Frankie Diamond. You know, I think the Saint and Frankie Diamond got something together. They used to work some numbers together, I know that, and I think they still got some action they're partners on. But how can you tell with Richie, he never says nothing. Anyway, I figure Frankie Diamond called Richie to tell him not to worry, Eddie's got nothing on yet, but that Eddie's pretty hot about his brother getting iced and after he stews on it awhile he'll probably want some blood. Frankie Diamond probably figured you'd wanna know that, so that's why he tells Richie."

"Yeah, Frankie's all right," Tony said judiciously. "So what happened?"

"Well, Richie tells us this and then we all go back out to this Leo Whatsisname, and he's eating up the whole fucking restaurant by this time. And then Billy—you know, little Billy, that waiter we got last month—he calls me over and he says, 'You know those guys?' and he shows me out the window where Tommie Minelli's sitting in this car there with his little shit of a brother. So I say, 'Yeah, I know them, thanks, Billy,' and I tell Richie. Richie says, 'Tommie Minelli is absolutely the dumbest little fuck I ever met. A real asshole. But he's one of Frankie Diamond's boys and Frankie says there's nothing on. Forget about him.'

"So I say, 'Then what's he doing out there, Richie?' and Richie says, 'I don't know what he's doing out there and he probably don't even know what he's doing out there. Probably trying to impress that little shitassed brother of his with how good he can sit in a car and look tough. You know, I keep telling Frankie to get rid of that creep. Fuck, this is nineteen seventy-five and this asshole runs around like it's Prohibition and he's George Raft. It's punks like that can get us all in trouble. I don't know what Frankie thinks he needs him for.'

"So I say, 'Well anyway, you watch out, Richie,' and Richie says, 'Me watch out for Tommie Minelli? You gotta be kidding.' And this Leo's listening to this whole thing and getting nervous and eating faster than he can chew, for chrissakes. Then Richie says, 'Come on, Leo, let's go.' And then he tells me, 'Jimmie, I just wanted you to know that Eddie's cool right now but he won't stay cool too long. You tell Tony that.' And then Richie and this Leo get up and go and the next thing I hear Richie's been put to sleep and this other guy too. Somewhere up by Tenafly. That's all I know, Tony."

Then Paulie Gagliano said, "Jimmie, let me have one of your cigars. I left mine in the car."

Monks handed him a cigar and no one spoke while he went through the ritual of lighting it. He took a deep slow drag and the three men all leaned away from the formica table. Tony the Lawyer was sifting what Monks had just told him and there was nothing to say until Tony spoke.

"That's good what you said about Leone," Tony said finally. "I talked to his people after you called and maybe we can work this thing out."

"Christ, I hope so, Tony," Monks said.

"All right," Tony said. "You guys want another glass a lemonade? Then we're going back to New York."

Gagliano sat up straight in his chair. "Now?" he asked, not liking the idea.

"Yeah," Tony said. "I set up a meet at Robustelli's place on the Grand Concourse. I told them eleven o'clock."

It was not unusual when middle-level Mafia leaders had a falling out for one of them to call a meeting of the local chieftains and to invite his rival. Each party to the dispute would present his side of the story for arbitration by this ad hoc jury. A lot of tough problems had been settled at these sit-downs, and the system was one of the things that had helped cut down on the internal warfare that had kept rival mobs at each other's throats from Prohibition down to the early fifties. Once in a while it didn't work, and then the papers were full of sensational headlines about gangland warfare, but for the most part it was an effective instrument of self-policing that kept things running smoothly.

On the way down to Vineland that afternoon, Jimmie Monks had tried to figure what Tony would do, but the idea of calling for a sit-down with Robustelli and Leone and Eddie Manzano never crossed his mind. The thing had gone too far for talking, he figured, but now it looked like he had been wrong about that and he was pleased.

"Gee, Tony, that's terrific," he said. "And Manzano really said he'd come, huh?"

"He wasn't invited," Tony answered sharply.

Monks was surprised again, for the second time in half a minute. So this wasn't going to be a real sit-down, he realized. "I don't get it," he said.

"Nothing to get," Tony the Lawyer explained. "I got nothing to talk to Manzano about and I got no quarrel with him. It's too bad about Richie Saint, but I'm not going to war with Eddie over Richie Saint. Besides, Eddie didn't have no order out on Richie. That was just that crud Minelli, the way I figure it. And I'll bet this house right now Eddie'll take care of that punk and his brother himself."

"Yeah, maybe," Monks said, "but it ain't whether you got a beef with Eddie but whether Eddie's got a beef with you. He figures you did a number on his brother."

"Yeah, I know. That's what I wanna see Robustelli and Leone for. I want them to know I had nothing to do with that thing, that's all."

Monks smiled for the first time since he heard about Richie Saint and rolled the two inches of cigar that were left around in his hand. He realized there wasn't a word of truth in what Tony had just told him and he looked into the ash and thought, Christ, Tony's smart all right. "I gotta give it to you, Tony," he mumbled admiringly, "you've got it figured."

"Nothing to figure," Tony said while Paulie Gagliano watched the two of them without understanding.

Monks, though, realized what Tony was doing. Robustelli was the biggest man in Harlem and the South Bronx and Leone was boss in Brooklyn. The meeting wasn't for Tony to present his case to them and let them settle it before it went any further. If he had wanted that, he would have had Eddie Manzano invited. And Eddie would have come because when someone like Robustelli or

Leone calls you and tells you to come over to sit down and work out some problem you got with someone you have to go. Then it would be all settled and Robustelli and Leone would see to it that there would be no trouble between Manzano and Tony. If Manzano didn't go along, he would have to answer to them for it. But on the other hand that would tie Tony's hands too, and he had been itching for a crack at Manzano for a long time. So he was setting up the meeting to line up Robustelli and Leone on his side. He had talked to them before about moving in on the Manzano brothers and they hadn't had any objections. Now whoever shot Big Sallie had given him his chance to make his move, only instead of there being two Manzano brothers to deal with there was only Eddie left. That made it easier.

Thursday, April 17

While Tony LaGarda, Jimmie Monks, and Paulie Gagliano were driving north to New York for their meeting with Robustelli and Leone, Eddie Manzano was sitting down to dinner at his brother's house. Eddie sat at the head of the table while his sister-in-law Ruth and his niece Helen, both still in black from the funeral, sat opposite each other. At the foot of the table, facing Eddie, sat Bob Bellini, Helen's fiancé. No one spoke through the whole meal and Naomi, the black maid, brought out and cleared dishes in silence. Upstairs, in Big Sallie's study, Frankie Diamond waited.

Eddie Manzano drank his coffee steaming hot just after it was poured and then pulled a leather cigar case from his pocket. "How about a cigar, Bob?" he asked, breaking the heavy silence for the first time as he slid a thick six-inch English market cigar from the case.

"No, thank you anyway, Mr. Manzano," Bob said. He had been with Helen since the morning, standing beside her at mass and at the cemetery and now for two hours at the house, and he hardly had said anything in all that time. His voice sounded strange to him and he thought he had stammered slightly as he spoke.

"It's good after dinner, a nice cigar," Manzano said.

"No, thank you," Bob repeated.

"Do you want anything, Ruth?" Eddie asked, turning to his sister-in-law. "Maybe a glass a wine? I'll have the girl bring you a glass."

"No, Eddie, I don't think so," Ruth said, reaching out to put her hand on Eddie's, which rested on the table.

Helen saw the gesture and knew it meant that her mother had taken all she could and might soon crack under the grief and strain. For three days the family had worried about Ruth, afraid she was on the brink of a nervous collapse, and their worry had preoccupied them, distracting them from too much thought about Sallie. Now Ruth was clawing nervously at the back of Eddie's hand and Helen said, "Mamma, maybe that would be a good idea. Let's have a glass of wine. It'll make you feel better."

Ruth turned to her daughter with a pained look, but she said nothing and so Bob Bellini rose from the table. "I'll get it, Mrs. Manzano," he said and went to the sideboard where the large crystal decanter stood. He poured four glasses of the sweet red wine and brought them back to the table. He set one in front of Mrs. Manzano, who looked up at him and smiled thinly, and another in front of Helen's uncle. Pausing behind Helen's chair, he reached over her shoulder to put the third glass in front of her and then ran his hand gently across her shoulder and to her neck. The smooth fabric felt warm to his touch but her throat was cool. He brushed her cheek gently with his fingers and then pulled up a chair and sat beside her. Eddie Manzano and Ruth were looking at him and he could guess what they were thinking.

"If you'll excuse me," Eddie said, pulling himself out of his thoughts, "there's someone waiting for me upstairs."

He walked from the room slowly and in the dining room they could hear each step as he lumbered up the large central staircase. When Ruth heard the door to her husband's study close behind him she began to sob silently. Her hands were wrapped tightly around the glass in front of her and she stared through tears into the deep ruby wine.

Upstairs, Frankie Diamond jumped to his feet as Eddie walked into the study.

"Eddie," he said.

"Yeah, I know, Frankie, I know."

Both were silent a moment, recognizing that no further condolence was necessary between them. Then Eddie walked to the stuffed chair and sat down and Frankie Diamond sat opposite him on the leather couch.

"Now what's this you said you wanted to tell me, Frankie?" Manzano asked.

"Well, Eddie, it's like this," Diamond began. "We got a problem I think you should know about." Manzano didn't say anything so Frankie went on. "The other night two of my boys did a stupid thing. I had nothing to do with it, Eddie, I didn't even know about it till somebody else told me."

Still Manzano said nothing, so Frankie Diamond said, "They hit Richie Saint."

Eddie looked up slowly and stared right at Diamond. He had a terrible hard stare that hit like a punch and then moved right through you. Frankie didn't want to say anything. He wanted Eddie to ask him something and then he would know how to answer. But Eddie didn't say anything and so Frankie had to.

"Eddie, I told them, like you said, I told them not to do anything. I told all my people that. I said Eddie don't want nobody to make a move till he tells you to. Just keep your eyes open, that's all."

"So what happened?" Manzano asked. Frankie was relieved to have a question to answer.

"Well, I figure that's what happened. They was just keeping their eyes open and I guess they was watching LaGarda's place and then Richie Saint comes out with this other guy and I guess they figure they'll follow him. Just see what he's up to. And then, you know how it is, one thing leads to another and they hit him."

"Who was it?" Manzano asked.

"Tommie Minelli," Frankie Diamond said softly. He knew this would get Eddie mad. Eddie had asked him a couple of times to get rid of the Minelli brothers.

"And his brother?"

"Yeah, the two of them."

"They hot?" Manzano asked.

"I don't know, Eddie. I had some people checking on that and I don't think so yet. They hit him right up here, somewhere on the Palisades Parkway, late at night. Probably no one around. No one could of seen it. They're crazy, Eddie, but they're not dumb. So I figure they're clean."

"I'm gonna get some heat for this, you know," Eddie said. His voice didn't sound angry so much as it sounded numb and sorrowful.

"Yeah, I know. I'm sorry about it, Eddie. It couldn't be helped."

Manzano shrugged slightly. "Every dumb cop in the world is gonna figure, with Sallie just buried and Richie Saint knocked over, that I'm in it. Shit, I want that Tony LaGarda. I'd even do it myself. I'd pull him apart with my bare hands and I wouldn't care if all the fucking cops in the world watched me do it. But I don't like taking heat for two fucking punks knocked off Richie Saint."

"It'll be all right, Eddie," Frankie Diamond tried to explain. "No way they can trace it to you. Let 'em think what they want. No way they can stick it to you."

Manzano knew he was right. Even if he had ordered the death of Richie Saint, and even if the police caught the Minelli brothers, they would never be able to make a case against Eddie. And he hadn't ordered it and probably they wouldn't catch them, so he was pretty safe. Still, if you order a job yourself you're in a better position than if you didn't, because then you're on top of it and you know how to handle it. But when dumb bastards like the Minelli brothers are making dumb moves on their own, they can get you in trouble and you don't even know what's going on.

"Where are these gangsters of yours?" Manzano asked. This was another question Frankie had been afraid of.

"I don't know," he confessed.

"You don't know!" Manzano exploded, showing his anger for the first time.

"Yeah, Eddie, I'm sorry but I don't know. Nobody's seen them since they done it. I've had a couple guys out looking for them and Phil Runelli has his people looking for them but no one's heard anything. They're cooling themselves off somewhere, I guess. And it's a good thing, too, don't you think?"

"No," Eddie said sharply, "I don't think it's a good thing. I don't think it's a good thing these bastards running around on their own and us not knowing where they are. I told you a long time ago, Frankie, that Tommie

Minelli is bad news. And I don't want him running around getting us into more trouble."

"Yeah, I know, Eddie, but he's not running around. If he was running around we would of found him by now. He's just cooling off somewhere."

"Yeah," Eddie said, "well he can't cool off enough for me. I want you to find him and I want you to put him on ice. Is that clear?"

"Yeah, Eddie."

"And you'll do it?"

"Yeah, Eddie, sure."

There seemed to be nothing else to say on the subject and both men sat tensely, not looking at each other. Then Diamond lit a cigaret and said, "There's something else I gotta tell you, Eddie, and you're not gonna like this either."

Again Eddie didn't speak, so Frankie had to.

"Al Palmini's gone," he said.

"Whatdya mean gone?"

"Well, he was staying at the Blackstone, you remember, like Johnny Lombardi said, and he ain't there now."

"Where the fuck is he?"

"I don't know, Eddie. He's just gone."

"Cops pick him up?"

"Naw, I don't think so, Eddie. If the cops pick him up they gotta let him call a lawyer and we'd of heard by now."

"Yeah," Eddie said, "that's true. So where is he?"

"I don't know. You remember what Johnny said, like Al was kinda crazy, like something popped in him when those guys opened up on him with that machine gun. Probably just flipped out. That's what it sounds like, don't you think? So he's probably scared shitless and he figured he had to go hide someplace else. He shoulda come to us, we woulda taken care of him. But you know Al was always a little weak in the head and if he just flipped out then maybe he's off somewhere else. I don't know."

"Jesus Christ," Eddie said, standing up and walking to the window. "This one goes crazy and kills a couple a guys on the Palisades Parkway, that one goes crazy and is holed up in some fucking hotel. Some way to run an organization, isn't it? Everybody's crazy. I'm supposed to be able to get things done when they gotta be done and I can't even find out where our goddamned people are. They just go crazy and we can't even find them. Some fucking business we're in, huh, Frankie?"

"Yeah, I guess so, Eddie."

Chapter 18

WE'RE TWO OF A KIND, Frank Hovannes thought to himself as he rolled onto his side and lay next to Emily. But he didn't believe it, because if that was true then how come they couldn't get along better together? Emily had grown, over the past few years, heavier and softer, he realized as his hands ran down her sides and over her hips, which were damp and smooth with sweat. Then he rolled all the way over onto his back and pulled his hands along his own chest and stomach and recognized that he too had grown heavier and, if not softer, at least less hard. Shit, Frank thought, it's been a long time, hasn't it?

Emily, he could tell, was asleep already, and he tried to remember if she had always fallen asleep so quickly afterward. He couldn't sleep and he thought for a moment about getting up and getting a cigaret but decided he didn't want one badly enough. Just what was their problem? If they had gone to a marriage counselor, he would have sent them home, told them to forget about it, that everything was all right. Hell, there probably weren't half a dozen newlyweds in the whole Department who had the sex life he and Emily had. And they had been together almost twenty-three years. It would be twenty-three in October.

After all these years they did still seem to want each other. Emily never said no to him, never showed any waning of interest in his body, his lovemaking. And just the other night—maybe it was last week?—when he felt restless and disinclined to sleep and had decided to stay up and watch television, Emily had gotten ready for bed and then called him to her. "Come to bed, Frank," she had said. "I'm not tired," he answered, and she had said, "Good," and laughed throatily. And this had happened more than once, happened frequently in fact.

But maybe that was it, he thought for the first time.

They still had their needs for each other, still desired each other. But it wasn't together anymore. Yes, certainly. Why hadn't he thought of it before? As he lay beside Emily, on his back, his leg following the line of her leg from where their hips met down to their ankles, it became perfectly clear to him that they had come to want each other separately. It was as though they had agreed, in some secret compact, never to want each other at the same time, as though their sex lives—what a strange term, "sex lives," but it was true, wasn't it, that their bodies had lives of their own, that their passions wove themselves in and out of their external lives, of their mere lives living together—it was as though their sex lives had come apart.

Was this true, he wondered. Was that what it was? He searched his mind for evidence, trying to remember when last he and Emily had just looked at each other or had simply touched and known, both together and at the same time without it being the desire of either one in particular, that they wanted each other. And he couldn't remember such a time. Emily would invite him, lure him, even seduce him, and he would think, Yes, that would be nice. Or he would hold her, pull her toward him, whisper suggestions to her, and she would respond, smilingly and willingly, yes, and lovingly, but it was a response to him, to his desire, not a response to the same desire in herself.

And then he tried to think. Was this bad? Did it really mean that something was wrong with their marriage? Hell, it wasn't like there was an absence of love, of passion, of needing. It was an absence of something else, and maybe not something essential. He comforted himself with this thought for only a moment, and then the thought came back that it must be something essential because he and Emily weren't happy together. So whatever it was, it was essential.

Now he wanted that cigarette and climbed carefully from the bed so as not to disturb Emily. But she sensed his movement and, without waking, pushed her leg and her hip toward where he had been. Standing over the bed, he looked down at her tenderly, saw the movement, and extended his hand to the side of her face. He pressed his palm against her cheek and she gave a soft, satisfied moan and then let her head sink deeper into the brown and gold pattern of the pillowcase. From the street light and

the high April moon there was enough light in the bedroom for him to see the colors, even the light brown of
her hair where it wasn't darkened by shadows in the nest
the pillow made.

Slowly Frank turned from the bed, straightened up,
and walked out of the room, picking his way in the dark
down the stairway into the living room and finding the
stuffed chair. He lowered himself into it, only to discover
that he was sitting on the newspaper he had left there,
and when he raised himself on his elbows to slide it out
from under him it clung to his sweaty thighs and buttocks.
With a momentary flash of annoyance at this interruption
in his thoughts and mood, he pulled the newspaper away
and dropped it beside the chair, then groped around the
table for his cigarettes and lighter. He lit a cigarette and put
his feet up on the hassock. There was more newspaper
under his ankles but he didn't bother to remove it. Then
he found the ashtray and rested it on his leg, the cold
glass sending a shock up his thigh in the darkness. When
the feeling of coldness passed he tried to bring his mind
back to where it had been when he was lying beside
Emily.

But everything was different now, and other thoughts
came to him. He found himself trying to go over the
whole thing to make sure he had all the pieces in place
and knew how he came to be here.

He had decided to become a cop in forty-nine, three
years after he got out of high school. He wasn't sure just
why he signed on, but the decision did put an end to three
years of aimless drifting in deadend jobs. He could remember that from the very start he had felt that being a
cop was like being a soldier. The academy was like basic
training and when he got his shield a few months after
his twenty-first birthday he felt like he would feel a year
later when he got his papers shipping him to Korea.

In his mind he skipped over the next two years of
fighting, not because he didn't like to think about them
but because they were so much a part of him inside that
he didn't have to think about them. When he got back
to the States he rejoined the force and had very little
of the trouble "adjusting" that some of his buddies told
him about. After a while, though, routine police work
began to frustrate him, and when he made the detective
division four years later he threw himself into the work

with a passion. In six years, first as a precinct detective on the Upper West Side, then with the Burglary and later the Narcotics divisions, he built himself a reputation as a daring policeman who wasn't afraid of what his colleages would think if his arrest records were twice as long as theirs. But he was restless and never stayed anywhere longer than two years.

In the early sixties—sixty-three it was—he succeeded in getting himself assigned to the Intelligence Division. Nicknamed the Red Squad because of its activities in infiltrating and investigation subversive groups, the Intelligence Division at the time was also the only unit in the Department with responsibility for policing organized crime. During the seven years Frank spent in Intelligence he learned to know what the soldiers in Vietnam were feeling, as opposed to how he had felt in Korea. It was not so much the unpopularity of the war, the fact that the "folks back home" didn't understand or appreciate what they were doing. That was only an excuse; civilians never do understand. No, it wasn't the limits put on the army he read about in the papers, any more than it was the Supreme Court decisions that cops like to grumble about. It was the nature of the warfare and the nature of the enemy. It was especially the fact that they seemed to be everywhere, that like some giant spongy thing in a science fiction movie they didn't seem capable of being hurt. The mob absorbed anything. Cut off an arm and it didn't even take the time to grow it back; it just flowed into the space and filled it up. Of course the small arrests of petty racketeers didn't make a dent—nobody thought they would—but even the occasional big busts didn't seem to have any effect. Whether it was because the bosses still ran things from jail or because the mob was so loosely structured that it was infinitely adaptable, it came to the same thing.

To make matters worse, the brass in Intelligence didn't seem to want to do anything except maintain a holding operation against the mobs. Whoever named that outfit knew what he was talking about, because all they were interested in was gathering information and never doing anything with it. The brass was all holdovers from the fifties, when politicians were running around saying there was no such thing as the Mafia and any cop who wanted to get anywhere went along with the game.

After the big Department shakeups in nineteen-seventy, when the Commissioner announced that he was forming an Organized Crime Control squad, Frank fought to get in on it. A squad like that would have to take organized crime seriously, and Frank figured that finally he would be able to find the kind of war he had always looked for in police work. He could remember how helpless and impotent he had felt during those last months in Intelligence, as he petitioned, cajoled, and prayed for his transfer to come through. He had never had a hook in the Department, because he operated pretty much as a loner, so there was no one to pull any strings for him. But still, he might get the assignment, and Frank knew it would be his last chance to make police work mean what he wanted it to mean.

Sometimes Frank thought that his problems with Emily had begun around then. There had never been a time in his life when he felt as alone as he did then, but he had to admit it was hard to blame her for that. She had been patient and uncritical, even supportive, if you could count as support her grim and silent recognition that he alone knew what he needed. If she couldn't understand his needs—for how could a woman be expected to understand a man who needed to have enemies—at least she was able to acknowledge that they were real. She gave him that much.

Sitting in his unlit living room, lighting another cigaret and dragging deeply on it, Frank felt it was somehow important to sort out the blame, and when he did he had to say in all fairness that it was he who had moved away from Emily and not she from him. That didn't leave her blameless, no, not at all, but it did make clear to him where the fault lay for whatever was going wrong with their marriage. She had wanted a baby so much, and had more or less given up hope, but maybe if he hadn't been so dead set against adopting they would be more in touch with each other now. The baby had certainly made a difference for Ernie, Frank thought. And then, bitterly, he wondered how much of a difference it was making for Dorothy now that Ernie was dead.

He squashed his cigarette in the ashtray, and as he did he began to feel a sort of nervous tenseness mounting from his stomach through his chest. Another minute alone, he knew, and his thoughts would carry him to that terrible

Thanksgiving Day last year. A restless stirring in his legs told him to get up and go back to Emily, because he could never think about that day lying with her. The pressure of her body against him somehow protected him from thinking about it. He blamed himself for what had happened that day, and he blamed Emily, and maybe that was why he couldn't think about it in her presence, because it was impossible for him to reconcile his bitterness with her, his angry and vindictive sense that she had been in some obscure way responsible for it, with the warmth and softness, the familiarity of her body.

But he didn't get up, and so the memory of last Thanksgiving flooded back to him, as perhaps he wanted it to do.

Chapter 19

THE MORNING AFTER Tony LaGarda got back from Vineland, Frank Hovannes came into his office to find Roberto Obregon already there and on the telephone. "Just a minute," Obregon was saying, "here's Inspector Hovannes now." Then he pushed the hold button and said to Frank, "Hi, Inspector, I think you should take this."

"Who is it?" Hovannes asked.

"It's this guy up at the four-two. Sergeant Fleckner."

"Four-two? That's up in the Bronx. What's he want?"

Obregon shrugged. "It's not good," he said.

Frank reached for the phone. "Hovannes here," he said.

"Inspector Hovannes? This is Sergeant Fleckner, forty-second precinct."

Oh brother, Frank thought as he waited for the thin wispy voice at the other end to continue. There was a ludicrously incongruous tone in the voice, as though he were trying to sound official and tough and wasn't used to it.

"We have something here that may be of some use to you," Fleckner said after a pause and then stopped.

Am I supposed to ask him questions or something, Frank wondered. He had had a bad sleepless night and wasn't in the mood for this sort of pussyfooting, so he said nothing and waited for Fleckner to get around to whatever he had called to say.

"Here's the story, Inspector. We usually try not to butt in on what you people are doing. We just try to keep our precinct under control and watch what's going on. Organized crime is your job and we try not to interfere, except to know what's going on in our own precinct."

"What are you talking about?" Frank asked, and immediately was sorry he had let his annoyance show.

Fleckner's voice moved a notch higher. "What I'm

talking about, Inspector, is the Dunbar Hotel. I take it you know what it is."

"Yeah," Frank said. "I know. That's Vin Robustelli's place. Grand Concourse, right?"

"That's right," Fleckner said, placated. "Robustelli lives there and he owns the restaurant downstairs. The Concourse Restaurant. Actually, his brother-in-law owns it, but it's his place."

"Okay, I know all that," Frank said, hiding his impatience a little better this time. "So what've you got?"

"Well, like I was saying before, we usually don't bother with these guys. As long as they don't make trouble in the precinct, we figure we'll leave them to you. That's the way the captain here wants it and that's what I tell my men. But I tell them to kind of keep their eyes open, in case they see anything interesting they can pass it along to you."

"That's terrific," Frank said, "and we appreciate it. If the whole Department worked that way it would make things a lot easier down here."

Obregon, who had never heard the Inspector talk this way, looked up from a report he was writing to see Hovannes making faces at the telephone. Frank motioned for him to pick up the other line.

"Thank you, Inspector," Fleckner was saying. "Well, last night one of our patrol teams was driving by the Dunbar Hotel, just a routine patrol, and the passenger officer saw something he just thought he'd take a look at. Nothing really out of the way, but he was just curious. He's a young kid but he'll be a good officer. Puerto Rican kid name of Ramos, but smart as a whip."

Frank looked across to Obregon on the other phone. He was blushing deeply and Frank broke into a broad grin which he just barely managed to keep from turning into laughter. Obregon scribbled something on a pad and passed it to Frank. It said, "All us Puerto Rican kids are smart as a whip." Frank nodded acknowledgment and then the two of them turned their attention back to Fleckner, who hadn't stopped talking.

"Well, what he saw was this big Lincoln pull up and three guys get out and he thinks he recognizes one of them. That's what makes him take a second look. This guy he sees is Carmine Leone, you know, the Brooklyn mobster . . ."

"Yeah, I know."

". . . and two of his men. Ramos thinks they're Anthony Basilio, a.k.a. Tony Basta, and Ilario Sciarra, a.k.a. Larry Boston. I don't know where this kid comes up with all these names, but like I said he's pretty smart. So anyway, he figures this is something to know about. Like I said, I tell my men to keep their eyes open for anything unusual and this is unusual. There's a lot of business going on at the Dunbar all the time, you know, but Robustelli doesn't usually entertain company like Carmine Leone. So Ramos and his partner pull over to watch for a while and they're not there five minutes when this big Imperial pulls up, and Ramos recognizes the occupants. This time it's Anthony LaGarda, a.k.a. Tony the Lawyer, and he's got with him Paul Gagliano and James Monaco, a.k.a. Jimmie Monks. Ramos doesn't know what all this is but it looks to him like they got some kinda little Apalachin going, so he gets on the radio and calls it in."

"When'd this happen?" Frank asked.

"Last night. He radioed in at, uh, ten fifty-four," Fleckner said, pausing to get the time off the report in front of him.

Jesus, Frank thought, this asshole really does have something. "What else you got?"

"Well, that's all. He stayed around there about an hour and a half and we sent another car around to the back of the place. Unmarked car, we sent two detectives. And they waited in back and Ramos and his partner were in front, but that's all they saw. No one else in or out."

"Tell me something, Sergeant," Frank said, his voice mockingly pleasant, "how come you're calling me on this now?"

"Well, I could see it looked like something important and I figured it's the sort of thing we should pass on."

"That's what I mean," Frank said. "Why the fuck didn't someone call last night?"

The voice on the other end stammered an incomprehensible explanation and Frank cut him off, saying, "All right, Fleckner. I'm coming up there with one of my men. I want to talk to Ramos and the other officer in the car with him and I want to talk to those two detectives you had watching the place."

"Ramos doesn't come on till four o'clock," Fleckner protested.

"That's all right," Frank said, "just get him there. We'll be there in an hour."

He hung up and so did Obregon.

"What's it mean?" Obregon asked.

"It may mean we're fucked," Frank said, his voice flat and expressionless.

Obregon didn't respond. As much as possible he liked to figure these things out for himself. That was one of the things Frank liked most about him. In his own way he was as curious as Savage, who was always asking questions, but he rarely asked anything. He watched and listened and you couldn't even tell whether he was taking in any of what was going on, and then he would ask something and you would know that he had been figuring it for himself and that his thinking was pretty far down the line.

Frank thought he understood Savage, who was kind of an idealistic guy, an old-fashioned cop with whom Frank could identify. And he was sure he understood Polito, because there wasn't that much to understand once you recognized that he was dangerous. Polito frightened him, and he had had his doubts about bringing him in on the operation. But he had no choice, and besides, he knew there would be things that had to be done that you needed someone like Polito to do. Killing Palmini for instance. But Obregon was another matter, and Frank suspected he knew no more about what made this intense young Puerto Rican detective tick than he knew about what LaGarda, Robustelli, and Leone were doing in the Dunbar Hotel last night.

Frank stood up slowly from his desk and walked across to where the coffee pot was plugged in. He lit a cigarette, which must have been his seventh this morning and it was only ten o'clock, and poured half a cup of coffee into his mug. Shit, he thought, this is gonna be a waste of time going up to the Bronx.

"Hey, Roberto," he said, still standing by the coffee pot, "you know if Lou is coming in today?"

"Don't think so," Obregon said. "I think it's his swing. He said he was going up to the Berkshires with his girl."

"The Berkshires? Where does he come off going up to the Berkshires?"

"I think he said they were going up to a concert or something. Didn't he say once his girl was a musician?"

"No shit," Hovannes said, drawing out the first word. "Well, see if you can get him on the phone and ask him to come in. Something I want him to do."

Obregon shrugged, picked up the phone, and dialed a few numbers. Then he hung up again.

"Hey, Inspector," he said, speaking slowly, "if they were having a sit-down, Eddie Manzano would have been there, wouldn't he?"

"Yeah," Frank said noncommittally.

"But that sergeant that called didn't say Eddie Manzano. He said LaGarda and Leone."

"Yeah," Frank said again, this time agreeing, "but that doesn't mean Eddie wasn't there. It just means your *paisano* Ramos didn't see him."

Obregon didn't say anything, but he didn't dial Savage's number either. After a minute he said, "If Manzano was there, then they were probably having a sit-down to bury the hatchet. Then LaGarda must've sold them on the idea that he didn't do the job on Big Sallie, or that anyway killing Richie Saint made it all even. In which case everybody's friends again and we're just back at zero, right? But if Manzano wasn't there, then what's LaGarda doing meeting with Leone and Robustelli?"

Frank didn't say anything.

"If Manzano wasn't there," Obregon continued, thinking out loud, "then our friend Tony the Lawyer must be lining up Leone and Robustelli so he can shaft Manzano." He paused. "How's that sound?" he asked.

"Sounds all right," Hovannes said.

There had been some talk on the street, Obregon remembered, about impending trouble between LaGarda and Manzano. The word was that LaGarda was planning to muscle in on some of Manzano's Manhattan business. LaGarda probably wouldn't have tried to make a move like that without clearance from higher up, so he must have talked to Leone and Robustelli already about plans to cut back on the Manzano brothers' territory. Then, when Big Sallie was eliminated, and after him Richie Saint, LaGarda might go back to Leone and Robustelli for an okay to go ahead with his plan. If he could convince them that he hadn't done the job on Big Sallie—and maybe that wouldn't be too hard, considering what Savage's informer had said about people in general not buying the idea that LaGarda was behind it—then he could bring up the Richie Saint business as proof that Eddie Manzano was dangerous and wasn't playing by the book, because you don't lay out a guy like Richie Saint on your own without getting the contract approved. Richie Saint was no street hood or common soldier. He had contacts with just about everybody, including Robustelli, and it would be easy for LaGarda to convince Robustelli that the hit on Richie Saint was a slap in the face to him personally.

So that's what it must have been, Obregon concluded. The Inspector's got it wrong, he thought. We're not fucked. If Manzano was at that meeting, then we'd be fucked because we'd be back at zero, but if Manzano wasn't there, then probably it means Tony the Lawyer's getting ready to go after Eddie Manzano, and that would be just beautiful.

Satisfied he had it worked out, Obregon picked up the phone and dialed Savage's number. A young woman's voice answered.

"Lou there?" Obregon asked.

"Yes he is." She had a pleasant voice, soft and friendly, and although her speech was completely unaccented the thought flashed through Obregon's mind that it was the voice of a *latina*. "Who's calling?" she said.

"Tell him Roberto."

"Uh-oh," she said. "I'll tell him, but we're going away till Sunday."

Then Savage came on. "What's up?" he asked.

"The Inspector wants you to come down here."

"Can't do it, Roberto. We're going up to the country. In fact we've already got our stuff in the car." Obregon didn't say anything. "Tell him we left already. If you called five minutes later you would've missed us."

"Yeah," Roberto said, "and if you didn't answer your phone you wouldn't have to come down here now. But you did. See you in twenty minutes."

Then Hovannes's voice was on the phone. "Lou, look," he said, "I'm sorry about screwing up your plans but something happened last night and you gotta do something for me. Last night Tony LaGarda was up in the Bronx meeting with Robustelli and Leone. We didn't even know he was back in town. A couple of patrolmen up at the four-two saw them. Roberto and I are going up there to talk to them, find out if Eddie Manzano was there, but I know we're not gonna get anything from them. If those assholes had called us last night we could've found out ourselves if he was there, but I don't know if those guys'd know him if they saw him."

"Yeah, okay, Frank, whatdya want me to do?" Savage said. Obregon, who was still on the line, could hear the girl say, "Shit!" in the background.

"I want you to find that guy you're using, the one told you about Richie Saint. See what he knows. Don't bother coming down here. Just get in touch with him, find out what he knows. Then call me back on it. If you can get him right away and if it's what I think it is, you can still get out of town today."

"Yeah, okay, Frank," Savage said and hung up. Then he explained to Celia as best he could what the situation was and she smiled and shrugged and said she understood.

"You'd make a great cop's wife," he said to her, but she ignored it like she always ignored it whenever he mentioned marriage.

"Do you think we might get to go anyway?" she asked, and when he said that maybe they could she said she'd leave the stuff in the trunk but wanted to go to the car and bring in the sandwiches to put in the refrigerator. When she left, Lou made a few phone calls and set up a meeting with Fran Marks.

At the same time, Obregon and Hovannes were on their way up to the Bronx. "Whatdya know about Lou's girlfriend?" Obregon asked, trying to sound as offhanded as he could.

"Not much. Met her once. Seems like a nice girl. Whatdya want to know—is she Puerto Rican?"

Obregon blushed and swallowed hard. "Naw, I just meant . . . Yeah. Is she?"

"Yup," Hovannes said.

"No shit," Obregon said and chuckled to himself.

Friday, April 18

Fran Marks waited for Lou Savage by one of the telescopes in Battery Park. He put a dime in the slot and bent over to look through the eyepiece. It was aimed at the Statue of Liberty, so he swung it around to look up the shoreline, straightening up a few times to peer over the instrument in order to find what he was seeing through the lens. Then he picked a target and tried to find it with the telescope, which needed oiling and was hard to move smoothly. After a few seconds of this he turned and walked away from the telescope before his dime was used up.

If he's calling me, Marks thought, this is gonna cost him fifty bucks. In four years of selling information to Savage he had never been able to get fifty bucks from him, but then Savage had never called him before. It was worth trying, he figured, as he wandered the sidewalk just above the water, stopping from time to time to lean on the railing and look out over the bay.

A black kid, maybe twelve or thirteen years old, was pedaling toward him on an expensive-looking ten-speed bicycle. "Hey, mister, got a cigarette?" the kid asked without stopping.

"Yeah," Fran said and the kid hopped from the bike, more or less vaulting over the seat without putting on the brakes, keeping his balance when he hit the ground and stopping the bike with his hands. Nice move, Fran thought, as the kid walked back toward him. He tapped two cigarettes from his pack and handed the kid one. "Need a light?" he asked, lighting one himself.

"No. Thanks, mister," the kid said. He put the cigarette over his ear, climbed on the bike, and pedaled off.

Fran watched him until he turned out of sight by the ferry depot and then resumed his walk along the shore. He finished his cigarette and threw the butt into the bay. Something about this whole business had been bothering him, and as he watched the butt floating in the water he felt good because he thought he had it figured out. He had walked all the way from Avenue D after Savage called, and on the walk he had begun to be suspicious of something. Marks made it a matter of principle always to trust his suspicions—in his business you had to—and so on the walk he had gone over his whole conversation with Savage from two days before, until finally he thought he understood what it was that was bugging him.

The first thing he had asked himself was what Savage might want. Maybe Savage just wanted to know if he had learned anything else about the Manzano shooting. From the way he talked last time, the cops must've been figuring it was Tony the Lawyer who hit him, and it would probably take them all the way from Monday to Friday to realize that that wouldn't wash. Shit, Marks thought, I told him that Wednesday, but it probably just dawned on those assholes that I was right and now they figure I gotta know something they don't if I'm so smart. Dumb shits.

But then he realized that that didn't make sense. The pigs aren't about to go busting their balls trying to figure out who killed a rat like Sallie Manzano. Especially that Hovannes, who'd just as soon he was dead anyway. The papers said he was in charge of this thing and what would he care who offed Big Sallie? Unless he wanted to give him a medal. Savage wouldn't be coming all the way down here for that, it wouldn't make sense. Besides, Savage is a narc. He doesn't work for Hovannes. So it couldn't be that.

Well, if it wasn't the Manzano thing, then what the hell did Savage want? At first Marks resigned himself to the fact that he'd have to wait till he saw Savage to find out. But whatever it was, it was gonna cost him. Shit, it's Friday and I'm supposed to see a man on Forty-third Street at four o'clock and instead I'm hiking down to Battery Park, so if there's one thing for sure it's that this pig is gonna have to make this worth my while, Marks thought.

Then another thought pierced through his annoyance, and he said to himself, Man, that's funny about Palmini. I told that prick Wednesday where he was, but they didn't pick him up. How come they didn't pick him up? He's gone now, and that's funny too, cause even Frankie Diamond doesn't know where he's gone.

Marks had been talking with Jack Kittens the night before, and Kittens said that Frankie Diamond had gone to the Blackstone to get Palmini out of there, only Palmini wasn't there. When Kittens told him this, Marks got a little scared, because Kittens might have been telling him for a reason. Did Kittens suspect he was talking to the cops, that it was he who had told the cops that Palmini was hiding out at the Blackstone? Was he telling him this to see his reaction, to see if he said something like, "The fuzz must've picked him up," which would be a dead giveaway because how could the cops pick him up unless someone told them where he was, and who else beside Frankie Diamond and Kittens and Marks knew where he was? So when Kittens told him this, Fran said only, "That's funny. I thought the guy was scared shitless. I didn't figure he'd ever come outta there."

Then he found out the cops hadn't picked up Palmini, and that was funny too. Maybe it wouldn't have been so funny if he was still there—like Savage said, they were in no hurry to get Palmini because what the hell could they do with him? You can't bust a guy for being shot at. But then why'd he leave? Someone must have tipped him that the cops knew where he was.

Holy Jesus, what a thought! Marks whispered under his breath, stopping in his tracks. By this time he was already down to Bridge Street, and he wanted to get it all straight in his mind before he got to the park in case Savage was already there. He stood without moving, except that his arms gestured as he talked to himself, thinking this thing through.

That would make sense, wouldn't it? I told Savage where Palmini was. The pigs'd probably want to pick him up, just question him or something. But he splits. So that means he's tipped they're coming. And that means Savage must have tipped him! What a fucking thought! Savage is working for Eddie Manzano, or maybe just Frankie Diamond. No, not Diamond, cause he didn't know where Palmini went. Unless Kittens was just putting me on about that. Either way, they got Savage working for them. So that's why he wants to know about who killed Big Sallie. Cause he's moonlighting for Big Sallie's brother. Crazy.

Fran Marks found this idea exhilarating in a strange sort of way. It was nice to know things really were as complicated as they seemed most of the time, and when he got to Battery Park he was feeling very confident and cheerful. That was why he had put the dime into the telescope, because it seemed like a nice thing to do. But then after the kid on the bike rode away and while he was watching his cigarette butt floating in the bay, it dawned on him that if all this was right, he was going to have to be very careful. Because if Savage is working for Manzano or Diamond, then they're going to find out that I'm selling information to the police. What a dumb, fucked-up situation, because it ain't gonna matter to them that the pig I talk to is working for them. They're still gonna have me down for a pigeon.

Man, this is bad, Marks said to himself and pulled another cigarette from the pack in his pocket. As he lit it he noticed his hand was shaking. Maybe he shouldn't talk to Savage, he thought. Maybe he should just split and get out of this whole scene. He had a nice little business going, and even though he needed the money from Savage he could live without it. It wasn't worth getting yourself whacked out for, that was certain. On the other hand, since he'd talked to Savage already on Wednesday, talking to him again today couldn't hurt. He wondered how long Savage had been on Manzano's pad, and whether everything he had been telling him all these years had been going back to Eddie. What were the odds that Savage just started working for them this week? Not very good. It was just as likely he had been on the take the whole time, or at least for a while. So Manzano might have known for a long time that Marks was a pigeon, and Marks was still alive. Then again, maybe Savage wasn't telling them who his line was. In fact that made a lot of sense, because Savage would have to protect his sources if he wanted to be able to get anything out of them.

Marks took a deep drag from his cigaret and noticed that his hand had stopped shaking. He decided it would be all right to keep the appointment with Savage that afternoon, and probably to keep working for him, but he made up his mind that he was going to be very careful about the whole thing. Very careful. In fact, maybe there was some way he could kind of cover himself with the mob. It probably would be a good idea to talk to Jack Kittens again, and he figured after he met his man on Forty-third Street he'd look him up. It couldn't hurt.

Chapter 20

Lou Savage stepped out of Frank Hovannes's office and took a seat next to Roberto Obregon at the table. Ron Polito sat opposite them. Except for the three of them, the wardroom was empty.

"Frank'll be out in a minute," Savage said.

"D'you know what's up?" Obregon asked.

"What's up?" Polito interjected. "What the fuck's ever up?"

Savage ignored him. He was annoyed at having to come back uptown to this meeting. By the time he got back home it would be after five o'clock, and at five on a Friday afternoon it would be impossible to get out of the city. So he and Celia would end up having their sandwiches in the house before they left, waiting for the traffic to die down. It would be midnight by the time they got up to the Berkshires and then they would have to find a room. This certainly wasn't the kind of weekend he had planned. Although he knew Celia wouldn't complain, he knew too that she would be disappointed and that was what annoyed him. So he passed over Polito's crack and answered Obregon.

"I don't know," he said, "there's a lot of things going on I guess, and he just wants to brief us before the weekend. You know about that thing up in the Bronx, don't you?"

"Yeah," Obregon said, "d'you find anything on it? We came up empty."

"What thing in the Bronx?" Polito asked. He didn't like the way things went on and he didn't know about them. He looked at Savage when he asked the question, but when Savage didn't answer he turned to Obregon.

"We got a call this morning from some desk jockey up in the Bronx," Obregon started to explain, but just then Inspector Hovannes came out of his office and took a seat at the head of the table. Obregon nodded toward Hovannes, indicating to Polito that the Inspector would fill him in on the details.

"Okay," Hovannes said, reaching down the table to slide an ashtray in front of him, "this shouldn't take long. I'm sorry about screwing up your weekend, Lou, but we should be out of here in about a half hour. There's some things going on I thought you all should know about. Then I think we can kind of coast for a couple days, let things settle in a little and see what's breaking. You've got the weekend off anyway, Lou, so maybe the rest of you oughta take your swing now too while we've got the chance. You may not get another one for a while. Then we can pick up Monday where we left off."

He paused to light a cigaret, took a deep drag, and exhaled slowly. "First off," he said, "let's see where we stand. We've been in business a week now and I think it's looking pretty good. Here's what we've got. Monday we hit Big Sallie, Silvera's still in the hospital, and you took care of Palmini on Wednesday, right, Ron?"

"Yeah," Polito said, smiling thinly, pleased to have his contribution acknowledged. "I wanted to ask you about that."

"Yeah, sure. It went all right, didn't it?" Hovannes asked.

"Oh sure, it went fine. Beautiful," Polito said, starting to get flustered. Damn it, why did he have so much trouble talking at these meetings? Who was Hovannes anyway? An Inspector—so what? It wasn't like he was the goddamned Commissioner or something. And it wasn't like Polito didn't have his own ideas on what they should be doing. He had ideas, plenty of them. But when they put him on a spot like this, like at a meeting, it was hard to get them out. "No, it went beautiful," he repeated, "but I was wondering about Silvera."

"What about him?" Hovannes asked.

"He saw you, Inspector," Polito said. "Don't you think maybe we gotta hit him?"

"Yeah, probably," Hovannes said casually without conceding anything, "but he's in the hospital now and he's not going anywhere till next week at least. There's no way we can touch him in there. When he gets out we'll have to think about that, okay?"

He paused, closing the subject. Polito wanted to say they should plan for it now, so they could hit him as soon as possible. He would be getting out of the hospital the middle of next week and it might be hard to find him once he was out. And he was more dangerous than Palmini, because Palmini was probably too dumb and too scared to get a look at Hovannes but Fat Louie wasn't that dumb and he would know Frank if he ever saw him again. So what was the sense in wasting Palmini and then letting Fat Louie walk out of the hospital alive?

Polito, though, didn't say any of this and Hovannes went on with the briefing.

"Okay, what else have we got? Monday or Tuesday LaGarda splits. Tuesday night somebody whacks out Richie Saint."

"I got something on that," Savage cut in. "Kind of interesting. The Richie Saint job was Tommie Minelli's work"

"That figures."

"No, but here's the interesting part. No one's seen Minelli since Tuesday and what I hear there's an open contract out on him and his brother."

"From Manzano?"

"Yeah, from Manzano."

Hovannes pondered this information for a minute. "Yeah," he said, "that *is* interesting."

"Be nice for us if nothing happens to those two boys," Savage said. "They could be a lot of trouble for Manzano if they ever figure out they're on his shit list."

"They must have figured that out already, Lou," Obregon interjected. "If nobody's seen them since Tuesday they must have figured it out right away."

Ron Polito was listening to all this and growing increasingly tense. He didn't understand why Eddie Manzano would put a contract out on two of his own men for hitting someone close to LaGarda and he was annoyed that Hovannes and Savage didn't bother to explain it to him. All right, they're big shit detectives and they know how these things work, but just because I spent five years in Tactical doesn't mean they have to treat me like a piece of shit, he thought. I was in on this thing before any of them—even Hovannes—he reminded himself.

As these thoughts ran through Polito's mind he lost the thread of the discussion and had trouble picking it up again. Hovannes was talking.

"Okay," he said, "put that with what we know about Thursday night and let's see what we've got. Thursday night Tony the Lawyer's back in town and he's up in the

Bronx with Vin Robustelli and Carmine Leone. What does that say to you?"

"Listen to this, guys, you're gonna like this," Obregon answered. He leaned back in his chair and doodled at arm's length on the pad he kept in front of him, his eyes following the random movements of the pencil as he talked. "When we got back from the Bronx this afternoon I did some checking. I thought I heard once that that place was staked out, so I checked with OCC in the Bronx. They said they used to have a window on the place but they closed up shop about a year ago. But the guy I talked to there, now get this, he says he thinks there are feds up there."

"Those pricks," Hovannes muttered. "You mean they've got a surveillance on Robustelli and they don't tell us?"

"They didn't tell *anybody*. This guy I talked to says they never heard a word. But his men used to see them there all the time. In fact that's why he closed it up. Figured if his men are watching the feds play Eliot Ness on the Grand Concourse, then Robustelli's watching it too, and he's got better things to do than stake out the FBI. Anyway, he says for all he knows they're still up there. So I give them a call and sure enough they got a twenty-four hour watch on the place. So I ask them what they know about Thursday night and about all they know is that it comes between Wednesday and Friday."

"They didn't make Eddie Manzano coming in or out?"

"Boss, they didn't even make Leone and LaGarda!"

Hovannes laughed and shook his head. "You gotta be kidding," he said.

"No, sir," Obregon said, raising his right hand above his head. "They are something else."

Hovannes laughed again and then the smile faded slowly from his face. "You see what we're up against, don't you," he said, and although he said it flippantly there was a cutting edge of scorn and derision in his voice that made it clear he wasn't joking.

Lou Savage slid himself closer to the table and sat up straighter, leaning on his elbows. The fire in Frank was so close to the surface that whenever it flared through, even in a small way like this, it excited Lou unaccountably, reminded him that in spite of everything he was glad to be working for Frank.

Even Polito noticed it, and for a moment his resentment drained away. He remembered his first weeks of patrol when he was just out of the academy, and then those first few weeks when he was transferred to Tactical. No one had helped him there either. Maybe that was just the way it was on the force, you were supposed to make it yourself. He had resented it then too, the way the older men assumed you were supposed to know what they knew already, what it had taken them years to learn. But he had made it on his own, hadn't he?—made it enough to be in on this assignment. So if Hovannes and Savage wanted to cut him out, to talk in front of him about things he didn't understand without even explaining, that was okay too. He would catch on.

Savage was saying, "So far as I can tell, Manzano wasn't invited to the party. My man didn't know anything about it and if Eddie was there he'd of known."

"Who's this?" Polito asked, giving his newfound commitment to start learning things a test run.

No one said anything.

"I mean, if it's someone close to Manzano maybe it's someone we can use or something," he stammered, starting to sense he had made a mistake.

Polito had no way of knowing how jealously detectives guard the identity of their confidential informants. Even Hovannes didn't know who Savage's source was and he would never ask. Every detective had run into this once in his career. An older man would be detailing information he had gained from an informant and the new man would say, "Hey, this guy sure knows a lot. Who the hell is he?" and he would be answered with silence. Maybe someone would say, "Look, kid, there are some informants we gotta keep confidential," or maybe nobody would say anything, but the message was clear either way. Now it was Polito's turn to learn this.

"Okay," Hovannes said to break the silence, "so what we got is this. Say Eddie Manzano wasn't there. That means it was a war council and Tony the Lawyer was getting the go ahead to fuck him over. Put that with what we know about those Minelli punks. If Eddie wants them iced it means he never authorized the hit on Richie Saint. Eddie's big on discipline. Which means that Eddie isn't ready to move yet. So that's your homework for the weekend. Tony the Lawyer's ready to go for Manzano but Manzano's still sitting tight. What I want you all to think about is do we want to keep it that way—let Tony make his move and see what happens? Or do we want to see if there's some way we can make this a two-way street, do something else to shake Eddie up? And if that's it, what? Have a nice weekend."

Frank stood up and walked back into his office.

"You still going outta town?" Obregon asked Savage.

"Yeah," Lou said. "Later. We'll probably eat home and wait till the traffic dies down. I hate trying to get outta town in all that traffic. Friday night it's fucking next to impossible."

Obregon had moved across the room to his locker while Lou was talking and he put the yellow legal pad with his doodles on the eye-high shelf and took out a shoulder holster. He put on the holster and transferred his gun to it from the waist clip he wore around Headquarters and when he wasn't wearing a jacket. Then he took a sport jacket from the hook, slammed the gray metal locker closed and headed for the door. "See you Monday," he said.

Savage waited till he was gone and turned to Polito. He was feeling good now because all the delays were over and he had only the weekend with Celia to look forward to. The operation seemed to be right on target, especially if it was true that Tony LaGarda was going to make some kind of move on Manzano. Anyway he had made it through the first week of Operation Counterthrust and he had no regrets. Getting into a thing like this was a scary business, and ever since he had given Hovannes his consent two months ago he had known that he wouldn't really know if he had done the right thing until he had been in it awhile. Now he was in it a week and it felt okay. Polito still bugged him and he couldn't say for sure that he didn't have any doubts about it. But if the doubts didn't get any worse than this he would be all right. Hell, you couldn't go into a thing like this without some doubts, could you?

He got up slowly from the table, pushing himself back from it like after a big meal. "Have a good weekend, Ron," he said and turned to leave.

"Hey, Lou," Polito said, "mind if I ask you a question?"

"No, sure."

"I was wondering, do you think Hovannes is right about Silvera?"

"Whatdya mean?"

"I mean, I don't know much about this, but it seems to me he's not taking that serious enough. I wasn't there and you were, so maybe I'm wrong about this, but didn't that guy get a look at Hovannes?"

"Yeah, I guess so."

"That's all," Polito said. "I was just wondering. Have a good weekend."

"Yeah, you too," Savage said and walked out onto Broome Street. It was only four-thirty and there were hours of daylight left, but it was starting to get cool already.

Friday, April 18

Shit, Ron Polito thought, this is no way to run an operation. Except for himself, the basement wardroom is the Broome Street Annex that Hovannes had requisitioned for Operation Counterthrust was empty, and that fact as much as anything else symbolized to Polito what was wrong with the whole operation. "I'm sorry about screwing up your weekend, Lou," Polito thought, mentally mimicking Hovannes's apology to Savage. What kind of operation was this anyway, closing down for the weekend like they were bankers or something? And Savage, picking up and going out of town with some girl he wasn't even married to. The whole thing was galling.

Still seated at the table, he glanced around the empty room and noticed that the door to Hovannes's office was closed. Hovannes was still in there, he remembered, and for a moment the thought of going in and talking to him passed through his mind. But what would he say?

He would tell him that this whole approach seemed wrong. All this business about strategy and counterstrategy and figuring out what the mob was doing and checking what was going on in the Bronx and who was at this meeting and who wasn't at that meeting was just a lot of bullshit. The idea was to hit the mob and hit them hard and keep hitting them and keep them spinning, wasn't it? At least that was what it was supposed to be.

The beauty of the operation was supposed to be that you could just open up on these guys. You knew who they were and now was your chance to get them without all the investigations and stakeouts and intelligence work that always kept things from ever happening. But from where Polito stood it looked like the same thing all over again. Shit, Hovannes had them waste months just finding out who it was they wanted to hit. And when you came right down to it, what the fuck did it matter? Endless debates about if you hit Sallie Manzano, would the street buy the idea that it was Tony LaGarda's job? Or if you hit Tony, would it look like it was Big Sallie behind it? Or what about hitting Robustelli? No, you couldn't do that because there was no one in the mob big enough to go for Robustelli. And because an investigation of a hit on Robustelli would be handled in the Bronx and Hovannes couldn't have control over that.

Okay, that made sense. Because you had to protect yourself and the best way to do that was to make sure that Hovannes headed up the investigation. But all this other shit about what the mob would think! Who cared what they thought? The idea was to waste them, then go ahead and waste them.

That was what he wanted to say to Hovannes now. He wanted to say, What is this horseshit about taking a weekend off and everybody going away and waiting till Monday while you tried to figure out what Tony LaGarda was doing up in the Bronx. And Monday, he could see it already, they wouldn't do anything either. They'd meet back here and talk about what they had figured out up in the mountains about what Tony LaGarda must be thinking.

And when you came right down to it, what did they know about what Tony LaGarda was thinking? He had seen guys like Tony his whole life, ever since he was a kid growing up on Orchard Street. He could remember how Saturday night he would go out to a restaurant with his old man and they would sit there the whole evening, his father talking Italian with his cronies and Ron not saying anything because he didn't speak Italian but understanding more of the conversation than he would let on. And then one of them would come in and everyone would stand up, and some of the old men would go over to his table to pay their respects. And he would sit there with his bodyguards, their guns showing through their jackets, lapping it all up, asking the old men about their daughters and their wives and their jobs like he gave a shit who they were. And even then Ron had thought, What do they do this for, why do they pay their respects to this pig who never did a day's work in his life? This pig who probably could have every man in that restaurant shot if he wanted to and wouldn't give it a minute's thought.

So what do guys like that think, and what does it matter what they think, and why does Inspector Hovannes give a shit? You got Sallie Manzano. Good. Now get his brother Eddie. And Frankie Diamond. And Phil Runelli. And Tony LaGarda. And Jimmie Monks. And Paulie Gagliano. Two weeks you could bag the whole lot of them. And that fat one in the hospital.

Especially him, Polito thought, and stood up from the table. He rolled down his sleeves and buttoned his cuffs. Then he walked to his locker and swung it open, pulled out the necktie draped on the hook and knotted it quickly. Especially him. Goddamn it, he had seen the Inspector. What did it matter that he wasn't getting out of the hospital? He had visitors there, didn't he? He could describe Hovannes and maybe someone he talked to would recognize him from the description. Hovannes had been dealing with these guys for years, so maybe someone would say, Hey, that sounds like that Inspector Hovannes. They could put two and two together. They'd say, Yeah, wasn't that his partner some of Sallie's guys wasted last November? And that would be that.

And what would be so hard about hitting him in the hospital anyway? There wasn't a guard around him. At least the police didn't have a guard around him, Polito thought. But maybe Manzano's people did. That was the real question, Polito figured, pleased with himself that he was thinking this thing through carefully.

He pulled his service revolver from his shoulder holster and checked it, then reminded himself that he wouldn't want to use that and slid it back into the holster. At home he had a forty-five automatic and it wouldn't take long to run up there and get it. What the hell, Polito thought, while he was there he could get his twenty-two target pistol too. The forty-five sounded like a cannon when it went off. If Fat Louie was just lying there like a target there was no reason you couldn't take him out with a twenty-two, even with all his blubber. Maybe I oughta bring a harpoon too, Polito told himself and laughed.

Yeah, Polito thought as he slipped into his jacket, there should be no problems. At least there'd be no problem getting into the hospital and checking it out. If Manzano's people were guarding Silvera's room he would have to figure out how they worked it and what kind of a schedule they were on and when to hit him. That might take a little time, but he had all weekend.

If Lou Savage wanted to go balling in the mountains that was his business, Polito thought. By the time he gets back, Louie Silvera is gonna be one dead fat man.

PART THREE

Chapter 21

EMILY HOVANNES HEARD the tires screech into the drive-way and sat up in bed. "Frank," she whispered urgently, and her husband sat up beside her. He took a few seconds to clear his head from sleep and then got out of bed when he heard a car door close. In the late night quiet the footsteps were clearly audible.

Naked at the window, Frank looked down to see a blue sedan he didn't recognize. The doorbell rang twice, two short blasts of noise. Frank pulled on a pair of pants, grabbed his shirt from the chair and his gun from the dresser. He hurried downstairs putting on the shirt as he went. Emily went to the closet for a robe.

"Who is it?" he asked at the door.

"Obregon."

Frank opened the door and his assistant stepped in. "We got trouble," he said. Hovannes turned and walked toward the living room without answering. Obregon followed him.

Emily, who had come partway down the stairs, stood watching them, holding her robe closed. When she heard the car pull up she had been afraid of God knew what, and now, seeing that it was Roberto Obregon, whom she recognized from her husband's squad, she didn't feel at all relieved. Whatever would get him waking them up at three in the morning couldn't be good.

Obregon nodded in her direction but didn't say anything. He was wearing a blue and white sport jacket that fit perfectly and mildly flared checked pants. It was the first time Emily had ever seen him dressed well, his short curly hair combed for a change, and she realized he must have been out on a date when something happened that sent him racing up to the Inspector's house. What did he tell the girl when he had to get rid of her so abruptly, she wondered. Then she heard her husband say her name and

179

she turned obediently and walked back up the stairs to the bedroom.

"Silvera's dead," Obregon said when he could no longer see the Inspector's wife at the top of the stairs.

"Killed?"

"Yeah, shot. Twice. I heard it on the radio. You'll probably get a call pretty soon."

"When?"

"Maybe forty-five minutes ago. I put my girl in a cab and came right up, figured you'd wanna know before they called from downtown."

Hovannes thought a minute, then he said, "Polito?"

Obregon nodded. "I couldn't come up with anything else," he answered.

"I'll be right down," Frank said and ran up the stairs. In the bedroom he pulled off his pants, put on a pair of shorts, and then put his pants back on. Emily, who had been standing by the window looking out into the clear half-moon night, went to the dresser to get him a pair of socks.

"There's been a shooting," he said, "I've got to go. If they call, tell them I'm on my way. Tell them Sergeant Obregon heard it on the radio and came to get me."

Emily walked to the bed and handed Frank the socks. She sat beside him as he unrolled them and pulled them on. "Be careful, Frank," she said.

He leaned over and kissed her lightly on the lips, then on the tip of her nose. "Tell them I left five minutes ago. Whenever they call, tell them five minutes ago, okay?"

"Sure."

"Don't worry," Frank reassured her. "The shooting's over."

Emily smiled weakly and followed her husband as he put on his shoes and hurried from the bedroom. "Frank," she called after him, stopping him when he was almost at the bottom of the stairs, "it wasn't one of your people, was it?"

Hovannes saw Obregon flinch but he knew what Emily meant and was pleased in a strange way by Obregon's momentary misunderstanding. It was like a reminder of normality. "No," he answered Emily, "it was that guy who was wounded in the shootout last Monday. The bodyguard. They finished him off tonight. I'll be back as soon as I can. Don't worry," he repeated.

Outside, as the two detectives walked to the car, Obregon said, "For a minute there I thought . . ."

"Yeah, I know," Hovannes cut him off. "You know where he lives?"

"Eighty-third, near Columbus."

Obregon raced down the West Side Highway, cut across town at Ninety-sixth Street to the park, and then down to Eighty-third. He didn't use the siren, but the warning light was flashing the whole way. When he pulled onto Eighty-third he turned off the flasher and removed it from the roof. "That's it," he said, pointing to a small remodeled brownstone on the north side of the street.

He pulled to the curb at the fireplug, got out of the car and came around to join the Inspector, who was already on the sidewalk. "Whatya gonna do?" he asked.

"What can we do?" Hovannes answered. "Let's see what it looks like."

"Inside, in the small foyer, the mailbox gave them Polito's apartment number, 3C, and Hovannes checked the glass inner door and found it was locked. He took out his wallet and removed his driver's license. Taking the license from its clear plastic sheath, he used the plastic to loid the door. Inside, they found a staircase behind a fire door opposite the elevator and walked up to three, Hovannes going first. At the third floor landing they both checked their guns but left them holstered.

The hallway was a little cube of space, not more than five by five, with four apartment doors opening onto it. C was on the same wall as the fire door, about three feet to their left in the corner. Hovannes knocked loudly, standing directly in front of the door—he had no choice—and Obregon took a position against the plaster wall between Polito's door and the door to the staircase.

A minute passed without any response, and then Polito's voice asked, "Who is it?"

"Hovannes. Open up."

The door opened as far as the chain lock would permit and Polito looked out, saw the Inspector, and closed the door again. The two detectives outside could hear the chain sliding in its receiver and the door opened again. Hovannes stepped in and Obregon followed, no one saying anything.

Polito's apartment looked like the furniture had come with it. Facing the entrance was a tiny kitchen, just large enough to stand in, with a half refrigerator built in underneath the sink. A brown bag with a couple of empty cans stood in front of the stove. The apartment itself was one room, with a bathroom off it. There was a couch on one wall, a bed on the other facing it, and a small formica table by the window in the far corner. The walls were bare.

"Lemme see your piece," Hovannes ordered.

Polito walked to a dresser by the door to the bathroom and took his off-duty gun, a heavy, nickel-plated forty-five automatic, from the top drawer. He brought it to the Inspector.

"This what you used?" Hovannes asked, removing the pistol and examining it.

"Yeah."

Obregon said, "Asshole, you must have waked up the whole hospital with that thing. You don't have anything smaller, huh?"

Polito shrugged. He had intended to use a twenty-two target pistol and had brought it with him. But when he found himself in Fat Louie Silvera's room he drew the forty-five without thinking. For a panicky moment he thought of putting it away and taking out the twenty-two. Silvera was just lying there and he had plenty of time to make a perfect shot, so the small caliber would have been enough. But he got off the two shots with the forty-five while he was still undecided and then ran like hell. Inside Silvera's room a door connected to the adjoining room and he raced to it. His luck was holding and it was unlocked. There was only an old man in the next room who couldn't possibly have seen anything, just waking up from the explosion of the shots. He passed through to the room beyond that, and then out to the corridor. Two nurses were running away from him, toward Silvera's room, and he made it to the stairway without being seen.

By this time he was thinking clearly enough to know he shouldn't take a cab home, so he walked across Forty-fourth Street all the way to Times Square, got the local up to Columbus Circle, and then switched to the IND. His first thought was to get rid of the piece, but it would be too easy to trace if it was found. In the end he decided they'd never do a ballistics check on his gun so the best thing would be to keep it.

Hovannes handed the gun back to him. "Don't use it," he said. "For anything."

"Yeah, sure," Polito answered, "sure."

He was still dressed in the clothes he had been wearing at Headquarters Friday afternoon. When he left the office he went straight home for his guns, leaving his service revolver in the dresser. Then he took a subway back downtown and walked across to the hospital, but there were too many people around so he went to the pay phone in the lobby and called the information desk to get Silvera's room number. Then he got a sandwich on Second Avenue and went to a movie, coming back to the hospital about nine-thirty. By that time the hospital had settled in for the night and he made it up to the seventh floor without attracting any attention. He looked into Silvera's room to check the layout.

Fat Louie was asleep and he could have done it then, but he figured later would be better, less people around, easier to get away. He left the hospital again, this time going out the rear entrance into the parking lot. Behind the parking lot was the FDR Drive and Polito found a footbridge over it and crossed into the park bordering the East River. He stayed there until after one o'clock, moodily pacing along the waterfront, resting from time to time on a bench from which he could see the looming bulk of the hospital. Except for a bunch of dog walkers between eleven and twelve, the park was mostly deserted.

Some time after one o'clock he went back to the hospital, surprising himself with how easy it was to get in and up to the seventh floor. He walked up, determined to call the whole thing off if he was seen, but everything went without a hitch. With the long walk to Times Square afterward—slow enough not to call attention to himself, but not too slow either—and the interminable waits for two subways, he hadn't been home more than a half hour when Hovannes knocked on the door. When he got home he just put his gun in the dresser, hung up his jacket, and sat on the couch, not waiting for anything really, but not wanting to sleep either.

As he went over the whole thing in his mind he was sure he had done everything right. Except for the gun, but even that worked out okay. When Obregon said, "Did anyone see you?" he answered confidently, "No, no one. It was perfect."

"Perfect!" Obregon shot back. "What was the big fucking idea anyway?"

Polito bristled. "I'm in this thing as much as you are," he said. "If that guy ever figures out who the Inspector is, it's gonna be my ass too."

Obregon started to answer him, but Hovannes cut him off. "Forget it," he said, "it's done." Then he asked Polito, "How'd you find out his room number?"

"I called from a pay phone."

"And you're sure no one saw you?"

"Yeah," Polito answered sharply. He had told them that already.

"Okay," Hovannes concluded. He turned and walked back to the door, Obregon following him. Outside it was starting to get light in the east, over Central Park.

On the sidewalk Obregon said, "That guy's gonna be trouble, boss."

"That guy *is* trouble, Roberto," Hovannes corrected. "But he's got us by the balls—we can't exactly book him for homicide, can we? At least Silvera's dead, you gotta give him that."

Chapter 22

JACK KITTENS SWUNG the door open just seconds after Frank Hovannes pushed the bell, but it was immediately clear that he was expecting someone else.

"This'll just take a minute," Hovannes said.

Kittens hadn't seen the Inspector since October, when they met near the top of the Empire State Building to talk about Sallie Manzano's hijacking ring, and there was no way Kittens wanted to see him again. Especially not showing up at his house like this.

"The fuck it will," he said. "I got no business with you."

"Invite me in, Jack, I gotta ask you some questions. The trouble with you is you're too suspicious."

"What kinda questions?"

"About Richie Saint."

"Oh—yeah," Kittens said, stepping back from the door to let the Inspector in. It stood to reason that Hovannes would want to question him about that—no harm in it. He looked into the hallway before closing the door, but no one was there. "That was too bad about Richie, huh, Inspector?" he said as he followed Hovannes toward the living room.

"Really, Jack? You'll do okay."

"Come on, Inspector, you got no call to talk like that," Kittens whined. "Richie was good to me, there was no reason he shoulda been hit."

Hovannes shrugged. The word was already out that Kittens was taking over Richie Saint's business, so his former manager's death had left him in a pretty comfortable position.

"If that's how you feel, Jack, maybe you can help us. You know who did it?" Hovannes asked.

"I know what I hear."

"Whatdya hear?"

"I hear Tommie Minelli."

Hovannes smiled. That was what he had heard, too, and

185

it was nice to know that Kittens didn't mind telling him. Not that Kittens liked helping the cops if he had a choice, but he had been very close to Richie Saint and probably didn't much care who got to Minelli first.

"Know where he is?" Hovannes asked.

"If I knew that I could make myself five grand. You want him, you're gonna have to find him, but you better hurry up."

"There's a contract out on him?"

"Look, Inspector, I wouldn't know a thing like that," Kittens said evasively. "I just know I wouldn't wanna be Tommie Minelli. You figure it out."

"This is a nice place you got here, Jack," Hovannes said, looking around. It was a lot more than he had expected and not at all the way he would have pictured an ex-pug like Kittens living. The floor was covered in a thick cream-colored carpet and the furniture was all very modern, a lot of chrome and glass and leather. From the window you could see all the way to the East River.

"Thanks," Kittens said. "Look, I don't wanna be rude or anything, but that's about all I can tell you. I'd help you on this thing if I could. Richie was good to me and I'd just as soon you got Minelli as anyone else."

"Yeah, I know," Hovannes said, turning from the window. It wasn't hard to like Jack Kittens. "There's some other things I gotta know, too, Jack. Why was he hit?"

"I told you—it was Tommie Minelli. You need a why?"

"Just Minelli? That's all there is to it?"

"Sure. Look, if Minelli was working under orders, you think Manzano'd want to have him hit now?"

"Manzano?" Hovannes said, pretending to be surprised.

"Sure, who else?" Kittens said, then realized that he hadn't wanted to tell Hovannes about that. "Look," he said, "forget where you heard that, will ya. I figured you knew."

"No sweat. But what's all this got to do with Sallie getting iced?"

"Hey, Inspector," Kittens protested, "you wanted to talk to me about Richie, I talk about Richie. Okay, that's police business. But I'm not on your pad. You forget about that thing last fall, you know what I mean. That was then, this is now. We got nothing to talk about."

"If that's the way you want it, Jackie," Hovannes said, moving for the door. "I figured you could help me, I could help you."

"What kinda help you talking about?" Kittens asked, interested.

"I'm talking about something's coming down between Eddie Manzano and Tony the Lawyer. One of them's gonna shaft the other, right? So if we get any kind of help at all we get whoever's left. That's what they call a golden opportunity for a guy like you, Jack."

Kittens didn't think about it more than five seconds. "You gotta get outta here, Hovannes," he said. "I got company coming. I'll get in touch with you. Right now I don't know that much, but I'll see what I can find out."

"You do that, Jack," Frank said.

As he put his hand on the door the bell chimed twice. Frank opened it and found himself facing a very tall young, man, slender, even skinny, with long greasy hair and badly pockmarked skin. He was about two or three inches taller than Hovannes, was wearing a plaid wool shirt and smelled bad. Frank didn't recognize him.

"This your company, Jack?" he said. "How'd he get past the doorman?"

Kittens didn't answer and the Inspector stepped past the stranger and walked down the dim, thickly carpeted corridor toward the elevator without turning back.

"Who was that?" Fran Marks asked after he had stepped into Kittens' apartment and closed the door behind him.

"The heat. Cmon in," Kittens answered matter of factly.

"A cop, huh? That wasn't Hovannes, was it?"

"Yeah, how'd you know?"

"Just a guess," Marks said.

The two police informants walked into the living room and sat down, Marks on the long couch and Kittens in a brown-orange chair with his back at the window. Kittens always handled his contacts with the FBI and with Hovannes carefully, and he never had any reason to fear that anyone knew he was an informant. But Marks seeing Hovannes at his house like that, and then his questions, put the ex-fighter on guard. So when Marks asked, "What'd he want?" Kittens' first response was, "Is that any of your business?" Then, immediately, he added, "He wanted to ask me some questions about Richie."

"What'd you tell him?"

"Didn't tell him shit, what could I tell him?" Kittens

said, and then tried to change the subject. "You said you wanted to see me. Whatdya want?"

"I been looking for you since Friday night. Where you been?"

"I've been staying up at Richie's place," Kittens answered impatiently. It seemed like Marks was pumping him. "It's empty," he added, "and I thought maybe I'd move up there. I'm getting kinda tired of this place."

Marks didn't say anything and Kittens began to get a little more edgy. There was no way this guy could know anything, he told himself. But then why is he coming out with all these questions? He decided to play it cool and see what Marks had to say.

On the other side of the room Fran Marks squinted across at Kittens, whose head, over the top of his chair, was framed in the brilliant blue spring sky. The tops of two tall apartment buildings rose just beyond his shoulders, to his left and right. But mostly what Marks saw was bright sky and he had trouble making out Kittens's punching-bag features in the shadowy living room.

Fran was nervous too. Ever since he left Lou Savage Friday afternoon he had been trying to figure out what he would say to Kittens. He wanted to find out if his suspicions were right that Savage was on Eddie Manzano's pad and if anyone knew that he had been selling information to Savage. But of course he couldn't come right out and ask without giving himself away. He had to be careful what he said or Kittens would start wondering.

Marks fished a cigarette from his shirt pocket and lit it. There was no ashtray around so he held the match after shaking it out.

"What I wanted to talk to you about, Jack, is this," he began. "All this shit that's coming down's got me worried."

"Got you worried!" Kittens laughed. "What's a little shit like you got to worry about?"

Marks didn't mind the insult. "Well, that's just it," he said "All I want to do is tend to business, know what I mean? I got a nice little business, you know, and if everything blows up I just wanna clear a space where I can land.

"It's got nothing to do with you, Francis," Kittens answered, relieved that that was all Marks wanted to see him about. "You come down the same place no matter what happens." He rose from his chair and walked past Marks to the entranceway, then came back with a glass ashtray and handed it to Fran. "Want a drink or something?" he asked.

Marks shook his head and took the ashtray from his host. He put it on the cushion next to him, rested his cigarette in it and pulled a wadded handkerchief from his pocket. He blew his nose with it and stuffed it back into his pocket, then wiped at his nose with the back of his hand. Kittens went back to his chair by the window.

"I don't know," Marks said when Jack was seated again. So far everything was going the way he had figured and he was confident that if he handled it right he could find out what he wanted to know. "Look," he explained, "I get all my stuff through Paulie Gagliano, right? If Eddie Manzano and LaGarda have it out, and if LaGarda goes down Paulie goes down too, and where does that leave me? See what I mean?"

"It leaves you working for Manzano. What the fuck do you care?" Kittens said impatiently. "You got some reason you don't wanna work for Eddie?"

"No, of course not," Marks shot back quickly. Was that a test question, he wondered. Was Kittens jiving him because he knew Marks couldn't possibly work for Manzano when Manzano knew he was a pigeon? "Of course not," he repeated. "But how do I know? What if Manzano wants his own people to run the business? Then I'm out on my ass."

Kittens shrugged. "It's happened before, Francis," he said. "Whatdya want me to say? Maybe you guys oughta unionize."

"I'm not joking, Jack," Marks said. "I'm worried, know what I mean?"

He tapped his cigarette toward the ashtray and missed, ashes splattering on the leather cushion. With his hand he brushed them away.

"Yeah, you're worried," Kittens said. "Everybody's worried. Like I said, whatdya want from me?"

Fran took another drag from his cigarette and then ground it out. Kittens' answer to the next question might tell him where he stood.

"Well, that's just it, Jack," he said. "I was thinking maybe it's not a good thing for me to stay with Paulie Gagliano. If he doesn't come through this thing awright I could be out of business. Then I got to thinking with Richie dead you'll probably be running his business. We've known each other a long time, Jack, and I was thinking maybe I could work for you."

Jack Kittens didn't like the sound of that and his suspicions started rushing back. He stood up and walked around the chair to face the window. With his back to the room he said, "I don't deal junk, you know that, Francis."

Marks stood up to and walked halfway across the living room toward Kittens, who turned to face him.

"Yeah, I know," he said, "but I could do other things too. I mean it doesn't have to be junk, know what I mean?"

That was the idea. If Jack took him on it would mean he hadn't heard any flak about Marks being a pigeon. But if he said no it might mean that Jack didn't trust him and wanted to keep clear. Might or might not.

Kittens, though, was looking at it from a different angle. What he had to ask himself was, Was this some kind of shakedown? If didn't make sense that a junk dealer like Marks would want to tie in with him. Everybody knew Richie Saint never touched the stuff and he didn't either, so there'd be no way for Marks to fit into his organization.

He turned away from Marks again, slid open the glass door to the balcony and stepped out onto it. The balcony was still in the building's shadow and it was cool. Thirty stories down he could see Ninetieth Street with its light Sunday traffic, and to his left was Central Park. A flock of bicyclists headed north up the main drive and beyond them the reservoir glinted in the sunshine. Then he turned the other way to face the East River.

Maybe that's what it is, he said to himself. This prick found out I was dealing with Hovannes—shit, I knew I never should of done it—and now he wants me to put him on the payroll to keep his mouth shut. Kittens glanced over his shoulder and saw Marks hovering just on the other side of the glass door. Francis didn't like being up that high and wouldn't have stepped out on that balcony for anything. Kittens looked at him contemptuously, from his oily face down to where his ratty tennis shoes ate into the carpet as he bounced nervously on his toes waiting for an answer.

How could this creep know, Kittens thought, and then

he reminded himself, What did that matter? Well, there was one way to find out—turn him down. If he was holding any trumps, he'd play them and then they could talk business. If not, he'd just go away.

Kittens stepped back into the living room, leaving the door open behind him, and walked to the sideboard near the entranceway. Marks followed him like a puppy. Jack pulled a pipe from the rack on the sideboard and stuffed it quickly with tobacco from the walnut humidifier. Then he turned to face Marks, who had been hanging just over his shoulder and stepped back instinctively.

"I'm sorry, Francis," he said. "I don't think so."

Oh shit, Marks thought, but he didn't say anything.

Chapter 23

MONDAY IS A QUIET NIGHT for the Caffe Fidelio, as it is for most restaurants. In the dining room there were only three couples and they were finishing their meals. Two waiters sat at a table by the door to the kitchen, talking about the Yankees, who were off to a good start, and killing time until they could clear the tables.

In the kitchen the cook sat on a short stool, his back against the stainless steel dish cabinet and his feet resting on the rim of a large plastic garbage pail. He was the second cook—Monday was the chef's night off—and he always enjoyed having nothing to do. His assistant was cleaning up, putting away vegetables that wouldn't be used until tomorrow. The potwasher had gone out, as he did whenever he could get a few free minutes.

"That Jerry, he's crazy I think," the cook said.

The assistant didn't even look up from what he was doing.

"The dice, always with the dice," the cook went on. "Cleans up from the soup and then"—pantomiming a crap shooter—"and then he runs in again. 'What's to do, Louie?' He washes three plates and he's gone again. He's crazy, what's he do it for?"

"Did you ever think maybe he wins?" the assistant said, moving toward the refrigerator with bundles of wrapped vegetables cradled in his arms.

"Pah!" The cook spat into the garbage pail, the large drop of spittle passing precisely between his feet. "If he wins, what's he washing pots here for, tell me that, huh?"

From the refrigerator the assistant said, "Whatdya have me take out so much stuff for on a Monday? Every Monday it's the same thing. Now I gotta put it all away."

"So? Put it away."

"Just makes more work," the assistant complained. "Whatdya gotta make more work for all the time?"

The cook wasn't thinking about that. "Ya know, I know

his Pappa," he said. "Maybe I should tell him. He's gonna get himself in trouble, always with the dice. Someone's gotta straighten that kid out."

Outside, Tommie and Mickey Minelli stood at the corner of Hester and Elizabeth streets. They had come by subway from the East Bronx because Tommie didn't want anyone seeing his car. He lit a cigarette and in a low voice he said to his brother, "Ya got it straight, Mickey?"

"Yeah, I got it straight," Mickey answered impatiently. "Let's get this over with."

He rubbed both hands hard against his thighs, drying them. He was afraid of what was coming next, but even more afraid to be standing out there on the street where anyone could see them and get a couple of bills for telling Eddie Manzano where they were.

Tommie took a slow drag from his cigarette and let the smoke curl from his lips. His eyes were trained toward the doorway to the Fidelio and his brother stood beside him. Without looking at Mickey he repeated, "I said, you got it straight, Mickey?"

"Yeah, I hold 'em in the kitchen. C'mon, Tommie," Mickey pleaded.

"What's the matter? You scared?"

"Yeah I'm scared. I'm scared shitless, aren't you?"

Tommie Minelli snapped his cigarette into the gutter. "C'mon," he said.

The two brothers walked west on Hester Street to Mott, turned down Mott, and then moved purposefully past three stores until they came to a narrow alley. A back door to the Fidelio opened onto the alley and when they were out of sight from the street they pulled their guns. Quietly, Tommie first, they approached the door. It was partly opened. Even before his younger brother realized it was happening already, Tommie stepped into the kitchen and Mickey had no choice but to follow.

In a very soft voice, Tommie said, "Don't move."

He said it so softly the assistant, who was wiping down a countertop, said, "What?"

The cook turned his head to look over his shoulder and saw two men, one behind the other, with drawn guns. His feet stayed on the garbage pail.

"I said don't move," Tommie Minelli hissed. This time there was something menacing in his voice and the assistant turned. When he saw the Minelli brothers he gasped involuntarily and froze where he was standing. The two brothers moved sideways along the wall until they had the cook and the assistant lined up in front of them. "Stay here," Tommie said.

Mickey's eyes darted in both directions as he checked to make sure he could see the swinging door to the dining room and the back door out onto the alley. He could. If anyone came in either way he could handle it. "Okay," he said.

Tommie stuffed his forty-five automatic into his belt and zipped his windbreaker closed just over the handle of it. Then he walked to the dining room door, which swung toward him when he was almost there. A waiter in a red jacket pushed through backwards, carrying a trayful of dirty dishes. As he pivoted clear of the door he spotted Mickey Minelli with his gun drawn in the middle of the kitchen, and then he noticed Tommie just a few feet away. His eyes went back to Mickey, who motioned him with his gun to move to the counter where the assistant was standing. No one said a word.

Tommie looked out through the glass porthole. There were two couples seated at tables. Another couple stood at the front of the restaurant, paying another red-jacketed waiter who stood at the register behind a short counter. Tommie stepped through the door and the waiter looked across at him briefly, then went back to counting out change. Minelli turned to his right and took four quick steps to an unmarked wooden door. In one move he pushed open the door with his left hand, pulled his forty-five, from his belt with his right and stepped into the office.

There were three men inside. They didn't say anything and Tommie Minelli didn't either. Tony LaGarda was seated at his desk, directly facing Minelli. Jimmie Monks was behind the desk, standing over Tony's right shoulder, also facing Minelli. Paulie Gagliano, who was in a chair to Minelli's right, turned to the door when he heard it open and saw the others look that way.

A few seconds passed while Minelli and his three hostages all took stock of the situation. LaGarda, Monks, and Gagliano quickly realized there was nothing they could do. When Tommie saw this he said, "Which one of you's Tony LaGarda?"

Monks and Gagliano both restrained an impulse to look at Tony.

"I'm LaGarda," Tony said without hesitating.

"I'm Tommie Minelli. I wanna talk." His voice went uncontrollably squeaky as he said it. He leaned his back against the door and it clicked closed.

"You got the gun, talk," LaGarda said, a faint edge in his voice that was perhaps sarcasm but not quite defiance.

"Eddie Manzano's got a contract out on me," Tommie began and stopped. He thought he saw Gagliano move, but it was nothing.

"Yeah, well, you don't need that thing in here," LaGarda said to him. "We don't want any of Eddie's money."

Minelli nodded but didn't put the gun away. It was still trained on Paulie Gagliano, but he could have hit any of the three of them in a second.

"Eddie Manzano's got a contract out on me," he repeated, "so now I'm working for you."

"You pull a gun on me and tell me you're working for me? What kind of a thing is that?" LaGarda said sharply.

Tommie wasn't really listening. "Me and Mickey," he added.

LaGarda didn't say anything and Tommie glanced nervously from Gagliano over to him and then to Monks and then back to Gagliano. He was pale as a ghost and his lips were cracked and dry. He had been hiding out since he killed Richie Saint last Tuesday, at first just to lay low for a while and then because he heard Eddie wanted to do a number on him. He knew there was no one he could turn to. Eddie's people were looking for him, Richie Saint's friends might want to get their hands on him, and maybe the cops too. So he and Mickey stayed in this empty one-room apartment in the East Bronx, sleeping on the floor and eating dry cereal from a bodega around the corner.

LaGarda said, "You don't give up any choice, do you?"

Minelli's tongue flicked across his lips but he didn't say anything.

"Okay," Tony said, like he had just thought over a proposition. "Whatdya have in mind?"

Again Tommie took his eyes off Gagliano to look at Tony and then Monks for a moment, but then his attention went back to Paulie. The gun had stayed on him all along. "Me and Mickey are gonna work for you," Minelli repeated.

While he talked to LaGarda he didn't stop looking at Paulie Gagliano. He was obviously confused and tense, and

Tony couldn't tell if he was stupid or just crazy. For a minute he thought that if he told him to go fuck himself the kid wouldn't know what to do. But it would be too risky, so he just repeated, trying to keep his voice flat and reassuring, "Sure, whatdya have in mind?"

"We'll waste Manzano for you," Tommie said.

Jimmie Monks grabbed his boss's shoulder impulsively. "Tony, it's a double cross," he blurted out, then fell silent.

Minelli's eyes and the gun swung around toward Monks, not really because of what he said—Tommie was hardly following it—but because of his quick movement and because his voice was loud and abrupt.

"You can do it?" LaGarda asked, ignoring Jimmie's warning.

Minelli nodded. Now it was Monks he wouldn't take his eyes off.

"Yeah, sure. You're dead if you don't," Tony said quietly, thinking out loud. Tommie nodded again, slowly, his head just bobbing slightly.

"This brother of yours," LaGarda asked, "where is he?"

With his gun in his right hand, Tommie waved toward the wall between the office and the kitchen.

"We'll work something out," LaGarda said. "Put that thing away."

Chapter 24

"HELLO, INSPECTOR, I'm glad you could come," Celia Maldonado said. "Sergeant Obregon's here already. He's in the living room with Lou."

Hovannes handed her his hat and waited while she opened a closet door and put it away. When she stepped out of the closet he was looking at her and she smiled awkwardly and then led the way to the living room.

The apartment was laid out in one of those unusual arrangements that sometimes happen in older buildings when large apartments are subdivided. The front door opened onto a long corridor, maybe eighteen feet, which was uninterrupted except for the closet door near the entrance. It was the sort of corridor that would look like a dark tube no matter what anyone did with it, but it was hung with half a dozen bright posters and a few other things that Hovannes noticed as he passed and immediately forgot. Toward the far end a door to the left opened onto a bathroom and right beyond that was the bedroom. Opposite the bedroom door was the entrance to the living room, a very large, squarish room with a small dining area and kitchen off it to the left.

Hovannes followed Celia, who walked rapidly in front of him. She had a small, well-shaped body, slender with rounded hips and a very thin waist. As she walked the cuffs of her widely belled pants rustled softly.

Frank caught up with her before they got to the living room and touched her lightly on the arm. She turned to face him.

"I was wondering," he said quietly so that Savage and Obregon wouldn't hear, "do you still feel the same way you did last fall?"

Celia knew what he was referring to but pretended not to. "What's that?" she asked. Her warm brown eyes locked on the Inspector's face.

She was prettier than Frank had remembered, but then

he hadn't seen her up this close last November. There was a firmness about her that was impressive—just in her body, as she stood directly facing him, feet slightly apart, but also in her mouth and eyes. He could tell she knew what he had been referring to.

"You said you didn't think Lou should be working for me," Frank reminded her.

"I said I thought he was doing more important work when he was in Narcotics," Celia corrected. "Yes, I still feel that way."

She turned and walked into the living room with Frank a few steps behind her. Lou Savage was at the opposite end of the room, sitting sideways in an old tan sofa with soft, frayed cushions. His back rested against the arm and his left leg was stretched across the cushion, dangling from the ankle. Obregon sat on the floor, resting against a blue stuffed chair. Neither got up when the Inspector came in. It was a social occasion and he wouldn't have expected them to.

"It's about time you got here, Inspector. Maybe now we can eat," Obregon joked.

Savage said, "I'm glad you could make it, Frank. Can I get you something to drink?"

"That beer looks pretty good."

Obregon said, "Yeah, it tasted pretty good too. I could use another."

Lou started to get up, but Celia stopped him. "I'll get it, I'm up," she said and went into the kitchen. A few seconds later she came back with three cans of Budweiser and a glass. "You still got half of yours," she said to Lou. "It'll only get warm."

Frank took a glass and one of the cans from her, pulled the tab and poured the beer quickly, straight down the center to make a thick head. Celia deliverd the second can to Roberto and opened the third one for herself.

For a few awkward seconds no one said anything. Celia went to the couch and sat at the far end from Lou, who moved his foot slightly to make room for her. Frank was still standing, with the empty beer can in one hand and the glass in the other, and Celia said, "Why don't you come over here, Roberto, and let the Inspector sit there." To Frank she added, "It's the most comfortable chair in the house."

"Do I look that old?" Frank asked playfully.

"It's not age, Inspector, it's rank," she answered, also playfully, but perhaps with a slight edge to it.

Obregon got up from the floor and walked to the couch, then sat back down on the floor by the corner of the sofa where Celia was sitting. Frank took the blue chair. It was comfortable. He put the empty can on the floor and looked across at the three of them. The fingers of Lou's right hand were tapping methodically in sequence on the thin upholstery and the nervous silence returned until Celia broke it by saying, "What Roberto said, Inspector, he was just kidding. We weren't really waiting. Dinner won't be ready for another half hour."

"Is it really *paella?*" Roberto asked.

"Sure, in your honor, Roberto," Celia said.

Frank said, "Is there anything in my honor?"

"Yeah, *paella*. It's in everybody's honor."

Hovannes and Obregon both laughed slightly, mostly for form's sake.

Lou said, "Have you checked the oven lately?"

"About fifteen minutes ago."

"Maybe I'd better check again," he volunteered, getting up and walking to the kitchen.

"This oven is worse than a geranium," Celia explained. "If you don't talk to it nice it does terrible things."

"A geranium?" Obregon asked, tipping his head back to look up at her.

"Yeah," she said, "if you don't talk to a geranium all it'll do is die. It won't ruin dinner."

"You talk to flowers?"

"Yes," Celia said. "They're not like people. You have to talk to them or they'll die."

As she spoke her voice seemed to get deeper and Frank thought he detected a trace of the rich Latin texture Obregon had picked up on the phone months before. He wanted to challenge her, to say, "And you don't have to talk to people?" But he decided against it and just said, "And when you talk to them they don't die, is that it?"

"No," Celia laughed, and the huskiness went out of her voice, "they all die anyway. But this way I don't feel bad about it."

"You're wise for your years," Frank teased and Celia nodded gravely, her lips pursed.

Just then Lou came back into the living room. "Sometimes I think Celia's a human defoliant," he said as he returned to the couch. "I figured out once if we ever really wanna put all the shit dealers out of business the thing to do is send Celia to Turkey to grow poppies."

It was a funny line but Lou didn't say it like it was funny and nobody laughed.

"Your wife has such a beautiful garden. Maybe she could give me lessons, Inspector," Celia said to cover over the blank.

"Frank," Hovannes corrected. "Yeah, I'm sure she'd be glad to."

"Maybe I'll do that," Celia said lightly. "In fact if that ivy dies, I'll definitely do that. Does she make house calls?"

"Only in emergencies."

Celia turned to Lou. "How was the oven?" she asked.

"It was a little hot. I turned it down."

"How hot's a little hot?"

"About four-fifty."

"Four-fifty? Maybe it's done already."

"No," Lou said. "Five minutes. Maybe ten."

Frank's glass was still half full and he finished it with a few long cold gulps. Celia stood up and walked toward the kitchen. "I've got to get the salad ready. Do you want another beer, Inspector?"

"Yeah, but it's Frank," he said, and to Lou, who seemed preoccupied again, he added, "You've got a terrific girl, Lou. Any girl who knows when a guy needs another beer, you oughta hold onto."

Celia stopped just short of the entrance to the kitchen. "Woman," she said. "If you don't say girl I won't say Inspector."

There was something about the arch way she teased that excited Frank in a strange way. It wasn't sexual, he was sure of that. He had only met her once before, and even then he had noticed a sort of assured self-possession about her that let her say things other people wouldn't know how to take. Frank had never put much stock in talking but Celia seemed like someone you could find a challenge in talking to. She was probably damned smart too, Frank thought, and was sorry he hadn't asked her whether people die if they're not talked to, or only plants.

"I keep forgetting," he apologized. "There's a lieutenant down at Headquarters, a woman, and she once sent out a memo about that. But I keep forgetting. Maybe it's my age. When you reach a certain age, Celia, everyone looks like a girl."

"Come on, Inspector," Celia laughed, posed at the entrance to the kitchen, her back straight, even slightly arched, and her feet apart. "Don't tell me you can't tell the difference between a girl and a woman."

She had lovely breasts, not large, but fuller than you might have expected on her slender body. Her shirt was a bright print in some kind of thin cottony material, and the shape of her soft nipples was visible through it. Hovannes didn't say anything, and Obregon joked, "If he can't I can, Celia. Does that get me another beer?"

"*Por supuesto,*" Celia answered. "*Dos cervezas.*"

After she brought the beers and returned to the kitchen there were only a few minutes until dinner. "I didn't get a chance to ask you," Obregon said to Frank. "Did Kittens go for the idea?"

"What idea?" Lou asked, dropping his feet from the couch and sitting up straight.

"The Inspector figured he could sign up Jack Kittens to keep us posted on what's going on."

"How's that work?" Lou wanted to know.

"You know who Kittens is?" Hovannes asked.

"More or less," Lou said, then added, "not really."

"He used to be Richie Saint's number one man," Hovannes explained. "Now he wants to be Richie Saint, and more if he can. Anyway, he's well connected, always knows a helluva lot. And I figured he'd keep us posted on what kinds of reactions we're getting."

"What's in it for him?"

Frank shrugged. "I told him if LaGarda and Manzano have it out, one of them's gotta lose. Then if he helps us we get the winner and that gives him a clear field."

"And he fell for it?"

"Nothing to fall for really," Hovannes said. "It's true. Anyway, I got the feeling he likes the idea."

From the kitchen Celia called them to dinner. In the center of the table was a gorgeous *paella,* full of shrimp and lobster pieces, chicken and sausages, the lemon-yellow rice studded with large green peas and chunks of bell pepper among the pieces of fish and meat. Celia was opening a bottle of white wine with a straight corkscrew.

Dinner passed with pleasant small talk, mostly between Celia and Obregon. Roberto tried to talk her into giving him guitar lessons, but she protested that she was a violinist and played the guitar only well enough to get by. Hovannes who had never had *paella* before and expected something very spicy, was pleasantly surprised by the onion and tomato mildness of the dish, which was almost sweet from the shrimp and an especially good lobster.

When they finished eating, Celia was the first one up from the table. "Lou, will you make coffee if anyone wants it? I have to go."

"Sure," Lou answered.

"You leaving?" Obregon asked, his disappointment obvious.

Celia looked at Lou for a moment without saying anything and then answered Roberto. "Yeah," she said. "I hate to run out like this. But I'm in a quartet and we've got to rehearse."

Hovannes and Obregon had stood up just after Celia did, but Lou was still seated at the table in the corner of the dining alcove, his back to the wall. His fingers were tapping slowly on the tabletop. Celia saw it and recognized his impatience. "I'm sorry but I really have to go," she said. "I'm late. I'm glad you could come, Inspector, and you too, Roberto."

She turned and left the room. Hovannes and Obregon both stood where they were as long as they could hear the rapid beat of her footsteps as she hurried down the long corridor. When he heard the front door close behind her, Frank was immediately aware that her departure changed the whole evening. Now he was the commander alone with his men. The dinner was gone and the uncleared plates on the table and the *paella* pan with a few spoonfuls of rice and a scattering of unclaimed vegetables looked like they must have been left by someone else. Was this what Lou had in mind from the start, Frank wondered. He had seemed preoccupied the whole evening. It would explain why he had asked him not to bring Emily.

"Do you wanna save this?" Obregon asked, indicating the *paella* pan.

Lou looked into it for a few seconds, like it had just said something to him he didn't understand. "Nah," he said, "it's just rice."

With a fork Obregon brushed what was left on the plates into the pan, stacked the plates, and carried them to the sink. Hovannes didn't offer to help and Lou didn't get up from where he was sitting.

"Where's the coffee?" Roberto asked when he was finished.

"Don't bother for me," Hovannes said. "I'd just as soon have another beer."

Lou said, "Yeah," and stood up heavily, using the table to lift himself. "What about you, Roberto? Coffee?"

"Beer's fine."

Lou walked to the refrigerator and took out three cold Budweisers, handed them around, and led the way to the living room. Obregon sat on the floor again, this time facing the couch, and Lou and the Inspector took the same seats as before. Almost in unison each pulled the tab on his can and took a long gulp of stingingly cold beer.

"Okay," Hovannes said, "what's the problem?"

Lou looked into the keyhole-shaped opening in the top of the can, which he held in his right hand while the index finger of his left hand traced three quarters of a circle back and forth around the rim. "I guess it's me," he said softly. "I think I gotta get out."

Obregon started to say something but Hovannes stopped him with a hand signal. "Why?" he asked. He didn't sound surprised and he wasn't.

"I think it's Polito," Lou said, looking up at the Inspector to see if he understood. Hovannes's face didn't tell him anything. "I know what you said," he went on. "You and I shouldn't come in unless I thought it was right. Well I did, at least I think I did, but I don't know anymore."

"Because of Polito?" Hovannes asked.

Lou was grateful for that—yeah, the Inspector understood. "He's bothered me all along," he said, mumbling his words in a tone that made them sound like a confession. "I mean, I know why I signed on. It seemed like it was the only way. I thought about it and it seemed like it was right. These guys are just fucking over everybody and somebody had to stop them. That seemed right, do you know what I mean? But that's not what it is with Polito, at least I don't think it is. And with someone like that in on it, it makes the whole thing different."

"Don't be dumb, Lou," Obregon said, jumping to his feet, his tone more impatient than angry. "All right, Polito's a thug with a shield. But that's what he was before we started. Did that make it wrong to be a cop?"

Lou looked at Obregon searchingly for fully half a minute before he answered. "Maybe it did," he said. "I knew a lot of guys in Narco who were on the take when I was there, and sometimes that's the way I felt. They made it wrong to be a cop, they sure as hell did. That's part of the reason I wanted to get out of there, and maybe that's why I signed on for this thing."

"We were pure, is that it?" Obregon said, almost taunting.

"I wouldn't put it that way," Lou answered. "But yeah, I think that's it."

"And with Polito it's not pure?"

Lou didn't answer this time. He turned to Hovannes, "I'm sorry, Frank, but I want out. Can you understand that?"

"No," Hovannes said flatly, "he's got nothing to do with you. I didn't know what to think myself after the Silvera thing, a guy who could just go and put two bullets in a guy in a hospital bed. And I couldn't touch him. I couldn't touch him because I put him in that position, put him where he had us by the balls and if we busted him the whole story would come out—you, me, Roberto, the whole fucking Department—and he knew it. So I gave him a license to go put two slugs into Fat Louie. But you didn't do that, Lou, I did. He's my mistake, but it's got nothing to do with you."

Lou stared at Hovannes for a few seconds without saying anything, feeling strangely cornered and at bay. He had known all along that the Inspector would say something like that and he didn't have an answer for it, but it didn't change the way he felt.

"It's not just the Silvera thing," he protested. "I had this feeling all along. I mean, the Silvera thing he was going against orders and you couldn't do anything about it. Sure, okay. But when he killed Palmini I had the same feeling. He's a killer, know what I mean? We planned the Palmini thing together. I would have done it myself if that was the way we worked it out. At least I think I would have, it wouldn't have bothered me. But something about Polito doing it gave me the creeps. You were with him when he did it, Roberto. What was it like? He's a killer, isn't that right?"

Obregon walked slowly across the room between the Inspector and Savage until he was at Celia's desk. His eyes scanned the two rows of books on shelves suspended from wall standards above the desk and he remembered that when Dumb Al Palmini saw where they were taking him, down along the abandoned piers and warehouses under the West Side Highway, he started to panic. Obregon was afraid to pull a gun on him because he knew that Palmini would be easier to handle if he just thought they were going to work him over. So he just hit him across the mouth and Palmini quieted down. Then Polito stopped the car and got out. He opened the back door where Palmini was sitting and Palmini started to climb out. His feet were on the ground and he was hardly off the seat at all when a bullet from Ron Polito's service revolver ripped into his stomach, dead center, fired from less than a foot and a half away. Palmini started to fall back toward Obregon, but Ron reached in with his left hand and caught him by the front of his shirt, pulled him from the car and dropped him to the ground. As he fell his head hit the metal panel under where the door closed. Obregon didn't move. From where he was sitting he couldn't see Palmini's body lying on the ground, couldn't tell if he was moving. There were two more shots and then Ron bent down and thrust his head through the open door where he had just pulled Palmini out. "Let's put him up there on that pier," was what he said.

Roberto turned from the bookcase to face Lou. "Yeah," he conceded, "he's a killer."

"Well, I'm not!" Lou shot back.

This time it was Hovannes who heard without knowing what to say. "What'll you do?" he asked. "Go back to Narco?"

"Yeah, I think so," Lou said dully. "Celia wants me to."

"What if we wrapped this thing up?" Frank asked. "I hate to lose you, Lou. Would you stay in OCC then?"

"I don't know," Lou said. "I don't think so. I'd like to tell you yes, Frank, but I don't know. Maybe."

Maybe was enough for Frank. He lit a cigarette and took a short sip of beer. "I wanna tell you something, Lou. You too, Roberto. Before Ernie Fleming was killed we talked about doing something like this. We both figured that if the case against Manzano fell through maybe we'd go out and take care of him ourselves. Remember that guy you told me in November got hit, Lou? You said you heard maybe some of LaGarda's people had gunned one of Manzano's soldiers. Well, that was Angie Morello. Ernie did it, I was there, down on Greene Street, that night we waited for the load from south Jersey and then they found the truck. I don't know why he did it, but I've got some pretty good ideas. Frustration in part. And maybe he wanted to show me it could be done, and prove it to himself. In a way I guess he was just declaring war. He was saying, I've had it up to here with this shit. Now me and my partner are coming down on you and we're coming down so fucking hard you cocksuckers won't know what hit you. It was all those things, but mostly the frustration, I guess. Anyway, we put Morello back in the warehouse and Billy Mazes probably found him the next day. They must've figured it was LaGarda's work. That's what everyone must've figured."

Lou nodded, remembering that that was what he had heard from Fran Marks.

"Anyway," Frank went on, "when Ernie got killed I made up my mind I was gonna go ahead with it. At first I thought I had to do it because they killed Ernie. But then I thought, Christ no, what's that got to do with it. You can't trade Sallie Manzano for Ernie, that doesn't even anything up. It can't be that kind of a thing. Then I remembered what you told me about the Morello business, Lou. I figured a hit on Sallie wouldn't prove anything. But if I got a couple good men, and if I didn't stop there, I could get all of them turning themselves inside-out. You stay ahead of them, figure out what their reactions are gonna be, who they are gonna think did it, get them at each other's throats—now that's something that can really screw up their operation. We've seen it already in the Richie Saint hit. Now we just know Eddie Manzano's not gonna sit still forever without making a move for the guy who killed his brother. Right now he still thinks it's Tony and Tony still thinks he thinks that, so Tony's not gonna sit still either waiting for Eddie to come get him. What I'm saying is this, Lou. Maybe we don't have to do anything else. Maybe all hell will break loose and all we have to do now is keep track of it and sweep up the garbage when it's all over. We're gonna need some good men for that, Lou. Can you give it another month?"

Hovannes stopped talking and Lou waited a few seconds before answering. In the pit of his stomach he felt like he was going to be sick, but he took a deep breath and said, "I can give it a month, Frank, if that's really the way it's gonna be. If it's really gonna be that way, okay."

Chapter 25

FRAN MARKS STOPPED at the luggage store on Broadway just north of Ninety-first and bought the cheapest cardboard suitcase they had in stock. It was closing time and the old man didn't want to wait on him. When Fran said, "I don't care what it looks like, just so's it's cheap. Just gimme any piece of shit you got," the old man thought, Uh-oh, stickup.

Luckily he had a tan and brown cardboard model with a damaged lock right behind the counter, which meant he wouldn't have to go to the back of the store. "The lock doesn't work," he said. "I can let you have it for five dollars." He tensed, waiting for what he was sure was coming.

Fran reached into his pants pocket and pulled out a handful of crumpled bills. He picked out a five, stuffed the rest back into his pocket, and handed the money to the old man, who took it and passed the suitcase over the counter. Then Fran turned and left. The old man hurried up behind him and locked the door.

Outside, on Broadway, Fran figured he still had a couple of hours to kill. He crossed to the west side of the street and went into the candy store. They had individual plastic-tipped cigars for seven cents apiece and he bought one, along with a Mounds bar, which he unwrapped in the store, leaving the paper on the countertop.

Outside again, he walked south on Broadway, more or less aimlessly, eating the candy bar and then stopping to light his cigar. A few blocks further on he paused to read the posters at the New Yorker and decided to take in a movie. It was some kind of a Japanese double bill, but that was all right. He just wanted to kill some time.

The girl in the booth stopped reading long enough to take his money and give him his change. "Smoking only in the last few rows," she said.

"What?"

"Smoking only in the last few rows."

Fran hesitated a moment and she went back to her book. "I'll be back in a few minutes," he said. She didn't respond. "That all right?"

She looked up slowly, annoyed. "What? Yeah, sure," she said and resumed her reading.

Marks decided to take a walk until he finished his smoke. Around the corner he set his suitcase down and passed a few minutes examining some magazines on the outdoor rack of the New Yorker bookstore. He leafed through a copy of *Screw*, amazed that they sold stuff like this out in the open. Must be paying someone off, he told himself, and put the magazine back in the rack.

Then he walked down to West End Avenue and watched for a few seconds while a small reddish dog waited at the curb until his owner told him it was all right to cross the street. "Good dog you got there," Fran said, and the woman thanked him, smiled quickly, and hurried to catch up with the dog. He watched her jog a few steps and thought. Nice pussy too, I bet.

When the cigar had burned down to the plastic Fran threw it into the gutter and went back to the theater. "Remember me?" he said to the girl in the booth. She looked up and with no sign of acknowledgment went back to her book. Fran pushed through the turnstile—there was just a turnstile outside the booth, they didn't give you a ticked—and walked in. The theater was mostly empty and the picture was somewhere near the middle. Fran took a seat about five rows from the front. For the first ten minutes he watched the picture and read the subtitles, trying to figure out what was going on. Then he gave up on the subtitles and watched without reading for another ten minutes, after which he fell asleep.

When he woke up it looked like about the same place in the picture as when he fell asleep. The theater now was more than three quarters full and he checked his watch. It was about a quarter to ten. He waited a few minutes until he was sure he was awake and then picked up his suitcase and left.

It had started to drizzle lightly and two hookers, good looking, well-dressed black girls with long shiny hair, talked and joked together under the marquee. One of them smiled at Fran but he didn't have time for that now. He pulled his jacket closed, hurried up to the corner to make the light, and crossed to the east side of Broadway. Then he walked quickly north a few blocks, his body leaning forward and bobbing from side to side with his long, loping strides. He turned at Ninety-first and went into the lobby of the Blackstone Hotel.

The clerk in the cashier's cage didn't see him for a while, so he rapped on the glass after he had waited long enough. The clerk dropped his newspaper on the desk and hurried to the window.

"Got a room?" Fran asked.

"Week or month?"

"Just overnight."

The clerk looked him up and down. "Just you?" he asked.

"So far," Fran answered.

The clerk didn't smile. "Fifteen dollars," he said. "Pay now."

Fran slid the money through the window and the clerk raised the grating for him to sign the register. He used his own name but for address he wrote General Delivery, Pawtucket, R.I. The clerk examined it expressionlessly, reached for a key on the board to his left, and handed it to Fran. "Elevator's right there," he said, sliding the grate down and turning to go back to his newspaper.

Fran took his suitcase to the elevator. The doors opened as soon as he pushed the button and he rode up to ten. He found his room in the brightly lit corridor, let himself in, and tossed the suitcase on the bed. Didn't even need it, he thought to himself. I shoulda known I wouldn't of needed it.

He went to the bathroom and looked at himself in the mirror. His hair was wet from the rain and he raked his hands through it to comb it back, then dried them with a few swipes at his pants. He reached into the tub and turned on the cold water, which gurgled for a few seconds and then poured out, rusty at first and then clear.

He went back to the bedroom and looked for the phone but there wasn't one. Mostly it was a residential hotel; if tenants wanted telephones they had to put them in themselves. Fuck it, Fran thought, went back to the corridor and pushed for the elevator. It arrived in a few seconds and he rode down.

"Hey," he called to the clerk as he stepped out into the

lobby. "The water's running in the bathtub and I can't turn it off."

The clerk walked slowly back to the window. "What's the problem?" he asked.

"The water's running in the bathtub and I can't turn it off," Fran repeated.

"Whatdya mean you can't turn it off?"

"The faucet's stuck. It won't turn. C'mon up and take a look."

The clerk looked Fran up and down again. He was a small, soft man and he said, "If you can't turn it off how'm I gonna turn it off?"

Fran said, "Beats me, but you gotta do something. Sounds like fucking Niagara Falls up there."

The clerk thought about it a minute. "Bring your key down and I'll give you another room," he said.

"I already unpacked my stuff," Fran answered stubbornly. "Look, isn't there a turnoff or something?"

The clerk brightened. "Oh yeah. There's a panel under the sink. Take it off and there's a handle in there. That'll shut it off."

Fran said, "You come up and do it. I'm no fucking plumber."

"Look, it's just a faucet," the clerk protested.

"Where's the night manager?" Fran answered. This guy was being more trouble than he had expected.

"I'm the night manager."

"That right?" Fran said, not fazed. "Well, unless you own the place too, you better get your ass upstairs."

The clerk came around and opened the door, pulled it closed behind him and checked to make sure it was locked. He rode up with Fran in sullen, pissed-off silence.

The door to Fran's room was open and the clerk went in first, heading straight for the bathroom. Fran was right behind him. They could both hear the water running. The first thing the clerk did was stick his hand under the water. It was cold. He reached for the cold water tap and it turned easily.

"Hey, what gives!" he started to say as he straightened up, but Fran grabbed his shoulders from the back while he was still partly stooped over the tub and pulled him violently backward until he slammed into the wall near the toilet. Fran was leaning against him, his left hand holding the little man's right shoulder to the wall and his right forearm pressing against his throat.

Fran bent down until his face was directly in front of the pasty little clerk. His breath still stank from the cheap cigar. He stared into the clerk's watery eyes until the clerk wanted to look away but he was afraid to.

"What happened to Al Palmini?" Fran demanded.

"Wha?" the clerk gasped. He tried to talk but couldn't with Fran's arm pushing against his throat. Fran lowered his arm just enough so it was still pressing against the frightened little man's collarbone and the clerk's head bobbed forward. He didn't want Fran's face right in front of him. "I don't know nothing about any Al Palmini," he said weakly.

Fran increased the pressure on his collarbone.

"Whatdya want from me?" the clerk complained. "Johnny Lombardi send you?"

"No. Why?"

"He was here asking the same thing," the clerk whimpered.

"What did you tell him?"

"What I'm telling you. Palmini was here and then he was gone. I didn't see him go. He paid in advance so it's no skin off my ass."

"That all?"

"That's all he asked," the clerk said. "And he just asked too, none of this strong-arm shit."

"Well I'm not asking," Fran said. His left hand let go of the clerk's shoulder and the heel of it came up to his forehead, pushing his head violently against the wall. Fran looked straight into his eyes while he stuck there like a butterfly. "Try again," he demanded, and the clerk knew he meant it.

"Awright," he whined. "Let go of me."

Fran gave a short, hard thrust with his forearm, just as a reminder, then let go and stepped back. The little man stepped sideways, away from Fran and the wall, and shook himself off like a wet dog. He wanted to go into the bedroom where there'd be a little more room, but Fran reached out to the side and swung the bathroom door closed.

"Two guys came and took him out," the clerk said, seeing there was nothing else to do.

"What two guys?"

"I don't know. They showed me badges, said they was cops. Said they'd get a warrant for the whole hotel if I didn't tell them where he was."

"One of them kinda short, maybe five-nine, five-ten, curly hair, kinda stocky?" Marks asked.

"Nah, it was a tall skinny guy, built kinda like you, and a Spic."

"You sure of that?" Fran asked, puzzled.

"A Spic's a Spic, whatdya want me to tell you?" the clerk said.

"Yeah okay. Then what?"

"They took him out, that's all. Then these two cops showed up. One of them looked kinda like what you just said, but this older one did all the talking. Asked for Palmini. I told him he was too late, told him what happened, and he said those first guys wasn't cops. Then they left. That's all I know."

Fran reached over and opened the bathroom door. "Thanks for your trouble," he said.

"No trouble," the clerk muttered and scurried for the door.

"You bet your ass it was no trouble," Fran called after him. "Didn't even happen."

"Sure," the clerk said without turning. "Okay."

He hurried out into the corridor and down to the elevator. When it didn't come in a few seconds he walked down the stairs to eight and caught it there.

In his room Fran thought to himself, Well, I was right and I was wrong. He had thought before that the cops hadn't picked up Palmini because Savage tipped him they were coming. Part of that still seemed right. The cop Savage showed up with must have been Hovannes. But Savage didn't tip Palmini, and the two guys who took him out of there, they weren't working for Eddie Manzano or Johnny Lombardi. They didn't have any Spics working for them. But Tony LaGarda did.

That was the tipoff. Savage must've called Tony and told him where Palmini was, that's the way it worked. Then Tony sent these two goons up there to take him. So maybe Tony was in back of the hit on Sallie Manzano after all.

Aw fuck it, Fran said to himself, what does that matter? What he cared about was what concerned him, and now he was sure he had it all figured out. Savage was on LaGarda's pad. Of course. That explained why no one ever knew what happened to Palmini. It also explained why Savage was so interested in the Manzano hit. Whether he was in back of it or not, LaGarda would want to know what the word was, whether people were fingering him for it.

In a way, Fran was relieved that he had all the loose ends tied together, but he knew that it was worse this way than what he had figured before. There was always a danger when you were talking to a cop on the pad that someone could find out you were ratting. If Savage was on Manzano's pad, like he had thought at first, that was bad enough. Some day Manzano might want something from LaGarda and he'd say, Look, do me a favor, Tony, and I'll give you the name of a pigeon in your organization. But with Savage working for LaGarda it was even worse. If LaGarda ever found out about it he wouldn't wait two seconds. He'd call up Paulie Gagliano and he'd say, Look, Paulie, one of your connections is a canary, take care of him. And that would be that.

Fran knew he had to do something to protect himself, and it didn't take him long to figure out what.

Chapter 26

"SAVAGE? I gotta talk to you."

"Okay. When?"

"Right away. You know that fort in Central Park?"

"Near the theater? Yeah."

"Okay. How long it take you to get there?"

"Maybe a half hour, but it's raining. How about some-place inside?"

"Wear rubbers," Fran Marks said and hung up the phone.

Fran figured it wouldn't take him a half hour to get there so he stopped on Broadway and had a well-done hamburger with a slice of onion for breakfast. Then he walked across Eighty-sixth Street to Central Park West and down to the Eighty-first Street entrance to the park. There was fairly heavy traffic going south on the Park Drive, but once he crossed it there was virtually no one in sight.

He passed the Delacorte Theater, an unroofed, horse-shoe-shaped amphitheater where they did Shakespeare productions in the summer, and walked around the side of the pond. To his left was a large, flat field with about eight baseball diamonds laid out on it. In the distance he could see a woman in a rubber raincoat carrying an um-brella and walking a runty little dog on a leash. Except for her and the dog, the park was deserted.

Circling to the south side of the pond, he climbed up the hill to Belvedere Tower, a fortresslike building in heavy stone rising above the high rocks at the southwest corner of the pond. Two antennas protruded out of the highest point of the tower and two cup-shaped wind gauges revolved restlessly in the drizzly breeze. A plaque on the side of the tower said that it had been built in 1869 as a lookout and the idea amused Fran. Lookout for what, he wondered. Were they afraid the spades were gonna in-vade them from Harlem?

On the west side of the tower was a flat concrete patio that provided a commanding view of much of Central Park. It was surrounded by a waist-high wall of foot-thick stones. From the patio Fran could see into the theater from above and behind the stage, and beyond that were the empty ballfields. He looked, but the woman with the dog was gone. The pond was maybe forty-five feet below him, gray-green and dimpled with the rain. He sat on the wall to wait, scanning the view in front of him for any sign of Lou Savage. Below his feet it was a fifteen-foot drop to the first rock outcropping, and below that more jagged rock and then the water.

After about ten minutes he saw a man come out from the trees just in front of Cleopatra's Needle. He walked rapidly along the east border of the pond and then Fran lost him in the trees. He couldn't tell if it was Savage. Then the man reappeared again, coming up the slope toward the tower. It was Savage all right and Fran climbed down from the wall to wait for him.

Lou came around the tower and walked up beside Fran. The two of them turned and leaned their elbows on the wall, looking out at nothing in particular. There wasn't much visibility in the overcast and drizzle, and Lou noticed he could barely make out the greenhouselike roof of the Metropolitan Museum less than half a mile away.

Lou was wearing a raincoat but he didn't have a hat and his normally curly hair lay flattened on his head. "This better be good," he said.

"Not good, bad," Fran answered.

Lou didn't say anything.

"Look, Savage," Marks said, "I know what's coming down and I wanna make sure I get my ass out of this alive."

"What's coming down?"

Fran turned his head to look at Lou for a few seconds, but Lou was still gazing straight ahead into the gray space above the park.

"I rat on my friends, you rat on yours. Everybody's gotta make a living," Fran said cryptically. "I got no quarrel with you."

Lou didn't understand what Marks was saying but he wanted to hear more. "What's your problem?" he asked.

"My problem is if LaGarda or Gagliano find out I'm

talking to you, my balls will be one place and I'll be someplace else."

"So?"

"So I don't want that to happen."

"If it makes you feel any better, Fran," Lou said, "I don't want it to happen either. How's that?"

"Not good enough," Marks answered quickly, turning and walking away from the wall. A stone staircase at one end of the patio led down to the highest level of the rocks and Fran walked down it. At the edge was a short wooden fence, more like a guard rail. Fran leaned against it on his elbows after taking out a cigaret and lighting it with his wet hands. In a few seconds he heard Lou come up beside him. "Not near good enough, Lou," he said.

"Down below he coud see two small turtles swimming in the soupy water. They were directly below him in a little cove cluttered with branches and beer cans. "Hey, look at them turtles," he said.

Lou looked and found them, a larger one maybe five inches across with a brown and white striped shell and a smaller one, rust colored.

"You're all right, Francis," Lou laughed and the two of them watched the turtles swim in circles for a short while. When the turtles disappeared down under the rocks Lou said, "Look, Fran, I know you've got a problem, but it's always been like that. I think we've covered ourselves pretty good. No one could have seen us. What have you got to worry about?"

"You, Savage," Fran answered sharply and snapped his cigaret out over the water. It floated down and fell in the little cove where the turtles had been swimming.

"What?"

"Enough's enough, Savage," Marks said, his voice heavy, weary and complaining. "I know you're working for La-Garda, I figured it out. Now what I wanna know is what have I got that lets me know you won't turn me over to Tony some day?"

"I'm not working for LaGarda, that's horseshit. Where'd you get that?" Lou protested, straightening up from the fence and turning to face Marks.

"I told you, I figured it out. Palmini. LaGarda's guys took him outta the Blackstone. Now how'd they do that if you didn't tip them, huh?"

Lou wanted to say, What would LaGarda want with Palmini? but he realized he was better off with Fran thinking LaGarda had done it than with him asking questions and finding out the real story. He thought quickly, trying to come up with something else. Then he said, "You know, Marks, if you knew where he was, a shitload of other people must've known. You're not exactly on their National Security Council."

"Maybe," Marks said dully, "but what does that do for my problem?"

"Doesn't do anything. You don't have a problem."

"Fuck it, Savage, I think I do. And if I think I've got a problem, then you got a problem. What are you gonna do about that one?"

"You tell me," Lou said.

Fran lit another cigaret and drew on it thoughtfully for a couple of minutes. "Look, Lou, I wanna get outta this scene," he said finally, and for the first time his voice sounded shrill and a little desperate. "You guys can fix it up, I know you can. Send me somplace. A little bankroll and a new identity. It's been done, I know it."

"Are you fucking nuts!" Savage exclaimed.

Marks looked at him without saying anything. The corners of his mouth twitched slightly and his eyes looked scared and hurt. Lou realized Fran had it all wrong, everything he had figured out was backward, but his fear was real and Lou didn't want Fran to think he was just brushing it aside.

"Vincent Teresa maybe," he tried to explain. "The feds did that for him, because he put a lot of important guys in the cooler for them. But Jesus, Fran, I don't even know if the Department could do it. And there's just no way a Narco dick could sell them on putting on a show like that for one of his canaries, no way. You know that. Come up with something else."

Fran's face had hardened again and the hurt look was gone. "No, you come up with something else," he said. "Here's my something else. Unless you give me something I can live with, I go to the commissioner or Nadjari or whoever the fuck it is you go to, and I tell them about you and LaGarda. I tell them I'll testify against you. Then the cops protect me, right?"

Lou had no choice but to surrender. "All right, Fran, I'll see what I can do," he said. "I could tell you I'll take care of it now but I'd just be jiving you. I gotta check it out, see what can be done. I'll get back to you."

"It's gotta be today, Savage."

Lou nodded. "Okay, today. Where? Here?"

"Yeah, here. How's six o'clock? That give you enough time?"

"Yeah, six o'clock," Lou said. He turned and walked up the steps to the patio level.

"Savage," Marks called after him, "if anything happens to me, there's a letter the commissioner's gonna get, know what I mean?"

Lou didn't answer. He hurried to his car in the Metropolitan Museum parking lot and drove downtown as fast as the late morning traffic would permit. One thing seemed clear to him: they would have to give Marks what he wanted, or at least enough to keep him happy and quiet. As long as Marks hadn't figured out about Operation Counterthrust, he wasn't an immediate threat. But if he ever brought his charges against Lou to the Internal Affairs Division they would investigate and might turn up the real story.

Down at the old Headquarters Lou found a parking space on Centre Market Street and went immediately to the Broome Street Annex. Polito was alone in the squadroom, sitting at the small conference table apparently not doing anything, when he came in.

"Hi, Ron. Frank here?" Lou said.

"Huh? No, he went out with Obregon, be back in a few minutes," Polito answered, glancing up and noticing that Savage looked disheveled and wet but not commenting on it.

Lou went to his locker on the wall next to the door and hung up his raincoat. He took a comb from the top shelf and pulled it through his hair to get rid of some of the water. Then he came over and sat down at the table with Polito. They had nothing to say to each other, so they waited a few minutes in silence until the door opened again and Hovannes and Obregon walked in.

"You been swimming or something?" Obregon asked jokingly.

"Yeah, I think so," Savage muttered absently and stood up. "Frank, I got a problem," he added in a low voice.

Hovannes looked at him and nodded. "Yeah, okay. In

here," he said, motioning toward his office at the back end of the squadroom.

Lou hesitated a moment. "I think it concerns all of us," he said. He would have preferred to talk to Hovannes alone or with Obregon, but on the ride down he had reminded himself that he had promised the Inspector last night that he would see this thing through, and that included working with Polito as long as the team was still together.

"Okay," Hovannes said, turning and leading the way, "why don't you all come in."

Polito got up slowly from the table as Savage and Obregon followed the Inspector.

"You didn't change your mind, Lou?" Obregon whispered as they stepped into the tiny office."

Lou smiled and shook his head. "It's not that," he said.

Hovannes sat down behind his desk. There were two straight-backed chairs in the office, which had been little more than a storage closet before Hovannes took it over for Counterthrust. Obregon took a yellow legal pad from the Inspector's desk and sat down in the chair just to the left of the door. He rested the pad flat on his lap and took out a ballpoint pen. Savage sat in the chair against the side wall a few feet from the corner of the desk. Polito came in a moment later, closed the door behind him, and remained standing, his back against the door.

"I've had this guy stooling for me a couple of years," Lou began as soon as the door clicked closed behind Polito. "Deals drugs, connected with the Gagliano outfit. He's the guy who told me Palmini was up at the Blackstone. I just had a nice talk with him up at the Belvedere Tower in the park. Somehow he found out two guys took Palmini out of there before we got there, Frank, and he's been trying to figure the thing out ever since."

Lou paused and looked straight across the desk at Hovannes, who was sitting forward, his heavy forearms resting motionless on the desk, his lips tightly clenched. To his left Lou could see that Obregon had stopped doodling on the pad and was looking at him expectantly. Polito was still leaning on the door between himself and Obregon. He hadn't moved.

"Well, what he came up with," Lou went on, "was a whole lot of horseshit, but it still could be some trouble. He got it into his head that I'm working for Tony La-Garda. The way he figures it, I told LaGarda where

Palmini was after he told me and then two of LaGarda's goons went and took him out of there."

"I don't see the problem," Obregon interrupted. "It still comes down to this guy thinking LaGarda's behind it one way or the other. So he thinks you're on the pad. He's not gonna tell the shooflies."

Obregon glanced from Lou to Hovannes to see how the Inspector was taking his rundown of the situation. Frank recognized that so far what Roberto said made sense, so he figured he hadn't heard the whole story. "Lou?" he said.

"Well, that's just what he is figuring to do," Savage answered, turning from Hovannes and speaking directly to Obregon. "What he's afraid of is if I work for LaGarda some day I might tell him one of Gagliano's dealers is a pigeon."

"I can see his point," Hovannes said and smiled wryly. "If you sell information to a cop who's selling it back to your boss, you can get it up over your hubcaps. What's he want?"

"Some kind of protection," Lou said. "Money maybe. Said he wants us to do the whole Vincent Teresa bit on him—bankroll him, give him some identification, send him someplace, the whole thing."

"Couldn't you convince him you weren't working for LaGarda?" Obregon interrupted again.

"I tried, but he wasn't buying. What was I gonna tell him—the guys who took Palmini out of his room weren't Tony's boys, they were cops?"

"Yeah," Hovannes agreed, "we're better off this way. What did you tell him?"

"I told him I'd see what could be done. I'm supposed to meet him back there at six o'clock with some answers. What are we gonna do?"

Frank leaned back in his chair and thought a moment before answering.

"There's only two choices," he said. "We either give him what he wants or we hit him."

He paused for a second waiting for Savage to interrupt him. Lou was looking across at him hard, almost defiantly, but he didn't say anything. "Well, it's something we gotta think about, Lou." Hovannes went on. "But first we gotta know who he is, who he's connected to, who else might know about his horseshit theories."

Savage's eyes moved off Frank's face and came to rest somewhere below the top of the desk. "His name's Fran Marks," he said, "but I don't know about hitting him. He said he left a letter with someone. If anything happens to him it goes in the mail."

"Was he bluffing?" Obregon asked.

Before Lou could answer, Hovannes said, "He probably was, but I don't want to find out. Besides," he went on, looking pointedly at Lou, "when we start hitting guys to protect outselves we're in a whole different ballgame. Fran Marks, does that ring any bells, Roberto?"

"Yeah, but it's just what Lou said," Obregon responded, pulling the information from his memory like he had Marks's file in front of him. "Busted a couple of times for street dealing but nothing recent. He's pretty much a loner from what I understand. Not many friends."

"Yeah," Lou agreed, "he gives that impression but he must know someone. He knows so fucking much sometimes it's scary."

"Okay," Hovannes said firmly, closing off that line of approach. "That leaves us choice number one, we give him what he wants."

"I was hoping you'd say that," Savage said, not hiding the fact that he felt relieved. "But can we do it?"

Hovannes shook his head. "No," he said, "but we can give him something, let him know we care."

"Like what?"

"Like a little identification. Driver's license, social security. How tall is he?"

"Six, six-one."

"Ron?"

"Yeah, about the same," Polito said from his station at the door.

"Heavy-set?" Hovannes asked.

"No, thinner than Ron, but not too much."

"No sweat," the Inspector announced. "Polito, you know where the detective division is down at the new Headquarters?"

Polito shook his head.

"It's somewhere on the third floor, you'll find it. Go down there and tell the desk officer I sent you. Tell him you want all the identification you can get. I'll call him, tell him you're doing some undercover for me."

Polito nodded but didn't move.

"You'd better get going now, Ron," Hovannes said. "I don't know how long it'll take them. Bring the stuff right back here as soon as you get it. Anything with pictures we can take them off, let him put his own on."

Polito hesitated a moment, then peeled himself slowly from the door and left the room without saying anything.

When the door closed Lou said, "I don't think a driver's license is gonna make him all that happy, Frank."

"Tell him you're gonna send him to Cincinnati or something, but it'll take till next week to make the arrangements. Whatever they give us from downtown, at least it'll show your heart's in the right place. How much do you usually give him?"

"Twenty, twenty-five."

"Well, give him fifty. The Department'll spring you for it. Think he wants a place to stay? I might be able to arrange that."

"He didn't say anything about it," Lou answered, going back over his conversation with Marks. "He probably wouldn't want to stay anyplace I put him—afraid I'd set him up or something I guess he'll just crawl into a hole somwhere."

"Yeah, fine," Hovannes concluded. "A little bread, a little identification—that ought to keep him happy. He's not an unreasonable guy, is he?"

"No," Lou said, remembering the way Marks had looked at him, begging for protection, "he's not unreasonable. Just scared."

Tuesday, April 22

After he left the stuff for Savage on Hovannes's desk, Ron Polito took the subway home, getting there about four-thirty. A little after five he went out again. Quickly, he walked the half block to Central Park West and then two blocks south to the Eighty-first Street entrance to the park. The rain had stopped an hour before and the sidewalks were still pockmarked with puddles.

Hurrying into the park, Polito passed a group of about eight or nine boisterous Puerto Ricans carrying baseball gear and joking in Spanish. At the park drive he had to wait while car after car swished by on the still wet pavement and the ballplayers caught up with him. As soon as there was a break in the traffic he crossed the drive and hurried up the shallow grade toward the Delacorte Theater.

Coming around on the far side of the theater, he could see carpenters on the stage working on an intricate scaffold set. He stopped to look up to the tower, but there didn't seem to be anyone there. Then he checked his watch—five twenty-five—and his right hand reflexively went to his armpit where it touched against the bulk of his heavy automatic with its long silencer through the fabric of his jacket. He had had to cut a large circle of leather from the bottom of his holster so that he could wear the gun with the silencer attached. It hung down his side almost to his lowest rib, but with his jacket unbuttoned and his left arm pressed to his body to keep it closed, he was sure it didn't show.

He looked around to get his bearings. The ballplayers had come up behind him again and were sitting on the grass, taking off their street shoes and lacing on their spikes. A couple of them were up already, playing catch as they worked their way toward the infield of the nearest diamond. One of the other diamonds further on already had a game going and as Polito watched he heard the dull thwack of a softball against a bat like a fist pounding into a mattress. There was shouting too, but it was in Spanish and too far away to make out.

About half a dozen people, maybe more, were walking dogs along the sidewalk that ran the perimeter of the softball diamonds. Fucking city does things to your head, Polito thought as he watched a collie-shepherd trotting along on the pavement like he didn't know there was short thick grass just a few feet to his side. Dumb dog doesn't know the difference between a sidewalk and a field, Polito said to himself and turned to look back up at the tower on the other side of the pond.

He still couldn't see anyone there. He retraced his steps, circling around to the west of the theater. He found a steep path that led up to the tower and hurried up it, his body leaning sharply forward with his long uphill strides. He was counting on Marks to get there early, ahead of Savage. But even if he didn't, Polito figured, it would be easy to trail him after he left Savage. And so it would come to the same thing either way.

Hovannes is an asshole, Polito said to himself. Sooner

or later they'd want to take care of all of them if they could, and it was just plain dumb to think that if this guy could make some trouble that gave you less reason, not more, to hit him. A fifth-rate crud like this guy Marks wouldn't have got himself high up on the list if he hadn't started making problems. But now he was a problem and it was clear to Polito that the only smart thing to do was to take care of him before he fucked up the whole thing. Who knows, they probably would have got around to him anyway sooner or later.

Polito came up on the west side of the tower patio. No one was there and he found himself a position near the tower where he could see all of the approaches for twenty-five yards or more. He was ready now and it was just a question of whether Marks got there before Savage. The underbrush south of the patio was almost jungle-thick and he decided that he would hide there if he saw Lou coming first. He felt loose and relaxed and he told himself it would probably be better if Lou got there first and he had to wait to follow Marks. That way he could pick his spot and he wouldn't have to worry about Lou showing up any minute.

He hadn't waited long when he saw a man hurrying up the hill from the east. He checked his watch—twenty to six—and leaned against the cool damp stone of the tower to wait.

Marks came around the corner of the tower and stopped in his tracks when he saw a stranger there waiting for him.

"Fran Marks?" Polito asked, calling the name loudly across the patio.

Marks looked at him suspiciously for a few seconds without answering. Then he decided he didn't want to get involved in anything that wasn't going the way he figured and turned to leave.

"Marks," Polito repeated firmly. "Lou Savage sent me."

Fran stopped and waited but he kept his distance and wasn't saying anything.

"I work with Lou, know what I mean? He told me to meet you," Polito said, much softer this time. He was still lounging against the wall standing on one foot, his left leg bent at the knee with his foot cocked backwards so the sole of his shoe was flat against the wall near the base.

"How do I know that?" Marks asked warily from twenty feet away.

Polito reached under his jacket with his right hand. He brought out a flat leather case and flipped it open. From where he stood Fran could see the tin shield shining at him as it caught the late afternoon sun over his shoulder. "What you asked for, you know," Polito was saying in a low voice that Marks had trouble hearing, "it's not easy to get without people asking some questions. He's working it out with a guy down at Headquarters, but the guy didn't want to see him till he got off duty, you know how it is. He might be a little late, he didn't want you to think he wasn't gonna show."

Just then a small black kid, maybe twelve years old, ran onto the patio from the west, where Polito had come up. His shirt was tied around his waist with the sleeves knotted at his stomach and he stopped when he saw the two men. Polito put his badge away quickly as the kid ran back down the hill. He pushed off the wall with his foot, turned and walked down the shallow stone staircase to the guard rail at the edge of the rocks. He could hear Marks following behind him and thought, A piece of cake. This won't take a minute.

Fran leaned against the guard rail next to Polito, as he had done with Lou that morning. "I don't know," he said. "That doesn't sound like what I had in mind."

"Yeah?"

"Look, I don't want a couple pieces of paper he lifts out of some desk, know what I mean? Christ, I can get that, anyone can get that. That don't give me no protection."

"Well what the fuck do you want?" Polito said sarcastically. "You want him to go to his CO and arrange it?"

"You better believe it," Marks answered bluntly, then added, "Look, I wanna be covered on all sides."

Polito shrugged. "How's he gonna do that, huh? You better take what you can get."

"Maybe I better talk to Lou," Marks said softly after a few seconds' thought.

"Maybe," Polito answered without looking at him. "You need some bread?"

"Yeah, but he's not buying me off for a couple bucks."

"Look," Polito shot back, "that's between you and Savage. I'm just up here doing him a favor, know what I mean? I asked you if you need some bread."

"Yeah, what've you got?"

"Fifty."

"Fifty!" Fran snarled, looking straight into Polito's eyes. "That's chickenshit. I'm not playing games."

"Take it or leave it," Polito said, returning his stare. "That's what he gave me."

"Yeah, all right," Marks conceded glumly, "but I wanna talk to Lou."

Polito reached into his pocket again with his right hand and came out with the automatic. Marks didn't move when he saw it. "What the fuck's going on!" he squealed, his voice going uncontrollably high and shrill. He took a step back from the guard rail but Polito made a short thrusting move with the gun that told him to stay where he was.

"Lou didn't send you," Fran said. There was a burning bitter taste in the back of his throat, like vomit. "What is this?"

Polito didn't answer.

"Look," Fran pleaded, "all I wanna do is get out of this. I don't wanna make any trouble, Lou knows that. I just didn't wanna be fucked over, but I don't wanna make any trouble."

Polito still didn't say anything and the gun didn't move.

"Let me talk to Lou," Fran begged. He could feel warm tears gathering in his eyes and he felt sick and dizzy. Dimly he could see the gun wave to the right and he obediently moved where it pointed, toward the guard rail. "Let me talk to Lou," he repeated desperately.

Polito's lips were closed tightly, sucked in between his teeth.

"Hey, Lou didn't send you," Marks repeated in his panicky confusion. "He didn't, did he? He'll be here in a little while. He wouldn't of done this, he'll be here at six o'clock. He didn't send you, did he?"

"Yes, he did," Polito answered softly.

He fired twice and Marks's jaw dropped open. His face still had that confused and uncomprehending look, like he wanted to say No, someone's putting me on. As he fell back against the guard rail Polito reached forward with his left hand and pushed at his chest. He toppled back and his feet came up, one of them catching Polito's elbow. Then he fell over the rail to the rocks and water forty-five feet below.

Polito looked up across the pond toward the fields. One of the ballplayers had seen the body falling and was already racing toward the pond, shouting. He was still a hundred yards away. Some others joined him running, and then a carpenter came out to the back of the stage at the theater and looked around to see what the noise had been.

Polito turned and walked away from the guard rail, up the steps and across the patio. Behind him and below he could hear voices shouting in English and Spanish, but he couldn't understand what they were saying.

Chapter 27

TONY LAGARDA, Jimmie Monks, and Paulie Gagliano sat at a corner table in the Caffe Fidelio. Each had a cup of coffee in front of him and an ashtray.

"It's quarter past eight," Tony the Lawyer said. "I thought you told them eight o'clock."

"Yeah, that's what I told em," Monks agreed.

"And Rusty from the Bronx, did you call Rusty?"

"Yeah, he said he'd be here too, him and Hector. Eight o'clock."

LaGarda looked at his watch again and took a sip of coffee. As an afterthought Monks asked, "What if Minelli doesn't go for it?"

"It's his idea. How's he not gonna go for it?" LaGarda answered, putting his cup carefully back in the saucer.

"No, I mean Rusty and Hector. Maybe he doesn't like working with Spics."

"Well, then he doesn't do it," LaGarda answered off-handedly. "Look," he went on to explain, "you know what this thing's gonna be like. Minelli doesn't care if he gets himself killed. He's dead anyway. If he pulls it off, that's nice. And if he doesn't, we haven't lost anything. I'm not gonna waste two good men on it."

Monks shrugged and reached into his pocket for a cigar. As he peeled the cellophane from it he saw the door to the kitchen swing open. Tommie Minelli stepped through with Mickey right behind him, catching the door and holding it open while his older brother scanned the crowded restaurant. When he spotted LaGarda he signaled with his head for his brother to follow and the two of them wove their way among the tables to where Tony was sitting. The kitchen door swung for a few seconds like a pendulum.

LaGarda stood up as the Minelli brothers approached. "Sit down," he offered. "You're late. Sit anywhere."

There were seven chairs at the large table. Tommie sat

at the foot of the table opposite Tony and his brother took the chair next to Jimmie Monks, who was busy lighting his cigar. The flame from the wooden match rhythmically flared up and banked down as he took short quick puffs to get it burning evenly.

"You want something to eat? I'll have the boy bring you something," LaGarda said. "Anything you want."

"Nah, just coffee," Tommie answered, seeing that the others weren't eating. His brother looked at him for a second but didn't say anything.

Tommie took out a pack of cigarets and tapped one out. He reached across his brother for the box of wooden matches in front of Monks. As he lit his cigaret his hand trembled slightly. LaGarda raised his hand in a signal to the waiter, and when he got his attention he called "Two coffee" in a voice loud enough to be heard halfway across the room.

"You don't look good, Tommie," he said, returning to a conversational tone. "You nervous?"

Minelli glanced up quickly from the ashtray in front of him. "It's my stomach," he said. "Haven't been eating good, I guess. My old man had ulcers, maybe I'm getting 'em too."

Be lucky if you do, LaGarda thought, but he said, "Well look, have something to eat."

Tommie shook his head.

"You?"

"No thanks, Mr. LaGarda," Mickey answered softly.

Tommie's tan suit looked like he had been wearing it for days and he needed a shave. His normally sallow complexion was the pale gray color of a sidewalk, and LaGarda, who was looking at him closely, noticed that he kept flicking the tip of his tongue at the corner of his lips, like a guy who had just been punched in the mouth.

When Tommie picked his head up to take a drag on his cigaret he saw LaGarda staring at him. For a few seconds he tried to return the stare, but then he broke contact and looked over at the two empty chairs to his left. "You said you was gonna get two other guys," he said.

"They'll be here."

Tommie nodded. The waiter brought two cups of coffee and put them in front of the Minelli brothers. "That be all, Mr. LaGarda?" he asked, but Tony waved him away.

Tommie took a couple of sips from the steaming cup while his brother stirred absently at his with a spoon.

After a few minutes the front door of the Fidelio opened and two Puerto Rican men in their late thirties stepped in. The smaller of the two was wearing a mustard brown suit with shoes and tie in the same color. The taller man, who stood behind him, had on a cream-colored shirt open at the neck and no jacket. It took them just a second to spot LaGarda in the corner and they hurried over.

Tony the Lawyer stood up again. "Rusty, Hector, this is Tommie and Mickey Minelli. You know Mr. Monks, Mr. Gagliano."

Rusty, the one in the brown suit, sat toward the head of the table near LaGarda and Hector took the chair to his right. When they were all seated LaGarda said, "Okay, Minelli. Rusty and Hector are gonna work with you. What've you got?"

Minelli didn't answer. He fumbled nervously for another cigaret and glanced at his brother.

"They're good men," LaGarda said, anticipating his objections. "Whatever you got planned, they're good for it."

Minelli looked hard across at Tony the Lawyer. He wanted to tell him to go fuck himself. It was easy to see what he was figuring, sending a couple of Spics on the job. He was figuring they wouldn't come out of it alive. Tommie took a slow drag on his cigaret and held it in front of his face, the side of his forefinger resting against his upper lip. The smoke washed in front of him and he didn't take his eyes off LaGarda.

This time it was Tony who broke the contact. "If you got any problems, Minelli, you can take your ass back up to the Bronx," he said.

Cocksucker, Tommie thought, you don't give me no choice, do you? "Friday night," he said softly, his hands still in front of his face.

The two Puerto Ricans nodded and Minelli went on. "Eddie has dinner Friday night at Valentine's. They're all there—Runelli, Diamond, Lombardi, and Eddie. We'll do it Friday night."

"Yeah. What time?" LaGarda asked.

"Eight o'clock, nine o'clock, I don't know," Minelli said. The ash fell from his cigaret onto the table. "We'll wait for him, whenever they get there."

"You gonna do it outside?"

"No, inside. Outside they could run. Inside'll be no problem."

"You wait for them inside?"

"No, they know me there. You have to know all this?"

"People work for me, I like to know what they're doing," LaGarda answered with a shrug. But he didn't care about the details. They were Tommie Minelli's problem.

"Well, I'm not working for you," Minelli said. "I just need two of your guns."

LaGarda folded his hands in front of him at chin level, his elbows on the table. "Fine," he said, "you work it out with Rusty and Hector. If you need anything, let me know."

"I don't need anything," Minelli said and his tongue flicked at the corner of his mouth. But his voice seemed calm and assured now, flat and toneless. LaGarda figured he was too busy being pissed off about the Spics to be nervous anymore.

"Rusty, Hector, Friday sound all right to you?" Tony the Lawyer asked.

The two men nodded gravely but didn't say anything.

"Jimmie? Paulie?"

Monks said, "Yeah, fine," and picked his cigar out of the ashtray.

"Paulie?"

"Are you gonna hit all of them or just Manzano?" Gagliano asked, turning to his left to look at Tommie Minelli through the cigar smoke.

"Manzano for sure," Minelli answered. "Frankie Diamond too. If we can get Lombardi and Runelli we'll get 'em."

"Yeah," Gagliano said, turning back to his boss, "Friday's okay."

"Any questions?"

No one said anything.

"You want some coffee, something to eat?" LaGarda asked the Puerto Ricans.

"Coffee, yeah," Rusty said. Hector nodded and LaGarda signaled the waiter again.

When the waiter came Gagliano stood up. "I got a man had to take care of a problem for me today," he said, excusing himself. "I gotta see if he worked it out."

Instead of going to Tony's office to use the phone there, Gagliano walked across the dining room to a pay phone in the corner by the restrooms. He took a dime from his pocket and dialed. The phone rang three times and a young girl's voice answered.

"Terry, is your father there?"

"No, he's out for the evening," she said politely. "Is there any message?"

"Tell him Paulie Gagliano called. How you been, how's your Mamma?"

"We're both fine. Do you want him to call you back, Mr. Gagliano?"

"Nah, I'll get in touch with him. Say hi to your Mamma for me."

He hung up, fished another dime from his pocket and dialed again. This time it was a man's voice that said hello.

"Jack?"

"Yeah. Who's this?" Jack Kittens asked.

"Paulie Gagliano. Listen, Jack, you do me a favor?"

"Sure, Paulie."

"Get in touch with Phil Runelli for me. He's not home and I can't keep calling. I don't want him calling me here. There's something coming down. Tell him to stay home Friday night."

"That's it?"

"Yeah, just tell him to eat dinner at home Friday night."

"Yeah, okay, Paulie," Kittens said and hung up.

Gagliano put the receiver back in its cradle and waited till the coin dropped. He walked back to the table and sat down between Monks and LaGarda. "Yeah, it's all right," he said. "He took care of it."

Tuesday, April 22

"Mrs. Hovannes, remember me? Lou Savage. I . . ."

"Yes, of course, Lou. Come on in," Emily said, stepping back from the door. "The Inspector's home. How have you been?"

"Fine."

"And Celia? We were hoping we'd see more of you."

"Yeah, she's fine. That'd be nice," Lou said absently, following Emily through the house to the kitchen.

Frank was seated at the table, halfway through dinner. "Lou," he said, not getting up.

Savage walked to the side of the table without acknowledging his greeting. He stood there a moment, looking grimly down at his boss, his face dark with barely controlled anger. It was a look Hovannes had seen before—years before, when he was on patrol, but he recognized it. A long time ago a woman had been killed in her apartment and when her husband found the body and reported, Hovannes was the first one there. The way the husband looked at him was the way Lou was looking at him now, with the anger of grief and betrayal.

Lou pulled a white business envelope from his pocket and dropped it on the table next to Frank's plate. "Marks is dead," he said.

Hovannes didn't touch the envelope. He knew what was in it—the papers Polito had picked up at Headquarters that afternoon for Lou to deliver.

"Shot?" he asked.

"He fell from the rocks near the tower," Lou said, "smashed up pretty bad. You can call the M.E. later, they'll find bullets in him."

Hovannes fingered the corner of the envelope without saying anything. From behind Lou, Emily asked, "Frank, was one of your men killed?" Her husband let Savage answer.

"No," Lou said. "He was a drug dealer. But I knew him for a long time."

Emily nodded but she didn't understand. "I have some work to do upstairs," she said, reaching around Lou to take her half-filled coffee cup from the table.

"I'm sorry, Mrs. Hovannes, I didn't mean to interrupt your dinner," Savage apologized.

"That's all right, Lou," she said and reached out to touch him lightly on the arm with her free hand. "It's not your fault."

She hurried up the stairs and Lou waited a moment until he heard a door close. Then he sat down heavily in the chair at the side of the table.

"That's not true, is it, Frank?" he asked. "It is my fault, isn't it?"

It would have been easy for Hovannes to say Not really, but he didn't and Lou added, "Yours too, you know."

"Yeah, I know," Hovannes answered.

"There were times I could have killed him myself," Lou said softly, speaking down to the empty space of table between his hands, more to himself than to the Inspector. "The only reason he talked to me was he wanted to be covered on all sides. That and the money. He was a dirty little rodent, you know that. But Jesus, Frank . . ."

Lou looked up without finishing the sentence. He was aware of the fresh pungent smell of oregano, like an irritant from the uncovered casserole in the middle of the table.

"I'm sorry I got you into this thing, Lou," Frank said.

"Nah, that's not it," Savage answered. "It didn't have to work out this way."

"No, that's true, it didn't," Frank said dully. "At least I think it didn't, but maybe it did."

The two detectives sat at the table a few moments without speaking and without looking at each other. Their minds were in different places. Maybe, Frank was thinking, it did have to work out this way. He was remembering Ernie Fleming silhouetted in the window late at night on Greene Street, his gun and silencer waiting for Angie Morello to walk in front of them, and superimposed on that picture he heard Ernie's voice say Jesus, Frank just before he died on Thanksgiving Day. Or maybe it was Lou's voice.

"It comes to the same thing," Lou said, breaking the silence. "Maybe the whole thing was wrong, maybe it just didn't work out. Maybe if Polito hadn't been in on it . . . I don't know. But this wasn't what we wanted, was it, Frank?"

Hovannes didn't answer. "Come on outside, Lou. I want to ask you a question," he said, standing up from the table. With Lou behind him he walked through the living room and slid the glass door to the patio open.

It was cool outside and the sky was dark already, ink-blue but not black yet. Hovannes took a pack of cigarets from his shirt pocket and offered one to Savage, who took it, then leaned forward to get a light from the match Hovannes held out for him in his cupped hands. Frank lit his own cigaret and tossed the match into the rock garden above the retaining wall.

"What would you have done if we decided this afternoon that we had to hit Marks?" Hovannes asked.

"What does that matter now?" Lou answered defensively.

"It doesn't," Frank admitted. "I just wanted to know. Don't you?"

"No," Lou said. "Why should I?"

"Because I almost said it. If you hadn't told me about the letter, that's what I think I would have done."

"Well that's your answer," Savage said. "Mine is I don't know. I really don't."

"Maybe it would have been all right this afternoon," Frank mused. "One way it's war and the other way it's just killing."

Lou said, "I don't know, Frank. Maybe."

In just the two minutes they had been outside, the sky had blackened into unambiguous night and the tips of their cigarets flared in the darkness.

Frank said, "I wish I could believe that. They're both killing. One way it's Polito and the other way it's us, that's all."

"That's a difference too, Frank," Savage said, his voice firm, convinced this wasn't just something he was clutching at. It was the difference that had been bothering him all along.

"Yeah," Hovannes conceded, "it is. Do you think you can stick it out?"

"No," Lou said. "Don't ask me to."

Frank nodded and flipped his cigaret to the side, where it continued to glow faintly on the patio stones. "I'll call Narco tomorrow," he said, "put through the papers. Who was your CO?"

"Hendricks. I'm sorry about this, Frank."

Hovannes smiled at him. From inside the house he heard the telephone ringing. "Celia'll be glad," he said.

Lou returned the smile. "Thanks, Frank," he said, and for some reason he thought of the two turtles in the Delacorte pond.

"Frank, there's a call for you," Emily's voice interrupted. She had stopped on the far side of the living room so as not to walk in on them while they were talking.

Frank stepped through the open doorway and Lou followed.

"He wouldn't say who he was," Emily said and turned to go back upstairs.

Frank walked to the phone on the kitchen wall. "Inspector Hovannes," he said.

"Hovannes. Jack Kittens."

"How'd you get my number?"

"Shit, Hovannes, there are harder things to do than that. Look, you wanted to know what's breaking. Something's on for Friday night."

"What?"

"It looks like the big show, fifteen rounds. I just got a call from Paulie Gagliano. I'm supposed to get in touch with Phil Runelli, tell him to eat dinner at home Friday night."

"What's that mean?"

"Paulie and Runelli were always pretty tight. I guess some people are gonna get wasted and Paulie wants Runelli home in bed when it happens."

"Okay, what do you figure?"

"Manzano, Diamond, Runelli—the whole lot of them— eat at Valentine's every Friday. This time it's gonna be the last supper. That what you wanted?"

"Yeah," Hovannes said, "thanks, Jack. Stay out of trouble all week, you'll be a big man come Saturday."

He hung up and turned to Lou, who was waiting by the dining room table. "Friday," he announced. "LaGarda's going to hit Eddie Manzano."

Lou looked at him impassively. His left hand lay on the envelope.

"Christ, I wanted him to do that," Frank said. "We know about a thing like this in advance, we should be able to bust LaGarda for the hit. Get rid of the whole filthy lot of them."

It *was* working out the way he had planned, he thought. Not all of it. But the important parts were right.

"Can you stick it out till Friday, Lou?" he asked. "Just till Friday. Then it'll all be over."

"Frank, I can't," Lou answered firmly. He picked up the envelope from the table and put it back in his jacket pocket. "You don't need me for this," he said. "It'll work out."

Chapter 28

"POLITO HERE yet?"

"Not yet, boss. Good morning."

"Yeah, good morning. As soon as he gets here, the two of you come into my office," Hovannes said curtly, walking past Obregon's desk in the squadroom into his own office. He closed the door behind him.

Coming around the desk, he tossed his hat on the windowsill, sat down and lit a cigaret. He smoked it through without doing anything, leaning back in his chair and tapping the ashes from time to time into the metal wastebasket to his right. When it had burned down almost to his fingers he sat forward and ground it out in the ashtray on the desk.

Sliding the shallow center drawer out until it hit the arms of his chair, he groped inside for the Department directory and pulled it free. He leafed through it until he found what he was looking for and dialed the number. A woman's voice answered.

"Narcotics, Sergeant Schmidt," she said crisply.

"This is Inspector Hovannes, OCC. I'd like to speak to Captain Hendricks."

"Just a moment, Inspector," she said and the telephone clicked dead.

A few seconds later a man's voice came on, deep and mellifluous, like a radio announcer.

"Frank, what can I do for you?"

"Just the opposite. That guy I took from you last fall, Lou Savage—you want him back?"

"What's the matter, he didn't work out?" Hendricks asked, a tone of cautious suspicion creeping into his voice. If Savage was a troublemaker, he was thinking, Hovannes could keep him.

"Nothing like that, he worked out fine," Hovannes answered to reassure him. "He just didn't like it here, that's all."

"No problems?"

"No problems. Look, I tried to talk him into staying, he didn't want it."

"All right, put the papers through," the Captain said.

"Thanks, Hendricks. How would it be if he reports to you right away for assignment?"

"Right away? It's gotta take a week. Sounds like you're in a hurry to get rid of him. You sure there were no problems?"

"I told you there were no problems. Whatdya say?"

"Yeah, all right," Hendricks conceded. "But look, Hovannes, if this guy's a troublemaker . . ."

"Thanks, Hendricks," Frank interrupted and then hung up.

He held the receiver pressed to its cradle for a few seconds and then picked it up again and dialed Lou Savage's number. Celia answered.

"Celia, it's Frank Hovannes. Is Lou there?"

"He's asleep, Inspector," she said, and then added, "he was up almost all night. What's the matter?"

"Nothing now," Frank answered. He wanted to say something reassuring but couldn't think of anything. "Don't wake him, but when he gets up tell him I called Hendricks and it's all settled. He's supposed to report to him right away."

"Oh, Frank, thank you," Celia blurted out. She sounded very young.

"It's all right," Frank said to her. "Keep in touch."

He was about to hang up when he heard Celia's voice and put the phone back to his ear.

"Frank," she said, "it was really me, you know. Lou would have stayed, I think. He really admires you."

"Thanks, Celia," Frank said. Admires was a funny word for her to have used, he thought. "Don't blame yourself," he added, and realized at once that that was a funny thing to have said too.

He hung up the phone and lit another cigaret. After a few minutes the door opened and Roberto Obregon leaned in.

"Polito's here, boss. Should I bring him in?" Obregon asked.

"Yeah," Frank said. He straightened himself in his chair and leaned forward over the desk while Obregon stepped back outside to get Polito. The two of them came in a moment later, Obregon first. As he always did, he took a pad from the Inspector's desk and sat in the chair facing Hovannes. Polito stood by the door as he had done yesterday.

"Sit down," Hovannes said tonelessly, motioning to the chair by the side wall where Savage had sat when they discussed the problem with Fran Marks. Polito hesitated a moment and then sat down.

Hovannes waited until he was seated. "First off I got some news. It looks like our ship might be coming in," he said. "Then afterwards I want to talk to you, Ron."

Polito nodded slightly, his eyes locked on Hovannes's face. The Inspector was probably pissed off about his hitting that junkie, he figured. But so what?

Hovannes looked away from him toward Obregon. "I got word last night," he said, "there's a hit planned for Eddie Manzano. I want any suggestions you got on how you think we should handle it. I'll tell you what I know, which isn't much. Friday night Eddie and some of his friends—that'd be Johnny Lombardi, Frankie Diamond, maybe Phil Runelli—eat dinner at Valentine's. That's a restaurant down on Cherry Street, it's Frankie Diamond's place," he explained for Polito's benefit. "This Friday night thing's been regular for years, except the late Sallie Manzano used to pick up the tab but now it's Eddie's turn. Anyway, he's gonna be hit there. Inside or outside, before dinner or after, I don't know. I don't know who the hit men are either. All I know is LaGarda okayed it and it's on for Friday night. Who's got some ideas?"

"We wanna let it happen, right?" Obregon asked.

"What have we been doing this last couple of months? Of course we want to let it happen. But what I want to work out is how we can cover it. We've got to be right there so we can nail whoever's doing the hit, but we don't want to scare them off. If they get away, all we've done is make a big shot out of Tony LaGarda."

"Ron and I could wait inside. None of them know us. Is there a bar there?" Obregon said.

"Yeah."

"Well, we could wait at the bar."

"You maybe," Hovannes said after a few seconds' thought. "I don't know about Ron. Most of the people at the bar are Puerto Ricans from the project. You'd fit in but Ron looks too much like a cop."

"Awright, maybe me and Lou inside," Roberto corrected.

"Lou's not in this."

Obregon looked up quizzically from his pad, but something in the Inspector's face told him not to push it.

"How come Lou's not in this?" Polito asked.

"We'll get to that later, Polito," Frank snapped at him. "Okay, you inside. But look, sit up at the far end of the bar. If you have to start shooting out of the middle of a crowd, somebody's going to get hurt."

"Okay," Obregon nodded. "I won't draw any fire unless I'm by myself. How's that?"

"Fine. Let them come out on the street if you have to."

"How many guys do you figure'd be in on a job like this?" Roberto asked.

"Two, three, I guess. Maybe four at most. If they leave a guy in the car, that means three inside."

"Any reason we can't use some other men on it? This is all kosher. There's nothing they'd need to know, just you got a tip there's gonna be a hit and they'd be covering it."

Hovannes shook his head. "I'd have trouble holding them back when the hit men went in," he said. "They might want to go in and get them before the shooting started. I don't want to have to explain later why I kept half a dozen troops sitting on their asses when I knew what was coming. Especially when it's Eddie Manzano that gets iced. You know how that'd look."

Obregon could see the Inspector's point. If he knew there was going to be a shootout, he should have men inside and out to keep it from happening. There'd be a lot of heat, maybe even Department charges, if it came out that the police didn't stop a gunfight with lots of innocent civilians around. "Yeah, okay," he said, "then it's just the three of us. I guess one of you has to take the front and the other the back."

"The back's no problem," Hovannes said. "It's just a little alley. Not more than six, seven feet wide, opens onto Water Street."

"Can one man cover it?"

"Yeah," Hovannes said. "If I remember it—we'll have to check this out—there's a door onto it from the next building, back door to a hardware store or something. It's in the side wall, maybe six feet from the kitchen door at

Valentine's. We could put Ron in there. We can't leave him in the alley because if they come in from the back they'd walk right into him. But if he waits in the hardware store till they're inside, he'd have an easy covered shot at anyone coming out."

"I could wear a wire, tell you which way they're coming," Obregon offered.

"Yeah, good idea. That leaves the front. You know, I was thinking, it's all old buildings down there. Cement block, two, three stories. How's this sound? I take over a room on the second floor right across the street. That way I'm out of the way when the hit men get there. I come downstairs when they go inside. Or if they do it on the street I've got them covered. Ron, you could be on the roof of Valentine's. That way you can cover the front and the back. If they do it outside we're on both sides of the street. If they do it inside, we'll know which way they're leaving—just see where they put the car. If they come out through the kitchen Ron can just pop them from on top as they come out the door. And if the car's waiting out on Cherry Street, I'll be down in front, you come around the front of the roof, and Roberto's on their tail inside. Three of us ought to be able to handle it."

"Sounds good," Obregon said.

"Ron?"

"Yeah, sounds good," Polito agreed. .

"Okay. Why don't you go down there, Roberto, and check the layout. See if we can do it that way. See what's right across the street too. Pick me out a good spot. But don't make any arrangements today, I don't want any chance of a tipoff. We can take care of that Friday. Okay?"

Obregon stood up and tossed the pad back on Frank's desk. He turned to leave but Polito's voice stopped him where he stood.

"How come Savage isn't in on this?" Polito asked.

"He's off the detail, that's all you need to know, Polito," Frank answered in a low voice.

"Yeah, but how come?" Polito said, his voice insistent but whining.

Hovannes stood up slowly and leaned forward on the desk, his knuckles pressed against the blotter. He looked at Polito a long time before answering. He wanted to say, Because of you, you little cocksucker. You killed a guy because he was afraid of Lou. But instead he just said, "He's off the squad. You don't need to know why."

"He didn't quit, did he?" Polito challenged.

Hovannes didn't answer. "You better get going, Roberto," he said, but Obregon didn't move.

"Look, I know what that guy was like," Polito said, his words rapid, his voice shrill. Obregon started to step toward him, but Hovannes motioned him with his hand to stay where he was and Polito went on. "I was afraid he was gonna quit all along. This thing was supposed to be for keeps. He wasn't right for this thing. He starts getting ideas, this is wrong, that's wrong. I mean, you're either in it or you're out. You can't just quit like you're not a part of it. We all signed on, we knew what we were getting into. Him too, he's no different."

While he was talking Hovannes came around the desk. He sat back against the corner of the desk and his hands, behind his hips, gripped the edges of the desk top hard. He was a foot and a half from Polito and he waited to let him have his say. Obregon came around to Hovannes's right.

"I know why he quit, too," Polito was saying. "It was because of that junkie. You said it yourself, we had to hit him to protect ourselves. I'm not going to jail because Savage all of a sudden thinks some fucking junkie is so precious."

He stopped talking and Hovannes's hands relaxed their grip on the desk top. "You finished?" he asked.

Polito looked up at the Inspector and for the first time he realized how close he was, almost as though he hadn't seen Frank come around the desk while he was talking. His head was at about Frank's chest level and for a moment he felt intimidated by the Inspector's size. He glanced over at Obregon and the thought flashed through his mind that the little Spic was going to try to hit him.

"No, I'm not finished," he said, looking back to Hovannes, his voice thin and reedy with fear and excitement. "Look, we're all in this together," he went on. "Like I said, a thing like this we've got to trust each other, know what I mean. If one guy breaks, we're all washed up. That's why we've got to stick this thing out to the end. If Savage thinks this kind of thing is wrong, he's got a right to think it, but he never should of come in in the first place. Now he quits and he thinks that gets him off the hook. But you know how it is with these guys. He's out of it now but he's gonna think about it some more and then he's gonna decide he's gotta come clean from the whole thing. Next thing you know he'll be telling that cunt he's living with all about it, if he hasn't told her already, and then he's gonna go to Internal Affairs with the whole story and we'll all be up on murder raps so that he can live with himself."

Hovannes had heard enough. Both hands flashed out and grabbed at Polito's shoulders, pushing him violently against the wall so that his chair tipped backward until his head and the base of his neck hit against the wall behind him. The chair skidded out from under him, toppling sideways to the floor. For a moment Polito hung incongruously, pinned to the wall and held there by the strength of Hovannes's hands until his feet, kicking among the chair legs, cleared a space for him to stand.

Hovannes pulled him upright until they were eye to eye. He relaxed his grip on Polito's shoulders without letting go, and Polito's hands came up, flailing like a girl warding off blows but unable to dislodge the Inspector's hands, which tightened into his shoulders as he struggled.

Hovannes didn't speak until Polito's arms dropped to his sides in surrender. When he did his voice was soft and forceful, ominous, almost a whisper. "Polito," he said, "I don't want any more mistakes. If anything happens to Lou, it won't be like Marks or Silvera. Is that clear? You're gonna have to take care of me and Roberto here too. I'll break you in half, so help me God I will. You'll go over for it, even if the two of us have to go with you."

Polito tried to look away to his right, away from Hovannes and Obregon, but the Inspector's hand, palm open, came up hard against the side of his head, catching him behind the left ear. Hovannes heard his cheekbone smash against the wall.

"Is that clear?" he said, his voice loud now, demanding but not as menacing as before.

Polito turned to face him. The skin below his left eye was scraped raw but there was no bruise. He nodded dumbly but didn't answer.

"You can watch this if you want to, I'm going to bed," Emily said. "I'm sure I've seen it before."

Frank looked up from the television to his wife. "Yeah, good idea," he agreed. "I'm kind of tired."

Emily walked into the bedroom. When she was out of sight Frank turned back to the television and realized he didn't know what the story was about. He was trying to decide whether he could afford to put taps on LaGarda's phones, at his house and at the Fidelio. They might come in handy. If the hit men were pros the chances of turning them around wouldn't be very good, and then tying it to LaGarda would be a hell of a job. Same if they were killed.

On the other hand, there was the same problem with bugging LaGarda as with bringing in outside men. Getting the court order would be easy. The petition could just say that a reliable informant had told him La-Garda was planning to have Eddie Manzano hit, no details. That would be enough for any judge. But what if the bug was too good and LaGarda laid the whole thing out for them? He'd have the same problem explaining why he didn't stop the hit since he knew about it in advance. No, Frank concluded, that won't work, it can't be a bug.

He could hear the water running in the bathroom sink and reached over the arm of the couch for the cigarets on the end table. The movie or whatever it was had ended and the news was on already. He watched for about half a minute—some footage of an angry crowd in front of one of the embassies, probably Jews, the Russian embassy—but it seemed very remote and when a reporter started interviewing some people from the crowd Frank's mind drifted back to his problem.

He snuffed out his half-smoked cigaret in the ashtray and gave up. LaGarda wasn't the important thing anyway, he told himself. He wanted him, and would take him if he could get him, but if Counterthrust ended with just the Manzano brothers out of the picture he could live with that. All Ernie had wanted was Big Sallie. When Ernie died Frank told himself he wanted more. Just revenge for

Ernie wouldn't be enough. If that was all he had wanted he would have been willing to just gun Big Sallie himself and take the consequences. And it might have been worth it. But the idea of Counterthrust was not simply to get rid of guys like Manzano but to mess up their operation as much as possible, get them going for each other.

And it had worked, too. Sallie was gone already, if the hit men knew what they were doing Eddie would be gone by Friday, and Frank knew he had a good outside shot at busting LaGarda for it. You couldn't ask for more than a good outside shot.

Then what was wrong, Frank asked himself. What was it Lou said last night? This wasn't what we wanted, was it, Frank? But why wasn't it? Because of Lou? Polito? Polito gave the whole thing a bad taste, but if it ended this way, what did Polito's hitting Silvera or Marks matter? It was ugly but maybe it wasn't too high a price to pay. The whole thing was ugly.

Of course Polito never should have been in on the thing in the first place, but Frank couldn't blame himself for that. Polito hadn't given him any choice. It was blackmail, either take him in or forget about it. Somehow Polito had found out about the plan from Ernie, and Hovannes didn't kid himself about what it meant; Polito was resentful enough to take whatever he knew to Internal Affairs if Sallie Manzano was killed and he wasn't a part of it.

Emily's voice interrupted from the bedroom. "Frank, are you coming?" she called. "I'm in bed already."

He pushed himself up from the couch and walked over to click off the television. On his way past the couch he checked to make sure his cigaret was out and turned off the lamp. The bedroom light was still on and he switched it off as he stepped into the room. Then he sat on the bed next to Emily, turned sideways so he could look at her.

"Something the matter, Frank?" she asked softly.

"No," he said evasively. "You surprised me. I didn't think you'd be this fast."

"And you're so slow," she said with a forced laugh. "What are you waiting for?"

He bent over to untie his shoes but then straightened up quickly. "There's something I've got to check," he said and hurried around the foot of the bed to the phone on Emily's side. He dialed Lou Savage's number and waited while it rang.

Emily rolled over to face him. She could see his outline standing over her in the dark but he seemed so far away from her that she didn't want to look and rolled back again.

He could do it anyway, Frank thought. The phone rang for the ninth, then the tenth time. He slammed the receiver down, startling Emily. She heard him walk to the dresser and knew it was for his gun. Then she heard his footsteps coming around the bed and past her, out of the room. He didn't even say goodbye, she thought, and started to cry. But then she heard him stop before he got to the top of the stairs and he said, "I'm sorry, Emmy. I've got to go."

She listened as he ran down the stairs and a few moments later she heard the door open and close and then the car door and then the engine starting. She couldn't stop crying, but it wasn't because she was alone. It was because she didn't know what his trouble, was, because he was alone.

Chapter 29

"SHE'S NOT in any danger," the doctor said softly, stepping into the hall and closing the door behind him. "She's asking about somebody named Lou. Is that the guy who was killed?"

"Yeah," Hovannes said dully. "Can I see her now?"

The doctor nodded and then walked away down the corridor.

Frank opened the door slowly, using both hands, and stepped inside. Celia was awake but she gave no sign of recognition. Her eyes followed Frank as he walked up beside the bed. Her arms were outside the covers by her sides, and under the blanket her body seemed stiff and awkward with discomfort, like she was trying to avoid contact with the bed.

Frank reached out for her hand and it softly returned the pressure of his grip. He was glad to see there weren't any tubes connected to her. She was very pale and had lost a lot of blood, but it didn't seem as bad as it looked last night when he found her. She was lying just inside the front door to the apartment, conscious but not moving. Her body was twisted awkwardly, crumpled. She must have been shot just as she came in, and the gunman had pushed her body aside with the door as he fled.

He rolled her onto her back to check the wounds. Her eyes weren't focused and he sensed she didn't know who he was so he said, "It's Frank Hovannes. You'll be all right, Celia. Don't try to move." There was a bullet wound in her chest below her right breast but toward the side. It may have got a lung but probably not; she seemed to be breathing easily. There was another wound below it, closer to center, just above her stomach.

Leaving her where she lay, Frank raced down the long corridor to find Lou. He saw him as soon as he got to the doorway to the living room and it was immediately apparent that he was dead. He lay on his back, stretched out full length just in front of the couch, his head against the apron of the couch, held up slightly from the floor. There was blood above him on the cushions, which must have splattered as he fell. There seemed to be two wounds, both in his face, above and below his left eye.

Frank ran to the phone and called an ambulance, then went back to Celia. Two patrolmen from the sixth got there first. The ambulance and a team of Homicide detectives arrived simultaneously a few moments later. Frank identified himself and gave them Lou's name and shield number. He told them he wanted the investigation handled from his office and asked them to have their CO get in touch with Assistant Chief Inspector Flynn at OCC. Then he rode to the hospital in the ambulance with Celia.

He stayed there all night, not really thinking about it but in the back of his mind surprised that no one had come looking for him. A little before nine o'clock the two Homicide detectives showed up to see if Celia could be questioned. Frank told them he'd handle it himself and sent them away. A few hours later, just after eleven, a nurse came and told him he could see her.

"Lou was shot," she said in a small voice, looking straight at Frank. "Is he dead?"

It was hard for Frank to look at her when he answered but he had to. "Yes," he said softly.

She didn't turn away, but her eyes closed for a moment and her lips tightened. She didn't want to cry.

"Who did it, Frank?" she asked. "Do you know?"

"No," he lied, letting go of her hand and turning around to pull up a chair next to the bed. He sat down. "A cop makes a lot of enemies. You know that, Celia," he said.

He reached for her hand again, and this time her fingers clutched for his and squeezed hard as soon as he touched her. Then her fingers relaxed, and her body too. She let herself sink into the bed, wincing at first from the pain but then accepting it.

"Can you tell me what happened?" Frank asked.

"Not really," she answered, her voice firmer now. "I was just coming home. I teach a class every Wednesday. It was a little after eleven—we went out for coffee after. I started to unlock the door but it wasn't locked—the bolt lock, I mean. I was just putting my key in the other lock when I heard these shots. I remember the first thing I thought was Oh God, Lou. He had been so unhappy lately, Frank. Then I ran inside. I mean, I just got the door open and I stepped inside and there was a man running toward me down the hall. I don't know what I was thinking, but I didn't want him to get away and I closed the door behind me and I stood in front of him. And then he shot me, that's all I remember, Frank. I remember the door hit me and it took him a long time to get it open. And when it closed I wanted to get up and find Lou, but I don't think I did. That's where I was when you came, wasn't it?"

Frank nodded. "You couldn't have helped him," he said. "Did you get a look at the man?"

"He was tall, tall and thin. He was wearing a suit—I mean, you know, a jacket and tie. I can't really describe him. Maybe I'd recognize him if I saw him, I don't know."

"That's all right," Frank told her.

"Do you know who it is?" Celia asked quickly. Her mind was alert and she noticed that he hadn't pushed her for a description.

"We have some ideas," Frank answered evasively. "It shouldn't take long. We'll get him."

Celia didn't answer for a long time. Then she said, "That's important to you, isn't it?"

Frank didn't say anything and Celia went on, speaking softly, to herself as much as to him. "I don't care, really. What happens to him, I mean. I want to understand it, why he had to kill Lou. I want to know who did it so I can understand why he had to kill Lou. But I don't care about the rest. Lou would have cared, he's like you. But I don't."

"I know," Frank answered her firmly, "but it does matter."

She wasn't looking at him any more and he stood up without letting go of her hand. "I've got to go, Celia," he said. "Is there anyone we should get in touch with—your parents, some friends, anyone?"

"No," she said. "There was only Lou. Will I be in the hospital long?"

"I don't think so, but you won't be able to move around much for a while. Maybe you'd want to come up and stay with Emily?"

Celia looked up at Frank and smiled. Her lips looked

pale and cold but there was strength in her smile and in her face.

Frank let go of her hand. "I'll be back tomorrow," he said, turning and walking to the door.

"Frank," she called after him. He turned back to face her. "I just want to know why," she said. "He was so unhappy."

There was nothing to say. "Tomorrow," Frank repeated and hurried from the room.

Thursday, April 24

"Now let me get this straight," Assistant Chief Inspector Flynn said from behind his desk. "Was this guy working for you or wasn't he?"

"Yeah, he was working for me," Hovannes explained patiently, going over it again. "I got him from Narco last fall on temporary assignment. Around the beginning of the year I put through a transfer. But he wanted to transfer back. I talked to Jeff Hendricks about it just yesterday. He was supposed to report to Hendricks for assignment. I don't know whether he did or not."

"I know all that," Flynn said. "I talked to Hendricks. He said you were in some kind of a hurry. What was that about?"

"Wasn't about anything," Frank answered. "The guy had been asking about the transfer for a long time and I kept putting him off. When he reminded me about it the other day, I figured I hadn't given him a fair shake so I tried to push it through, that's all."

Flynn looked down at his desk. His fingers flicked nervously at the tab of a green file folder in front of him. "You sure that's all?" he said.

"Yeah, look, I didn't want to lose him. That's why I stalled off putting the transfer through. He was a good man."

Flynn looked up. "A good man," he snorted. The file folder flipped open and Flynn slid a sheet of paper across the desk toward Hovannes.

Frank picked it up and looked at it. It was the letter Fran Marks had warned about. After he read it he tossed it back toward the Chief.

"So what's this," he said scornfully. "You see what the guy's got. After Sallie Manzano was hit a week ago Monday one of his bodyguards went on the lam. This guy knew where Palmini was and he told Savage and Savage told me. The two of us went up there to get him but somebody had taken him out of there already. So this guy gets the cockeyed notion that Savage must have told Tony La-Garda where Palmini was. But you know who this guy was—he was a fifth-rate connection. If he ever picked up a kilo, he'd rupture himself. So if he knew where Palmini was, everybody but us must have known. Could have been a hundred guys tipped LaGarda."

"That's true," Flynn agreed, "and it could have been like it says here."

He put the letter back in the folder and flipped it closed, then looked up at Hovannes. "Know what I think," he said almost belligerently. "I think your man was up to his ass in trouble and I think you know more about it than you're telling me."

"How do you figure that, Flynn?" Hovannes said without flinching.

"Let's say it was like this guy Marks says," Flynn answered, backing down slightly, his tone less challenging. "This Marks was shaking him down. They set up a meeting, and the next thing Marks is going face first into the water."

"Okay," Frank interrupted, "but Savage didn't kill him. The guy was shot with a forty-five. Savage has got a Browning, but it wasn't the gun that killed Marks. You can check it out."

"We already did," Flynn said coolly. "You're right on that, but let's take this a little further. Say Savage is on LaGarda's pad and this guy Marks is shaking him down, awright? LaGarda finds out about it and he doesn't like the whole scene. He doesn't like a little shit like Marks pushing his cops around and he doesn't like paying a cop who can't take better care of himself. So he has both of them wasted. You buying that?"

"No," Hovannes said flatly but didn't elaborate. He waited for the Chief to continue.

"Savage and Marks were killed with the same gun," Flynn said. "What does that tell you?"

"It tells me they're connected, but we already know they're connected," Frank answered quickly. "Look," he added, "I knew Lou Savage. He wasn't on anybody's pad. I'll put every man I've got on it and we'll come up with something better. But I'm telling you now Lou Savage is clean."

"I hope so, Hovannes," Flynn said. He swung around sideways in his chair, pushed his glasses up on his forehead, and rubbed at his eyes with the heels of his hands. "I don't want you handling it, Hovannes," he said with his hands still in front of his face. "Let Homicide take it."

Frank shrugged. It didn't matter to him who handled the investigation. "If that's the way you want it, Larry, it's okay with me," he said. "There's a couple of things I want you to do, though. There's a good chance the girl's in danger, whoever did it. She say's she might be able to recognize the killer, and if he finds out she's alive he might want to get rid of her. I want a twenty-four hour guard on her room."

Flynn nodded. "I'll do it right away," he said, turning back to his desk and reaching for the phone. "Special Services all right?" he asked as he dialed.

"Sure."

Flynn got a captain from Special Services on the phone and explained the detail to him—two-man shifts around the clock. Before he hung up Frank said, "Let me talk to him," and reached for the phone. The Chief leaned forward to hand it to him.

"This is Inspector Hovannes. Look," he said, "tell the men you put on that detail that I don't want anyone getting in there. I mean anyone. I don't care if they're guys Savage worked with. She doesn't want condolence calls. No exceptions, that clear?"

"No exceptions," the Captain on the other end of the line repeated.

"What was that about?" the Chief asked as Frank stretched forward to hang up the phone.

"I just don't want to take any chances."

"You think it could have been a cop, is that right?"

"Look, I don't know, Larry. Maybe Savage told somebody else in the Department about Palmini. Maybe Marks was right, only he had the wrong cop, I don't know."

"That's not bad, Hovannes," the Chief said slowly after contemplating the possibility a few moments. "It could be. You're really sure about this guy Savage, huh?"

Frank nodded. He had been up all night and it showed.

"Yeah, okay, look, if the guy's clean he's clean," Flynn said. "I'm sorry about what I said before, Hovannes. The whole thing's such a fucking ugly business. Why don't you go home and get some sleep."

Frank pushed himself heavily from the chair and left the Chief's office without a word. Out on Centre Street the brilliant sunlight stung his eyes. It was the middle of the afternoon and he hadn't eaten all day, but he was too tired to be hungry.

He walked to the Broome Street Annex and went to the basement squadroom. The door was locked and he let himself in. He had never noticed before how damp the room felt. Shivering involuntarily, he took a deep breath to stop it, then locked the door behind him and walked to the small conference table in the middle of the room. He slid one of the metal frame chairs up to the table, sat down and felt for his cigarets. He took out the pack but changed his mind and left it on the table. It bothered him that he had to lie to Celia. Pushing the cigaret pack to the side to clear a space, he leaned forward until his face rested against the cold metal of the table. Like a kindergarten kid taking a nap, he thought, and fell asleep.

When he woke up the room was dark. He checked the high, sidewalk level windows at the side of the room and saw that it was late but there was still a little daylight left. His watch said twenty to eight. He stood up slowly, his neck and back stiff, and walked purposefully to his office. Inside, he clicked on his desk lamp, reached for the phone, and dialed. It rang about five times and then a man's voice answered and said, "Yeah?"

"Polito, I meant what I said yesterday," Frank began. He knew what he was going to say, the whole thing was clear in his mind. "You should have gotten rid of the forty-five after you hit Silvera. It was dumb to hold onto it, but maybe it's not too late now. But you can't do anything about your service revolver, Polito, and that's what I'm going to get you for. We've got ballistics samples from it, you know, and they'll match the slugs in Palmini."

Frank stopped talking and the phone at the other end clicked dead. He stood up, turned off the light and hurried out to the street. His own car was still in front of Savage's so he hailed a cab and had the driver take him up the West Side Highway to the Seventy-second Street exit. He got off at the traffic circle and walked down to the river, following it south past the boat basin until he got to the abandoned shipping yard where Obregon and Polito had taken Al Palmini.

There was no sense trying to find the body, he figured, so he picked out an open corrugated tin shed on an old pier and went inside to wait.

Chapter 30

Ron Polito hung up the phone and reached up with his right hand to steady himself against the wall. He stood there for fully a minute, his mind racing with inarticulated thoughts. Then he let go of the wall, went into the kitchen and turned on the cold water tap. Taking a handful of ice cubes from the freezer, he dropped them into a yellow plastic tumbler and filled it with water. He waited a moment until the water cleared and got cold, then drank it down and refilled the glass, which he carried to the living room.

He sat down in the middle of the couch, holding the glass in both hands between his knees. First thing, he told himself, was to get rid of the forty-five. That wouldn't be a problem, drop it in the river somewhere. Hovannes knew that already. That's why he didn't mind reminding Polito about it. He must have been figuring he didn't need the forty-five to make a case. Yeah, Polito thought, okay, that's what I'll do.

Putting the glass on the floor, he stood up, walked to the dresser and slid open the top drawer. Both guns were there and the sight of his service revolver startled him, almost as though he had expected it not to be there. He picked them up, one in each hand, and carried them back to the couch, where he sat down and examined them for a long time, trying to figure out what to do with them. The two guns confused him and he forgot for a few minutes that he had already made up his mind about the forty-five.

While he was thinking he suddenly remembered the silencer he had used when he hit Marks. Laying the guns on the floor near the water glass, he went back to the dresser. He shoved the top drawer closed and opened the one below it. Pushing aside some shirts and underwear, he found the imitation leather case and pulled it free.

Back on the couch he sat awhile, looking at the two

guns and the case grouped in a little arc on the floor in front of his feet. The case might float, he reminded himself. Maybe it was wood or cardboard under the vinyl. He picked it up and opened it, took out the heavy piece of metal and put it in the space on the floor where the case had been. Then he examined the case but there was no way to tell. The vinyl went around all the way on the inside. He knocked against the cover with his knuckles and it sounded hollow, rigid, but not as rigid as wood. Still, it might float. Not with the silencer in it, but if the latch got wet it might open and then the silencer would fall out and the case would float up above it, marking where it lay.

He inspected the case closely for any identification that could tie it to him, but there was none. Fuck it, he thought, I can ditch it in a garbage can. Then the forty-five and the silencer could go in the river. That still left the thirty-eight, and he didn't have any ideas—except one that he didn't want to think about.

Maybe Hovannes was bluffing about the ballistics samples, he thought. But maybe not. He had to qualify with the gun twice each year. It didn't seem implausible that they would keep a slug from the target for identification, put the blow-up in his file right with the firearms issue receipt he had signed. He thought about calling someone to ask, but he didn't know anyone he could trust and it might be incriminating later.

Bending forward to the floor, he put the silencer case down, extending the arc, and picked up the thirty-eight, which he examined for a few moments, his mind blank. One thing at a time, he told himself, and carried the service revolver back to the dresser, replacing it in the top drawer. He walked back across the room and squatted in front of the little arc on the floor. There was a space where the thirty-eight had been and he pushed the silencer case around to fill it in. It all looked compact and orderly, which made it easier to be decisive.

Satisfied, Polito stood up quickly and walked to the closet. He slid the door open and took out a dark green nylon windbreaker with a matted pile lining. It would be cool near the river. Then he went to the kitchen and pulled a folded brown supermarket bag from the pile where he kept them. He hesitated a moment with it in his hand as an idea came to him. Then he flapped it open and set it on the floor next to the bag half filled with garbage. Dumping the garbage into the clean bag, he carried the old one into the living room. People rummage around in garbage cans, he reminded himself, but they were less likely to open an old greasy bag than a clean one.

He put the silencer case into the bag and folded it tightly closed. The silencer went into the left-hand pocket of his windbreaker and he tucked the forty-five into his belt, then zipped the jacket closed over it. He stood there a moment to test, holding the brown paper bag in front of him in both hands, his left elbow against his side to keep the slash pocket of the jacket closed. He let go with his right hand and dropped the bag to his side. That still kept the pocket closed and it didn't look unnatural.

At the door, he suddenly thought, What if Hovannes is outside waiting? He thought of going back for the service revolver but decided against it. It would be too much hardware to carry. Instead, he zipped the jacket down until it was just a quarter of an inch over the handle of the gun in his belt. He picked up his key case from the telephone table by the door and walked out into the little square hallway. He pushed for the elevator, waited and rode down when it came.

At the glass door in front of the building he hesitated, looking out carefully before opening it and walking to the sidewalk. He held the bag in front of him, supported by his left hand with his right hand behind it, against his stomach, just a fraction of an inch from the gun.

Hovannes wasn't there. No, it figured he wouldn't be, but still it was smart to be careful.

Polito walked west on Eighty-third Street toward the river, down the long blocks to Columbus, Amsterdam, Broadway, West End, and then Riverside. It took him almost twenty minutes to get there. At Riverside he stopped, looking for an entrance to the park. There was one just across the street a little to his left. He crossed the wide avenue and hurried down the hill into the park. To his right was a long promenade, two concrete sidewalks with a broad grass median between them. After walking a few minutes, he saw a stairway on his left. It led down to a walk that went under the West Side Highway and came out by the river. Good enough, Polito thought, and hurried down the steps.

He dumped the paper bag with the silencer case into a trash basket along the path and kept walking until he came to the river. There was a heavy wire mesh fence at the edge of the sidewalk with a wooden railing at the top. The tide was fairly low and the water level was about eight feet below him.

Reaching into his pocket with his left hand, he gripped the silencer like a baton and pulled it out. Transferring it to his right hand, he quickly heaved it out over the water and it splashed down maybe fifteen feet out and sank immediately. Then he took the forty-five from his belt and flung it, a high arching overhand shot that carried it even further from the water's edge. In half a minute there weren't even ripples anymore and he turned to go back home.

It had gone smooth as glass, he thought, congratulating himself as he hurried through the park and back into the city. At first he felt euphoric, but that wore off quickly. As he approached Columbus Avenue it suddenly occurred to him that Hovannes might be waiting for him now, when he didn't have his gun. Fuck, I should have taken it, he said to himself, his lips moving although he didn't articulate the words.

He stopped where he stood, across the street from the post office, trying to figure out what to do, but he was panicky and light-headed and not thinking straight. He realized he hadn't eaten yet, and maybe that's what the trouble was.

The restaurant on Columbus was almost empty when he walked in and sat at the counter. He ordered a breaded veal cutlet and spaghetti. Although he ate there often, the coutnerman didn't know his name and never bothered him with small talk. Ron watched as he took a breaded cutlet from a package in the refrigerator, dropped it in the frying basket and lowered it into the oil. Then with a large fork he drew a mound of spaghetti from the pot, transferred it to a heavy china plate and evened it with his fingers. "Coffee?" he asked, and Ron nodded.

The counterman poured a cup and carried it to where Polito was sitting. He pulled out some silverware from under the counter and then went back to the fryer. He lifted the basket and let the oil drain off for a few seconds, then slid the cutlet onto the mound of spaghetti and ladled tomato sauce over the whole thing. "Cheese?" he asked as he set the plate in front of Polito. Ron shook his head and the counterman wrote out a check and slid it face-down in front of him.

Polito ate slowly, cutting the spaghetti with his knife. After a few bites he realized he felt better, the light-headedness was gone. He was able to put everything out of his mind while he finished his meal, and when the spaghetti and cutlet were gone he drank down the cold coffee and asked for another cup. The counterman brought it and added the price to the check, then walked away.

If he's there he's there, Polito told himself, looking into the cup. Tiny rainbowed droplets of oil swirled at the surface of the steaming coffee and from the other side of the counter Ron could hear the sound of the counterman scraping at the grill with a wide spatula.

Yeah, that was a mistake, he reminded himself, his lips moving silently. But he had to get back home to get his piece. He didn't even ask himself what he would do then.

He tried a sip of the coffee but it was too hot to drink and he didn't want to wait any more. The bill was two-forty-five so he left three singles on the counter and walked out to Columbus Avenue. The clock in the dry cleaner's said a quarter past ten. He crossed Columbus and started up Eighty-third, on the south side of the street. Cars were parked on both sides but there was no sign of Hovannes. Moving cautiously and checking ahead of him to make sure none of the cars were occupied, he kept walking until he was directly across the street from his building.

"So far so good," he said, this time out loud. He took a deep breath and hurried across the street. His keys in his hand already, he unlocked the front door and raced to the fire stairs. No point being careful now. If Hovannes was waiting here he had him trapped good, and the only thing to do was get inside as fast as possible. He ran up to the third floor, shoved the fire door violently open and checked the hall.

No one. He stood there a moment as the door swung back to him, then caught it with his left hand and stepped around it. He unlocked his own door, went inside, and double locked it behind him. Now there was nothing to be done except figure out what to do about that goddamned thirty-eight.

He had to assume Hovannes wasn't bluffing about the

ballistics sample, so there was no sense getting rid of the gun. That meant he'd have to get rid of Palmini or the slugs. "Shit, it's probably a trap," he said, talking out loud again. "There's probably thirty cops down there right now with searchlights looking for him. Or maybe just Hovannes waiting. Yeah, that's probably what it is, just Hovannes waiting."

He took a drink from the plastic tumbler of ice water on the floor. Drops of moisture had collected on the outside and he rolled the wet tumbler against his forehead. The cold felt good, but after a few seconds he put the glass down and wiped at his forehead with his jacket sleeve.

"I bet there aren't cops down there," he said. "If he blows the whistle on me he's gotta tell the whole story and they'd suspend him so fucking fast. He wasn't kidding when he said he wouldn't mind going to jail, but he wouldn't want to get himself pinched before tomorrow. He's so fucking righteous about Savage, but he wouldn't blow his chance to be there when they hit Eddie Manzano."

Polito stopped talking. What does it matter, he thought. If there's a bunch of cops there looking for Palmini's body, they're gonna come for me when they find it anyway. So if I go down there I just save them the trouble.

But the more he thought about it, the more convinced he became that that wouldn't be the way it would happen. It's just gonna be Hovannes waiting, he told himself. He's gonna be there, just him. He wouldn't have told me about it if he wasn't.

"Well, Hovannes," he said, speaking out loud again, "it's gotta be. Might as well be tonight."

His mind made up, he walked slowly to the dresser. He took out the thirty-eight, flipped it open and spun the chambers, then snapped it closed and stuffed it into the right-hand pocket of his windbreaker. He scraped around in the drawer and found a small box of shells, which he put in the other pocket. Then he left the apartment quickly and started the long walk back to the river.

He walked down Broadway this time to Seventy-second, then turned west, crossed Riverside Drive, skirted around the traffic circle on the sidewalk, and headed for the river the same way Frank Hovannes had gone a few hours earlier.

He passed the boat basin. It was still early in the year

and there were only a few cabin cruisers bobbing at the pier. A little farther south there was a softball field right under the highway and just beyond that the old shipping yards began. His right hand was in his pocket, his finger on the trigger ready to fire, and he walked slowly. Hovannes could be anywhere.

The first couple of piers had small tin sheds on them, but Polito ruled them out. Hovannes would have no way of knowing which way he was coming. If he had gone around to come in from the south he'd never get as far as these piers and Hovannes would be completely out of the picture.

Still, he walked quietly, although it was impossible not to make any noise on the gravelly cobblestones. He stopped to listen, but the only sound was the traffic hissing evenly on the West Side Highway above him. He might even be behind one of the highway struts, Polito thought, and moved on again. There was a set of railroad sidings with freight cars on them about fifty yards to his left, but they were too far away to get off a good shot in the dark. He wouldn't be in one of them.

Polito crossed two sets of half-buried tracks cutting down to the piers. The pier just to his right was completely burned out, the wood flaky and charred, the old metal shed on it twisted and warped beyond recognition, making a ten-foot high pile of rubble, like it had been bombed. A hundred yards beyond it was another burnt pier with its own pile of rubble and Polito stopped, expecting to hear Hovannes's voice any second.

Nothing moved. He could hear the traffic above him and sea gulls squawking from the water. Okay, he said under his breath, and hurried the last hundred yards. He stopped when he got to the pier. Fifty yards further on there was a corrugated tin shed on the next pier, a big one completely intact, spanning two piers. Maybe that's where he is, Polito thought, or maybe he's right here with Palmini, waiting for me.

It doesn't matter now, we'll find each other one way or the other, Polito thought, and started picking his way through the debris toward Al Palmini's body.

Frank Hovannes stood behind the wire mesh door of the large shed. He heard the sharp clank of metal but couldn't see anything. That's got to be him, he thought. Opening the door carefully, he stepped out onto the boards and waited. He could hear pieces of metal grating against each other and timbers slipping. He walked to the side of the pier to listen, but the sounds had stopped. Except for the gulls and the water lapping against the concrete sea wall it was quiet.

"Polito!" he called loudly across the water between where he stood and the next pier. Dimly, he could see a man's shape rising on top of the ten-foot pile of rubble fifty yards away.

He raced to the front of the pier, leaped down from the boardwalk onto the cobblestones, and ran toward Polito. He heard a shot but it didn't bother him. There was no way Polito could hit a moving target in the dark at this distance. He ducked behind some shoulder-high rusted metal crates and then, using crate after crate as cover, he made it to within ten yards of the foot of the pier where Polito now was trapped. After that there were no more of the big crates.

Carefully, he raised his head enough to look out over the top of the crate. He could see the pier clearly, but there was no way to spot a man's shape in the middle of all that twisted metal and lumber.

He dropped to the ground and crawled on his stomach to get closer. The ground was rough gravel here, littered with rocks and broken shreds of wood from old crates. Crawling slowly and stopping often, because there was no hurry now and he didn't want to make a sound, Frank took almost fifteen minutes to cross the last few yards to the foot of the pier. The only cover in front of him now was a few low pieces of tin.

He realized he was pretty much out in the open while Polito had good cover, but he knew it was Polito who was trapped. He waited without moving for about five minutes, then ten. The traffic on the highway above and behind him was thinning out and he could hear individual cars instead of the steady hum of a half hour ago. There wasn't a sound from the pier in front of him.

"Polito," he called, "I'm right here. Do you want to come out or do you want me to come and get you?"

There was no answer.

Okay, Frank thought, reaching for his gun in the belt clip at the small of his back. Pushing himself up with his hands, he crouched on all fours and saw he had maybe another eight inches of cover above his head. He sat up straight and looked over the top of his rusted shield. Then he raised his gun to his side and stood up. From the chest up he was unprotected.

"I'm here, Polito," he yelled again and a shot answered him. It missed by more than ten feet and Frank dove forward and sideways for cover. That was what he wanted to know. Polito didn't have to show himself to get off a shot.

On his stomach again, he crawled forward toward the corner of the pier, well protected. Keeping low, he made it all the way to the boardwalk where the corner of the shed had stood. He pulled himself up to the boardwalk and lay still a few minutes, waiting and listening. All that stood between him and Polito now was the forest of tin and timbers. The two of them couldn't have been ten yards apart.

"I'm here, Polito," Frank taunted again, his voice getting lost in the maze of rubble.

Another shot answered him, a wild shot out toward the foot of the pier where he had been fifteen minutes ago.

"You better reload, Ron. I can count," he said. "You'll be dead if you wait till your last shot."

Another shot rang out. This one passed twenty feet to his left. Polito still hadn't located his voice, but he was coming closer.

Frank inched carefully further out along the pier. He didn't want to go too far, because that might give Polito a chance to make a run for the front. He gripped one of the timbers in his left hand and the burnt wood crumbled in his fingers and fell. Reaching higher up, he found a firm grip and stood up straight. He tried to look through the mound of timbers to see if he could see anything, but it was too thickly interlaced. Polito had to be just on the other side of it, looking through, trying to see him.

To his right Frank saw it was fairly clear footing along the edge of the pier all the way to the back. It was time to come around, he decided. Without hesitating, he ran the length of the pier, his feet clattering loudly on the loose boards. He rounded the rubble pile at the back, behind the fallen shed, and headed for Polito's side.

Confused by the sudden noise, Polito couldn't tell which way Hovannes was running and froze where he stood, waiting for something that would tell him where the Inspector was.

Frank didn't mind stepping out into the clear. They'd both be in the open, so that much they'd be even. When he came around the corner he saw Polito standing in front of him, still peering into the pile of debris. Frank raised his gun to shooting level and waited.

Five seconds went by, maybe a little more, and then the silence got to Polito. He looked around nervously, first toward the front of the pier and then to the back. When he saw Hovannes he started to raise his gun and turn, and Frank hit him then, three times. He went down without getting off a shot.

Frank walked up to him to make sure he was dead. He took the gun from Polito's hand and put it in his jacket pocket, returned his own gun to its clip, and then walked from the pier.

Chapter 31

THE YOUNG BLACK PATROLMAN JUMPED to his feet when Hovannes identified himself. "That's all right," Frank said. "Anyone been in here?"

"There's a nurse in there now, Inspector. The doctor was here about ten o'clock, and two Homicide detectives about an hour ago."

Hovannes nodded. The guard was pointless now but he didn't want to have it pulled off just yet.

"You said no one was supposed to go in, Inspector," the guard went on, offering a needless apology. "We held them up till we could clear it with Chief Guerrin."

"Who's that?"

"That's our commanding officer, sir, Special Services. He tried to find you, I think, but I guess he couldn't. He cleared it with Chief Inspector Flynn."

"Good work," Frank said, moving around him and putting his hand on the door.

"They were pretty pissed off, sir. The detectives, I mean," the patrolman said sheepishly.

"They had no call to be," Frank answered flatly. "You were doing your job. Don't let it bother you." The patrolman nodded, standing almost to attention as the Inspector opened the door. "Look, I'll be here about a half hour. If you want to get some lunch, go ahead," Hovannes added.

"Thank you, sir," the patrolman answered enthusiastically, not moving.

"That's all right, officer, go ahead," Frank encouraged, then waited while the guard stooped to pick up his hat, which lay on the floor between the feet of his chair. When he stood up, Frank asked, "Your partner go for lunch already?"

"Yes, sir."

"Well, go find him," Frank said, checking his watch. "The two of you be back here by one-thirty."

He stepped into the room. A slender, sour-looking

nurse turned to face him as he swung the door closed behind him. "All right if I come in?" he asked.

"Frank? Yes, of course," Celia called from the bed.

He walked around the nurse and came to the head of the bed, where he stood looking down at Celia without saying anything, smiling a greeting. Her color had returned and she looked days better than yesterday. She smiled in response and for a few moments neither spoke.

"If you don't need anything else, Miss Maldonado," the nurse muttered perfunctorily.

"No," Celia answered. "Thank you." Even before the door closed behind the nurse, Celia turned to Frank. "She doesn't approve of me," she said lightly. "She said she heard about me on the news last night. I can't tell whether that's why or because I was living with Lou."

"They're both serious," Frank answered, catching her tone and echoing it. He reached around to slide up a chair and sat down.

"I'm glad you could come, Frank. There's so many things I want to ask you. Two detectives from Homicide were here questioning me. How come you're not handling it, Frank?"

He had known before that when she had time to think about all that had happened she would have a lot of questions. But he wanted to tell her everything in his own way, so he answered evasively. "It was a homicide, Celia," he said. "And Lou was one of my own men. That's the way they handle it."

She thought about it a moment and then tentatively accepted his answer. "Were the guards your idea?" she asked.

Frank smiled in spite of himself, thinking it was like Celia to put it that way. "Yes," he said. "They're not really necessary, it was just a precaution."

"Don't try to reassure me, Frank," she said sternly. "I know what it means. All day yesterday I was thinking. It must have been someone Lou knew. He let him in and they were in the living room, weren't they? Maybe even someone I know. And then when the guards showed up last night, I knew you were thinking the same thing. Is it someone I know?"

Frank didn't answer. He had to tell her everything but it wasn't going to be easy. So he waited. Her eyes, bright and demanding, focused firmly on his face, but when she saw his resolve not to answer she relented and looked away, readying herself for his explanation.

"Celia," he said, "I have a lot to tell you and there's not much time. Are you sure you want to hear it?"

She closed her eyes and nodded, her face toward the ceiling. A strand of black hair hung across her forehead and he reached to brush it aside. Her eyes opened but she didn't respond to his touch.

"You remember last fall when you and Lou came up to my house?" he began, but stopped himself immediately. No, that was going back too far, he thought. It wasn't justification he wanted, but only for her to understand.

She nodded and rolled her head on the pillow to face him, encouraging him to go on.

"No, never mind that," he said. "I can tell you what happened but I don't know if I can explain it. If you think about it, maybe you'll understand. We do what we have to. At least what we think we have to—it comes to the same thing. I've been on the force a long time, Celia, and you see a lot of people get pushed around, killed, I don't have to tell you. After you've seen enough of it you have to do something about it. I'm not talking about some gunman who sticks up a bodega and kills the old man behind the counter, I'm talking about professionals. These people are protected up and down the line. It's nobody's fault, but I've watched it for years and I had to do something about it. Last fall my partner was killed. Ernie Fleming. I don't know if you ever heard Lou talk about him. It would be easy for me to tell you that what happened was because of that, but it wouldn't be true, not really. Ernie and I talked before he died and we decided that someday we were going to put a stop to it. Not all of it, no one can do that, but we were tired of beating our heads against the wall. When he died I figured it was time. I wanted to get those people and there was only one way I knew to do it."

"Oh, God, Frank," Celia exclaimed. For a horrible moment—hardly a moment, just a crazy thought that ran through her mind—she thought Frank was about to tell her that he killed Lou. Lou found out what he was doing and he killed him. Then she remembered the tall man in the suit running toward her with his gun and she gasped with the aftershock of what she had thought.

Frank guessed what was going through her mind and

took it without objecting. He could see under the covers that her body was trembling and he waited a moment, hoping she would look away from him. When she didn't, he went on.

"I think it was right for me to do it," he said. "I thought it at the time and I still do. The idea I mean, not the way it worked out. I wanted some men I could trust around me to help me with it. You don't have to know who they were, but Lou was one of them."

He paused to see if she wanted him to go on, but she gave him no sign. She was thinking about a talk she had had with Lou months before about conscience and breaking the law. She hadn't understood it at the time but she did now, and to her it meant that she was in some measure responsible for what happened.

"Do you want to hear the rest?" he asked.

"Yes," she said, trying to put her own role out of her mind. There would be time enough for that later. "Roberto was the other one, wasn't he?" she asked.

"There were two others," Frank answered. "It wouldn't be right for me to tell you who they were. But there were some problems and you may have to handle them. I think you should know as much as possible about it."

"What kind of problems?" Celia asked. It seemed strange to her that Frank would expect her to handle them.

"I'll get to that," he said. As briefly as possible he told her about the hits on Sallie Manzano and Al Palmini. Then he told her about Fran Marks, about how he told Lou where Palmini was and then began to get suspicious when somebody got to Palmini before the police.

"Basically, he wasn't that far off," Frank explained. "He knew two guys took Palmini out of the hotel where he was staying before the police got there and he figured Lou must have tipped them off. And he was right, but he had no way of knowing the two guys were also cops. He figured they must have been hit men from the LaGarda outfit and that scared him, because that meant Lou was selling information to the mob he worked for. He was in a tough position, you see that, don't you? He was stooling for Lou and he thought Lou was working for his boss. He was afraid that some day Lou might give him away."

"So he killed Lou," Celia said, her voice low and weary.

It all seemed so small and ugly. "What are you going to do to him?" she asked.

"No," Frank said, "he didn't kill Lou. I wish it was that simple. Do you remember I told you when we shot Manzano there were two bodyguards? One of them was the one we took out of the hotel. The other ended up in the hospital, wounded. We talked about what we should do with him and we decided not to do anything, at least for the time being. But one of my men had different ideas. Maybe he was unstable, I don't know, I'm no psychiatrist. I think he just discovered he was free to kill, I don't know how else to explain it to you. He went up to the hospital and he shot the bodyguard. I hadn't authorized it, but he knew there wasn't a thing I could do about it."

"Authorized!" Celia exclaimed, for the first time giving voice to the indignation that she hadn't recognized until this moment as part of what she was feeling as she listened to Frank. "Who do you think you are, Frank? You can't authorize people to kill."

Frank didn't answer and didn't look away from the piercing stare of her eyes, which were hard and cruel with judgment at that moment. He had known when he decided to tell her the whole story that she would be judging him, and a part of it for him was accepting her judgment.

"Maybe you're right," he said after a long silence. "I just want you to know what happened. When Lou found out about the shooting in the hospital he wanted to quit, to go back to Narco. I guess he saw a difference that you don't see between what that guy did on his own in the hospital and what we all did together. I see it, I still see it now, but maybe you're right, there isn't one. Anyway, I talked him out of it," Frank went on, careful to avoid mentioning that this discussion had taken place the night Celia made *paella* for them. "I don't think that mattered. It might have come to the same thing anyway. I thought it would all be over soon and I wanted Lou to stick with it to the end. Then maybe we could just forget about it and go back to being cops. Lou was a good cop, I liked him, I wanted him to stay with me after it was all over."

He paused to collect his thoughts and then quickly told her the rest, about the demands Fran Marks had made and their decision to buy him off, and about Marks being shot while he waited to meet Lou.

"This was Tuesday night," he said, "and after Lou found his body he came up to my house. He wanted to quit and I didn't try to talk him out of it. I put through the papers Wednesday morning, that's when I called you. Then it hit me late Wednesday night that Lou might be in danger and I came down to your place, but I got there too late."

He stopped talking. Celia was sobbing silently but there were no tears. Frank didn't say anything else because there was nothing left he had to tell her. He waited for the tears to come, but if he had known Celia better he would have known that they wouldn't.

"So it was a cop who killed Lou," she said at last, her eyes on his, hard and bright. "And now you've killed him, isn't that right, Frank?"

This time he did look away. "Yes," he answered softly.

"What are you going to do now?" she asked gently, the hardness suddenly gone from her voice.

"It all would have been over tonight anyway," he answered, keeping his eyes on the space of floor between himself and Celia's bed. "The two gangs are going to have it out and I've got to be there."

Celia nodded. She thought she understood. There were tears in her eyes now and she didn't say anything.

Frank looked up at her. Telling her had been like making a confession and he felt tired and drained, confused by the story he had just unfolded to her and very much alone. In a way that even she wouldn't have understood he was grateful that she was crying for him and he wanted to thank her but didn't know how.

For a few minutes she cried freely, easily, but then she began to struggle against it. "You said there was something you wanted me to do, Frank?" she asked, barely able to get the words out.

"Yes," he said, glad to have something concrete, some plan, some action to talk about. "Lou's informant, the one who was killed in Central Park, sent a letter to the Department before he died. It's what I told you, his suspicions that Lou was on a mob payroll. And the Department is checking it. They have to, it's all so confused. I don't know what they'll find, but I don't want the story to come out that way. There's Lou's name to think about, and there's another man who's still alive and I don't want him to be hurt. You'll be out of here soon. I want you go to to Bob Halloran. He's retired, he used to be Assistant Chief Inspector. We didn't get along very well, but he wouldn't want anything to happen to hurt the Department. Tell him the whole story, but tell him there were three men, not four. Tell him he'll find Palmini's body and the man I killed on one of the burnt-out piers below the boat basin. There's a gun in my locker. It belonged to the man I killed, it's the gun he shot Palmini with. I don't think they'll find the gun he used to kill Lou and the informant and the bodyguard, but he can check and he'll see that they were all killed with the same gun. I think when you tell him all that he'll stop the investigation."

"It doesn't matter about Lou," Celia said, "but if you think I should do it for the other man I will."

"Yes," Frank said. "I've got to go."

He stood up, wanting to be able to say more to her, even just to touch her hand and feel it clutch his in fear and loneliness the way she did yesterday. But he didn't think he could do it and he turned and walked away from her.

"Frank," she called after him as he opened the door to her room. "Does your wife know about this?"

"No," he answered softly. "I don't want her to."

Friday, April 25

There were less than a dozen young children playing in the small park on Catherine Street. For some reason the older kids didn't use the park but Cherry Street seemed almost crowded with Puerto Rican, black, and Italian teenagers from the project lounging on the sidewalks and against the buildings in segregated groups. An Italian kid with no shirt on, maybe thirteen or fourteen years old, was slamming a hollow rubber ball at the base of the windowless wall at the corner of Cherry and Catherine while two fielders across Cherry Street waited for the high arching rebounds to come down to them. When he hit it right he could drive them all the way back to the plate glass window of the hardware store across from where he stood.

The boy grunted with each throw, a sharp, exhilarated

punctuation of his effort, just before he released the ball, just before it thwacked against the bricks. But his outfielders moved laconically, one of them smoking a cigaret, holding it loosely in his lips as he went after a fly, then flicking the ashes after he returned the ball. There was a difference of some kind between these kids, Frank Hovannes thought as he watched a few more throws, admiring the sheer force in the boy's long skinny arms. Each time he listened for the grunt, which in just a few minutes had become for him a part of the sound of the game.

When the ball got away in the outfield he had no interest in watching the boy with the cigaret chase it down, loping easily along the gutter, and he walked quickly on, past the impatient thrower toward Valentine's.

Just beyond the restaurant was a glass and wood door and Hovannes stepped through it. He was in a small foyer, three by five, with a row of doorbells on the left and a bank of mailboxes on the right. The small metal brackets below the doorbells were mostly empty, but that didn't mean the apartments were unoccupied. Down here a lot of people didn't put their names on their doors.

He tried the inner door and it was unlocked. There was a staircase to his left with an old-fashioned wooden bannister and he hurried up it, not stopping until he came to the steel-plate door that led to the roof. It was closed with just a hook and eye. Frank unlatched it and shoved the door back. The air felt good after the sour smell of the stairs, and there was still a lot of sunlight left.

Stepping onto the roof and pushing the door closed behind him, he walked to the front of the building. It was easy to see the whole length of Cherry Street over the belly-high parapet. Now there was nothing to do but wait. It was six-thirty, maybe a little later, and it might be eight o'clock before anyone showed up.

Down the street to his left he could see the boys playing a pantomimed, noiseless version of the game he had watched. Once in a while, when the traffic sounds were briefly quiet, he could hear the impact of the ball against the building but that was all.

Two or three times in the next few minutes he felt an impulse to check his watch but he restrained himself each time. Years ago he had trained himself to forget about time on a stakeout, and he wanted this to be no different. He walked to the back of the roof, which reached halfway through the block to Water Street. He didn't have a clear, unobstructed view of the whole block but he could see enough. If the hit men came that way, the chances were he would be able to see them.

He stood directly above the narrow alley that led out to Water Street from the kitchen door of Valentine's. He didn't think he'd be on the roof when the time came, but if he was, anyone coming out that door would have to make it twelve yards right under him before he could find cover out at the sidewalk. Putting Polito up there would have been perfect, he thought, finding a wry satisfaction in the fact that they had worked it out correctly. But now, with only one man to cover the whole operation, he recognized that staying on the roof was at best an outside possibility. It wouldn't make sense unless the getaway car waited on Water Street, which wasn't very likely. To do it that way the hit men would have to go out through the kitchen, and it made more sense to go out the front.

Unless, of course, they came in through the kitchen. If they did it that way, one of them would have to stay there, holding the kitchen help at gunpoint. Figuring four men, one of them staying in the car, that would leave only two for the hit. The front door on Cherry Street was a better bet.

Leaving his vantage point over the alley, Frank walked back to the front of the building. Most of the kids were gone from the street now and it was strangely quiet. There was less than half an hour of daylight left and Frank killed it pacing the roof, coming back to the front every minute or so to make sure that nothing had changed. He continued his pacing as the sky turned slate-gray, heading toward black, but after it got dark he kept to the front wall of the roof, expecting that he might see something any minute.

He wasn't worried. One way or the other it would work out. The only thing that concerned him was Obregon. What if he hadn't believed Frank when he called him to tell him the hit was off. He had already heard about Lou, of course, and he guessed that Frank had already taken care of Polito. "I've been trying to find you ever since I heard," he said, "but I didn't want to keep calling your house. I wanted to go with you for Polito, but I guess it's too late for that, huh, boss?"

"Yeah," Frank had said, "thanks, Roberto. Look, I got

a call from Kittens. He tells me the hit is off. Runelli must've told Manzano and they're not going there. Whatdya say we pack it in for the weekend. I've got no stomach for anything and just want to get some sleep. I'll see you Monday."

It was a transparent lie and Frank was sorry now he hadn't come up with anything better. In the first place, even if Kittens had conveyed Gagliano's warning to Runelli, Runelli never would have warned Eddie Manzano. They'd only do the hit some other time, except the second time Gagliano wouldn't make the mistake of letting him know it was coming. Runelli wouldn't want to see his boss get killed, but he had to know he was better off letting it happen some time when he was somewhere else. And in the second place, if Roberto was trying to get Frank and couldn't, how could Jack Kittens?

Maybe Obregon was too upset to notice these things. Not likely, Frank reminded himself. But if he was smart enough to figure it out, he was smart enough to see that Frank wanted to do this alone. He was a sensitive guy and he knew his boss better than any of the other men, better even than Ernie in a way. He'll understand, and he'll respect it. Frank told himself, not fully convinced but wanting to believe that Obregon wouldn't show up.

Leaning against the parapet, looking out to the right and across the roof, Frank could see the spires of the Brooklyn Bridge, all the way down to the roadway. The cars coming in from the Brooklyn side had their headlights on now, and Frank watched absently for a few minutes, much as he had watched the kids playing on the sidewalk. It was a kind of contact that was comforting, reassuring.

If he doesn't show up in the next few minutes, he's not going to, Frank thought, his eyes still on the headlights as they moved distinctly toward him out of the scattering of window lights in Brooklyn Heights. If he does, I'll just station him up here, that's all, he told himself to put the problem out of his mind.

He turned back to face Cherry Street and was just noticing that he hadn't seen or heard a car in maybe fifteen minutes when a gray Cadillac eased around the corner from Market Slip to the north and pulled to the curb dirrectly opposite Valentine's. Frank tensed, waiting. The driver's door opened first and Johnny Lombardi got out.

A moment later he was joined in the street by Frankie Diamond from the back seat. Then the two doors on the far side from Frank's vantage point opened and Eddie Manzano climbed from the front seat, Phil Runelli from the back.

Three stories above them, Frank crouched low behind the parapet to make sure he couldn't be seen from the street. He watched as Lombardi and Frankie Diamond walked around to join the other two on the sidewalk and he chuckled to himself. So Kittens never called Runelli. That figured. He had no reason to want Runelli around trying to piece together what was left of the Manzano operation. He watched until the four men disappeared as they moved in under him. Now the only thing to do was to wait for the hit men.

He stood up and backed away from the wall, reaching around for his gun in the waist clip at the small of his back. Early this morning, just before it got light, he had gone to the office. From a locked desk drawer he took out the fourteen-shot Browning automatic he had bought in January. It was a heavy gun but designed flat and he had already checked to make sure it would fit into his clip. He put Polito's gun and his own service revolver, the one he had killed Polito with, in the drawer and locked it.

With the Browning in his hand he stepped back to the parapet to wait. He guessed it was maybe eight o'clock, maybe a little later, when Manzano showed up. Every few minutes he hurried to the back, staying there just long enough to make sure there was nothing happening on the Water Street side.

Time passed quickly, a half hour, maybe more. A few times cars passed beneath him, but they all turned left at Catherine and went on, nothing suspicious. Then a yellow Buick drove down the street and hesitated briefly next to the Cadillac. Yes, Frank thought, but as he crouched to get out of sight it drove on and rounded the corner. He watched it go without any feeling of disappointment. If it wasn't this car it would be the next, or the one after that. There was no point being impatient.

He didn't have to wait more than a few minutes. The yellow Buick rounded the corner again and this time it stopped across the street from Manzano's Cadillac and a few doors to Frank's right. The back doors opened first and two Puerto Ricans got out, a tall well-dressed man on the driver's side and a younger one from the opposite door. Frank didn't recognize them. Then the passenger door in the front opened and Tommie Minelli stepped onto the street.

Jesus Christ, Frank thought, this is good. Sure, it made sense. That punk had even more reason to want to get rid of Manzano that LaGarda did.

Minelli stood in the street by the open car door for what seemed a long time. His eyes ran the length of the block, down past Valentine's and then back. Then he stepped forward and slammed the door closed. As if on cue, the Puerto Rican on the side of the car toward Frank reached down and opened the driver's door. He waited while Mickey Minelli stepped out, then took his place behind the wheel. Mickey hurried around the front of the car and joined his brother and the first Puerto Rican. The three of them walked together the few yards to the door of Valentine's.

Frank hesitated a moment to give them time to get there, and then he headed for the steel door and the stairway. The driver would be to his right as he came out, facing him, and that was bad. The doorway he would come out was right between the car and Valentine's, so he would have to turn his back to the driver. But maybe he wouldn't do anything. If he figured cops when he saw Frank, maybe he'd just get the hell out of there. No one would figure there'd be just one cop alone.

Frank vaulted down the stairs. Just as he got to the front door he heard shots, a lot of them, maybe ten. He charged out onto the sidewalk, his gun drawn, glancing to his right to see what the driver was doing.

Roberto Obregon was standing on the sidewalk next to the car, his gun in his right hand, his left reaching in through the open window to handcuff the driver to the steering wheel and take his gun and the keys.

"Cover the back!" Frank shouted, racing for the door to Valentine's.

Just before he reached the door it swung toward him. Frank fired, hitting the Puerto Rican gunman straight on as he came through the doorway. His momentum carried him forward and he fell to the sidewalk toward Frank, who leaped for the gutter to get a better angle at the door.

Mickey Minelli stood exposed in the doorway, frozen

for a fraction of a second. Frank and Minelli fired at the same time. He felt Mickey's shot slam into his left shoulder, hitting bone, and his left arm dropped to his side, useless. His own shot was wide but he got off two more and Mickey fell sideways, back into the restaurant, his gun going off as he hit the floor, sending a bullet keening along the sidewalk.

The door swung closed and Frank ran for it. Tommie was going for the back and the only question now was whether Obregon would get there before he did. Frank lunged against the door, hitting it with his full weight to knock Mickey Minelli's body out of the way. As the door gave way he raised his gun to shooting position. "Don't move! Police!" he yelled, an automatic warning.

Ahead of him, all the way at the back of the restaurant, Tommie Minelli stood at the door to the kitchen, frozen in indecision. Then he pushed through it and Frank ran after him.

Before Frank got to the end of the bar he heard two shots. That meant Roberto had made it around in time. Then there were two more. He didn't know what they were, but he kept moving toward the kitchen door.

In the corner, under the clock, he saw Manzano's table. Phil Runelli was slumped on it and the other three lay on the floor, all dead. Frank reached the kitchen door and hit it with his dead left shoulder. It swung free but before he could even see what was on the other side he heard three shots and felt them explode in his chest and stomach.

As he fell, face forward, he realized what had happened. He went over it in his mind quickly, before it was too late. Minelli must have seen Obregon coming down the alley as soon as he opened the back door. So the first two shots were Minelli's, Frank thought, desperately trying to get it straight. And the second two were Obregon's. But maybe there weren't two other shots. Or maybe they're just happening now. Yes, there were more than two. Four, five, six—Frank heard them and counted, and then in his pain and confusion he gave up trying to understand.

What seemed like a long while passed, but it was only seconds. And then he was fighting to hold on to a little more consciousness, a few minutes more, while Roberto knelt next to him on the kitchen floor. He was saying something but Frank couldn't hear the words.

THE BIG BESTSELLERS
ARE AVON BOOKS

A NERVE-SHATTERING THRILLER...

SOON A MAJOR MOTION PICTURE FROM COLUMBIA ARTISTS!

AVON

27136/$1.75

GREGORY MCDONALD

"I WANT YOU TO MURDER ME..."

Irwin Fletcher. A down-and-out beach bum among the drug-ridden human wreckage on a sunny California beach. Except that Fletch is a crack undercover reporter hot on the trail of the most sensational story of his career...

Until millionaire industrialist Alan Stanwyk makes him an offer his reporter's instincts won't let him turn down: commit a murder and collect a safe full of cash.

But the victim is Stanwyk himself, and Fletch has just seven days to find out why a guy who has everything wants to throw it all away. Day by day, minute by minute, FLETCH races across a sprawling canvas of California decadence and electrifying human intrigue, toward a stunning unguessable climax!

* * * *

"IT'S A HARD ONE TO RESIST!"
—The New York Times

FL 3-76